Praise for
Dragonspell

"In *Dragonspell*, Donita K. Paul has created an amazing world of fantasy adventure. From riding on dragons to jumping off cliffs to moving mountains, this story is sure to spark a reader's imagination—young and old. And with a message of identity transformed from slavery to servanthood, it's a book families will love reading and discussing together."

—CHRISTOPHER P. N. MASELLI, children's author of *Reality Shift*
and founder of TruthPop.com

"A reluctant heroine, her fainting dragon, and an assortment of colorful companions make for a delightful read in Donita K. Paul's *Dragonspell*. This is adventure and fantasy at its finest—a must-read for the imaginative soul."

—LINDA WINDSOR, award-winning author of *Along Came Jones*
and the Fires of Gleannmara trilogy

"*Dragonspell* is a fine, well-written tale guaranteed to entertain both old and young alike. This was proven in our household when our eleven-year-old son snatched up the book and devoured it. Upon returning it, he exclaimed, 'It's good!'—high praise from a rabid fan of Tolkien, Lewis, Jacques, and company. I can only nod my head in agreement."

—CHRISTOPHER A. LANE, author of children's and adult fiction,
and winner of Gold Medallion and C. S. Lewis awards

"Inventive, engaging, witty, insightful, touching, and profound—*Dragonspell* is all this and more. If Donita K. Paul's only intention was to create a world where readers encounter novelties and wonders at every turn, then she has succeeded admirably. But she actually does much more than that: She enables us to see our relationship with God and His world through new eyes. A delight for all true fans of fantasy literature."

—JIM WARE, author of *God of the Fairy Tale* and coauthor
of *Finding God in the Lord of the Rings*

"Enchanting! A perilous quest, a timeless battle, an unlikely heroine, and a rousing adventure in a world of magic and mystery—Donita K. Paul has concocted a tale brimming with eternal truth and seasoned with delightful and amazing characters that linger in the senses long after the last page. *Dragonspell* is destined to become a classic for a new generation of adventurers!"

—SUSAN MAY WARREN, award-winning author of *Happily Ever After*

"The greatest thing any author can do is to catch you up and transport you right into the very scene, the very action, the story…in such a way that you live the book, not merely read it. That is exactly what Donita K. Paul does with *Dragonspell*. For a few hours, you will take a journey to a place you have never been, with a story you will never forget. Enjoy the trip!"

—STEPHEN BLY, author of *Paperback Writer* and *The Long Trail Home*, winner of the Christy award

"*Dragonspell* is a tightly written fantasy quest set in an extraordinarily rendered storyworld. With seven intelligent races, seven evil races, several delightful dragons, one weird wizard, and an endless supply of exotic plants and animals, you will *not* be bored."

—RANDY INGERMANSON, author of *Oxygen* and *Premonition*, winners of the Christy award

"No one will ever be able to read this and doubt that Christian fantasy is a viable genre for spreading God's Word."

—CHRISTINE LYNXWILER, president of American Christian Romance Writers

"Charming, well-drawn characters, a story chock full of adventures and misadventures, a land populated with dragons, doneels, emerlindians, grawligs, and all sorts of other fascinating inhabitants—I ask you, what more could any reader want? With *Dragonspell*, Donita K. Paul has nailed a complex and engaging fantasy world. Whether nine or ninety, you won't be disappointed."

—KATHLEEN MORGAN, author of *Consuming Fire* and *All Good Gifts*

"*Dragonspell* has a heart-thumping, page-turning plot that is sure to captivate and enthrall even the most reluctant reader!"

—PEGGY WILBER, author of *Reading Rescue 1-2-3*

DRAGONSPELL

To a fantastic reader

DRAGONSPELL

Blessings!

Donita K. Paul

DONITA K. PAUL

WATERBROOK
PRESS

DRAGONSPELL
PUBLISHED BY WATERBROOK PRESS
12265 Oracle Blvd., Suite 200
Colorado Springs, Colorado 80921
A division of Random House, Inc.

Scripture quotations are taken from the *New American Standard Bible*®. © Copyright The
Lockman Foundation 1960, 1962, 1963, 1968, 1971, 1972, 1973, 1975, 1977, 1995.
Used by permission. (www.Lockman.org).

The characters and events in this book are fictional, and any resemblance to actual persons
or events is coincidental.

ISBN 1-57856-823-4

Library of Congress Cataloging-in-Publication Data

Paul, Donita K.
    Dragonspell / Donita K. Paul.— 1st ed.
        p. cm.
    ISBN 1-57856-823-4
    1. Young women—Fiction. 2. Master and servant—Fiction. I. Title.
    PS3616.A94D73 2004
    813'.6—dc22

                                                                2003027715

Printed in the United States of America
2005

10 9 8

God has blessed me by bringing young people into my life. This book is dedicated to my first readers. They kept me on my toes and the story progressing.

Mary and Michael Darnell
Regan Gibson
Alexandria Gray
Ryan Haas
Kristianna and Kaleigh Lynxwiler
Jason McDonald
Lynette Nelson
Robert Mikell Rogers
Allison Rozema
Stephanie Desha Veazey

Contents

Acknowledgments

Where there is no guidance the people fall,
but in abundance of counselors there is victory.
PROVERBS 11:14, NASB

Each of these people at one time or another offered wisdom, encouragement, practical help, or inspiration to me in developing *Dragonspell*. Thank you.

Donna Abitz

Bonnie Aldrich

Amy Barr

Evangeline Denmark

Kory Denmark

Jan Dennis

Bonnie Doran

Sara Diane Doyle

Kathy Egeler

Barni Feuerhaken

Jane Gibson

Cecilia Gray

Rachel Hauck

Kay Holt

Diann Hunt

Sandra Moore

Scott Myers

Anne Napierkowski

Jill Nelson

Elnora Paul

Sarah Pottenger

Carol Reinsma

Helen Schnieder

Nan Seefluth

Heather Slater

Tom Snider

Armin Sommer

Faye Spieker

J. Case Tompkins

Vikki Walton

Peggy Wilber

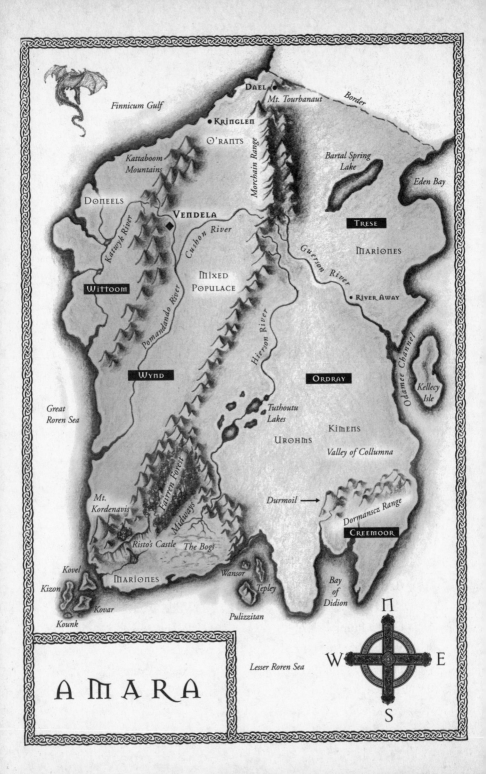

Almost There

"Are ye sure ye won't ride all the way into the city?"

Kale hardly heard the farmer's question as she stood beside his wagon-load of barley grain. Her eyes looked over the crude cart she'd traveled in and then turned to the dazzling metropolis across the wide valley. The sun sparkled on Vendela, a city of sheer white walls, shining blue roofs, and golden domes. Many spires and steeples and turrets towered above the city, but in a vast variety of shapes and colors. More than a dozen castles clustered outside the capital, and more palaces were scattered over the landscape across a wide river.

Seeing Vendela reminded Kale her life had changed forever. Her hand rose to her chest and rested on the small pouch hidden under her clothes.

I have a destiny. The thought scared her and pleased her too. After being a village slave all fourteen years of her life, she'd been freed.

Well, sort of free.

Less than a month ago she'd left River Away, her village of two dozen homes, a shop, a tavern, and a meetinghouse. In maybe another week, she'd go through the tall gates of the most beautiful walled city in all of Amara, quite possibly in the entire civilized world. It would take a week to get used to the clamor. She could feel it from here.

I'd go mad in my head if I stepped into Vendela tonight.

The city pulsated with thoughts and feelings of more people than she could count. On market day in River Away, she endured thirty or forty people close enough for her to feel their lives bumping against the walls of her inner person. But Vendela…

I might smother. I'll go slowly into that city. Nobody knows I'm coming. I don't have to hurry. A mile or so a day. Slow, till it feels comfortable.

A lot of things worried her. It was easy to say you were glad not to be a slave any longer. It was hard to walk alone into a place you'd never been before. Nobody knew or cared about her in Vendela. In River Away, most everybody cared, even if the caring revolved around whether or not she worked hard.

"Girl!" The old man's bark jerked Kale from her thoughts. He scowled at her. "I'm going right into the city. Ye might as well ride with me."

"Thank you, Farmer Brigg, but I'd just as soon walk the rest of the way. I can look at how pretty Vendela is."

She smiled up at him, feeling some affection for the gruff old man. She'd ridden the last leg of her journey beside him on the wide wooden seat. He'd been kind to her, sharing his bread and cheese and stories of all the wonders in the great city. Nevertheless, Kale would not be rushed into entering Vendela. She'd do it in her own time.

"Ye're headed for The Hall, aren't ye?" His pale blue eyes twinkled under bushy gray eyebrows.

Kale didn't answer. To say yes would give away more about herself than she intended. Not such a good idea, trusting someone outside your own village, even a grandfatherly, talkative old farmer.

"Well, I see ye're not going to tell me." He winked at her and then looked off at the city, his expression growing grim. "Should ye get in trouble, go to The Goose and The Gander Tavern, North City. Ask for Maye. Tell her ye're a friend of mine, and she'll help ye if she can."

"I will," said Kale, and waved good-bye to the old man before trudging up the hill, away from the road. She listened to the squeak of the axle and creak of the wheels but didn't turn to watch the farmer's wagon lumber down the sloping road. Among an hour's worth of advice, Mistress Meiger had said to keep her focus on what's ahead.

Kale sighed. *Mistress Meiger knows best.*

Lush gorse bushes covered the grassy slope. The hill nestled right against one of the mountains. Farmer Brigg had known the names of all the peaks in the Morchain Range. His stories of how these names came to be fascinated Kale, but it was tales of Vendela that caught her attention. After all, Vendela would be her home.

Just over the rise, she found a place to settle. She sat with her back to a gum tree, her bare feet propped up on a stone outcropping. She rested her arms on knees pulled up to her chin and her chin on her folded arms. Then Kale took a long peaceful breath of the hot summer air and allowed herself the luxury of gazing at beautiful Vendela. The twisting spires and floating spheres were beyond anything she had imagined. The whole scene looked like a magical picture, clean and bright and full of promise.

Pulling the thong at her neck, Kale drew out a soft scarlet pouch. She placed it between her hands, gently rubbing the material, enjoying the satin finish, elated by the secret of the stonelike egg within. The egg warmed, responding to her excitement. It thrummed. The gentle vibration communicated joy and anticipation through Kale's sensitive fingers.

With her eyes back on the city, Kale talked aloud. "In a week we'll be going to The Hall. I'll be a servant of the people then, not a slave. That's higher class than I ever dreamed of being. Fancy food, fancy clothes, fancy education."

She smoothed the silky cloth at her throat with one rough hand. Mistress Meiger had given her the long blue scarf the night her husband, Chief Councilman Meiger, told Kale to go to Vendela. The rest of Kale's homespun attire reflected her social status. Her trousers had two patches, one at the knee and one at her seat. She wore a shirt, a tunic, and the blue scarf. Travel dust covered every inch of her. She'd find a stream and clean up before entering Vendela.

A new life awaited her in that beautiful city. Not one person in all of River Away remembered a time when a local had been sent to The Hall. Master Meiger said to hold the honor tight. Kale held it tight all right, if only to convince herself she wasn't scared like a squawking peeper fallen out of the nest.

Focus on what's ahead.

"We'll travel and do Paladin's bidding." She grinned at that. "Sounds pretty high and mighty for the likes of me."

For a few moments, she stared at the fairy-tale castles surrounding the walled city. Seven bridges in jewel colors crossed the Pomandando River on the eastern side. Each bridge led to a towering entrance to the inner city.

"People from each of the seven high races cross those bridges at one time or another," she whispered.

The wall in the River Away Tavern had a mural of a brotherhood marching across a mountain pass. Each of the races was represented. Crudely drawn, the figures nonetheless looked excited to be adventuring.

Kale imagined a similar procession crossing one of the great bridges. "Bantam doneels, giant urohms, the elegant emerlindians, fighting mariones, tumanhofers, swift kimens, and o'rants." Kale sighed. "O'rants, like me. Chief Councilman Meiger said he thought I was an o'rant though he'd never seen one. Another reason for me to go to The Hall, he said."

She squinted as a large, dark shape swooped over the far mountains and headed for Vendela. She jumped to her feet and could not keep from bouncing on her toes as she recognized a Greater Dragon. It circled the city, a dark silhouette passing in front of the iridescent white towers.

Kale tucked the pouch safely back into her shirt and scrambled up the steep hillside, hoping for a better view. She stopped and gave a whoop as she saw two more of the majestic creatures crest the mountains and make a downward approach to Vendela.

Climbing the sharp incline on her hands and knees now, Kale grabbed branches and jagged rocks to hoist herself up. She topped the embankment and rolled over the edge.

Guttural shouts greeted her arrival. Rough, hairy hands grabbed her arms and legs. A putrid smell filled her nose, and her mouth watered in revulsion. Her stomach lurched. *Grawligs?*

Kale had heard tales told in the tavern. Nothing smelled as bad as the mountain ogres. She saw dark hairy legs, a leather loincloth, tattered cloth hanging over a barrel chest, fat lips, yellowed teeth, a grossly flabby nose, and tiny eyes, solidly black. *Grawligs!*

Two of the mountain ogres flipped her through the air. Her muscles tightened as she expected to come crashing down among the rocks. Instead, another grawlig snatched her before she hit the ground, and a screech ripped from her mouth. A burst of raucous laughter greeted her alarm. Her captors joyfully sped up their game of toss.

One grawlig claimed her as his prize. He slung her over his shoulder, his hard muscles smashing into her middle, forcing the air from her lungs. He gave a hoot of triumph and ran around the crude camp with the others chasing him. Kale hung upside down with her arms dangling. Her face bounced into the oily, matted hair on his back.

They'll kill me! They'll play with me, then kill me.

The grawlig's beefy hands tightened on her thighs, and she felt herself swung in an arc over his head. He jumped and twisted, performing some kind of ritual dance with the others howling and gyrating around them. Kale desperately tried to pull in one cleansing breath of air.

"Stupid o'rant. Stupid o'rant." The ogre's taunt filled her ears. "We heard you coming."

He released Kale and launched her frail body across the clearing toward the ridge she had climbed. Just before she sailed over the thirty-foot drop, another grawlig caught her by an arm and the back of her tunic. He swung her over his head, chanting.

"Stupid o'rant. Stupid o'rant. We heard you coming."

He changed the angle of the swing. Now her head came within inches of the ground and then high above the grawlig's massive skull. Pain roared within her head with every sweep. On the next swing downward, she fought darkness closing in around her. She lost.

2

Into the Mountain

Old leaves, moldy and partially decomposed, softened the ground beneath Kale. Her nose wrinkled against the musty smell. Her head felt like a cracked melon, and her eyes refused to open. Her stomach wanted to heave. The putrid smell of rotting garbage tormented her.

She shifted. A hard lump pressed against her rib cage. The egg! The rock-hard egg was still intact. Kale tried to sit. Bindings around her wrists and ankles stopped her. *Grawligs!*

She remembered the huge hairy grawligs and their rowdy game. She felt again the helplessness of being tossed from one rough ogre to another. Terror sickened her. They hadn't killed her, but she felt that every muscle in her body had been stomped on.

She slitted her eyes open and peered at her surroundings. Grawligs lay sprawled around a campfire. Beyond the light cast by burning logs, night shadows hid the forest. Two females turned spits, roasting what looked like large deer. A group lounged almost in a pile under trees across the clearing. They made loud rhythmic noises Kale assumed must be a song.

No one seemed to be interested in the captive trussed up and lying under a bush. Two grawligs sat just a few feet away as if they'd been set to guard her. Even they ignored her. They picked over a knee-high pile of dirty mushrooms, popping them into their drooling mouths, smacking their lips as they chomped on the treats.

Kale closed her eyes against the sight, hoping to protect her stomach. The repulsive smell of the grawligs could not be shut out so easily. To distract herself, she searched her memory for tales of the mountain ogres. *What's true and what's fable?*

In the stories, they eat anything they catch. Lucky for me, it looks like they prefer roasted venison to roasted o'rant.

Dumb and vicious. I think I can testify to that much.

Afraid of tight places? Maybe.

Clumsy with their fingers.

Moving her head just enough to look down, Kale examined the cloth binding her hands together. She wiggled her wrists, and the loose knot unraveled.

Well, they don't tie knots very well.

She glanced up at her guards to see if they'd noticed her movements. They were still bent on stuffing the forest fungi past their flabby lips.

Carefully, she moved her ankles apart an inch, and then back and forth until she could slip her bare feet out of the binding.

Can I escape?

She watched the two grawligs push dirt-encrusted mushrooms into their mouths. Their pile dwindled with every minute. Soon they would have nothing to distract them. Could she crawl away? Would they turn and catch her? Should she wait until the females declared the roasting deer done and passed the meat around?

If I wait too long, I'll probably be dessert.

Kale made her decision. Rolling onto her stomach, she crawled deeper into the bushes surrounding the camp. The grawligs' caterwauling covered the crunch of leaves and twigs under her as she slithered away from the light. On the other side of low bushes she found herself against boulders, part of the mountain looming over the smaller hills.

She rose to her hands and knees and crept another ten yards. Then on her feet, but still nearly doubled over, she followed the jumble of rocks. Her muscles protested, but she pushed on.

Distance muffled the noisy voices of her captors. Kale breathed more deeply, begging her body to relax. Surely tension caused as much of her pain as the injuries inflicted by the grawligs.

A shout went up from the camp, followed by a clamor of voices and howls from the angry brutes.

Kale quickened her pace, looking over her shoulder, expecting to see dark, hairy shapes rising out of the forest to chase her. One misplaced foot slipped into a hole, and she found herself sliding, not away from the rocks and down the mountainside, but into a narrow opening under a huge boulder. She grabbed for roots to try and break her fall. Loose dirt rained down around her as she continued to scrabble, sliding ten feet farther before landing on a hard rock floor.

The impact jarred her aching body. She clenched her teeth and squeezed her eyes shut against the pain. Debris still showered on her head. Instinctively, she lifted her arms to cover her hair.

The last trickle of dirt slowed and then settled. Kale relaxed her jaw and opened her eyes. Pitch dark surrounded her. She listened and heard the *plink* of dripping water somewhere behind her. She shivered. Goose-bumps rose on her arms.

Cold and frightened, she looked around for a means to escape. Peering upward, she could make out the opening and the starry sky beyond.

A cave. This may be good. Aren't grawligs afraid of closed-in places? I sure hope so.

A scuffling warned her that the grawligs were tramping around in the forest above her.

Maybe they'll just pass on by.

She heard branches snap, grunts and low voices, and an excited exclamation. She'd been found. The heads of three ugly grawligs blocked out the dim light from above.

They chanted, "Stupid o'rant. Stupid o'rant. We smelled you."

Kale slumped in a heap, clutching her knees, and leaned against the cold rock wall. Too tired to think, too tired to fight despair, she allowed the tears to come.

"Stupid o'rant. Stupid o'rant. We smelled you."

The chant grew louder as more tormenters joined the first three grawligs kneeling by the hole. A hairy arm reached down and groped along the sides of the rock. More dirt, leaves, and twigs fell on Kale's head.

The young o'rant girl curled tighter, shrinking from the voices above. Her hand searched for her treasure, pulling it out by the leather cord. She grasped the smooth cloth of the drawstring pouch. At first the egg inside lay cold and unresponsive. Gradually, it grew warm. Kale concentrated on the soft thrum in her hand, blocking out the "stupid o'rant" chant of the grawligs.

Pain and fatigue, fear and panic drained away. She shifted around to find a fairly comfortable position on the stony floor. With the pouch gripped in her hand and pressed against her cheek, she fell asleep.

When she opened her eyes once more, streams of light shone into the cave at three spots. The first was directly above her. A head covered with matted brown hair lay partially inside the hole. Kale could see a large hairless ear and part of the loose lips of the beast. Rough snores rumbled above.

A beam no more than a hand's width descended from a second hole in the ceiling. The third opening on the opposite side of the dismal cave showed more promise. Not only was the hole big enough for Kale to wiggle through, but also large boulders like uneven stairsteps made climbing possible.

She stood and stumbled across the uneven cave floor. She looked up and studied the hole she hoped to use for her escape. Since the ceiling of the cave sloped upward, it would be a long climb compared to the slide last night.

"I'm thankful that's not the hole I fell through," she whispered.

Tucking her treasure inside the neck of her blouse, she started climbing. She placed each foot carefully and tested each ledge before shifting her whole weight. She didn't want to cause a landslide for two reasons: *I don't want to wake those grawligs, and I don't want to be buried under a ton of boulders. I want out of here alive. I want to get to Vendela in one piece.*

Warm air touched her hand as she placed it on the next rock. Contrasted with the chill air surrounding her, it felt like a breath from the mouth of a huge animal. She pulled her hand back and listened. Faintly she heard the coarse snores of grawligs and the morning chatter of birds in the trees outside, an odd combination. Within the cave, only the drip of water from a far corner reached her ears.

Cautiously, she eased up to peer over the rock. A narrow passage stretched back into the darkness. Moist air flowed steadily from the opening.

I wonder what's back there.

Again she tilted her head and listened intently. No sound came through the tunnel opening, no sound at all. Curiosity niggled at her thoughts.

What's in that tunnel? How far back does it go? Why warm air?

She found herself crouched next to the hole and leaning in. She'd have to crawl on hands and knees. If she had a light of some sort, she could go in. She put a hand on the floor of the tunnel and placed her head within the opening.

What am I doing? I don't want to go in there. I want to get away from the grawligs.

She drew back as if she'd nearly stepped off a high cliff. Her breathing came in quick, panicked puffs. Clenching her fists, fighting the urge to plunge into the tunnel, she remembered Mistress Meiger's stern face.

Focus on what's ahead.

Kale stretched a hand up and grabbed a rock ledge. In a minute she'd be out of the cave.

Still she wanted to turn back and explore the tunnel. The powerful urge to go through that underground passage scared her. It made no sense.

She climbed the last few feet to the top of the cave with firm determination. Kale cautiously poked her head and then her shoulders above the ground. Squinting in the bright morning sun, she considered the bushes around the rocks where she had fallen into the cave. Her present outlook was higher and a good twenty feet west of the sprawled grawligs. Not all of them had fallen asleep around the hole. That meant some were out of sight.

Awake or asleep? And how many?

As near as she could count, eleven uncouth ogres lay in piles in and around the bushes. Last night dozens of grawligs had gathered in the camp.

Where are the others?

She surveyed the surrounding area, first the low ground ahead. Then she turned and peered above her. The best route of escape lay over the rocks going west.

At least that looks like the best way.

She looked again at the beasts below. The grawligs might sleep for some time. They had feasted late and probably guzzled brillum, a brewed ale that none of the seven high races would consume.

Five, maybe ten minutes, and I'll be in and out of that tunnel.

She slipped back into the cave and into the stone burrow before she could think twice about what she planned to do.

Thick, moist air settled on her skin as she groped her way in the dark. A sweet fragrance grew heavier as she moved farther and farther away from the cave. The dark, the smell, the damp, all screamed danger in her mind. Her arms and legs kept moving. She argued with herself, trying to force her body to back up and leave both the tunnel and the cave. None of her words, muttered softly in the cloying atmosphere, reached her ears.

Enchantment! she realized with a groan. She could not resist whatever pulled her into depths of darkness.

Trembling, she hoped fear would cause her to collapse.

Then I'd stop. Then I couldn't go one bit farther.

But I probably couldn't scoot backward either.

I'd be stuck. Stuck until I die.

3

BLUE CAVERN

Darkness in the tunnel pressed against Kale. Each time she tried to stop, her arms and legs ached to move forward. She bit back the whimper that rose to her lips.

Whining never got me out of a lick of work as a village slave. It won't help here... Focus on what's ahead.

Oh no! Somehow focusing on what's ahead doesn't seem the right thing to do. I don't want to follow Mistress Meiger's wise advice.

I mustn't give up. The things I learned in River Away are a part of me, and those things are good and strong and pure. What did she say? What did she say? 'Focus on what's ahead. Use what is behind.' Use what is behind. There is always something from your past that will help you with your future. Use what is behind.

Perhaps when she got to wherever this force pulled her, she would have a chance to defend herself.

She tried to imagine herself swinging fists at some unseen foe. Bolley and Gronmere often fought in the square of River Away, showing off their talent as fighting mariones. She tried to picture how they held their short, muscular bodies as they prepared to lunge at each other. Instead, she saw Mistress Avion's chicken coop.

More enchantment. I can't even see in my mind what I want to see.

She groaned again and hunched down so that she was almost on her belly. She squirmed through the narrowing tunnel. The rough walls came closer together, and still she crept forward. The heavy smell of minerals choked her, and still she couldn't stop. Inch by inch she moved into the darkness.

I'm probably in the middle of this mountain by now.

Her knees hurt from scraping over the uneven rock surface, and the tops of all ten toes felt raw. Instead of slowing down, she moved faster. The enchantment grew stronger, urging her on.

I hope there's no hungry beast waiting for me. I don't want to be somebody's breakfast.

Her own stomach grumbled. Farmer Brigg's bread and cheese were a distant memory.

A soft, azure glow appeared ahead. She breathed a sigh of relief.

The end of the tunnel. Whether it's good or bad, it's better than crawling through this tiny space, wondering and worrying.

The bluish light continued to beckon. Excitement overcame the dread in her heart. The cramped passage abruptly opened up to a vast underground chamber. She twisted to put her legs in front of her. As she hopped down into the cavern, she saw lights glistening from millions of tiny sapphirelike stones embedded in the rock walls. An additional glow emanated from icicle-like formations hanging from the ceiling and thrusting up from the floor.

They look like sharp dragons' teeth.

The bubbling of an underground hot spring distracted her for a moment. The steam that rose from a foamy surface smelled sweet like syrup boiling in the spring after the trees had been tapped.

The enchantment pulled her attention away from the odd formations in the cavern, and she walked unerringly through the maze of pointed columns to a niche in the opposite wall.

Seven small, oval stones clustered together in a nest of hardened broer.

Dragon eggs! Her hand went automatically to the pouch hanging around her neck. *Now I know why I saw Mistress Avion's chicken coop. This is too much like gathering eggs for breakfast to be real. Am I dreaming?*

She touched one of the glowing stones, felt its cold, rough surface, and saw the light turn part of her hand blue.

I'm awake.

She whipped the scarf from her neck and stretched it out on the floor.

She picked up each egg and held it with wonder before placing it on the soft blue material. When she'd lined up all seven eggs, she sank to the ground beside them, sitting cross-legged and admiring her find.

"Seven!" She breathed the word. She pulled out her treasure and opened the pouch. She placed the dragon egg she had been carrying next to the others. "Eight. I have eight dragon eggs."

Chief Councilman Meiger had had a fit when he saw one.

"How did you find it, girl?" he'd asked.

"I went to the stream to gather rushes for Mistress Avion. I waded into the water, and my skin began to tingle."

"Tingle?"

"Yes, tingle."

"Go on, go on." He placed his hands upon his ample hips and glared at her.

Being a marione, he didn't have much height, only a few more inches than Kale. But his ominous expression made the village slave feel small and vulnerable. She swallowed hard before continuing.

"I waded under the bentleaf tree to the boulders. The egg was in a hole there."

"Where?"

"Under the water."

"Under the water?"

"In the rocks. I reached in and pulled it out."

"How did you know it was there?"

"I didn't."

"Why did you stick your hand in a hole?"

"I don't know."

"There could have been a blattig fish in there with sharp teeth ready to gobble your fingers."

Kale didn't have an answer. She didn't dare scoff at the fabled fish that ate children when they fell in the river. She hadn't believed that old wives' tale since she was old enough to gather reeds for basket making.

"Humph." Master Meiger sat down hard on the bench by his front door. "There has to be a meeting," he'd said after a moment of contemplation. "We must decide what to do with you."

"May I keep the egg?"

"What?"

"May I keep the egg? It's mine, isn't it?"

"See how much you know? Nothing! No one owns a dragon egg."

Kale had been disappointed. Besides her clothes, she didn't have a thing that was her own. She told herself being allowed to keep the egg had been a small hope, and therefore, losing what wasn't even hers had to be a small disappointment.

"You can't stay here." The councilman's words shocked Kale. "You have to go to Vendela, girl. But the village council must meet first." He had stood and walked away, but more words drifted back to her as he shook his head and glowered at the ground. "Shocking! Never in River Away. Never this far south."

Kale looked at the blue scarf and the eggs nestled in its folds. She counted them again. In the pale light of the cavern, each shimmered a faint blue. In the sunlight she thought they would be alabaster white like the egg from River Away. Her breath seized in concern as she spied her treasured egg. She picked it up and examined it more closely. The egg from River Away had tangles of fine, dark lines crackled over the surface. The lines had not been there a month before.

The council told me not to take it out of the pouch until I reached The Hall in Vendela. Could I have broken it just by taking it out? I thought it was too hard to break. What happens if I did break it? What will the wizards of The Hall do to a village girl who broke a dragon egg?

She turned the egg over in her hand, hoping she would see some sign that this promise of a new life was not damaged. The dragon egg warmed and began its gentle thrum.

"Maybe it is just the light in here."

She relaxed and enjoyed holding her treasure. After only a moment, her ease gave way to amazement. The weariness and aches that had overcome her body were vanishing. The hunger squeezing her middle was gone as well. Her eyes opened wide as she watched the small scrapes and scratches on her bloody toes and knees heal over. The damage to her body disappeared as if it had never been, but the torn cloth of her trousers was as ragged as ever.

When the last break in her skin closed, she stared at the egg in her hand as if she had never seen it before. If her clothes hadn't been tattered and bloody, she would have thought she'd dreamed the injuries. As her excitement grew, the egg jumped. She tightened her grip to keep it from falling.

"I guess you aren't broken," she said with a grin.

She tucked the egg back in its pouch and pushed the bag inside her shirt. She moved the other eggs onto the rock and tied a knot in the scarf about a foot from one end. She tucked one egg in next to that knot, folded the soft cloth around it. Using a length of thread from the unraveling edge of her tunic, she secured the egg and tied a knot. She placed another egg on her makeshift sling and tied it in. When finished, she had a ropelike object with seven bulges. She tied the egg-bearing blue scarf around her waist, next to her skin, under the tunic and shirt.

"Now, let's get out of here."

She stood and trotted across the floor of the cavern, neatly dodging around the glowing columns. Just as she reached the opening of the tunnel, she had a thought. She turned to search the area around her.

Spying a fist-sized rock lying on the ground, she rushed to pick it up. Dozens of crystals shimmered from the rough stone. She smiled and carried it into the dark tunnel.

The way back didn't seem nearly as long. The enchantment, which had pulled her in, had disappeared when she touched the first egg. No dread of what was ahead plagued her thoughts. The rock glowed in the tunnel. She could see several feet ahead of her, although it was awkward to hold the rock and crawl.

She pushed on, eager to get to the cave and climb out the top. The thought of the grawligs awakening helped her to hurry. She halted as soon as her head poked through the opening from the tunnel to the dimly lit cave.

Three beams of light still fell in straight shafts from the outside. They'd shifted with the movement of the sun.

Her ears told her something else had changed. She tilted her head, trying to identify the clamor. The grawligs no longer snored. Instead she heard metal clanging against metal, angry shouts, frenzied commands, and roars of fury. If she was not mistaken, sounds of battle echoed from all three openings of the cave.

4

FRIEND OR FOE?

This time Kale raised her head out of the hole even more cautiously. Judging from the tumult, she had expected an army to be facing the grawligs. Kale spotted only three attackers—two mounted on dragons. Most of the noise came from the mountain ogres.

The third attacker stood within a circle of the grawligs and felled them right and left, wielding a sling-type weapon with a spiked ball at the end. She recognized him as a fighting marione like the race of people populating River Away. His muscled frame, short and blocklike, stood solid against the onslaught. Known as farmers and fighters, the mariones could make any ground productive and defend any ground against invaders.

The dragons in the air were not as big as the Greater Dragons Kale had seen fly into the city. One large milky-white beast carried a giant warrior in armor and chain mail. As the dragon swooped and soared over the battling grawligs, the rider hurled lances with deadly aim. The insignia of a royal house emblazoned his helmet and riding gear. Two large quivers hung over the dragon's shoulders just in front of the knight's knees.

Kale watched the other dragon's aerobatics, stunned by her beauty. The red wings glistened as if covered with tiny rubies. Her chest and stomach pulsated in blue and purple shimmers. Sunlight reflected off blue-green scales on her head, tail, and hind feet.

A small furry rider wore bright colors, almost as flamboyant as his mount. Shouting terse words Kale could not understand, the man cast yard-long lances among the grawligs.

"I am Leetu Bends. We came to rescue you."

A female voice uttered the words directly into Kale's thoughts. The o'rant girl jerked in surprise.

A mindspeaker! She looked around trying to decide who had spoken.

"Go now, while we have the grawligs' attention. Go west, over the ridge. Follow the stream down the mountainside. We'll catch up with you."

Kale still held the glittering rock she'd picked up in the cavern. She opened the neck of her shirt and dropped the stone under the frayed material. It settled against the bulge of dragon eggs tied to her waist.

She pressed her palms into the rim of the hole and hoisted herself over the edge. Without stopping to watch the combat, she scrambled over the rocky terrain away from the fighting.

A battle cry rent the air. Kale turned to see the rider of the smaller dragon slide off his saddle into a knot of grawligs.

He fell!

The miniature warrior, dressed in vibrant shades of green and gold, disappeared into the snarling melee of brown and black beasts.

Kale imagined the little man ripped in pieces as the ogres tore at his arms and legs. She ran toward the clutch of tangled fighters until she stood on an outcropping just above. The grawligs made hideous noises. Dust rose, obscuring her view of the valiant little warrior. She saw flashes of color from his clothing, but not the man, nor how he defended himself.

They're killing him. I've got to do something!

Kale picked up a rock and hurled it. It bounced off a grawlig head. He grunted and swayed, but returned to his efforts to pummel the enemy in their midst without even looking up to see what had hit him.

Kale threw one rock after another as fast as she could pick them up and as hard as her muscles would allow.

"What are you doing? Get out of there. Dar knows how to fight. He doesn't need you. Go! Quickly! Before they turn on you."

Kale hesitated.

"GO!"

She heaved the rock in her hand and took off toward the crest of the ridge.

I don't like this. Not one bit. In River Away everyone always yelled at me, "Go! Come! Do this! Do that!" But at least I knew who was ordering me about.

At the top of her climb she paused to look over her shoulder. Fierce fighting still raged in the gully below. She didn't want to be chastised again, so she turned away from the battle and stomped over the ridge.

A stream sprang out of the rocks in the midst of a copse of evergreen shrubs. Kale followed it easily. The noise of enraged grawligs battling her rescuers soon faded. The breeze whispered through the trees, cooling her as she trudged along. The sun sparkled off the brook as it foamed over its rounded-rock bed. Birds sang in the forest as if nothing so ugly as raiding grawligs existed in the whole of Amara.

She marched along, muttering about grawligs and voiceless orders and not knowing where she was going. As she tramped beside the stream, her anger faded. A yawn stretched her mouth. Her eyes drooped. Then her legs grew rubbery, making it hard to stay upright. She stumbled more than once over terrain that should have been easy for her to cover. Jumbled thoughts broke her concentration, and she kept losing her balance.

She said they came to rescue me. Who are they? How did they know I was in trouble? How did they know where I was? Could Farmer Brigg somehow have known? No. How could he?

I'm so tired. And I'm getting hungry. How long before they catch up to me? What if they lost that fight with the grawligs, and the grawligs catch up with me instead? What if... I'm so tired. My whole body hurts.

Kale sank down on the mossy bank. *I'll just rest a minute.* She pulled the pouch from beneath her shirt and soon fell fast asleep with it tucked under her cheek.

——

The whistling first sounded like a double-crested mountain finch, but then a few too many high notes warbled at the end of the call. Kale's eyes sprang open, and she sat up. A doneel sat on a log by the stream. From his finger, a string dangled over the edge of a rock into the water. His clothes were tattered but bright in hue between the smudges of dirt and blood. His whistle changed to the song of a speckled thrush.

Kale compared the look of this real-life doneel to the painted figure in the mural at the River Away Tavern. This whistling doneel sat, but she was sure if he stood, his little frame would not reach four feet. His tan and white furry head sat on a well-proportioned body. His large eyes hid under shaggy eyebrows that drooped down his temples and mingled with a long mustache. His broad nose stuck out like the muzzle of a dog, and his black lips met with hardly a chin at all underneath. Dressed in rich fabric of glorious colors, he was far more interesting than the blurry image on the dark tavern wall.

"Hungry?" he asked. Smiling, his face became round, half of it the huge mouth. Two ears covered with soft fur perched on the top of his head near the front. They twitched and turned as he listened.

"Only a little." She had never talked to a doneel. Only mariones and a few kimens came to River Away. Kimens were smaller than doneels, but their bodies were much more delicate, almost wispy looking. They wore forest colors in loose, draping material. And a kimen's face had what Kale thought was a more normal set of eyes, ears, nose, and mouth—although she had to admit she thought their raggedy haircuts and lack of eyebrows made them look perpetually surprised.

"You are very hungry," said the doneel. His voice rumbled a bit over the words.

"I am?"

"Yes." He nodded decisively. "When was the last time you ate?"

Kale remembered the bread and cheese Farmer Brigg had shared. "Yesterday noon."

He jerked on his line and pulled out a brook dabbler, its scales silver on the belly, its back coal black, its fins the colors of a sunset.

"You've been battered by grawligs," continued the fisherman as soon as he had his catch off the hook. "You fell down in a cave and healed yourself using magic."

"I did?"

The doneel cast her a skeptical glance. "You did."

"Magic?"

"The egg."

"Oh." Kale put her hand on the pouch. How much did this odd little man know about the dragon egg? All the questions that had disconcerted her as she followed the stream came back. What if this doneel meant to steal the egg? Did he also know about her new find? Surely, eight dragon eggs would be very valuable. How did he even know about the first? She hadn't told a soul since leaving River Away.

The doneel stood and brushed off his torn and dirty pants. "My name is Dar."

Kale stood as she had been taught. "I'm Kale."

Again the doneel's smile almost overcame his entire face. "Pleased to meet you."

He crossed to a pack left on the ground and pulled out a cloth-wrapped bundle. Untying it, he revealed some flattened rolls. He handed them to Kale.

"Eat. The magic makes you think you aren't hungry, but your body needs nourishment, especially when it has been busy repairing bruises and scrapes."

Kale took the offering and sat again, this time beneath a borling tree. Dar gathered sticks and laid a fire while she ate. Kale watched him with suspicion. He whistled and hummed and didn't seem to mind her silence. Kale had never been much of a talker. Slaves weren't encouraged to enter into conversations. But the questions boiled inside her, and she thought she'd scream if she didn't get at least some of the answers.

"Where did you come from?"

Dar crouched beside a pile of sticks he arranged with great precision. "The Hall."

"Why did you come to help me? How did you know I was in trouble?"

"Actually, I didn't know, but Merlander did."

"Who's Merlander?" The words came out louder than she expected, and she cringed. None of the villagers would have forgiven such an outburst.

Dar seemed unconcerned. "My dragon."

"The beautiful one?"

Dar grinned again. "She is something to look at, isn't she? But vain. Don't say too much about her being pretty when she's around."

Kale nodded, agreeing to his request as if she understood all the intricacies of owning a dragon.

"You said 'my dragon.' I was told that no one could own a dragon."

"Oh, I don't own Merlander. I say 'my dragon' in the same way I would say 'my friend' or 'my sister.' She would say 'my doneel.' We've been together five years."

Kale gulped and almost choked on the bread. Dar came over and slapped her on the back. When she was breathing easily again, he got a heavy ceramic mug out of his pack and brought her cool water from the stream.

"She talks? Your dragon talks?"

"No, not like you and I. She knows my thoughts and I know hers. She told me a new dragon was coming from the east, over the Morchain Mountains. As you carried the egg closer, Merlander knew when you were tired or excited or frightened. The dragon embryo in your egg already reflects your disposition. My dragon knew what your dragon felt. When you were terrorized by the grawligs, we knew. But we couldn't come to you when you were unconscious. We had no beacon. Then you were awake and hurting. We knew. But after a short while, you went to sleep."

"You knew all that?"

"Merlander knew."

Dar lit the fire and cleaned the fish. He hung the brook dabbler on a metal brace he plucked out of his pack and placed over the fire.

Kale puzzled over all the information Dar had given her. Councilman Meiger was right. She didn't know anything.

"So," she asked the doneel as he slowly turned the cooking fish, "will you take me to The Hall now?"

"No," said Dar. "I was sent to keep you from going to The Hall."

5

New Friends, New Enemies

Kale stood in a panic. This little doneel was not what he seemed. Where could she run?

She'd been told where to go by the elders of the village. To Vendela. She *must* follow their instructions. Should she go to The Goose and The Gander and look for Maye? That was what Farmer Brigg had advised. Always before, she had only to listen to instructions and do what she was told. Nothing complicated ever came her way.

Maybe being a slave isn't so bad. If I can just get to The Hall, I'll be a servant. That's enough like being a slave that all this adventure with grawligs and doneels, running from danger and battles, will just cease to exist.

She looked at Dar and his diminutive frame. His short legs would never keep up with her. She surveyed the forest and wondered which way to run.

A hailing cry came from the sky. Putting a hand at her brow to shield against the sun, Kale scrunched up her eyes and saw Merlander with her beautiful red wings swooping down. Again the dragon called with a round melodious tone. Dar waved a greeting. The whoosh of the last beat of Merlander's wings ruffled Kale's hair like a spring breeze. The dragon folded her wings against her sides.

A young woman riding the dragon's back threw her leg over the arching blue neck and slid down glittering scales to the ground.

"I'm Leetu Bends," she announced with a nod in Kale's direction. Then she turned a scowl on the doneel. "Dar, what did you say to her?" And before he could answer, "What foolishness. How clumsy."

Dar dipped his head, hiding his expression. His ears drooped.

"I'm sorry." Leetu turned to Kale. "Dar teases, among other disreputable things. Think of him as an older brother who has no sense of decorum. Or no sense, period. Paladin has urgent need of your skill. That is why you must turn aside and leave going to The Hall until later."

Kale stood rigid in her confusion. This was the commanding voice she had heard as the grawligs battled—the one who said they had come to rescue her. Kale looked back to the repentant doneel and then to the self-assured young emerlindian. She did wear the colors of The Hall. Her tunic was a mellow, golden tan of ripe wheat, and her breeches, the rich brown of the earth.

But how could Kale know for sure who Dar and Leetu were? What did they really want? Were they here to help or hinder her?

Leetu Bends came up only to Kale's shoulder, yet she had a dominant presence. White-blond and blue-eyed in a slim frame, Leetu did not look a bit delicate, but rather tautly muscled, ready to spring into action. She was a young emerlindian. Chin, nose, eyebrows, and ears all slightly pointed, her beauty was sharp, drawn with clean lines.

Kale had heard stories of emerlindians. The race was born almost pure white. As they aged, their skin, hair, and eyes darkened. They lived a long time, hundreds of years. Wise brown grannies were both male and female and cherished by the younger generations. But even older than grannies were a few black grands, emerlindians who supposedly neared a thousand years in age. Generally thought to be noble, kind, and benevolent, the emerlindians possessed interesting mental powers.

Kale winced at the knowledge. *This Leetu Bends reads my thoughts. She knows I don't trust her.*

Kale cast her eyes down to the forest floor, concentrating on the leaves scattered at her feet.

Is it possible to block her reading my mind?

Leetu laughed. "Yes, it is. And it's a technique I'll teach you as part of your training. For now, you can't throw up a barrier."

Kale looked up. Merlander had settled, lying down at the edge of the clearing. Dar stood beside her neck, his head just coming to her glistening cheek. He leaned against her comfortably as if welcoming her back. Kale could feel the peace between them.

Leetu Bends had not moved. Her bright face, radiating warmth and friendliness, no longer held the stern and autocratic look she had given Dar when she first arrived. Kale wanted to like her.

Could she trust these two? The elders had told her to go to The Hall. Did she dare put aside Councilman Meiger's instructions? Why would Dar want to keep her from going where she was supposed to go? Leetu said Paladin needed her skill. What skill? Kale let herself collapse in a rather undignified heap on the ground.

"I know it's overwhelming," said Leetu.

The emerlindian's comment did little to ease Kale's mental struggle. Since she'd left Farmer Brigg's wagon, nothing had gone as she'd expected. Life was much simpler in River Away where Mistress Meiger told Kale whose house to go to, and the mistress of that home ordered her about all day.

Leetu came and sat beside her. "Try to relax. Let us take care of you. Dar's a good cook…when he doesn't get distracted and burn everything."

The doneel jerked to attention, rushed back to the fire, and turned the fish.

Leetu grinned and returned to her quiet talk with Kale. Her low, reasonable voice soothed Kale's anxiety. "You do need food. You've been relying on magic to sustain you, and it won't, you know. Well, you wouldn't know that yet, but you'll learn. Your skill is in finding dragon eggs, and there is an egg that *must* be found."

Leetu pulled a green parnot fruit from the pouch at her hip and handed it to Kale. "We'll eat and talk," she said. "You can ask as many questions as you like, and then we'll start off on our quest."

It sounded so rational, and yet it didn't. Kale bit into the sweet fruit.

The elders had given her instructions to go to The Hall, but the elders were far away. Kale had enough experience to know that ignoring what you were told to do often led to trouble. She trusted the elders, for although they had never acted as parents to her, they had treated her fairly. They saw to it that she had food, something to wear, and schooling, such as it was. They allowed no villager to take advantage and work her too hard.

She was free now. Well, sort of. She still had to go where she'd been told to go, and when she got to The Hall, she would probably *still* have to do what she was told to do. But it was different somehow. Being a servant was better than being a slave. Wasn't it?

Leetu Bends had said she could ask as many questions as she wanted. In River Away she had never been encouraged to ask questions. That much was different at least. But a problem remained. Would she know what questions to ask?

The small party ate without much conversation. Dar finished first and took out a foot-long metal harmonica. He settled against a tree trunk and began to play quiet tunes.

"Digestive music," said Leetu. "Doneels believe strongly in the correct type of music to accompany each of their activities."

Kale nodded and continued to eat the delectable fish. Pretending to concentrate on her meal gave her an opportunity to think over just what she wanted to know. After each thought, Kale examined Leetu's face for some indication that the emerlindian knew what was going through Kale's mind. Her stomach knotted. She put her dinner aside. Nothing inside her head made any sense.

I never had big things to think about in River Away. Is this what I really want? To be surrounded by people I don't know, who might be friends or might be foes?

Her companions set to doing chores. With the few dishes washed and stashed in a canvas pack, Leetu and Dar sat down on either side of Kale. Her thoughts still jumbled every which way, but she couldn't stall any longer.

"You must ask your questions," said Leetu. She gestured with a graceful hand at the three gathered around the doused campfire. "We must be on our way."

Kale looked to the dragon laden with bundles of supplies. "Where are we going?"

"First, to find Wizard Fenworth."

Kale didn't know one wizard from another. Weren't there wizards enough at The Hall? "Why?" she asked.

"He has been chosen to take care of the dragon egg once you have found it."

"How do you know I can find it?"

"You have the gift," said Dar. "Didn't you walk right to the egg you carry in the pouch? Didn't you put your hand on it before you even knew why you were reaching?"

Kale's hands clenched on the edge of her tunic. It wasn't fair that they should know so much about her and be confident in all they did. She didn't know anything. "How do you know about me?"

Leetu slapped her hands on her knees and shook her head. "Paladin knew. We can't tell you how Paladin knows things. He just does."

Kale blinked at Leetu's agitation, but having been given permission to ask questions, she just couldn't keep from asking another. "Why am I the one Paladin has chosen to go look for this egg?"

Leetu stood and paced. "Another question that we cannot answer. Once you have been in his service for a while, it will cease to amaze you that he knows so much." Leetu looked away for a minute as if to summon up words to make it easier on Kale. She sighed her frustration and turned back to her listener. "Let me tell you about the egg, and why it is so important."

Kale nodded.

"First, it is a meech egg."

"Meech?"

Dar jumped in. "The highest order of dragon, the most powerful. A female meech may lay three eggs in her entire life span, over five hundred years. The eggs are rare."

Leetu put up her hand to stop Dar's lecture. "This egg was taken by Risto."

"Who?"

Dar squirmed with his lips pressed firmly together as his eyes darted from Leetu's face to Kale's. He just couldn't keep quiet and burst out with the information Kale needed. "An evil wizard! Risto's an evil wizard."

Leetu cut him off with a look. "Risto does not wish to hatch the egg, but to use the power of the egg to cast a grandiose spell."

"Of course," said Dar. His ears twitched, and he licked his lips as he stared at Kale. "His spells are evil." The little doneel's eyebrows came together in a fierce frown. "If he needs the power of a meech egg to get it done, there's no telling what contemptible transgression he's plotting."

"You mean you don't know what evil spell he's going to cast? How can you be so sure it's dangerous?"

Dar bounced to his feet, flinging his arms wide. "Because it's Risto. He doesn't do good things. He has all the evil traits that taint the seven high races. Pride, greed, deceit, faithlessness." Dar sputtered in his outrage. "He's cruel, power-mad, cunning—"

"He's evil," Leetu interrupted. "In the use of power from the un-hatched egg, Risto will destroy the life within."

"You see," said Dar, stamping his foot for emphasis. "Evil! No respect for Wulder's handiwork. Risto must be stopped, and Paladin sends us to do it."

"With Fenworth," Leetu reminded the doneel.

Dar screwed his face into a grimace of disgust. "Having that wizard along will lead to disaster."

"Why?" asked Kale.

Leetu sent Dar a warning look before answering. "It's best you wait and see, Kale."

6

A Dozen Delays

"Merlander can't carry three passengers," explained Leetu. "She's too small."

Kale watched as Dar and the emerlindian woman untied bundles from the dragon's back.

"Dar," asked Leetu with a frown on her face and a quick shake of her head, "did you bring your entire wardrobe?" She gestured to the piles of parcels at his feet. "We have miles to walk. You can't carry all that, and neither I nor Kale will carry it for you. These things aren't necessary."

Dar bristled and muttered beneath his bushy mustache. "A person needs to look sharp, well groomed. We represent Paladin. Who knows who we'll run into on an important quest? We may be called upon to negotiate with rulers of distant realms."

"We're going through forest and swamp. You don't need fine clothes in brilliant colors fit for a ball. Pick out sensible clothes in greens and browns, if you have any."

Leetu left the last canvas bag she'd removed from Merlander's back and came to stand before the grumbling doneel. With her hands on her hips, she looked over his collection. "Two bags, that's it. Two bags light enough for you to carry on your own."

"We could stop at the next village and acquire a donkey," suggested Dar.

"Two bags," said Leetu.

Dar turned large, pleading brown eyes toward Kale. "Kale would carry a bag for me," he said.

"Kale will have enough to carry. Quit this, Dar. Send the extra clothing back to The Hall with Merlander."

With what sounded very much like a growl, the doneel conceded.

Now that Leetu had won her point, she sat down against a tree and exhibited an amazing amount of patience. She pulled out a book from her pocket and thumbed through the pages until she found a place to begin reading.

Dar fiercely sorted through his belongings, working to pack as much into two bags as he could. He fussed over the bits and pieces of clothing, even trying on a rich, green velvet coat, a silk shirt patterned in blue, and a crimson vest.

"Too bright," said Leetu, barely glancing up from her book.

Dar sighed as he packed away the vest. He added a matching scarlet jacket, another vest, this one purple, and a green and gold pair of knickers. He muttered about people who did not appreciate the value of being properly attired and not having a mirror to help make important decisions.

Kale watched with amusement for a time. She had to admit the bright colors and fine fabrics attracted her, too. For a moment she allowed herself to hope, envisioning herself walking the marble corridors of The Hall, wearing flowing garments of brightly colored silks.

Eventually, she turned her mind to remembering the geography of Amara. The only map available in River Away belonged to Dame Blezig, the schoolmistress. It had been several years since Kale studied the yellowed parchment, but she recalled the two mountain ranges running north and south, islands off the coast, volcanoes in the southeast, and massive forests in the northeast and southwest. A place called The Bogs covered a large area in the southwest.

Her eyebrows shot up as she realized the only place where they could walk through both forests *and* swamps was in the southwest, nearly a thousand miles away.

We're going to walk to The Bogs?

Leetu's head jerked as she looked up from her book and stared at Kale.

"You very nearly shouted that at me," she said and closed her book. "Seems I'd better pay more attention to you. You'll need to be able to contain your thoughts before we enter Bedderman's Bog."

"Why? What's in Bedderman's Bog?"

"It's best you wait and see, Kale."

Kale didn't like the vague answer this time any more than she had the last. What about the promise to answer all her questions? She would try once more to get a straight answer.

"Are we going to walk to The Bogs?" she asked, looking toward the doneel, hoping he would blurt out his thoughts. He seemed more willing to impart usable bits of information than Leetu.

Dar, fretting over his bundles, didn't interject an answer.

"Yes, we'll walk," said Leetu. "But we'll go through a gateway."

Kale's mouth dropped open. Gateways were part of fairy tales. Heroes escaped through gateways or sprang upon unsuspecting foes from gateways. Gateways went hand in hand with talking animals and magic amulets.

Gateways are real?

Kale closed her mouth and slowly shook her head from side to side. Councilman Meiger was right. She didn't know anything.

"I'm ready," announced Dar. He gave Merlander a pat on her neck, and the dragon rose to her feet. The doneel stepped back to avoid being struck by her wings. She lifted into the air with his extra packs lashed firmly to her saddle. Dar watched her climb high into the cloudless blue sky and set off toward Vendela. He turned a grumpy face to Leetu Bends and Kale.

The emerlindian sprang to her feet and hoisted a pack into the air. She pitched it to Kale, who caught it with a grunt. Without a word, Leetu grabbed two more bundles and swung them over her shoulder. She started down a path beside the stream. Kale scrambled to her feet just in time to follow Dar as he plodded down the trail.

They trekked on, the sun warming their backs, birds singing in the towering trees, and the brook babbling among the round rocks. Occasionally, the knotted roots of giant evergreens extended into the stream. Here the water frothed and churned through the bare, brown footing of the mighty trees.

Soon Dar began to hum and then sing softly under his breath. He'd regained his good humor. He sang louder, and his songs grew livelier as they marched along. Kale's spirits responded to the happy tunes of the legendary heroes among the seven high races. Dar also sang of farmers and other ordinary folk caught in funny circumstances. She laughed and gasped at all the trials that could befall a traveler.

They rambled down the mountain, then across a valley, and started climbing again. Dar ran out of breath as the path grew steeper. They could no longer step lively to his cheerful beat. Kale, though used to working hard, was not accustomed to long treks. Her legs protested. She very much wanted to rest.

Dar stopped suddenly, and for a moment Kale thought she'd get her wish. But the doneel lifted his nose to the breeze and closed his eyes. Leetu stopped and turned.

"Grawligs," she said, obviously reading his mind. "How far do you think?" She looked at Dar.

"Half a mile."

"Which direction?"

Dar puzzled over that a moment, sniffing the air. "We're surrounded."

Kale thought she'd been too tired to go much farther, but now a shiver of fear energized her muscles. She was ready to run as soon as Leetu gave the order.

The emerlindian examined the trees and bushes surrounding the small clearing.

"We'll make our stand here."

Surely they should run. Kale opened her mouth to protest. Nothing but a croak came out.

Impatient, Leetu beckoned with a brusque gesture, and Kale hurried to the emerlindian's side. Leetu threw her own burden into the bushes, then snatched Kale's bundle from her back and hurled it into the undergrowth as well.

"Dar, you take the center of the clearing," Leetu ordered. "Kale, climb this tree."

Kale looked at the thick trunk of a towering evergreen. She'd seen several of these imposing trees on the trail she'd taken through mountain passes. None like it grew around River Away.

"This is a rock pine," explained Leetu, again demonstrating she knew Kale's thoughts. "Its name doesn't come from growing in rocks. Those prickly pine cones are as heavy as stones. Climb as high as you can. Take off your tunic and wrap it around your throwing hand. When the grawligs attack, start pelting them with the rock cones. Hit anything you can, but aim for the grawligs' ears. They're tender."

Leetu made a boosting step with interlaced fingers. Kale put her foot into Leetu's hands and felt herself thrust into the air. She grabbed the lowest branch and clambered up the tree. The grunts and coarse mutterings of the approaching grawligs inspired extra speed.

Once perched on a high branch, she could see dark forms advancing from all sides, completely encircling them.

"How many?" asked Leetu from below.

Kale scanned the area. "Twelve."

"That shouldn't delay us too long," said Dar.

Branches in a tree next to Kale swayed. She made out the slender form of Leetu as she climbed to a branch thirty feet above the ground. Below, Dar stood in the center of the clearing with his ears perked, listening to the approach of the marauding mountain ogres. Kale wanted to shout, "Climb a tree!"

"He'll be all right." Leetu's calm voice reassured her. *"Just watch. He'll throw up a magic shell and fight from beneath."*

At that moment four grawligs crashed through a line of brushwood and entered the clearing.

Dar hunched over, and a shimmering shell appeared over his body. It hovered above him like an inverted glass bowl. Kale could see the doneel's movements within. Two daggers flashed in his hands.

The grawligs gave a roar and charged. They beat on the shell and tried to pry it up. Dar's hands whipped out from the lower rim. His daggers slashed and poked at the grawligs' toes as well as their fingers when they gripped the edge of his protective armor. The grawligs hopped around amid yips and howls but didn't give up. As one fell back to suck on his injured fingers, another took his place.

"Now!" cried Leetu's voice in Kale's mind, startling her so that she almost lost her grip on the branch. More of the mountain ogres poured into the clearing. Their massive legs tore through the thick underbrush. They bellowed a war cry, and Kale clutched the tree trunk, thinking the horrendous shouting would shake her out of the tree.

Dar disappeared in the middle of a dozen raving grawligs. Arrows from the emerlindian's bow rained down upon the ogres' heads.

I can't just sit here. I'm supposed to help.

Kale wiggled out of her tunic and wrapped it hastily around her right hand. She grabbed a pine cone and had to twist at the woody, seed-bearing orb to make it come loose. Even with her hand protected, she felt the pricks of the barbs. She hurled the rock-heavy cone down wildly and managed to hit one of the grawligs on his hairy back. The cone clung to the matted hair.

Over the next few minutes, her aim improved as did her ability to twist the cones in just the right way to pull them off the bushy, needle-laden branches. She climbed to different limbs several times in order to reach more clusters of the spiny weapons.

Kale began to see the advantage of Leetu's strategy. While Dar, in the relative safety of his shell, inflicted grievous wounds on the ogres, Leetu peppered them from above with arrow after arrow.

The rock-hard pine cones Kale threw bruised the ogres but did not impede their attack. Nonetheless, the cones stuck, and Kale saw that was a good thing. Most of the hairy grawligs carried the extra weight of ten to twenty rock cones. She thought the beasts were incredibly stupid. Their focus remained riveted on the doneel they thought they had trapped on the ground.

Eventually, the assault from above bothered some of the grawligs enough that they stopped to gawk at the trees. Leetu took advantage of the upturned faces. Her skillful aim sent several grawligs howling into the woods, pulling at arrows embedded in their flesh.

Kale marveled over each direct hit on a grawlig's ear. They reacted with shrieks of anger and pain. Often the wounded ogre left the foray with a massive hand covering the side of its head. All the grawligs were limping painfully from the wounds inflicted to their feet by the doneel.

She redoubled her efforts to make a bull's-eye, then laughed to herself and corrected the phrase. She wanted to hit a grawlig's ear, not a bull's eye.

The skirmish was soon over.

Dar was right. They're leaving! And none too soon. My arm aches from throwing all those heavy cones. I must have thrown a couple hundred. And my hands feel like I've been squeezing pincushions.

She reached inside her shirt and pulled out the red pouch to cradle between her palms.

For a moment Dar, Leetu, and Kale remained still, listening to the grawligs scrambling through the forest, howling and snarling and making just as much noise in their departure as they had in the attack. As the sounds faded, Dar released the protective shell. It vanished. He stood and sniffed the air.

"They're gone," he announced. He cleaned his bloody daggers, wiping them on the trampled grass. They disappeared into his sleeves, and the fussy doneel inspected his spattered knickers.

Leetu slithered from branch to branch and landed lightly on the ground.

"Messy work," she commented and began to pick up arrows that had bounced off the grawligs' hard heads or been pulled out and thrown down by the angry beasts.

Kale came down from her tree more slowly. She'd been in a battle! If she wanted to believe it a dream, she couldn't. Splashes of grawlig blood spotted the little clearing. She crept to the far edge to sit apart from her companions. Her stomach felt queasy, and she didn't want to talk to anyone.

Dar had already pulled off his boots and socks and had one of his bags open, looking for clean clothes.

"It's all right." Kale heard Leetu's calm voice in her mind but could not bring herself to look up at the emerlindian's serene features. Instead she

studied the twigs, dirt, and pebbles between her feet. An insect crawled across an open space and then disappeared underneath a trang-a-nog leaf.

Kale deliberately answered Leetu with her thoughts. *One of the fighting mariones from River Away had been to the borderlands and fought blimmets. He said killing blimmets was no more bothersome than swatting flies.* His *stomach didn't turn at the sight of blood. If Paladin expects me to fight in battles, maybe he picked the wrong o'rant.*

Leetu's voice penetrated her mind. *"Don't feel bad about being sick over this sort of thing. Don't ever get used to killing. If you do, then no matter how high you were born in the seven races, you'll slip down to the level of those born of Pretender's evil mind."*

Paladin approves of killing? asked Kale.

A long pause followed.

"Paladin believes in protecting his people."

What does that mean?

"It's better you wait and see."

Kale growled under her breath and heard Leetu's answering chuckle in her mind as well as in her ears.

7

Granny Noon

After Dar changed his clothes, they resumed their journey, Leetu in the lead, Kale trailing behind. The forest grew thicker, darker, mustier, quieter, colder. The footfalls of the three travelers made a shushing sound on the thick carpet of old leaves.

Kale's gloomy thoughts blocked out her surroundings. She mulled over every aspect of her pilgrimage from River Away to where she had left Farmer Brigg on the road to Vendela.

If I'd stayed with him, I'd be safely inside the walls of The Hall by now. It's my own fault. I didn't follow the elders' instructions, and now look where I am.

She bumped into Dar before she realized the doneel had stopped in his tracks. "Sorry," she murmured.

He did not respond but peered into the thick vegetation before them. Leetu had disappeared. Kale noticed the chill in the air and shivered. She wrapped her arms around her middle, tucking her hands between the rough cloth of her sleeves and her tunic. She started to ask if something was wrong, but the furry little man held up a hand and whispered, "Shh!"

Kale's throat closed, her muscles tensed, her heart beat like a drummerbug. She clenched her fists, not knowing whether she should be ready to fight or run. She preferred running. She forced herself to scan the area around them with just her eyes, keeping her head perfectly still.

There's not two inches between those tree trunks. How did we get this far? Were we following a path? Where's Leetu? What's Dar staring at? Will something spring out of that wall of leaves? Why are we standing here?

She heard the rustle of leaves first and then saw the wall before them quiver. The branches shimmered, turned silver, and began to glow. Gradually, the light intensified. Kale squinted and covered her eyes with one arm. The air warmed, the brilliance faded, and Kale smelled the pungent aroma of freshly plowed dirt after a rain. She lowered the shielding arm and opened her eyes.

Leetu stood in an open archway of flowering vines where the solid wall of leaves had been. Beside her another emerlindian, wrinkled and darkened with age, nodded a greeting. Her rich brown hair hung nearly to the ground. Dark eyes flashed a welcoming smile.

Kale took in a shaky breath. "A granny," she whispered as she exhaled.

"Yes, dear. I'm Granny Noon. Welcome to my home."

Dar stepped forward and offered a courtly bow in greeting.

Granny Noon laughed. "Dar, I can always count on you to bring elegance to my humble abode." She turned to Leetu Bends. "Bends, how you've darkened since I last saw you. I ran into your parents at Summer Solstice Feast Day. Your mother said you still read every chance you get."

Even Kale knew that was true. She glanced at the young emerlindian and saw her blush.

"They were well?" Leetu asked, and Kale figured she didn't want to discuss her reading habits.

"Oh, yes, definitely," said Granny Noon as she linked her arm through Kale's and gave her a gentle tug toward the opening. "And proud of their offspring." She patted Kale's arm. "Come, child, you're nearly exhausted, and I've baked nordy rolls."

Kale heard Dar smack his lips behind her and decided the rolls must be something special. Within a few steps, the leaf covering on the walls began to dwindle and packed dirt showed between the sparse vines. The floor gradually sloped downward. Thick roots occasionally crossed the incline and then formed a steep stairway deeper into the ground.

Light came from rocks similar to the ones Kale had seen in the mountain cave where she had found the clutch of dragon eggs. These luminescent stones were not embedded in the walls but roosted on elaborately carved wooden shelves at intervals. Behind each, a curved mirror reflected the lightrock's gentle radiance outward. Leetu's blond hair, as well as the patches of white in Dar's fur, shimmered a lovely cerulean. Each bit of pale clothing worn by the small party also reflected shades of blue.

At the bottom of the root stair, the yeasty smell of fresh baking wafted from the dim corridor ahead. They proceeded just a few more yards before coming into a cozy room with a green moss carpet, walls lined with books, a blaze flickering in a snug fireplace, and wood furniture cushioned with plump pillows. In the center of the room, three-legged stools surrounded a table set with elegant china and tall candles in shining silver holders.

Kale's stomach rumbled at the sight and smells of delicious food. Granny Noon gave her arm an understanding squeeze. Her milk-white teeth peeked out between smiling bronze lips. Even in the shadowy light of the underground home, Kale could see the warmth and affection in the old woman's face. For the first time since the o'rant girl had encountered the grawligs, she felt a measure of safety. She allowed the peace to settle in her heart. Her tense muscles relaxed, and she didn't stiffen as Granny Noon laid an arm across her back.

"You can wash up in the room through there." She gestured with a nod to a solid wooden door. "I'll just put the kettle on for tea."

Minutes later, Kale sat down to a table crowded with warm dishes. Rather than snatch up any of the tasty-looking items, she forced herself to exercise self-control. She'd learned manners serving at the better homes in River Away. But now she wanted to gobble the tiny sandwiches of crusty toasted bread filled with thin slices of meat and cheese. Granny Noon lifted the ceramic head off a rabbit-shaped tureen in the middle of the table and ladled fragrant vegetable stew into bowls.

Dar slurped and Leetu frowned at him, but Granny Noon did not seem to notice. She passed out sweet brown rolls, which must have been those she mentioned at the arched entryway. Dar cut his in two and lathered each half with butter. Granny cleared her throat. Dar looked her way, and then he graciously offered one half to Kale.

"Thank you." She took the warm bread and savored a whiff of the aroma rising from the dark portion in her hand. Kale bit into the nordy roll, and a wonderful nutty taste flooded her mouth. She closed her eyes and chewed slowly, wondering before she even swallowed if she would be allowed another, or maybe two more.

"Eat your fish, dear," Granny Noon's voice urged her. Kale opened her eyes to see a new plate before her with a slice of pure white fish and a mound of mashed pink potatoes. Kale had only had the rare pnard potatoes when they were left over from festival dinners. Pnard potatoes were so delicious, most people scraped the bowls clean and left none for the slaves.

By the time Kale put down her fork, her middle bulged uncomfortably against the blue scarf tied at her waist.

"Thank you, Granny Noon. That was the best meal I ever ate."

Leetu and Dar echoed her appreciation.

The old woman smiled and nodded. "We'll leave the cleaning up for a while. It isn't good to scurry around the kitchen when you need to relax and digest your supper. Perhaps Dar will play for us."

The doneel beamed at being asked and went immediately to fetch his bag. He sorted through a number of small instruments and selected a flute. Granny Noon settled Kale on cushions in front of the fireplace. Leetu chose a book from a nearby shelf and sat closer to a branch of candles standing among the glowing rocks. Granny lowered herself into a rocker and pulled a piece of knitting from her basket. Within minutes Kale's head nodded, and she laid her cheek against the velvety soft fabric of the cushion.

She wanted most to stay here in the cozy underground home of the oldest, kindest person she had ever met. To forget about Vendela, quests, dragon eggs, wizards, and grawligs—especially grawligs. To perhaps stay with Granny Noon and be her servant. That would be a dream come true.

8

EXPLANATIONS

"Kale."

Kale didn't want to wake up. She moaned softly. No bright morning light fell on her eyelids. The room was dark. It must be long before dawn. She shifted and felt the hard floor against her hip. A log popped and hissed in the fireplace. Mistress Meiger didn't like her to put pine in the fire. The wood burned too hot, and the resin trapped in the wood snapped and sparked when the flames licked it. Kale opened her eyes.

I'm not at home.

"No, you're not." Granny Noon's voice came into her thoughts. *"I can't let you sleep any longer, dear. I've too much to tell you before you begin your journey. Get up now."*

Kale sat up and saw the older emerlindian standing across the room. She beckoned Kale to follow and opened a door to another chamber. Light spilled out of the door, falling like a path to where Kale sat among the cushions. Dar's muffled snores rose from a plush rug across the room. Leetu was nowhere in sight.

Kale tiptoed to the door and entered cautiously.

"I've a warm bath for you and new clothes." Granny Noon's soft voice came from behind a screen. "Come here, child. I've packed a bag for you to take, and I put pockets in the lining of a cape for you to carry your dragon eggs."

She knows!

"Of course, dear, and I'm very excited for you. What a treasure! What a responsibility! What fun you're going to have raising those precious creatures."

Kale smiled and felt a ripple of joy in her heart. She approached the screen and peered around the edge. Steam rose from a tin tub. Granny Noon laid out a washrag, a lump of mottled soap, and a huge drying towel. She patted a stack of folded clothes. "Put these on when you're finished. I'll sit and spin while you bathe. And I'll tell you some of the things you've been aching to know. Don't forget to wash your hair. Wait. Sit here, and I'll cut it first."

Granny Noon pulled long, shiny shears out of her apron pocket. She pointed to a wooden stool, and Kale reluctantly perched on it. She cringed as Granny Noon attacked her curly hair. The flashing silver blades clipped at her locks with amazing speed.

"Sit still," ordered the tiny old woman. "Let's see…where to begin? First, don't be intimidated by your gift. You will gain mastery over the pull dragon eggs have on you."

"I didn't like going through that tunnel to the cavern."

"Of course you didn't, dear. Very sensible of you. Sticking your hand in holes, crawling into unlit underground passages. Risky undertakings. You'd be well advised to be a bit more cautious." She shook her head and tsked without once missing a beat with the shears.

"I couldn't help myself. It was scary. In the tunnel, I couldn't stop."

"Yes, well now you know more of what it's all about. Your mind was trying to tell you even then."

"It was?"

"The image of Mistress Avion's chicken coop was the only thing that your previous experience could identify. If you had been able to relax, you probably would have conjured up an image of the egg you already had, and then by putting two and two together, you would have understood you were going toward a clutch of dragon eggs."

"You think so, Granny Noon?" Kale shook her head. "I don't think I'm that smart."

"Keep still." Granny Noon lightly thumped her on the head with the side of the shears. "Yes, I think so. All you need is experience in the service of Paladin."

Granny ran her fingers through Kale's curly hair, and then sharp scissors snapped around her ears. Kale squeezed her eyes shut as if that would protect her from being nipped by those shiny blades.

"Discernment is what you need," said Granny Noon.

Kale wished the old emerlindian would just concentrate on the haircut and not try to talk at the same time.

"I wish I could give you discernment, but you must learn it. Step by step. Experience by experience. They should have chosen older companions for your journey."

"Dar and Leetu are older."

Granny laughed. "Leetu is a lot older, but still a child emerlindian. And Dar is no better. Sending three children out to find Fenworth. Of course, he's as old as the swamp, so that should give you a balance of wisdom."

"I'm afraid I don't understand."

"Of course not, dear. That is why I am saying you need discernment."

Kale crushed down a remark that sprung to her lips. Didn't anyone outside of River Away know how to properly explain anything?

"The two who came to rescue you with Dar and Leetu Bends," continued Granny Noon, "were Lee Ark, a marione general for Paladin, and Brunstetter, an urohm lord and ruler of a small province in east Ordray. I can't believe Bends never got around to telling you these things. That girl! And she informs me that she has given you no instruction on your mindspeaking abilities."

"Me? Mindspeaking!"

"Of course, dear." The shears' snapping slowed now into a rhythmic beat as Granny Noon circled Kale. "How did you feel when you approached the city of Vendela?"

"A little scared," Kale admitted.

"No no, besides that. Didn't you feel crowded? As if there was a hum of noise, like bees bumping against your brain?"

Kale drew in a sharp breath. That was exactly how it had felt as she sat in the wagon approaching Vendela. And in River Away, too, on market days.

Granny Noon continued as if Kale had answered. "You see, that's because you're a mindspeaker. Of course, a mindspeaker is also a mind-listener, so to speak." She giggled, and the air quivered around Kale as if Granny Noon's joy actually enlivened everything in the room. "Now look down, dear, so I can get these scraggly wisps of hair at your neck."

Kale dropped her chin, and Granny Noon talked as she snipped. "Living among the mariones was a disadvantage. Very few of that race are proficient in conversations of the mind. And they're among the most difficult to read even if you're talented. You've had no training, but your skills will develop quickly now that you're with Bends. Just the practice you get listening to her and sending your thoughts will do the trick."

"I did that!" Kale jerked around to see Granny Noon's face. "I did! Right after the last grawlig attack. She said not to worry about being sick to my stomach, and I asked her how Paladin feels about killing."

Granny Noon nodded and then placed her hands on Kale's head, firmly moving it so she could continue shaping the side cut.

"You see, you're already picking it up. Now for guarding your thoughts. It's best to put this little measure in place and keep it there. You never know who'll be listening."

"Is it difficult? Can I do it right away? It *is* uncomfortable knowing Leetu can hear everything I think."

"Well, she doesn't."

"No?"

"No. Most of the time, Leetu Bends is thinking about something else. Unless a thought is startling, listening to another's mind requires focusing. Now, to guard against eavesdropping, say this in your mind, 'My thoughts belong to me and Wulder.' "

"That's all?"

"Did you expect some long chant of mumbo jumbo?"

Kale quickly repeated the phrase to herself and then answered her mentor's question.

"I thought I'd have to imagine walls or something."

Granny Noon chortled and put the shears back in her ample pocket. "Well, you will learn."

Again, I see how right Master Meiger was. I don't know anything. As soon as the thought crossed her mind, she looked to see Granny Noon's reaction.

The old woman dipped a hand in the tub, then shook droplets from her fingers as she pulled it out. She twisted her face in disgust. "Too cold. I'll add some more hot water."

It works! Kale hid her smile by ducking her head. Then she saw the pile of dark curls circling the stool. Her hands flew to her hair, and her fingers explored the soft ringlets covering her head in a snug cap. A small mirror hung on the wall. Kale hopped off her seat to take a look.

"It's practical," said Granny Noon.

"I look…"

"Well?" Granny Noon stood with a hand on her hip, and her serious face tipped toward Kale as she waited.

Kale gazed in the mirror, unable to form exactly what she saw into words.

"Ahem!" said Granny Noon as she turned away. "You look pretty, child. Without all that wild hair taking over the looks of you, you can see the fine eyes, the pert nose, the strong chin, and the lovely smile."

The old emerlindian stepped over to the fireplace. With her hand protected by a thick cloth, she picked up a large kettle, one that seemed too big for such a small lady. She had no trouble hoisting it high and pouring steaming water into the tub. Kale had lifted many such kettles as a village slave. She knew how heavy they were and wondered again just how old the dark emerlindian could be. Granny Noon put the kettle aside and sat at her spinning wheel.

"You get yourself into that tub before the water gets cold again." Her bossy voice held a mother's note of tenderness.

Kale went behind the screen and shed her clothes, listening to Granny Noon's melodious words as she climbed into the warm water.

"To get into a mind that is blocked, you think these words, 'In Wulder's service, I search for truth.' If you are going to listen to the thoughts of someone you know is wicked, you must protect yourself. Say, 'I stand under Wulder's authority.' Of course, you don't have to say these things precisely as I teach them to you, but it's good to stick pretty close to the original, so you don't accidentally leave yourself vulnerable."

"But what if someone wicked wants to hear my thoughts? Can't he just say those words and get into my mind? What good does it do to block someone who knows how to unblock the block?"

Granny Noon's soft chuckle mingled with the whir of her spinning wheel. "Child, the forces of evil *cannot* call upon Wulder's authority and use His power. Now, Kale, repeat the three phrases I've told you so far."

Kale leaned back in the tin tub. Her head rested against the rim, and she closed her eyes to concentrate.

"My thoughts belong to me and Wulder. In Wulder's service, I search for truth. I stand under Wulder's authority." *I guess Wulder is going to be pretty important in my life from now on.*

"Now, dear, that's truth, pure and lovely."

The gentle hum of the spinning wheel accented the silence that fell over the room. Kale rested in the aura of peace radiating from the old woman.

Granny Noon's sigh swept through Kale's contentment. Her sweet serenity swayed, buffeted by a hint of warning. The vague disturbance didn't destroy the pleasure the young o'rant felt, being alone and cosseted by the old emerlindian. Kale couldn't tell if the disquieting sound had come to her through her ears or through her mind.

"Child, Pretender will also be more active in your life."

Kale shivered. Pretender? No one in River Away had talked much of either Wulder or Pretender. The very name Pretender had always made Kale feel he was make-believe, not a real source of evil. But it seemed, like gateways, Pretender *was* real and not just part of tales told in the evening around the fireplace.

What have I got myself into, Granny Noon?

The answering laugh, soft and reassuring, echoed gently in Kale's mind.

"Nothing you have to face alone, child." The quiet room felt like a sanctuary until Granny Noon's voice returned to Kale's thoughts with a solemn message. *"This quest you go on is nothing you would have chosen of your own free will."*

Dangerous?

"And then some."

Why me?

"Because you've been given a gift, and those that get a gift must use it."

Must?

"Must!"

9

Neither Here nor There

Kale puzzled over the fine cape Granny Noon had given her. Draped around her shoulders, it fell to the floor and swayed gently as she moved. Something odd happened to the color every time she glimpsed it out of the corner of her eye.

I'm not used to such elegant clothing, that's all.

That could be the explanation, but still something about the cape made her vision kind of muzzy.

She stood in the center of the snug sitting room, marveling at the feel of her new clothes. Everything—her undergarments, stockings, boots, skirt, blouse, and cape—smelled new. Soft colors of brown, beige, and white enveloped her small frame from shoulders to toes. Kale couldn't help the grin on her face. She liked looking clean and neat. She'd be warm, and she'd look respectable. But the cape...

Inside the lining, Granny Noon had sewn pockets in two rows down each side of the opening. From her waist to the hem, eight pockets, four on each side, held one dragon egg each. Two deeper pockets hung in the side seams at her hips. Granny Noon called them *hollows* and had Kale stuff them with objects she said were essential for a quest. With all the things they'd slipped into those pockets, the cape should have bulges. It didn't.

I may not know much, but I know pockets should look full when they're full.

Granny Noon had explained each item, but the familiar objects had bizarre purposes. Before Granny tucked the last feather into the right side pocket, Kale knew her mind was muddled with bits and pieces of information she didn't understand. She tried to sort out Granny Noon's instructions as the others busied themselves with their own preparations.

Dar stood beside an ironing board, pressing out wrinkles in clothes he had washed and dried. Leetu studied the bookshelves, looking for a book to borrow. Granny Noon bustled from cabinets to the table, packing provisions for their journey.

Kale patted the smooth surface of the cape where a "hollow" pocket lay underneath. *The beans will grow breakfast. The dried yellow leaves cure headache. The dried pink leaves cure stomach pain. The twigs tell which way to water. The white feather is a peace token. The black feather signals trouble. The gray feather means "follow me." What is the little shell for?*

Kale stared at the fire trying to remember. *Oh yes, to summon a crow. But I don't remember why I would want to summon a crow.*

She slowly turned her head, watching the others in the room and wondering how she could ask Granny Noon without alerting Dar and Leetu Bends to her inability to remember simple instructions. She could try to speak to Granny Noon's mind. How could she block Leetu's hearing and reach Granny?

Her eyes caught her reflection in the mirror, and she snapped to attention. For just an instant, she had seen only her head...

The cape! There *was* something odd about the cape. The light gray fabric shimmered in the light—rippled, really—catching the colors of other things as if the material reflected images like the old mirror on the wall.

Dar broke the comfortable silence of the room. "Granny Noon spun the cloth from moonbeams."

"Moonbeams!" Kale cried out. "Cloth made from light?" She stroked the smooth, warm fabric, tilting her head to examine it even more closely.

"Dar, you're incorrigible," said Granny Noon. She cast a frown in his direction and then looked over her basket at Kale. "It's a type of bush with round white flowers. Thus the name, moonbeam plant."

"Why does it look so strange?" She moved her arms to hold the cape away from her body. Squinting, she tried to see what she had seen just a moment before. She sighed, shaking her head in bewilderment. "And then it looks normal."

"When you move, the material looks like any other cloth," explained Granny Noon as she went back to wrapping small bundles with gauzy white cloth. "But when you stand still, you blend into your surroundings."

"I'm invisible?"

"No, not invisible. More like a chameleon, well hidden. And you would need to put up the hood to keep your head and face out of sight."

Kale reached over her shoulder and pulled up the soft material that lay like a rumpled collar around her neck. The hood surprised her by dropping over her face as well as her head. She peered through the loosely woven fabric.

"That's it," said Dar. "Now tuck your hands under and keep still." Kale heard him clap his hands together. "That's it! You're gone."

"Really?" The folds around her face muffled her voice. Her warm breath came back to tickle her cheeks.

"No," said Leetu. "Dar, you're going to give her too much confidence in that cape, and then she'll get into trouble." Leetu carried three books in her hands as she crossed the room to stand in front of Kale. "The cape is more effective in shadows or at night. In the blazing sun, your outline will be clearly visible. Never risk your life, thinking the cape will save you. It's one of the first rules of service to Paladin. Trust in what is real, not illusion."

"Finally!" Granny Noon came over to hug Leetu. "I was beginning to think we were mistaken to send you as mentor to this o'rant child."

Leetu's face clouded over as she shrugged out of Granny Noon's embrace. The young emerlindian handed the three books to Kale. "Here, stick these in your cape hollow."

"My pockets are full," said Kale, looking at the titles: *The Care and Feeding of Minor Dragons; Training for Performance—An Overall Guide to Dragonkeeping;* and *Pitfalls of Magic.*

"Your hollow isn't. They'll fit," said Leetu. She crossed the room with a few graceful steps. Even when irritated, she moved like a leaf floating on a gentle breeze.

"Don't mind her." Dar approached, speaking too softly for Leetu to hear. He handed Kale her own blue scarf, laundered and ironed. "She's miffed because Lee Ark sent her with us instead of taking her to defend the southern border from an invasion of quiss."

"Quiss? Sea creatures?"

"Nothing but rumors," said Dar. "The quiss migration isn't due for another year. Leetu will likely see more adventure with us than patrolling a remote seashore."

Kale looked at her scarf folded in a neat square. Why had Dar done this kindness for her? He was not a slave or a servant. Why?

Grawligs and gateways, mindspeakers and grannies, Pretender and quiss. All of this is more than I bargained for when I left River Away. Is anything normal out here?

She felt the smooth cloth Mistress Meiger had given her. The beautiful blue scarf had been in a sad state last time she saw it. She looked at the doneel's friendly face. He stood next to her, eyeing her expectantly.

"You washed my scarf?" she asked, still not quite believing that someone would do this menial task for her.

Dar looked away, apparently embarrassed.

"Thank you," said Kale.

He nodded with a smile quirking the corner of his mouth, gave a courtly bow, and then returned to his ironing.

Granny Noon put her hand on Kale's shoulder.

"To a doneel, clothing is symbolic. He saw me throwing away your old clothes and salvaged the scarf. It would be important to him to carry or wear something from his home."

Kale looked from Leetu's rigid back to Dar's small figure. The emerlindian again examined the bookshelves as the doneel meticulously pressed a crease in a pair of trousers. Leetu might be worthy of wearing the colors of The Hall and heading their expedition, but Kale was very glad Dar would be along.

10

Through the Gateway

Kale's foot hit a loose rock in the shadowy tunnel as she followed the others into the depths of the mountain. The stone rattled and clattered as it bounced against the rough surface of the path ahead. It bumped off Dar's polished boot and rolled to the side.

Dar's back kept a steady distance ahead of her. His yellow jacket glowed green in the pale blue light. She only rarely caught a glimpse of Leetu farther ahead. And she hadn't seen Granny Noon in quite a long time. The elder emerlindian headed the small procession.

Kale's skirt felt cumbersome. She had never worn anything but short trousers that hit just below her knee. Granny Noon had given her a long skirt and soft leather boots that came up her calves. Her legs tangled in all these trappings. She constantly tripped. And it seemed she was always clumsiest when Leetu watched.

Then there was the cape. Kale liked the way the material flowed around her. But she constantly felt the need to gather it close, keeping it away from the dirt and rock walls in the narrower passages. Never before had she been concerned about her clothing getting soiled.

She didn't like wearing the new clothes in these awful underground passages. She didn't like the clammy dirt, the musty smell, and the shadows. She didn't like not being able to see all the time, and she didn't like not knowing where they were going.

To the gateway. But where is this gateway, and how long will it take us to get there? I don't like being so deep in the mountain at all.

The bright burrow leading down to Granny Noon's rooms had been clean and comfortable. Someone had placed large, glistening lightrocks on convenient, man-made shelves. But in these tunnels, light shimmered in uneven intervals along the walls. Embedded lightrocks glimmered in a natural scattering. Some parts of the passage shone brightly where the rocks clustered. Sometimes the travelers walked in deep shadows with only small, faint lightrocks marking the way.

At first the tunnel had been cool and fresh. Now the hot, moist air stung Kale's nose and left a metallic taste in her mouth. She thought they might end up clear on the other side of the world if they kept going, down and down, always marching down, deeper into the mountain.

Dar entered a darker section of the passage, and Kale walked a little faster. She didn't want to be left behind. Something smacked against her ankle. She whirled around. Snarling teeth flashed close to the ground. She jumped back. A dark animal, no bigger than a rat, skittered into the shadows. She pivoted on one foot and ran after Dar.

"What is it?" he asked as she came up behind him.

"An animal." She panted, not from the short run, but from fear. "Dark, quick, ugly teeth."

"A druddum." Dar kept walking, no faster than before. "They won't hurt you as long as you're with someone."

She pushed her nervousness aside and concentrated on Dar's thoughts. She didn't pick up any words, but she got the impression of the doneel chortling.

He's teasing me again.

"Tell me the truth," she insisted.

Dar gave her a quick look of mischief over his shoulder. His shaggy eyebrows waggled, his ears perked up and twitched, and his mouth opened in his extra-wide grin. Then he shrugged and turned back down the tunnel, walking steadily on.

"They don't hurt anybody," he said over his shoulder. "However, they do steal things. Food, naturally. But they also take things just to look at them or feel them. They have hoards, and they *will* bite if you try to take something from their cache."

Dar adjusted the pack he had been carrying across his chest so that it hung over his shoulder. Another druddum barreled around a turn in the tunnel. Both the small animal and Kale let out a high-pitched squeal. The druddum flipped in the air and took off in the direction it had come from. Dar laughed.

"I once came upon a druddum's nest," he said. "I stopped short before it saw me and watched awhile. It had a piece of smooth cloth and turned that scrap over and over in its paws, stroking it like a pet. Its eyes were half closed, and it hummed one note almost the way a cat would purr. That druddum sat on a mirror, and lots of shiny things poked higgledy-piggledy out of the dried grass of his bed."

Kale didn't care what a druddum's nest looked like. "They won't attack?"

"No." Dar stepped over a large rock in the path, and Kale followed. "They run through these tunnels at great speed and sometimes run smack into walls. That druddum probably scared itself spitless by running into you."

Reassured by Dar's words, Kale nonetheless stayed close behind him. "How far until we reach the gateway?" she asked.

"I've never been to this gateway, so I don't know."

"Dar, do you read my mind?"

"Nah, I don't have the talent."

"Not at all?"

"Not even a whisper."

Kale concentrated, staring at the back of Dar's head. Again she heard no thoughts but felt his general excitement and knew he was eager to go through the gateway and begin the quest for the meech egg.

"Dar, can you block me from reading your mind?"

"No, but doneels are harder to read than mariones." He looked back and flashed her another wide grin. "It's the thick heads." With a wink, he turned back to follow the others. "After you've been in training for a time, you'll be reading my mind and telling me what to do, just like Leetu Bends."

"Oh, I don't think so." Kale couldn't imagine ordering anyone about, and certainly not with the audacity of the young emerlindian.

Dar quickened his pace. Kale scurried to keep up. It amazed her how quickly the doneel moved on his short legs. He never stumbled either. All her muscles were tired. She wanted to crawl back into the comfy bed at Granny Noon's.

It was exciting to get up before dawn and have Granny Noon talk to me and just me. But now I wish I'd slept more. And my muscles are sore again. I've done more climbing, running, falling, hiking…more everything!…than I ever did in River Away. I thought I worked hard as a village slave, but at least I got to sit and peel vegetables once a day. I even got to sit when I milked cows. Don't these people ever sit down and rest?

Her hand went to the pouch that again lay under her blouse. Fumbling with the cord, she pulled it out to hold as she walked. Just before they left Granny Noon's, Kale had slipped her special egg, the first one she'd found, back into the pouch Mistress Meiger had given her. The egg belonged there, not in any pocket. Its presence comforted her, hanging around her neck, sometimes bouncing against her chest. In the pocket of the cape she couldn't feel it, and sometimes she wanted to feel it.

Like now.

She clasped the egg in the pouch and felt strength returning to her legs and energy pumping through her body. She soon felt she could follow for another day if she had to.

Granny Noon had explained how the magic of the egg worked to heal her. Kale thought over the words carefully. Granny Noon talked a lot about Wulder, and she always talked in a tone of voice that gave Kale the shivers. A nice kind of shivers.

The old emerlindian spoke of a great mystery, one revered for ages and ages by people Kale had never heard of. She knew the things Granny Noon said were true, but they didn't seem to have anything to do with a slave girl turned servant. She thought the words Granny Noon used must have come out of distant places and wondrous times.

When the storytellers and minstrels tell of legends in the tavern on a Saturday night, they use words like "long ago and far away." But Granny Noon talks as if that "long ago and far away" is here and now.

Kale clutched the rock-hard egg in its pouch and felt the dragon within respond with a steady thrum. She kept her hand there and tightened her grip with a jerk every time they encountered one of the hasty druddums. She did manage to keep from squealing as the lightning-quick hairy bundles barreled around the corners. But when they careened off her legs or came in groups of a dozen or more, she plastered herself against the wall and called out to Dar.

"Come on," he urged. "If we stop for you to recover every time we meet something unpleasant, we might as well give up the quest now."

Kale bit back a response. *Well, Master Dar, I didn't really ask to be included in this quest. I had a destiny, and that destiny was to go to The Hall, not follow some fancy-dressed doneel through endless tunnels with nasty rat-things running crazy—*

"We're here," Granny Noon's soothing voice announced from just in front of Dar. The dark emerlindian, small and fragile, looked as much at home in the eerie light of the tunnel as she had beside her own hearth many miles behind them. Leetu stood to one side of the passage under an outcropping of lightrock. Her face and hair reflected the blue luminescence. Kale looked past her companions for a door, a gate, an opening, but saw none.

"You will now pass out of my authority," said Granny Noon, "into realms that hold danger, not only for you, but for all of the seven high races. I am not to walk with you, but I do follow you with my hope. You will be strong. You will be courageous. Each of you will give of yourself for the good of the others. Do not let fear enslave you. Do not let frenzy bind you. Seek truth. Seek honor. Obey your call to serve Paladin."

The air beside Granny Noon quivered. Ripples of iridescent colors radiated from the stone floor to the arched ceiling.

Granny Noon embraced Leetu Bends, patted her on the back, and kissed her cheek. The young emerlindian returned the affectionate gesture and then silently slipped into the shimmering air. The lights held her for a second, and then she was gone.

Dar stepped up and bowed with his usual grace and flourish. Granny

Noon chuckled, leaned over and hugged the doneel, pressing her brown cheek to his furry side whiskers where the drooping eyebrows mingled with his long mustache.

Kale watched Dar leave Granny Noon's side and walk into the gateway. Again, the radiance sparkled and held his figure for a moment before he moved to beyond where Kale could see. Kale stared as if she would suddenly be allowed a glimpse of the other side.

"Well, young o'rant girl," said Granny Noon, "are you frightened?"

"Yes, very."

"Excited?"

"That, too."

"You will do well, Kale Allerion."

Kale's eyes snapped from watching the shimmering gateway to the face of Granny. "Allerion? I've never had any name but Kale."

"Now you do." Granny Noon came close, embraced Kale as she had Leetu, and gave her a parting kiss. "Go, child. Your destiny is on the other side of the gateway."

Kale hung back. "Granny Noon, I'm not worthy."

"None of us is, dear."

Kale looked into Granny Noon's dark, dark eyes. Kindness, strength, and courage shone in their depths. Kale nodded with a jerk and turned to the gateway.

Mesmerized by the constant ebb and flow of prismatic colors, she felt Granny Noon's presence behind her. Granny Noon rested her small, strong hands on the o'rant girl's slender shoulders. She felt reassured by her gentle squeeze.

"Trust Wulder," said the old woman's mellow voice in her ear. "Follow Paladin's lead. That's best. You'll be fine." The pressure of Granny Noon's fingers on her shoulders eased up. "Take a deep breath now, and go. Sometimes the passage kind of pinches your lungs."

Kale inhaled deeply, lifted her chin, squared her shoulders, and stepped forward.

†HE LEGEND OF UROHM

Leaving behind the azure glow reflected off cold stone walls, Kale entered a kaleidoscope of colors shot through with tiny explosions of light. The air thickened around her. Her body pushed through the lights and colors and sticky air and emerged under a sunny sky, surrounded by trees and the fragrance of fresh rain and sweet flowers. A soft breeze brushed against her cheeks and tousled her short curls.

"Breathe!" shouted Dar. She barely heard him over a thunderous rushing noise in her ears.

Pressure built in her chest, and her lungs felt coated with fire. Her eyes stung, tearing up, blurring her vision.

"Breathe!" Dar repeated.

He sprang to her side and thumped her on the back between the shoulder blades. Kale coughed and drew gulps of air through her mouth and into her lungs. Her breathing came rapidly and took a minute or two to regain a natural rhythm. Dar guided her to a log and had her sit.

Gradually, she noticed the rich and varied greens of trees and underbrush and the lush display of giant wildflowers on prolific vines. The vivid colors made her blink. The roar in her ears separated into birdsong—sharp caws, twitters, chirps, whistles, and melodious trills. A legion of forest insects added to the din.

"We'll eat our noonday meal here," said Leetu, lowering her pack to the ground. "After a little rest, we'll begin our trek to The Bogs."

"Where are we?" asked Kale.

"Fairren Forest," answered Dar. "About five miles west of Bedderman's Bog. Granny Noon wouldn't put us down in the swamp. Too easy to step right out of the gateway into something nasty." Dar chortled. "Or even someone nasty."

"What kind of creatures live there?"

"Not as many flesh-eaters as you would think."

"*Dar!*" Kale heard Leetu's reprimand given directly to the doneel's mind.

His response was muffled as he ducked his head and rummaged in his pack, "Well, it isn't completely terror-free. But there's a good chance we won't be accosted by gruesome bisonbecks or odious mordakleeps."

"Dar…" Leetu glared at the little doneel.

"What?" He spread his hands in a gesture of innocence.

"Eat your lunch," she commanded.

"Fine, if you see no reason to worry about bisonbecks who do the bidding of Risto"—he sat down on a log and pulled out his lunch—"or mordakleeps who team up with anything nasty and currently have a wonderful working relationship with that same evil wizard Risto, then why should I worry? Why should we warn Kale?"

Leetu's scowl turned darker.

Dar lifted his sandwich to his mouth, but had one more thing to say before he bit into it. "Actually, I agree with you. Worrying now over an encounter that might occur later would only ruin our digestion."

Leetu threw her hands in the air in a gesture of exasperation. She turned away from the doneel and faced Kale.

"Just eat," she commanded. "We have a long way to go. It isn't necessary to conjure up visions of disaster. Paladin has equipped us to handle whatever comes."

The emerlindian sat down and pulled out a book as well as a packet of food. She glared once more at Dar, who chewed contentedly without showing the least concern that he had upset the leader of their expedition.

Kale reached into the left-hand hollow inside her cape and pulled out one of the packets Granny Noon had provided. When she opened the bundle wrapped in a gauzy cloth, she found a sandwich made of tasty jimmin poultry. The lettuce popped with freshness when she bit into it, and tomato juice ran down her chin.

Her stomach rumbled in appreciation, but her mind dwelt on something other than her hunger. She firmly ignored Dar's hints at danger. She didn't want to think about whether or not he was teasing. Or how much was teasing and how much was real. The fact that she had "overheard" Leetu admonish Dar was much more comforting to think about.

I heard Leetu mindspeak to Dar. She called his name, sharp and angry. I heard the tone as well as the words, and it was definitely with my mind and not my ears. She wasn't mindspeaking to me, but to Dar. I didn't know I could listen like that to another's conversation.

Probably, I couldn't before.

Granny Noon said my talent would develop by being around Leetu. I guess this is the kind of thing she meant would happen.

Kale watched the emerlindian turn the pages of her book while she ate.

I wonder if I can listen to Leetu's mind while she reads.

Kale chewed her own sandwich slowly as she reached with her mind to Leetu. For an instant, printed words flashed in her mind. The page from Leetu's book blurred, and Kale saw Leetu's thoughts, images of mighty urohm soldiers mounted on gigantic horses moving in formation across a plain. In the distance, a dozen dragons flew in a line with one shimmering silver beast in the lead. Their destination was a bleak mountain range of obsidian black and ash gray. Storms shrouded the crater tops. The roiling clouds sent jagged bolts of green and purple lightning across the sky in all directions, accompanied by a menacing rumble of thunder.

Kale knew this was the ancient legend of the Battle of Ordray. She had heard the tale once in the tavern and had no idea what the army looked like. Nor could she imagine the landscape of the great conflict on her own.

Leetu's imagination, fed by her knowledge of the race of urohms, formed the pictures Kale viewed. Leetu had also seen the Valley of Columna. The beauty of the flowered meadows ended abruptly at the foot of the dark ridge of mountains. Kale closed her eyes and took in all the details Leetu summoned up as she read her book.

The leader of the urohm forces, Corne, sat with the diminutive kimen, Ezthra, before him on the neck of his war-horse. A few days before, Ezthra had arrived with an urgent plea.

Kale relished the story as she partook of Leetu's imagination. This was one of the most exciting accounts of Wulder's directly intervening on behalf of His people. The kimens' request and the urohms' response had earned Wulder's pleasure, and His reward was astonishing. Kale leaned forward and forgot to eat as Leetu continued to read.

When Ezthra first arrived, frazzled by fear and exhausted by a long, treacherous journey, he told Corne and the other urohm leaders his tale. The kimens, the smallest of the seven high races, had suffered through three dry years. A bisonbeck slave of Pretender had sought out the kimen high council and delivered an ultimatum. Pretender, through his messenger, revealed he had control of their weather, and unless they pledged allegiance to him, he would rain fire from the sky to finish the destruction of their forests and grasslands.

The kimens doubted Pretender's claim. Wulder commanded wind and rain and sun. They sent back a defiant reply.

Two kimens discreetly followed the bisonbeck to spy and bring back news.

One returned.

He reported to Ezthra and the other elders. The spy had no news concerning Pretender's claim to have gained control over the elements of weather. But he had seen armies of bisonbecks ready to descend upon the kimens. He'd crept into the field tent of a commander and listened to their plans to capture and enslave the kimens, destroy their homes, and stamp out their culture.

Bisonbecks, the most intelligent of the seven low races brought forth from Pretender's evil mind, were a hideous enemy. Rock-hard of muscle, thick-skinned like a crocodile melon, known for strength and endurance, the bisonbecks added an unholy rage in battle to their formidable ability to wipe out anyone who opposed them. What chance did the gentle, peace-loving kimen people have against them?

Kale had seen a few kimens. They used to come into River Away. She always marveled at the tiny creatures and had to stop herself from staring. Kimens stood a little over two feet high in delicate bodies that were sometimes lifted by a strong breeze so they appeared to fly.

In Leetu's book the storyteller explained that the kimens could hide, but that would be their only defense. In hiding, they would most likely prolong their existence. However, with bisonbecks occupying their lands, the kimens would be caught one by one. Those who remained free would bear untold hardships and slowly starve. If Pretender did rain fire upon them, the kimens would most certainly perish.

Pretender had in no way threatened the urohms. The storyteller made that clear as he related the legend. Corne stood up and spoke for his people. His compassionate response to the plight of the kimens provided the lyrics to many tavern songs. The urohms would not stand by in safety behind the black ridges of Dormanscz. The urohms would not allow one of the seven high races to suffer and expire.

They sharpened their wood-cutting axes to take into battle. They brought out their hunting weapons, made more arrows, and honed the edges of their small blades. Wives and daughters sewed makeshift armor out of thick leather hides. In three days they were ready to march against impossible odds.

As the men slept a final night in their homes with their families, Wulder came among them and increased the size of these valiant people to match the compassion of their hearts. They arose in the morning as warriors twelve- to fourteen-feet tall with new fighting skills breathed into their minds and souls.

Their clothing, livestock, and weapons had increased in size as well, but their homes and furnishings remained the same. Even today, the urohms build all but their beds on a smaller scale to remind themselves of the mighty gift bestowed upon them.

The legend unfolded on Leetu's pages. Kale relished the march across the Valley of Collumna. In the air, Wizard Dayen rode a regal dragon. He and eleven other wizards under the authority of Paladin had been summoned to flank the ground warriors. Even with this unexpected reinforcement, the battle undertaken proved to be costly.

Kale anxiously awaited Leetu's turning of the page. The hazy memory of the legend Kale had heard several years before came to life with Leetu's reading. She saw the awakening urohms' bewilderment and then felt their new courage as they realized Wulder had given them an extraordinary gift for battle. When the urohm leader Corne first spotted the battalion of regal dragons coming to join their forces, Kale thrilled with his expectations and rising hopes.

The images stopped. Kale opened her eyes to see Leetu had laid her book in her lap. The emerlindian glared at Kale.

I'm sorry! Shame washed over Kale. She'd been eavesdropping. Sneaky. Stealing Leetu's pleasure. It wasn't sharing; it was trespassing. Despicable. "I'm sorry."

Leetu closed the book with a snap, jumped to her feet, and strode away to a large trang-a-nog tree. She slapped her hand against the smooth green bark and stood rigid, staring into the junglelike woodland.

Kale looked over to Dar and saw him watching Leetu. He turned back to Kale. "What happened?" he asked quietly.

"I have offended her. She is justly angry with me."

Dar sat back against a tree, relaxed, and apparently examined the fabric of his linen shirt.

He doesn't care. Why should he?

Loneliness shrouded Kale's heart. Frustration, too. She wasn't very good at this questing business. Not any better at being comrades.

Dar cleared his throat, looked speculatively at Leetu, and then addressed Kale in a voice that could be heard by both of the girls.

"It is hard to win back the trust of a friend. But we live by the code of Paladin, and Leetu, although young, is well versed in his way."

What should I do?

"*You've said you are sorry. Wait.*" Kale heard his words clearly but could not take pleasure in another step of progress in her mindspeaking abilities.

Kale waited, her half-eaten sandwich forgotten in her hand. Leetu stood as a statue. Only the breeze lifting strands of her wispy white hair and pushing against the cloth of her tunic proved she had not turned to stone.

Eventually, her shoulders moved as she took several deep breaths. She turned, and Kale was relieved to see the ominous, cold expression had relaxed on the emerlindian's face. She stood as Leetu walked purposefully across the forest glade. Kale swallowed back another hasty apology when Leetu stopped two feet in front of her.

"I owe you an apology," Leetu began, and Kale caught her breath. She started to interrupt, but Leetu held up a hand. "Yes, it is I who must apologize, though I will wrest one from you, as well.

"Granny Noon reprimanded me on being lax in my obligation to you. She is right, as usual."

Leetu shook her head slowly and shrugged. "I've never seen myself as an instructor, and when given this assignment, I agreed with my lips but not with my heart." She looked away from Kale and then back. Leetu focused on Kale's face, deliberately making eye contact. "Just now I was angry because you experimented with your untrained talent and intruded on my privacy. Had I taken the time to guide you, this would not have happened. I apologize."

Kale stood looking at the emerlindian's colorless face. Her eyes were earnest. Her pale lips twisted in a slight grimace, showing her distaste for this conversation.

Dar tugged at Kale's sleeve. She jumped a little. She had not seen him come close.

"Accept," he urged her.

Kale nodded and looked back to the leader of their quest. "I accept."

Leetu let out a sigh. "Now for the intrusion. You have realized, have you not, the error of seeking the thoughts of a comrade to idle the time away?"

"Yes," said Kale. "It made me feel awful when I realized what I'd done. I *am* sorry, Leetu."

"Fine. Finish your sandwich as we walk. Dar can lead. You and I will discuss etiquette, among other fine points of your talent. Dar, keep an eye out for mordakleeps. Rumor has it they've been spotted near waterways farther and farther from the swamps."

12

SHADOW IN THE BOGS

The first thing Kale noticed as they went from Fairren Forest into The Midways, an area surrounding The Bogs, was the change in the scent of the air. Fairren Forest had smelled fresh with a breeze carrying the fragrance of tropical flowers. Now warm air lifted a musty smell of rich humus from the black ground beneath their feet. Not a whisper of wind cooled the sweat on their faces as the three stepped over hummocks and around knots of tumpgrass.

The trees in Fairren Forest had been alive with brightly colored birds and small furry animals of so many types Kale had only been able to name one or two. Dar offered to tell her the names of all the plants and animals, but Leetu hushed him.

"On another trip, Dar," the emerlindian had said. "Now Kale and I must work to equip her for this journey."

Leetu did not get distracted during the uncomfortable hike in the sweltering afternoon sun. She drilled Kale on the contents of her cape hollows, making sure Kale knew the identity and use of all the things Granny Noon had provided. Leetu also put Kale through some exercises in mind conversation, inserting from time to time the proper way to do things in a mindspeaking society.

Kale and Leetu communicated exclusively through mindspeaking. Leetu apologized to Dar, saying they did not mean to talk behind his back, but she wanted to give Kale as much practice as possible. Where Leetu had been negligent before, now she was conscientious, to the point Kale's head ached from all the mental exercise.

Bedderman's Bog began as abruptly as Fairren Forest had ended. After they had crossed the wide-open space of The Midways, the land dipped, and marshy patches squished under their boots. Kale gladly accepted the hazardous swamp as a reason to concentrate on where she put her feet instead of Leetu's lessons.

Massive swamp trees surrounded them. Their roots, partially entrenched in mud and murky water, made up a portion of the travelers' walkway. When the soggy ground gave no footing, Dar led them across the roots humped above the water like steppingstones.

In Fairren Forest, the vines had been crowded with thick green leaves. In The Bogs, large swamp vines with sparse, pale leaves roped around tree trunks. Tangles of thin, willowy vines draped over all the larger branches in gray-green clouds that looked like dripping foam. Dar said it was moss and burned well in a campfire.

Leetu took over the lead. As gracefully as she had climbed a tree before the grawlig attack, the emerlindian stepped from root to root and hillock to hillock. Dar adroitly followed. Kale, at the end of the procession again, hoped she would not land face first in the marshy water.

As Kale passed under a cluster of low-hanging moss, she heard a hiccup behind her. She turned abruptly, caught her foot on a vine, and sat down hard on the root of a cygnot tree. As much as the knobby wood hurt her backside, her main concern was the hiccup she heard again. She looked toward the sound, heard a definite hiss, and thought a shadow moved among the shifting shades of green a few feet away.

"What's wrong?" asked Dar just behind her.

"I thought I saw something."

"So you sat down to watch for whatever it is?"

Kale took hold of a vine roped around a tree and pulled herself to her feet. Balancing on the root, she still stared at the trailing moss.

"Kale." Dar tugged at her sleeve.

"What?"

"There's nothing there."

"I heard a hiccup."

"A hiccup?"

"Two, and a hiss."

"Two hiccups and a hiss." He put a hand in the crook of her arm and pulled her around to face the direction they should be going. "Come on, Kale. It was probably a beater frog."

"I saw something move, and it was too tall to be a frog."

"Okay." Dar's tone said he was going to be patient. "Use your mind. Reach out and see if there is anything besides Leetu Bends and myself close by."

"I don't think I know how to do that."

Dar shrugged and started after Leetu.

"Wait," Kale called, and he stopped. "Couldn't you smell something? I mean, you smelled the grawligs coming."

"Everything in this swamp smells the same." Dar wrinkled his nose. "Well, I suppose I'd smell a grawlig. Nothing can disguise the smell of a grawlig. But right now, Kale, all I smell is wet and mildew and stagnant water and decaying vegetation."

Kale sniffed the air and looked around. "It doesn't smell *that* bad."

Dar clicked his tongue and shook his head. Once again he started after Leetu, speaking over his shoulder, "Oh, to have the horribly deficient olfactory equipment of an o'rant."

Kale gave one last look at the place she thought she'd seen something and followed Dar. After only a few minutes, she felt the little hairs on the back of her neck rise.

Someone is watching us.

She stopped and listened. She heard the footfalls of Dar ahead of her but nothing from the nimble-footed Leetu. Insects and birds sounded natural enough. Occasionally, she heard a distant splash as if a small fish had jumped, or something fell in the water. Nothing like the human hiccup and the snakish hiss she'd heard before. As if conjured up by her thoughts, a shiny green snake slithered along a tree limb to her right. Her eyes went from the snake to Dar many yards ahead of her. Kale gave up trying to figure out anything but how to keep up with the doneel.

The trees grew thicker and the water deeper. Less land poked up through the marsh, and Leetu led them upward to walk through The Bogs on the lowest branches of the cygnot trees. At regular intervals on each huge trunk, limbs stuck straight out and twined with the limbs of neighboring trees. This made floors of tightly woven greenery in a network of strong branches.

Walking over this network was actually easier than walking among the roots and water below. Usually the space from one layer of branches to the one above was five or six feet. Dar and Leetu were both short enough not to be bothered much by the limbs above. Dar, surefooted as he was, had no problems. And of course Leetu's foot landed without fail on a strong branch.

Kale struggled. Her skirt and cape caught on twigs and wrapped around her legs. She was just tall enough that her hair got snagged, and occasionally she had to crouch. Between watching where to put her feet and keeping her head out of the upper layer of branches, she fell behind.

Each time she approached the trunk of the next tree, the thicker limbs provided easier steps, and she hurried. Most often the trees grew close enough together that it was hard to tell where one tree left off and the other began. But a few cygnots were spaced far enough apart that thin limbs interlaced in a shaky floor. Here Kale knew one misstep would send her crashing through to the water below. She had just eased herself over one of these areas when she glanced up to see how far ahead Leetu and Dar had gone.

A dozen feet ahead, a man stood in her way. She saw his feet first. The brown boots sagged around his ankles. Green-gray robes hung like wrinkled bark from narrow shoulders. His head disappeared into the cygnot branches of the level above. A long moss-colored beard and wisps of scraggly gray hair tumbled over his chest.

Kale blinked. The man was still there.

She retreated one step and lost her footing. She fell backward toward the thinner branches. They gave way but snagged her clothing so she hung suspended.

Kale struggled to hold on to the swaying structure and managed to hook an arm over a branch. Sunk beneath the level of most of the leaves, her vision was obscured, but she could hear.

"Oh dear, oh dear, tut-tut, oh dear." The muttering came from the man she'd seen.

"Help me!" she demanded.

"Oh dear."

Kale managed to get her hand through the foliage and grab a branch to hoist herself higher. She looked in the direction where she'd seen the old man and saw only a tree trunk with a massive cascade of moss where she thought she'd seen a beard.

Dar and Leetu were running back through the cygnots.

In moments they lifted her, Dar pulling her up while Leetu unsnagged her clothing.

"Did you see him?" Kale gasped.

"Who?" asked Dar.

"The old man."

Dar and Leetu looked around.

"Where?" asked Dar.

"He was there." Kale pointed to the tree trunk.

Leetu shook her head. "Just a trick of the light. No one's around."

"He spoke!" Kale insisted.

"What did he say?" asked Dar.

"Well, he said, 'Oh dear.' "

"Is that all?"

Kale felt her face grow warm in a blush. "He said, 'Tut-tut.' "

Leetu reached down and helped Kale to her feet. "Sounds like bird noises to me."

"It wasn't a bird. It was a man. An old man. A tall old man."

"Where did he go, then?" asked Leetu, once more scanning the area.

Kale looked around hopelessly. *Where did he go?*

A bird fluttered through the canopy and landed close to the trunk Kale had believed was a man. It preened a moment, running its bright yellow bill over ebony wing feathers.

"Tut-tut," it twittered.

Kale stamped her foot on the thick branch beneath her, and the leaves shook in protest all around.

"Oh dear, tut-tut." The bird bobbed its head and looked askance at the people invading its territory. "Tut-tut-tut-tut-tut-tut..."

"Oh, go away, you stupid bird." Kale balled up her fists and then folded her arms in front of her. *I will not cry.*

Dar took a step toward the bird and gave it a speculative look. "Maybe it's Fenworth," he said.

"The bird?" asked Kale.

"No, not the bird," said Leetu, and she began examining the area more closely. "But Wizard Fenworth has a reputation..."

The bird flew away as she walked up to the tree trunk and placed her palm on the bark. Dar took Kale's hand and pulled her to stand beside Leetu.

"Fenworth?" Leetu's voice sounded soft and persuasive.

"Wizard Fenworth," said Dar. "We really do need to speak to you."

Kale felt she must add to their pleas, but couldn't think of a thing to say. "Sir?" she croaked.

From a distant branch the bird watched. "Oh dear, oh dear, oh dear, oh dear, oh dear, oh dear, oh dear, tut-tut-tut."

"I think we're talking to a tree," said Dar and turned away.

Leetu sighed. "He's the master of The Bogs. We won't find him unless he wants to be found." She went to pick up the pack she'd dropped when she ran to rescue Kale.

"So what are we going to do?" asked Kale.

"Keep walking," answered Dar.

"Where to? For how long?"

"It doesn't matter where. And how long? Until Wizard Fenworth decides we can find him."

"Aren't there any other choices?"

"No," said Leetu and Dar in unison.

13

Dangerous Shadows

Dusk in The Bogs brought out a multitude of insects. They chirped, chittered, and clicked in the vegetation. They buzzed and whined around the travelers' ears. Some of them stung and bit. Kale hated it when they crept across her skin.

Dar, Leetu, and Kale stopped for the night, setting up camp in the thick branches near the trunk of a cygnot tree. The foliage thickly intertwined to make a secure floor. Kale had no doubt she would sleep soundly if she could ignore the bugs. Spreading her cape out over the springy limbs, she settled down to eat her next meal wrapped by Granny Noon in the loose-woven cloth. The lettuce still crispy, the meat as fresh as when first cut, the sandwich satisfied her hunger.

Dar came over.

"Tired?" he asked.

"Yes," admitted Kale.

He handed her a waxy bar. "Rub this on your face, hands, and ankles. It keeps the bugs away."

Kale gratefully took the thick, sweet-smelling stick and scrubbed it over her exposed skin.

When she gave it back to Dar, she noticed his clothes.

"You changed."

The doneel wore green trousers that hung loosely on his short legs. Over a crisp white shirt, a long emerald jacket flowed to his knees.

"I don't like to wear the same thing at night as I did all day. I don't sleep well in dirty clothes." He sat cross-legged beside Kale and fingered the material of her cape. "This didn't tear when you fell through the cygnot flooring."

"No, but my skirt has big holes in it."

Dar's ears perked up. "Give it to me, and I'll mend it."

Kale stared at him.

"Really," Dar insisted. "I like to sew. Many in my family are tailors."

"Is that what you would like to be?"

Dar shook his head. "No. Unfortunately, I was born with the wanderlust. It happens sometimes with doneels. If you have the spirit of adventure, it's painful to have to stay in one place."

"So that's why you're in Paladin's service?"

"I'm an adjunct."

"I don't know what an adjunct is."

"I am officially accompanying you and Leetu because the meech egg was stolen from the doneel region of Wittoom. I am not officially from The Hall."

"Oh, I thought you were."

"I know." Dar looked over to where Leetu sat reading a book. She had a lightrock in her lap, and the glow lit both the pages of her book and her face. He picked a broad leaf from the floor and bent it back and forth in his hands. "Someday I hope to be accepted at The Hall as one of their warriors. But there is a prejudice against doneels. We are considered too fastidious. Our love of music is supposed to be at odds with a desire to fight for right." He sighed and tossed the leaf away. "How silly!"

"I agree," said Kale. "I've seen you fight against the grawligs, and you *are* a brave warrior."

Dar winked at her and grinned. "But I do like to look nice."

Kale smiled back. She leaned closer to whisper, "I like to look nice too."

"Then give me your skirt, and I'll fix it."

Dar jumped up and turned his back.

Kale stood and untied the cord at her waist. When she removed the torn and stained skirt, the blouse Granny Noon had given her hung down to her knees like a nightshirt.

"Here," she said.

Dar reached a hand back over his shoulder. Kale placed the skirt in his fingers and sat down as the doneel walked away. Dar's skillful whistling drifted over his shoulder. Fiddlers had played the same elaborate tune at the River Away Tavern. The sound reminded her how far she had come in such a short time. Her old home seemed a different world to her now.

Will I ever get to my new home?

Reaching into a hollow in her cape, she pulled out her lightrock and one of the books Leetu had given her at Granny Noon's. *The Care and Feeding of Minor Dragons.*

The first chapter described the different types of dragons, their nesting habits, and the expected hatching patterns. Kale identified her eggs as those of minor dragons. These creatures would hatch thirty-three days after they had "quickened." To quicken a dragon egg, a warm-blooded creature must provide nurture. As Kale read, she realized she had done this with the first egg. By placing it in a pouch and hanging it next to her skin, near her heart, she had quickened the embryo inside.

Two weeks? With careful fingers, she touched the spot where her blouse bulged slightly from the egg pouch underneath.

I found the egg and showed it to the village council. Then they had to think and talk and think some more and talk some more to decide what to do. That took three days. I traveled for twenty-seven days. I spent the night in the cave and traveled another day. And today is one more. Thirty-two!

Kale pulled the egg pouch from under her blouse and hastily opened the top. When she slipped the egg out into her hand, she saw a fine network of cracks covering the shell. The egg had once been alabaster white. Now it appeared bluish-gray even in the azure light from her rock. As she held the egg tenderly in her palm, she felt movement within.

"Oh. Oh!" she whispered, barely containing her excitement. She glanced around to see if the others had noticed what was happening.

Dar bent over his sewing; Leetu's nose was in her book.

Should I show them? Kale looked back at the egg. *No. This is between me and the dragon inside.*

She held the egg close to her chest with one hand and picked up the book with the other. She needed to read more. What should she do when the shell cracked open? What should she feed the baby dragon? Should he be wrapped warmly or kept cool?

She read as long as she could keep her eyes open. Finally she tucked the egg back in its pouch, slipped the pouch securely beneath her blouse, and put the book and lightrock away. Even as she closed her eyes, she wondered about the baby dragon.

Will I be able to take care of it well enough? Did Wulder really decide I should be the one to raise the dragon? Is it a girl or a boy? What do you name a dragon? If Wulder gave me this responsibility, will He also tell me how to do a good job? When Mistress Meiger gave me a new task, she always made sure I knew how to do it. Surely Wulder is smarter than Mistress Meiger.

⊹┝━━┥⊹

Sunbeams filtered through the dense branches above and made a dappled green light in the bower around the three travelers. Kale opened her eyes, touched the pouch beneath her blouse, and sat up. The egg was still whole, Dar and Leetu were awake, and Kale was starved. Beside her, the skirt lay folded neatly. She shook it out to put it on and discovered Dar had remodeled it with his needle. Now she had a pair of knickers.

"Dar!"

He looked up at her call and grinned, the comical smile spreading from ear to ear. "Do you like them?"

"This is wonderful." Kale stood as he turned back to his breakfast. She pulled the knickers on, then tucked in her blouse. Twirling around on the thickly woven branch floor beneath her feet, she laughed. "This will be so much easier to walk in."

"Put on your boots," ordered Leetu, but Kale saw the friendly smile on the emerlindian's face. "Eat breakfast, sleepyhead. We have miles to go today."

Kale sat down again and pulled on her soft leather boots, tucking the new pant legs into the tops. "Do we know where we're going?" she asked.

"No," admitted Leetu. "But I aim to waste no time getting there."

Dar laughed. He had a bowl in his hand and spooned up what looked like porridge. Kale eyed his breakfast, and her stomach rumbled.

Again the cheerful doneel laughed. "There's plenty for you, if Leetu will wait long enough for you to eat."

Leetu had her bags packed. She sat down, rested her back against a trunk, and pulled out her book.

Kale smiled at Dar and winked. "I think I have time."

She savored the warm pudding, which tasted of cinnamon and apples, while Dar heated water for washing in a kettle over the fire.

The doneel took the dishes when she finished eating. "I'll go below with these and use swamp water to rinse off the worst of the leftovers." He disappeared through a gap in the flooring.

Kale put on her cape and then took out the egg to have one last look before they began the day's journey. As she cradled it, three sharp taps bumped against one palm. Then the dragon within lay quiet for a moment. The taps occurred on the other side of the egg next.

Just like the book said. He, or she, is twitching and turning. Maybe today the egg will hatch. She looked over to where Leetu still read. *Maybe I should tell her. Suppose we ought to stay in one place to let the dragon rest instead of being jostled around all the time?* She remembered the page that said dragons traveled well, but she couldn't help but think of how fragile a chicken egg was. Of course, a dragon egg was more like a stone.

She ran her finger across the crackled surface of her egg and realized the shell felt more like leather now than rock. Out of the corner of her left eye, she saw movement. Dar had gone down to the marsh level on her right. Why would he be coming up a different way?

She turned her head and saw only a dark shadow across the leaves. It rippled some, much like the other patches of dark and light cast by the sun and branches above. A shiver of fear ran down her spine. The shadow moved toward her emerlindian friend.

"Leetu!" Kale screamed.

Leetu sprang to her feet, a long-bladed dagger in her hand. The shadow rose up and formed a hideous monster. Tall and massive, the black shape seemed to fill up the small bower. Now that it stood upright, Kale could see arms reaching toward Leetu, a bloblike head silently wagging back and forth. He stood on two thick legs. A thin tail disappeared through the leaf floor at the spot where the shadow had first appeared.

Mordakleep!

Still clutching the precious egg, Kale looked around for some kind of weapon. Dar's sword lay in its scabbard across his packs. She leapt to grab it. For a few costly seconds, she struggled to release the blade from its sheath. When she turned with the sword in her hand, she saw that two more mordakleeps had oozed up through the floor and were taking shape around Leetu. The mordakleeps made no noise but plodded purposefully. Their grotesque mouths chomped, lips slapping against each other, teeth showing sharp and yellow. They looked eager to take a bite out of anything in their way.

Swinging the sword wildly before her, she charged the monsters attacking Leetu. Her blade cut through the nearest mordakleep. Black goo spurted, then splattered the front of her cape, her arms, and her boots. The liquid sizzled as it hit the moonbeam material and evaporated in a noxious fume. The globs of black drops pooled and skittered away like mercury.

The monster whirled around and clipped her chin with a backhanded swing of one of his massive arms. Kale flew backward and landed against a cygnot trunk. She gasped for breath and then shrieked again as she saw the mordakleep bend over and scoop up the egg she'd dropped from her hand.

Cold terror and then a sick emptiness seized her heart. Tears streamed down her cheeks as she stood to face the monster advancing toward her. Now she could see the features of his face, the gray hollows from which small red eyes glared, the wide mouth with a green tongue flicking over thin lips.

He silently lurched over the intertwined limbs, his great weight making the whole floor undulate like waves on an ocean. Clenching Dar's sword around the hilt with both hands, Kale waited for the monster to lumber close enough for her to hit. She saw the flurry of activity beyond. Leetu battled three creatures. Two more mordakleeps emerged from the cygnot floor. Dar had reappeared to help in the fight. But Kale's attention focused on the ugly mass of black slime menacing her.

"Dar, it has my egg!" she cried, and then the creature made a lunge for her throat. Instead of swinging the sword, she ducked and rolled to one side.

"Cut off its tail," Dar yelled. He had a gleaming dagger in each hand and rushed the monsters attacking Leetu.

Kale tried to work her way around to its back, but the mordakleep, in spite of its size, twisted and turned cleverly. Dar stood behind a monster hovering over Leetu. He swung his dagger down in a wide arc and sliced off its long black tail. Without waiting to see the body of the creature dissolve into a puddle and drip through the leaf floor, he circled around and lopped off the tail of the next mordakleep.

Kale jumped and stabbed at the monster coming toward her, its hands poised to grab and tear her into pieces. More often her blade swiped thin air instead of the flesh of the mordakleep. At last the creature stumbled just as Kale fell to one side. Horrified, she found herself lying on the black beast's slimy tail. With one whack, she severed the ropelike tail. She rolled away, gasping as the noxious smell rose from the dead creature.

Like the other monsters, this mordakleep disintegrated, once deprived of its tail. As the black form melted into a shadow and then seeped through the cygnot floor, it left behind the egg. Kale snatched it up, wiped the last drips of ooze from the shell, and held it against her chest.

Dar knelt beside her. She looked around and saw that all the monsters had gone. He rested a hand on her shoulder. Kale's sobs almost prevented her from speaking.

"Did it k-kill the egg?" she asked. "Did it kill the b-baby dragon?"

"I don't know," Dar answered.

"Will Leetu know?" Kale again looked around the empty bower.

Dar squeezed Kale's shoulder. "They took Leetu."

In Wulder's Presence

Kale peered along the tangle of cygnot corridors as if she would catch a glimpse of Leetu and her captors. The dim light of the shaded level revealed nothing more than straight branches connecting trunks at various intervals.

It's hopeless.

"What can we do?" she asked.

Dar sat down beside Kale. "First, reach with your mind. Try to contact Leetu."

Of course.

The words sounded hollow in her mind. She knew this would be the right thing to do.

How simple.

But Kale's bruised spirit could not jump to the challenge. Fear and sadness fought inside her. Tears already overflowed, and the sobs that just a minute before had hindered her speaking threatened to return.

I have to calm down. I can't do anything in a dither like this.

She closed her eyes. Dar still had a hand on her shoulder and his touch comforted her.

Leetu?

Darkness washed over Kale. She bent forward, then collapsed in a heap, pulling herself into a ball. She wanted to escape the anguish tormenting her. A void filled her soul. Emptiness pressed at her from every side. Oblivion threatened to hold her against her will in a place of no color, no sound, no life.

Kale cried out, calling for help in a twisted syllable that could not be formed into a word.

She felt Dar's hand upon her shoulder and a violent shake. "What's wrong?" He grabbed her other shoulder. "Kale, stop!"

She collapsed, stretched out on the bower floor. Gasping for breath, she opened her eyes and saw Dar bent over her with worry etched on his hairy features.

"I can't do it," she cried. "I can't. When I reached out, I didn't find Leetu but something hideous. I felt like my heart was being squeezed, and I couldn't breathe."

"It's all right. There will be another way." Dar sat back on his heels and seemed to consider the situation. "I'll fix you some tea."

Kale nodded. She wasn't thirsty, but a cup of tea was normal. A cup of tea was something she used to have in the afternoon after midday chores and before supper chores. She'd had a cup of tea at Granny Noon's. A cup of tea would be nice.

She didn't move as she watched Dar make preparations. He set up a tiny cookstove from his pack, lit it with a match, poured pure water from their bottled supply into the two-cup teakettle, and then pulled out his flute to play as he waited for the water to boil.

Kale clutched the cold dragon egg to her chest in a hand cramped by fear and strain. Every bit of the mordakleep remains had seeped through the floor and disappeared. No stains splattered the leafy floor or the rough cygnot trunks. Grawlig blood had been a gruesome reminder of their battle when the three had fought off the mountain ogres before reaching Granny Noon. Dying mordakleeps left no blood.

Kale shivered, remembering Leetu efficiently shooting off arrow after arrow into the melee of grawligs below the tree where the emerlindian perched. Kale had thought Leetu invincible, a mighty warrior from The Hall, Paladin's capable servant. Where was Leetu now?

"Is she alive?" The question burst from her lips. She hadn't meant to speak her doubt aloud.

Dar stopped blowing across the small hole in his silver flute. The lilting tune cut off on a high note. "I don't know."

"Will we be able to find her?"

Dar slipped the long, shiny instrument into its velvet case. "Wulder knows where she is. He knows our concern."

"But what good does that do us?" Kale's voice came out strident, loud, and impatient.

"Us?" Dar shook his head and reached for his pack. "Kale, in your mind you've made us the center of what is happening. Wulder is the center."

Kale's head pounded.

"Wulder knows what happened." Dar put tea leaves in the kettle and took it from the small fire. "We need to wait, Kale. Paladin, no doubt, has a plan, but we don't know it. We wait. In his time he will show us the way."

"We have to wait here?" Kale looked around the empty bower. Leetu's book lay open near the place where she was attacked. Her packs waited for her to pick them up to resume their journey. "I don't want to wait here."

Dar came to her, holding two heavy ceramic mugs. Spirals of steam drifted up from the dark liquid within. "I put lots of sugar in it." Dar smiled, not his usual face-splitting grin, but a tight smile. He handed her a cup. He then sat down beside her to sip from his own mug.

"Waiting is a state of mind," he said. "The point isn't whether we are moving or not, but whether we have made our own plans with insufficient information. Sometimes people make plans just to be doing something."

"I've never been in charge of making plans," said Kale.

"Good." Dar winked at her. "It's a bad habit."

She didn't think the village council would agree. They spent hours making plans, unmaking previous plans, remaking plans.

A small smile lifted the corner of her mouth. She felt a little better. She tipped the mug to her lips. The hot, sweet tea felt good in her mouth.

"Dar, why did you tell me to cut off the mordakleeps' tails? Why did that kill them?"

"Mordakleeps have hundreds of gills on the tips of their tails. A foot or so from the tip are their lungs. Mordakleeps must keep the end of their tails in water all the time, or they suffocate. Fortunately for them, they have very long tails that stretch even longer. Unfortunately for them, if the tail is severed from the body, they die instantly."

"How did you learn all these things?"

"I like to learn. I listen. And I figure any bit of information that comes my way is not by accident. Paladin has a way of giving his servants what they need."

"He teaches you?"

"Oh, yes." Dar drank from his cup and smacked his lips. Kale knew Leetu would have frowned at him. She didn't want to think about Leetu.

"I thought you had to go to The Hall," she said.

"To learn?" Dar looked genuinely surprised. "No, Kale, Wulder is everywhere, therefore His lessons are everywhere."

"I know Wulder made all things, and Pretender tries to copy His work. But I didn't know Wulder is everywhere. How could that be?"

"You're thinking of Wulder as having a body and moving from place to place." Dar stood and pivoted in a circle with his arms outstretched. "Wulder is everywhere. You can see His power by recognizing His work. When a flower opens, that's His work. When the stars twinkle at night, that's His work."

He paused, facing her. He let his arms fall to his sides. "Look at me, Kale. Right now, I am standing with Wulder all around me. I'm under His protection, within His will, standing on His pledge. And Wulder is, at the very same moment, in me."

"Me, too?" asked Kale.

"Yes." Dar knelt in front of her, his earnest face only inches away.

She looked into his dark brown eyes and saw strength and peace. She wondered at his patience with her. Often her marione masters gruffly explained things they thought she should already understand.

Dar winked before he continued, his funny face serious and yet cheerful at imparting what must be old knowledge to him. "So many people don't know who Wulder is or what He's capable of doing. Their ignorance doesn't make Wulder less of a being; it makes them less. Until they know, they can't be whole."

He leaned back and sighed, spread his arms out in a gesture of explanation, and continued, "It's so simple, Kale. Everything hinges on His willingness to be involved with our world. When a mountain stands instead of tumbling down, He's holding it there. If He were to leave…" Dar shook his head. "If He were to leave, all that He holds in order would spin out of control. But He will never leave."

"How do you know?"

"He made a pledge…and He sent Paladin."

"You must think I'm awfully stupid."

"No, Kale. How can you know things that haven't been told to you? Where you lived, no one knew the things you are destined to know. You're special, Kale. Wulder's guiding you on a special path."

"I don't know if I want to be special, Dar."

Dar grinned, put down his empty mug, and pulled out his flute. "Yes, you do, Kale. I want to be special, Leetu wants to be special, you want to be special. Wait until you meet Paladin."

"Why? What difference will that make? And besides, someone like me is not likely to meet Paladin."

Under Dar's breath, the flute let out a short, happy trill of notes. A mischievous grin stole over his face.

"Should I tell her?" he asked no one in particular. Then he blew a light warble from his silver fife.

Yes! I want to know!

Kale pressed the egg hard against her chest until the smooth roundness of it hurt. She reached with her talent and gasped as she encountered a wild rhapsody in Dar's mind. His joy flowed from him and washed over her. With so much excitement buzzing through her, she could no longer just sit. She jumped to her feet and stood awkwardly for a moment like a marionette just before the puppeteer moves her strings.

Then the music lifted her and directed her steps. At first it felt as if someone else was helping her keep time to Dar's melody. Someone else controlled each leap and pirouette. Gradually, she knew she was the one responding to this extraordinary elation. She danced around and around the bower.

Dar's jubilant song poured out through his silver flute. It filled the air and flowed into Kale's heart. Within the rhythm of the music, she embraced freedom, freedom to respond to the presence of Wulder.

Out of the shadows of the trees came kimens. First one and then three, then six, and then a dozen. Light as down feathers, they swirled in and out of the branches, around Kale and Dar. They fluttered in the dappled light of sunbeams filtered through layers and layers of intertwined cygnot branches.

Kale paused to watch the dizzy dance spiraling around her. She'd seen kimens occasionally in River Away. Then they were dressed in greens and browns, the floating material of their clothing fluttering with each breeze. These dancers wore pale colors glimmering with a special light that for moments rippled in rainbow hues before gleaming white, silver, yellow, and gold.

Kale looked down at her moonbeam cloth cape. It too had taken on the wondrous colors. She lifted the egg high above her head and rejoined the dance. Nothing was more important than expressing the celebration sweeping through her heart, her veins, her whole body.

She became aware of the kimens' singing. Their voices blended with the notes of the flute. She wanted to understand the phrases, but she didn't recognize the language. She wanted to sing the song, but she didn't know the words. Still, nothing dampened her joy. She danced.

The melody soared and then calmed. Like autumn leaves floating on gentle zephyrs, the dancers drifted, skimmed, fluttered, and settled on the cygnot floor.

With her eyes closed, Kale lay still. The last notes of heavenly music faded and floated away through the branches above. She breathed rapidly and deeply, but her body was not tired. She listened to the leaves rustle, or was it the kimens' tiny breaths? The sound faded, and she knew without looking that the delicate creatures had left the arbor.

She could feel her own heartbeat, the *thump, thump* in a vein in her neck, the steady pulse in the palm of her hand.

Her eyes flew open and focused on the egg.

"Dar," she called. "He lives. The egg is hatching. Dar, come quickly."

15

One Dragon

"What should we do?" Kale asked.

Dar sat down beside her in tailor-fashion with his legs crossed. "You're the one who read the book."

"Wait, just wait," said Kale. "That's all we can do. The book said to be patient."

"Sounds like good advice."

She realized Dar had given her this same advice earlier. She looked up to see a familiar wide grin breaking over his face. She smiled back.

"The book said to let the dragon hatch out on its own. I can hold the egg, but not peel back any of the bits and pieces of the shell as they crack."

"How long will it take?"

"Fifteen minutes to an hour and a half."

"Time for another cup of tea." He got up and went back to his cookstove.

Kale cradled the egg, intent on watching every moment.

A crack widened, and a wee bit of shell pressed outward.

"Dar, there's a hole. A tiny hole."

He looked up from dropping tea leaves into the kettle. "Can you see the dragon?"

Kale examined the grayish membrane exposed by the hole. "I think so."

"What color is it?"

Is that the dragon's skin? "I can't tell."

"I bet it'll be green."

Kale remembered what she'd read only the night before. The minor dragons had different abilities. All could fly. All could mindspeak with people. But some were fighters, some peacemakers, some masters of fire, some healers, and the list went on. The color of their scales indicated which subspecies they fell into. Thinking of the times she'd been healed by holding this egg, Kale nodded. "A healing dragon? Green. Yes, I think so too."

Dar brought her a fresh cup of tea while she watched, but he didn't hover over the egg as she did. Out of the corner of her eye, she saw him go back to his cookstove. He poured oil into a small pot and, out of his provisions, made a soft dough.

Kale heard a sizzle. She lifted her eyes to puzzle over what he was doing. He rolled dough into a thin rope and dropped it into his pot. An aroma of sweet bread arose with another rush of furious sizzling. She had no idea what he was making. Her attention went back to the cracking egg.

"Dar, it just broke out a piece the size of my thumbnail."

"Can you see the color now?"

Kale wrinkled her nose. "A dull green. Not nearly as pretty as your Merlander. But the book said the color will brighten after it hatches."

Dar brought her a tin plate piled high with finger-sized crispy bread. She took it absent-mindedly, placing it on the leafy floor beside her. She put one of the skinny fried sticks in her mouth.

"Mmm, this is good," she said, but her eyes were still on the egg cupped in one hand.

"Fried mullins," said Dar.

Kale nodded.

"Granny Noon gave me the recipe."

Kale nodded again and took another bite. Dar shrugged and walked back to his improvised kitchen. She noticed he looked dejected when he sat down and pulled out his harmonica.

"I'm sorry, Dar. They really are good."

Dar chuckled. "Don't worry about it, Kale. It's only right that your attention is on the hatchling. Let me see if I can come up with a tune suitable for the emergence of a minor dragon."

He placed the wide instrument to his lips and blew a reedy scale, then settled on a stately melody known as "The Dragon Dance."

Kale watched as another piece of the egg broke away. Anxious not to drop the baby should he suddenly tumble out, she placed her other hand beside the one holding the egg. The dragon's head pushed through and slid across her wrist. Its wings emerged and then tiny front legs. It rested. Kale watched it take a long breath and let it out. Another and another. Then with a jerk, its hind legs kicked the shattered shell away.

"He's out," she whispered. "He's out."

With eyes still closed, the baby dragon rubbed his ridged chin over Kale's skin. She cradled him with one hand and picked away the bits of discarded shell with the other. Soon she felt the familiar thrum she recognized from when the dragon had first quickened in the egg. It lay in her hand, gently stretching, rubbing its scaly skin against her roughened palm. It twisted on its side and then its back, seemingly trying to move every bit of its hide into contact with Kale's hand.

As she watched, the gray-green color took on a richer hue. Shades of emerald green appeared on its back. Lighter, brighter shades lined its sides. Its underside glistened with the pale green of a new leaf. She marveled at its miniature claws and the delicate membranes stretching over its wings.

The dragon opened tiny eyes, dark and glittering, and looked directly into her face. Its eyes locked with hers, and she took in a sharp breath as she felt the mind connection snap into place.

"It's a boy," she told Dar in a soft voice. "His name is Gymn."

Dar's music stopped. He slipped the harmonica into his jacket pocket and came to admire the newborn.

"He's a beauty, Kale."

The dragon flipped over on his belly and stretched. Kale felt his tiny feet pushing into her palm. He raised up on hind legs and cautiously his wings unfolded, stretching into a six-inch spread. The leathery membranes darkened to almost black but still the tinge of green held.

"Let him hear your voice, Kale. Sing to him."

"What shall I sing?"

"Anything."

Kale searched for something she knew all the words to. Ordinarily, a slave was not encouraged to sing, but she'd rocked many a fussy baby for the dames of the village, and those were times she was allowed to croon.

She began to hum a harvest tune about seeds and sun, rain and grain. Dar pulled out his harmonica and joined her. Encouraged, she sang,

"Dry seed planted in the ground,
Wait for sun and rain to come 'round,
Hope in the future, rest in the land.
You are part of Wulder's plan.
Toommba la-la, trillo coom day.
Toommba la-la, sen-sa-may.
Toommba la-la, trillo coom day.
Toommba la-la, sen-sa-may."

Gymn perched in the palm of her hand, swaying gently in time to the music. Then his outstretched wings moved up and down with a rhythmic swish-swish. Kale felt his hind leg muscles tense as she started the second verse. Suddenly, he leapt into the air, flapped his wings with more strength, and landed on her shoulder. She laughed out loud as the tiny green creature snuggled up against her chin and rubbed her cheek affectionately.

Dar lowered the harmonica and smiled. "When will he be hungry?"

"Tomorrow," Kale answered, "according to the book." She reached up one finger to stroke the baby's soft green belly.

"Then let's get moving."

"Moving?"

"I told you I have the wanderlust, Kale. We'll explore The Bogs. We might find a trace of Leetu Bends or a clue as to where to find her."

Kale's heart plummeted. How could she have forgotten? Leetu was in danger. She closed her eyes and reached with her mind, hoping she'd brush against the presence of the emerlindian.

Darkness hit her. Gymn squeaked and fell from her shoulder into her lap. She opened her eyes to see his limp body across the fine material of one knickered leg.

"Dar?" Kale squealed.

"Don't panic, Kale." Dar leaned over the baby dragon. "He's still breathing."

16

Finding the Trail

"What happened?" Kale tried to keep the panic from her voice.

Dar ran a finger down Gymn's back.

"Watch his tail," he said, and again stroked the length of the animal's back. When he reached the vertebrae at the base of the tail, Gymn's tail tip twitched. "There! He's unconscious, but there's no bad damage if his reflexes are still good. He's breathing, too, without any raspy noises or gasping. I think he'll be okay."

"But what happened?"

"I don't know, and there's not much point in guessing."

Dar and Kale continued to watch the baby dragon. Soon his eyes fluttered, and he looked up at Kale. Immediately, he sprang to his feet and scrambled under the edge of her cape and into the top pocket.

"He's afraid," said Kale. "I can feel it."

"What's he afraid of?"

Kale thought about the sequence of events.

"I reached for Leetu, and that same ugly darkness met me," she explained. "That must have been what happened." She paused, cupping her hand over the cape where the baby dragon shivered in the pocket underneath. "I think he fainted."

Dar chortled. "Well, I've never heard of a dragon fainting before, but he *is* just a baby."

Dar got up and went to pack away the rest of his equipment.

"Do you want to go up a couple of layers in the cygnot? The air will probably be cooler and fresher."

"Are you hot?" asked Kale.

"I'm not wearing a moonbeam cape, Kale. I am very hot!"

She stared at him, not understanding.

He let out an exasperated sigh. "Stick out your hand. Stretch it away from the cape. Feel the air."

Kale did as she was told. Her fingertips touched the air a foot beyond the moonbeam material. The hot, moist atmosphere of the swamp coated her hand. She drew it back quickly. Within a circle around the cape, the air cooled to a pleasant temperature.

Startled, she glanced up at Dar and saw a peculiar expression on his face. She reached to his mind and caught the last of a thought.

"...lot to learn."

I know. Councilman Meiger said I didn't know anything.

"First off, it's rude to come into my mind like that. You are supposed to be learning manners as well as controlling your talent."

I'm sorry. I didn't think first.

"Second," Dar went on without acknowledging her apology, *"there's no crime in not knowing something. However, it's a shame to turn away from an opportunity to learn. Not a crime, but definitely a poor choice.*

"Don't worry about what you don't know. Just think about how much you've learned in the last few days. You keep up at this rate, in a week you'll know everything there is to know in the universe."

Kale watched a big teasing grin take over her friend's face. Even if he was poking fun at her in his big brother way, she liked him, and she liked what he said. It was true. She had learned an awful lot since she left River Away. And now she was responsible for a baby dragon.

That thought made her smile. And she had seven more dragon eggs that would someday hatch. She couldn't help the glow that settled on her. But her next thought snuffed out the light. She was also supposed to find one wizard who didn't want to be found, a meech egg held by the evil Wizard Risto, and Leetu who might be dead already.

She saw Dar latch the straps of his pack and swing it onto his shoulder. He picked up Leetu's bundles as well. One he handed to Kale. The other he tucked under his arm.

"Dar?"

"One thing at a time, Kale. We do the one thing that is in front of us to do and trust Wulder to lead us to the rest."

"Are you sure you don't read my mind?"

"No, but your face is pretty easy to understand. You looked happy, then worried, then panicked."

Kale nodded.

Even encumbered by so many packs, Dar made a courtly bow in her direction. "Shall we go, my lady?" He swept one arm toward the treetops. "Our destiny awaits us."

He had at least made her feel more cheerful. Kale softly laughed, patted the pocket holding the cowering dragon, and got to her feet.

"How do we get up there?"

"Climb," said Dar. He walked closer to the nearest trunk and then peered upward. "There." He bent his knees for a second and then sprang straight up, catching an overhead branch on the first try. Without a struggle, he chinned himself on it, and then poked his arms through the foliage. In only a moment, he wiggled through to the next layer.

Kale watched his feet disappear and almost panicked again.

Stop it! she told herself. *He's out of sight, not gone. You'll be up there with him in just a minute. You're taller than Dar, and you've climbed lots of trees. You can do this.*

Dar's smiling face appeared, hanging upside down from the hole he'd made.

"Coming?"

"Yes."

She moved underneath him. He put an arm down to help.

"I can do it," she protested.

The arm disappeared, and the branch trembled as he moved away. Kale's head brushed the lowest hanging leaves. She pushed her hands and arms through the hole and realized the opening was only big enough for the smaller doneel. She'd have to force her body through, enlarging the hole as she went.

Twigs and rough limbs scraped and poked as she hoisted herself, using her arms.

I can't get stuck. It would be too embarrassing.

She reached out and grabbed a branch woven into the cygnot floor, and by pulling on it, she inched higher over the edge. Another stout twig jabbed her stomach. Rolling sideways, she managed to unhook herself from that snag only to find her blouse caught again.

Well, I said I could do it myself, but he doesn't have to ignore me.

She craned her neck around to the left. No Dar. She looked to the right. No Dar. Startled, she scrambled out of the hole, heedless of the grabby branches.

"Dar!"

"Up here."

Kale looked up to see his face showing through the next layer of branches. Biting back angry words, Kale stood and leapt at the hole. This time the branches were more than a foot above her head, but her irritation toward the doneel gave her a boost. She squirmed through the hole quickly.

"Good," she said. "You haven't had time to vanish."

He looked puzzled. "Vanish?"

"Never mind." She stood and brushed loose bits of leaves from her clothes. "Are we going up again?"

"No, I think this will do. Let's go."

"I want to check on Gymn first."

Dar sighed but didn't object.

Kale opened the cape and peeked into the top pocket.

"He's asleep."

"Ready now?"

Kale didn't answer. She looked around. "I can stand up straight here, and the upper limbs won't catch in my hair. It's lighter, too. More sun gets through." She lifted her face and closed her eyes. "And there's a breeze." She opened her eyes to look at Dar. "Why didn't Leetu bring us up here sooner?"

"Look down," said Dar.

Kale immediately saw the difference. "Oh."

These limbs were thinner with less foliage. Big holes gaped in the flooring, and some places looked as if the branches might give way under any weight at all.

"Leetu wanted you to have a chance to practice walking where it was easier," Dar explained. "The cygnot floor is called planking. Each time you go up a level toward the sun, the planking is less firmly woven together. The branches are younger, more supple. They bend and slip to the side when you step on them. You've practiced below. Now with a little more practice, you'll master this planking as well."

"It would have been more comfortable for you and Leetu up here."

"Yes, but not if we had to keep dragging you back up through several floors of the cygnot forest."

Kale nodded agreement with Dar's explanation, but she suspected Leetu had thought mostly of making the journey easier on a poor, untrained o'rant girl.

"Well," she said, "let's get started. Which direction?"

Dar pointed. "That way. Deeper into The Bogs."

"Can the mordakleeps get up here?"

"Yep." Dar headed out.

Kale followed, watching every step and cringing a little when the intertwined flooring sank under her feet. Several times she hopped to a bigger branch just as she felt she was sliding through the planking.

Kale stopped occasionally as the day progressed to peek at the newborn dragon. Mostly Gymn slept. Once in a while he stretched and turned over.

He seems comfortable. The cape is probably making his little pocket den just the right temperature. She slapped at a bug as it landed on her face. *At least he'll be able to catch enough food for himself. I hope he has a hearty appetite.* She slapped at another insect, and waved her hand beside her ear where something small buzzed. *I'll have to ask Dar for that stick that keeps the bugs away next time we stop.*

"Kale." Leetu's voice, weak and distant, called to her.

Kale stopped in her tracks. "Dar!"

"What?"

"I heard Leetu."

Dar sprinted back from his position in the lead.

"What did she say?"

"Just my name, and then nothing."

"Concentrate."

"I am. I mean, I will."

Dar stood perfectly still and stared at her. Kale closed her eyes so she wouldn't have to see him and his expression. He looked as if he expected her to know where Leetu was and whether she was all right and if they could get to her. And oh, how she wanted to know all those things too.

With her eyes closed, she reached out to Leetu. She hesitated. That awful dark emptiness might be out there ready to swallow her up.

It hits so hard when it comes. It hurts. It's like a nothingness, an emptiness, a...something I can't name. But it hurts all the way down to my heart.

Stop it! Stop it! I've got to quit thinking. I've got to try. Leetu spoke to me. She did. I didn't imagine it. And if she spoke to me, she needs me. She's someplace where Dar and I can help her. I've got to quit thinking about doing it and just do it.

Gently, Kale reached. Slow. Careful. Like reaching out in the dark, she felt ahead of her, not rushing. She didn't come up against the ugly, terrifying blackness. She reached and stretched, and her mind penetrated all directions at once.

Then she knew.

Her eyes flew open and she looked toward the setting sun. Small pink splotches of sky peeked through the overhead branches.

"That way," she said.

"That's where we just came from."

"Leetu is somewhere in that direction."

"Are you sure?"

Kale started to say yes and then stopped.

Am I?

She reached with her mind again but focused west.

There. She felt it again. Leetu. Not her thoughts, but her person. No words, just a longing to be free, to escape.

"I'm sure, Dar, and we have to hurry."

Tears filled her eyes. She didn't know if the desperation was her own feeling or Leetu's.

"We have to hurry."

17

LOOKING FOR TROUBLE

Dar wasted no time. With a nod to Kale, he slung his knapsacks across his back again and headed in the direction she had indicated. Kale followed, glad that she had picked up some skill in walking the treacherous planking at this altitude.

Leetu, we're coming.

No response.

I wonder if she can hear me?

Leetu?

No answer. At least Kale hadn't been slapped in the face with that horrible darkness.

She blanked out all thoughts and tried to hear Leetu mindspeak. With her mind on her friend instead of the planking, Kale's foot hit a thin spot. She plunged through the branches, catching herself with her arms. Dar sprinted back, grabbed her shoulders, and helped her struggle back to the level where they were traveling.

"You all right?" He picked a caterpillar off her arm and placed it on a branch.

"Are you asking *me* if I'm all right, or the caterpillar?"

Dar's eyebrows shot up and his ears flattened. "Not all right." He shook his head and turned away, already resuming his quick stride. "Definitely grumpy."

"I'm not grumpy!" she called after him. She glared at him for a moment, then realized she was wasting more time. His back couldn't see her scowl.

"I'm not grumpy," she muttered and took three tentative steps after the doneel. The branches gave way under her, and she hopped to a sturdier limb.

I'd better pay attention to my feet. I wonder if we should go down a level. The problem is speed. Where can we travel the quickest?

The problem is me. She sighed. *Dar could reach Leetu faster without me. I'm slowing him down, falling through the planking.*

She followed Dar, wondering if she should suggest moving down. She could move faster on a level below, provided she didn't step wrong in the dimmer light. Here she could see better, but it was tiring to have to be so cautious.

Too bad there isn't a river and a boat. Too bad we don't have riding dragons like Dar's Merlander. Even a dirt road and a farm horse would move us faster than this.

She came to a thicker patch of cygnot forest and took advantage of the more closely woven planking to catch up to Dar. He moved at the same pace whatever the quality of planking beneath them.

They stopped for a quick meal late in the day. Inside the gauzy wrapping, Granny Noon's sandwiches were still fresh. Gymn came out of his pocket-den and sniffed at her bread, cheese, and sliced jimmin but didn't take a bite. He skipped up her arm and perched on her shoulder until she finished eating. When she stood up after her meal, Gymn dashed back into his pocket-den.

"Let's keep moving as long as we can," said Dar. "Do you still think Leetu is in that direction?" He pointed through the trees.

She allowed her mind to test for Leetu's presence and felt a faint nudge, much less pronounced than before.

Is she weakening? Is she farther away? Is she dying?

Leetu?

No response. At least she knew which direction to go.

She nodded in the direction the doneel still pointed. Dar shouldered his pack and struck out.

Soon daylight faded. The moon's soft glow did little to help her distinguish between dense clusters of leaves and a solid branch. The swamp bugs became more aggressive. She'd forgotten to ask for the stick that discouraged bugs. Dar's furry covering didn't appear to be as attractive to them as her exposed skin.

Big and small flying insects tormented her, distracting her from the serious business of putting her feet down in the safest spots. Kale slapped at them and vowed that as soon as Dar stopped for the night, she would ask him for the stick. She wouldn't ask now. They must reach Leetu.

After Kale stumbled several times, Dar found a place to camp. He said nothing about her clumsiness. She was too tired to even be embarrassed that they had to stop because she was falling on her face every couple of steps. She spread out her cape close to a cygnot trunk where the planking was thick and solid.

Dar handed her the insect repellent. Kale muttered a thank-you. She rubbed the fragrant bar over every bit of skin sticking out of her clothing, even in her hair.

She wanted to talk to Dar, ask him some things. How far? How soon? Would the mordakleeps be there? But her tongue wouldn't form the questions. As soon as she curled up on the moonbeam cape and pulled it around her like a gray cocoon, she fell asleep.

<hr />

Kale opened her eyes to a misty morning. Hazy sunlight filtered through the branches above. A small creature scuttled across her shoulder and down her back. The tread of the animal raced down her leg and back up. As it reached her thigh, Kale sat up with a jerk. She relaxed when she saw it was Gymn. He scurried in another direction, made a leap, and caught a bug. He chewed only a second before he swallowed and then went in pursuit of more breakfast. He never ventured more than a couple of feet away from Kale.

The aroma of sweet porridge drew Kale's attention. Steam from Dar's cooking pot swirled around his hand as he stirred with a long-handled wooden spoon.

Kale rubbed sleep from her eyes and crossed her legs.

We should get up and move. But Dar's fixing breakfast, and there's no hurrying him. She sniffed the air and smiled as she watched him. *He'd say, "Doneels take their meals seriously." And, "You can't expect to think and act your best on an empty stomach." I know a lot about him and how he'll act. I think I know more about how he'll act in a crisis than I know what I'll do. I'm willing to sit here and wait for him to produce some delicacy. I do want to find Leetu, but I'm afraid of what we'll find with her.*

Her stomach rumbled. Oats fortified with dried parnot fruit tantalized her nose with a savory odor.

"I had a dream last night," she said, trying to get her mind off food.

"An interesting dream?" Dar lifted his stirring spoon to his lips and tasted.

"I don't know."

He took a pinch of white powder from an open packet beside the small cookstove and dropped the grains into the pot. He stirred slowly. "What was it about?"

"A dragon."

"A meech?"

"I don't know. I've never seen a meech. This dragon is larger than Merlander, though."

Dar nodded. "Not a meech."

Kale tilted her head and thought. "It's funny, Dar. I can still see her. It's kind of like the dream is still going on, even though I'm awake."

Dar's ears perked up, and he stopped stirring. "What is the dragon doing?"

"Nothing much. She's sad and lonely. She's wounded."

"Where is she?"

"In a barn."

"What else is in the barn?"

"Nothing. I mean, no animals, no hay. It's empty. The gray boards in the walls have gaps so I can see outside. The air is cool and dark and damp."

"That's not a dream, Kale." Dar sounded excited. "You've connected with a dragon. Don't lose her."

"Lose her? How can I keep from losing her? I don't know how I got her. Or even what it means when you say I connected with her."

Dar dished up lumpy porridge into a bowl, stuck a spoon in it, and hurried over to serve Kale. "Eat this. We have to go."

Something about his expression worried Kale. "To find Leetu, right?"

"No, to find that dragon."

"Leetu is more important."

Dar hurried back to his cookstove. He extinguished the flame as he ate hasty bites of breakfast straight from the pot.

"Bigger than Merlander, you said. She can probably carry both of us. Kale, if we find this dragon, we can fly to where Leetu is, and just as important as getting to her in time is being able to get away once we rescue her. And we need to get away fast. Doesn't a dragon sound pretty convenient for this type of mission?"

"But she's wounded."

"You have a healing dragon."

A dozen more arguments popped into Kale's head. They didn't know for sure where Leetu was or where the dragon was. What if Leetu died while they made this detour to find a dragon who might not want to help them?

She opened her mouth to speak, but Dar interrupted her before she got out one word.

"What's her name?"

Kale stared at him, surprised that she knew the answer. She swallowed hard. What was going on? "Celisse."

Dar whooped and made a leap into the air. "She knows you're coming, Kale. She's given you her name. What's she doing now?"

Gymn slowly settled on Kale's knee. He stretched out with his body along her thigh. His legs and tail went limp, and he closed his eyes. Kale took one finger and gently stroked his back. He sighed and rolled over. His swollen belly looked like a round pomegranate. Obviously he'd found enough insects to make him content. Kale looked at Gymn, but in her mind a large shadowy image hovered behind the minor dragon. A massive, placid female dragon swayed her head back and forth.

"She's humming," Kale answered Dar's question.

⊹⊱⊰⊹

Soon after they began their trek, they had to descend to the swamp. The cygnot forest thinned at the edge of The Bogs. Kale followed Dar, hopping from one root curved up out of the water to the next until they began to find patches of sodden earth and then dry land. Dar and Kale came out of Bedderman's Bog and clambered up the embankment. Muggy fog blanketed The Midways.

"Which way?" asked Dar.

Kale nodded one direction. "Leetu is there." She turned and nodded in another direction, not quite opposite. "Celisse is there."

"Which one is closer?"

"The dragon."

"Let's go then." Dar started off, wading through the tall, dew-drenched grass. He disappeared into the cloud hovering on the ground.

Kale planted her feet and didn't budge. "We can't even see where we're going."

She heard him stop. He muttered something under his breath and came back.

"It doesn't much matter if we can see or not," he said. "It's not like we know where we're going. We don't have to look for landmarks. We just have to follow your instincts. *You* will take us to the dragon, and then *you* will take us to Leetu."

Kale started to object, then swallowed the words that came to her mouth. Dar was right. For this one time, she had to lead.

"This is my destiny," she whispered.

"This is only the beginning, and we're going to miss it if you keep lally-gagging. Come on."

They marched through the field until they came to a road.

"Which way?" asked Dar.

Kale clearly felt the wounded dragon's misery and nodded toward Celisse.

Several miles later, the morning mist had still not burned off. Kale took hold of Dar's sleeve and slowed to a stop.

"We're close, Dar," she whispered, "but there are other creatures here."

"Animals? A barn should mean there are animals around."

"These aren't farm animals."

"Then protect yourself before you reach into their minds."

"What?" Kale's fingers dug into Dar's arm. "Reach into their minds? No."

"Would you rather walk into a trap?"

Kale was silent.

Dar put a hand on her arm. "Do you remember the words Granny Noon told you?"

She nodded.

"Say them."

"I stand under Wulder's authority."

"Go ahead then," Dar urged her.

Kale sank to her knees and concentrated. She felt a malevolent force batter her mind, but she repeated the words, *I stand under Wulder's authority.*

"Four," she told Dar. "Bisonbeck men. They are to guard the dragon and not let her escape." Kale gasped. "Oh Dar, they shoot her. Twice a day, they shoot her with a poison arrow. They come in with a big, ugly crossbow and shoot her while she's still helpless from the last arrow. It keeps her docile. Wizard Risto is coming to enslave her with his magic. Tonight. He'll be there tonight."

Kale then turned her mind to Celisse, deliberately allowing herself to touch the dragon's feelings. She recoiled from the encounter. "Oh, Dar. She's so sick she can hardly move. I'm glad we came to rescue her."

"Concentrate on the bisonbecks, Kale," Dar ordered. "Do you know where they are standing guard?"

Kale nodded, her eyes still closed. "One in front, one in back. The other two are sitting by a burned building, a house."

She opened her eyes to watch Dar as he thought. His serious expression told her he was plotting out what they would do. His mustache twitched. His ears lay back flat against the top of his head, almost disappearing in his mane of hair. She waited patiently.

After a while he nodded, rubbed his hands together, and then turned to look into her face.

"You will sneak into the barn."

Kale felt her eyebrows rise. A lump formed in her throat.

Dar patted her shoulder. "You'll be fine. Whenever you get scared just stop and be still. The cape will hide you."

She allowed her head to bob up and down slowly in agreement, but she couldn't work up any enthusiasm for his plan.

Dar continued. "Once you're inside the barn, you and Gymn will heal her."

"You mean Gymn will heal her."

"No, I mean you and Gymn." He let out an exasperated sigh. "Gymn is small and young. Celisse is big and wounded...and poisoned. With your talent, you will magnify Gymn's gift and be a part of the circle that heals Celisse."

"Oh." Kale wanted to ask a dozen questions, but she feared she wouldn't understand the answers. Maybe she would understand better after she'd been in the barn, been part of the healing, and escaped with Celisse and Gymn.

At the beginning of their journey into Bedderman's Bog, while she had listened to Leetu explain a hundred different things, she had found all of it together boggled her mind. But at the same time, her simple o'rant mind accepted small things easily if she ignored the overwhelming bulk of ideas. Then as she understood the small things, the larger things began to make sense. As an o'rant slave in a marione village, she had never felt her mind was very useful. Now she began to wonder if her mind was just different, not inferior.

Dar continued explaining his plan. "After you have told Celisse what we're going to do, mindspeak to me that you're ready. I'll create a distraction, you open the barn door, and you and the dragons fly out. Simple."

"Simple," Kale repeated, a squeak breaking the word in two.

Dar clapped her on the shoulder like he would a comrade-in-arms. "Nothing to it."

"Nothing to it," repeated Kale, and this time the words barely rasped out of her throat.

"Fine, then. Let's go," said Dar. "We want to do this before the sun burns off the mist."

Kale looked at him with wide eyes. She didn't *want* to do this before or after the sun burned off the mist.

18

THE DRAGON'S LAIR

They may not see me in this cape, but they for sure will hear my heart thumping.

Fog obscured everything beyond two feet in front of Kale's nose. She didn't feel invisible and therefore safe. She felt as if someone could sneak up on her out of the hazy surroundings.

Tall, sun-bleached stalks clustered behind her in a field where the corn had been stripped from the plants and the poles left to wither and die. Her head jerked every time she heard a faint rustling in the dried leaves. In the eerie half-light, Kale could not see how far the old cornfield stretched out behind her in acres and acres of cold soil. She knew the dead corn went on for miles. She'd walked around this field, petrified ever since she left Dar's side. There might not be one living creature hidden among the dry stalks, or there could be thousands. Kale shivered.

Dar had not let her come through the field. He said the noise she'd make as her footsteps crackled on the old foliage would give her away. That started her thinking about who, or what, was out there to hear. While she circled the farmer's harvested land, she took care every step of the way to make no noise. She'd listened for evil beings prowling around the countryside, looking for easy prey.

Looking for someone like me. Easy prey. That's what I am. Gullible, too. I shouldn't have let that crazy doneel talk me into this.

Surprised that she'd made it this far, Kale wasn't about to let herself get caught now. She knew the barn was close, because from where she stood, she knew exactly where the riding dragon was. She hesitated at the edge of the barnyard, close to the dragon, but also just as close to the four guards.

Kale cocked her head and listened, holding her breath. Her ears strained to pick out a sound, hopefully a normal sound. Did she just hear a whisper in the field? She waited. Nothing. Pent-up breath eased out between her teeth.

Inside his pocket-den, Gymn wiggled.

You just be patient. I'm not ready to step into the open.

The moonbeam cape covered her from neck to toes. She pulled the hood up and let the filmy material drop in front of her face. Blinking, she discovered she could see more clearly through the light fabric.

I should have worn the hood all along. Why didn't someone tell me the moonbeam cloth would make me see better? Dar or Leetu? Or Granny Noon? They probably forgot how little I know.

She moved her head slowly, looking at every feature of the open space. Cornstalks stood as if looking over her shoulder. A rutted road ran past her into the shrouded horizon.

With trembling fingers, she fastened all the buttons on her moonbeam cape.

I hope I really am invisible.

Two long slits enabled her to reach through the sides of the cape, but she didn't want her arms exposed. She pulled them inside and wrapped them around her middle, trying to hold the butterflies in her stomach still.

Gymn wiggled again.

I'm not asking your opinion, Gymn. Your job is to be quiet and stay out of the way until it is time to heal Celisse. My job is to help Celisse escape.

Kale rubbed her hands together. The cold came from her fear within, not the damp air without. She would have to be brave.

Her foot responded sluggishly as she tried to take a step. She was *so* close. The barn, hidden under a blanket of moist air, housed Celisse. Kale felt the dragon waiting for her. Two bisonbeck men dozed by a smoldering fire. She smelled fresh smoke as well as an acrid odor rising from the burnt timbers of the house and charred furniture.

One man paced behind the barn, pivoting with military precision as he reached the vacant pigsty and striding back to the empty corncrib where he turned again. Kale knew his thoughts were on battle. He resented guarding a barn. The other guard stood stock-still and thought of food—lots of food…and rich wine and sweet mead…and a certain barmaid.

Kale hoped he concentrated on that maid's green eyes and smiling lips and didn't notice one o'rant girl creeping up to the barn.

As she tiptoed into the farmyard, Kale peered into the grounded cloud and finally saw a dark building loom in the mist. She moved silently, following a railed fence. The barn stood gray and battered, its huge front doors closed. Two openings into the hayloft gaped as square black holes. To Kale, they looked like sinister eyes watching her movements.

The front peak of the roof displayed a weather vane tilted at an awkward angle as if it had received a blow. The roof curved down on both sides to about six feet from the dirt, then went off in straight lines to stop abruptly over ramshackle side walls. Here, a normal-sized door offered Kale an entry into the dragon's prison.

Gratefully, she saw that the heavy wooden doors that allowed wagons and animals entrance to the barn swung outward. The metal brackets that would have held the bar to bolt the door were empty.

These bisonbecks must be pretty confident their prisoner is too sick to break out.

Kale could see the man guarding the front. His massive dark shape leaned against a wagon some distance across the barnyard. He shifted. She heard armor grate, hard leather creak, and boots shuffle in the dirt. His head remained still, his eyes facing front. Kale inched to the edge of the barn. Only three more feet and she would be at the smaller door.

I hope it isn't locked.

I hope the hinges are oiled.

I hope the guard doesn't see me.

She sighed.

I hope I don't die of fright.

She put a foot forward. The guard suddenly stood at attention. Kale lost her nerve. She froze. She felt Gymn stiffen in her pocket.

The warrior flexed his shoulder muscles, bent his head to one side until his ear almost touched his metal armor. He straightened his neck and tipped his head the other direction. Then he marched in place for a minute, lifting his knees high. At no time did his attention leave the barn.

This isn't going to work. He doesn't see me now, but when I move to the door, he will. I need Dar to create a distraction. But if he raises a ruckus now, then he'll have to do it again later. And it might not work a second time, and that's when Celisse and I will be ready to come out of the barn.

Kale watched the guard as he returned to his casual stance, still conscientiously observing the old wooden structure.

Suppose I mindspeak to that guard and tell him to go somewhere. No. Why would he follow my orders? Maybe I could make him think it's his idea. Oh, I don't know what to do.

She went over the mind exercises Leetu had drilled into her head.

A picture! I'll create a picture of something crawling on the other side of the wagon. And a sound! He'll go look.

Kale imagined a man, a young, strong marione man. As she filled in the details, she realized she was picturing Bolley, one of the best fighters in River Away. When satisfied with the vividness of her image, she projected it to the guard's mind and, at the same time, imagined the sound of a rock scraping against metal. Only the soldier would hear the created sound.

Kale nearly bounced with delight when the guard crouched. He lifted his battle-ax to a ready position and stealthily crept to the end of the wagon, looked, and then moved around the corner beyond Kale's vision. She scooted to the door and pushed with her shoulder. The door opened with only a slight protest of rusty hinges. She bolted into the barn and eased the door shut.

The dragon inside crowded the open space between the walls lined with stalls. Her tremendous bulk blocked everything on the other side of the barn. As far as Kale could tell in the gloomy light, the dragon was black and gray with no glistening streaks of vibrant colors like Merlander.

Celisse greeted Kale with a mellow call like a mourning dove's coo.

The dragon's memories washed over Kale. She tried to comprehend the fast flow of information. Sorrow and rage pulsed in the dragon's account of the tale.

The people of the house were all dead. Celisse grieved the loss of her "family," and Kale's tender heart ached with the dragon's.

A detachment of soldiers had burned the house. Rough bisonbeck men carried off all the farmer's crops. Ropmas, another of Pretender's low races, had driven off the farmer's livestock to feed Wizard Risto's people.

Celisse's torment tangled the account of her defeat into a disordered mess. Now Kale saw images of a battle in the farmyard. Celisse had returned from a trip to town with the farmer and his oldest son on her back. They'd swept into the yard and fought the squad of soldiers left behind to complete the pillaging and torch the farmhouse. The farmer and his son were no match for the ruthless warriors. Soon only Celisse raged against them. She eventually sought refuge in the barn and struck out at those who tried to enter.

Evidently, messages had been sent to the main body of the army. Risto's men did nothing to keep their plans secret, and Celisse's keen hearing picked up many conversations. A crossbow marksman had arrived with special arrows. The man had no trouble shooting the cornered dragon with a poison that kept her mind fogged, her body in agony, and her will to live sapped.

Celisse knew Risto himself was coming to claim her for his own fleet of dragons. Her resistance dwindled with each poisoned arrow. Every time she felt her strength returning, the soldiers reopened the barn doors, and the marksman stepped into view, firing another arrow into her flesh.

This had started several days before. Wounded and hungry, Celisse didn't think she'd last much longer. But with the arrival of Kale, her will revived. If she lived, Celisse wanted to join allegiance with the mighty Dragon Keeper.

Now the dragon's hope soared and invaded Kale as the o'rant touched Celisse's thoughts. Kale trembled as she tried to sort through the dragon's turmoil.

In addition to the emotions transferred from the dragon, Kale's heart responded to the story of Risto's callous destruction of the honest farmer and his family. She had to deal with her own feelings of disgust and anger. She understood Celisse's desire to join forces with those who opposed Risto's evil. She, too, felt an outrage against his crimes.

However, one aspect of Celisse's determination to seek revenge puzzled Kale. The o'rant girl had never heard of the "mighty Dragon Keeper" and could only guess his identity.

Paladin? she quizzed the dragon.

The dragon's thought pattern rippled with laughter. *"You are the mighty Dragon Keeper."*

Kale's mouth dropped open, and she closed it with a snap.

"That's ridiculous. I haven't even been to The Hall yet." She spoke sternly to Celisse and moved closer. In the murky gray light, she could see an odd spiny growth on Celisse's back, over the left wing, and behind a shoulder blade. She studied it for a moment and then let out a horrified gasp.

The poisoned arrows! Long barbs stuck out of swollen flesh like pins in a cushion. Kale's stomach turned just the way it had when she had to pull a fishhook out of little Dubby Brummer's thumb.

This would be worse, much worse.

19

HEALING

Kale's memory latched on to one of Leetu's instructions.

The purple root cleans a wound and kills the pain.

Kale tore the buttons of her cape out of the buttonholes and whipped the special garment off her shoulders. She turned the cape inside out and laid it on the barn floor. Kneeling, she began to empty the two side hollows. Gymn poked his head out of his pocket-den and watched intently as Kale sorted through the many different items.

"Where is it? Where is it?"

Finally, she pulled a purple tuberous root out of the pocket.

"A knife. I need a knife."

Gymn darted out of his hole, dove into a hollow, and came out seconds later with a pocketknife in his mouth. He dropped it in front of Kale and lunged back into his own pocket.

Kale muttered, "Thanks," and picked up the knife. By scraping the root with the edge of the blade, Kale made a pile of creamy violet powder. When she had a handful of the precious medicine, she took it over to Celisse.

"I think you'll have to lay on your side in order for me to reach the wound," she told the huge beast.

The dragon, already in a prone position, shifted, and her bulky torso rolled over. Exhausted, she stretched out her neck and closed her eyes. Her shallow breathing barely stirred the bits of hay on the dirt floor. Occasionally, a moan escaped her throat.

Kale went right to work. She spread the powder over the swollen flesh, around the protruding arrow shafts, and put an extra amount where heat radiated from pus-filled sores.

"I suppose it would have been better to make a poultice, but we don't have what we need." She spoke aloud, but when she looked at the dragon's face, the huge beast seemed to be unconscious.

"I'm doing the best I can, Celisse."

I really hope it's enough. Granny Noon, you should be here.

Kale remembered something the old emerlindian had said as they parted at the gateway. "My hope goes with you."

Kale leaned against the ailing dragon's side.

"Will that help? Will Granny Noon's hope help?" she asked in the cool, dark barn.

Kale waited. The medicine needed some time to work, but not much. Leetu had said powder from the purple root worked quickly. While the minutes ticked by, Kale went over some of the other medicinal objects Granny Noon had put in her hollow pockets. She remembered a brown vial with a cork stopper. She returned to the cape to rummage through the collection.

"Here it is."

She walked back to the dragon, pulling the plug out of the neck of the bottle as she went. She held it under her nose and sniffed. Her head jerked back, and her nose wrinkled at the strong odor of scarphlit.

Kale inspected the open wound where she'd applied the purple root powder. It already looked better.

She started to pour on the oil and then paused to speak to the dragon, "This won't hurt."

Celisse didn't seem to hear.

Kale dripped the oil from the small brown bottle on the wooden shafts of the arrows where they entered the dragon's body. Then she sang ten verses of "The Beggarman's Wife" in her head, using the tune to measure off the twenty minutes needed.

The wounded flesh felt cooler under Kale's fingertips. She carefully pulled on the first arrow and mentally thanked Granny Noon for the oil when the rod slipped out with no problems. In a few minutes she had extracted all of the huge poison darts.

"Now for the healing." Kale went back to her cape and tenderly took Gymn from his pocket-den. "I don't really know what I'm doing. I don't suppose you do either. We'll both touch her and touch each other because Dar said something about a circle. Then all we can do is leave the rest to Wulder."

Kale leaned against Celisse's side near the wound. She placed Gymn on the beast's dark, scaly skin but kept her hands cupped around the tiny dragon. Then Kale relaxed. Her body molded against the hard-muscled Celisse, and her mind wandered much as it did when she was tucked in bed and ready to sleep.

In this half-awake state, she began to feel the same surge of energy she had felt when Dar played praises on his flute and the kimens appeared to dance in the cygnot bower. The feeling rose and fell, swelled up and drew back, much like Dar's music. Kale liked both the calm parts and the wild, energetic surges. With joy, Kale realized Wulder was part of the healing circle. Celisse, Gymn, Kale, and Wulder. The truth nearly took her breath away; it was so wonderful.

Then the feelings left, drained away, leaving only a hum of gladness in her soul.

Celisse stirred, raised her head, and yawned. Kale saw new skin where the horrible infected wound had been. The healing had worked.

Kale moved back to her cape and sorted through the various objects she'd left in a heap. Gymn zipped back into his pocket while she tucked items into the cape hollows.

She heaved a big sigh. She had accomplished one part of her mission. Time to let her doneel friend know what was happening.

She's healed, Dar.

"Good. But I think more time has passed than you're aware of. It's afternoon. The fog is holding. It's a very sticky cloud we've been blessed with this day. But still we must get away."

I understand.

"See if Celisse can fly."

Before she could even ask the question, the riding dragon conveyed her enthusiastic answer into Kale's mind.

Kale grinned. *Dar, she can!*

"Well, get busy!"

"We can't waste time," Kale spoke to the dragon. "Where's your saddle?"

The dragon thought of her saddle, and Kale sensed the location. She moved into a stall, dragged out the heavy leather contraption, and pulled it toward Celisse.

Gymn came out of his pocket-den and climbed to perch on Kale's shoulder. His eyes grew big as he saw Celisse wide awake and moving.

Celisse stretched her neck out until her huge head hovered directly over the minor dragon. She sniffed the little creature. With a whoosh, the air at Kale's shoulder drew into the large dragon's nostrils. Gymn gave a short, shrill cry and collapsed in a heap. Kale caught him as his little body slid down her chest. Startled, Celisse backed up.

In the dim light, Kale examined the baby dragon.

"Fainted again." She went to her cape and carefully placed Gymn in the inside pocket he had claimed as his den. Then she returned to her most pressing problem.

"This is where Dar's fine plan begins to fall apart," she grumbled as she examined the odd contraption on the ground. The saddle had a place for two people to sit, one behind the other. Lengthy straps ran out of every large flap of leather. "I told him I've never been near a riding dragon, let alone put a saddle on and climbed aboard. I've never even saddled a horse." She turned the saddle over and investigated the underside.

"'You can do it. You can do it,' he says. And I say, 'What if we get into the air and this thing comes loose? Then what will happen, Master Dar?'"

Kale turned the saddle over once more. "I think this is the top and this is the front." She looked at the large dragon. "How am I supposed to get this on you? You're as big as a barn." She looked around at the empty stalls and the bare hayloft. "Well, almost as big as a barn."

Dar?

"What?"

Tell me how to put this saddle on Celisse.

The dragon lay down on the dirt floor. Following Dar's instructions, Kale stood on Celisse's leg. The small o'rant girl heaved the cumbersome double-seater over the dragon's back, between her wings. The riding dragon stood to allow the buckles underneath to be secured. After several tries, Kale finally had all the straps going the right direction and fastened to the correct places on patient Celisse's body.

I'm ready, Kale announced to Dar.

"Have you unlatched the barn doors and climbed into the saddle?"

No, just a minute.

Kale ran across the dirt floor. She put her eye to the crack, trying to remember if she had seen anything propped against the outside of the doors to keep them from opening. *No, I remember the door was clear, and the bar brackets were empty.*

One glance told her that no one had since barred the door. The afternoon haze swirled between her and the charred ruins of the farmhouse.

A breeze!

A patch of sun broke through the thinning fog. She could clearly see the bisonbeck on guard.

They were running out of time.

20

First Flight

Dar?

"I'm here."

We're ready.

"Good. This fog is going to blow away in the next few minutes. I'm moving into the farmyard. Don't come out of the barn until you hear a long blast from my trumpet. When you come out, fly high and don't look back. Got it?"

Got it.

Kale put on her cape and approached Celisse.

"Now, I've never done any riding of any kind unless you count riding in a wagon, and I wouldn't count that if I were you. So I'm not going to be good at this. I guess I'm saying I'm a bit nervous."

Celisse sent Kale an image. The huge, matronly dragon relaxed in the sun with numerous small children clambering over her. Then Kale saw the dragon in flight with a small boy clinging to Celisse's saddle. The o'rant girl breathed a sigh of relief and climbed onto the dragon's back.

She hooked her knees over hard leather braces on each side of the saddle horn. These braces made a three-quarter loop, providing a sturdy anchor for her legs to squeeze during flight. Kale assumed that she would clutch this safety device and any other within reach as soon as they were airborne. The saddle horn had two padded handles. A second seat, attached to the first, extended out behind her. The farmer's saddle had no fancy scrolling in the leather—no ornamentation at all—but it was strong, well put together, and in good repair. Kale thought it was a splendid saddle.

No reins extended from Celisse's head to Kale's hands. The thought of using reins to direct a dragon was ridiculous. A dragon rider communicated to a dragon through mindspeaking. The dragon followed suggestions, if it desired. Dar had given Kale rudimentary instructions on flying with a dragon. No one thought of the dragon rider as master and the dragon as beast of burden. The two formed a team, and that was only if the dragon so chose.

Kale heard the rapid blasts of a trumpet. She recognized the melody within the first distinctive notes. "March of the King of Lightyme" was a popular tavern tune.

"What's that?" a soldier's rough voice bellowed.

"Music," another bisonbeck answered with a sluggish voice as if he'd just awoken.

"I know that, you clout. Where's it coming from?"

"Well, would you look at that?" exclaimed a third voice.

Kale very much wanted to see what was going on. To do so, she pictured the soldier who stood guard by the wagon. She repeated the words Granny had given her for protection in an evil mind and entered the man's thoughts just as the soldier announced Dar's arrival.

"It's a fancy-dressed doneel!"

Through the soldier's eyes, Kale saw Dar in brilliant yellow and blue court dress with a horn pressed to his lips. The little doneel came high-stepping out of the fog, playing the small silver trumpet as if he were leading a marching band. He strutted right into the open area in front of the barn.

Kale held her breath, wondering what her little friend would do next. He had never divulged the details of the distraction he would create.

"Oh, be careful," she whispered. She watched through the mind's eye of the soldier as two bisonbecks circled and flanked Dar. She squealed when they charged. Celisse shifted nervously beneath her. Gymn curled into a tight ball in his pocket-den. She felt him tremble. But Dar leapt into the air as Kale had seen him do before, and the two soldiers collided with each other instead of trapping the doneel.

Dar lost not one note in his tune as he landed and continued his cocky march around the farmyard.

"Why, you little—" The soldier on guard by the wagon suddenly charged Dar. Kale threw the enemy bisonbeck an image of blinding light just before he would have tackled the doneel. Unfortunately, she also blinded her vision of the action being played out in front of the barn door.

A long blast interrupted the pleasant tune from Dar's trumpet.

"Oh," said Kale, startled. "Let's go!"

Celisse needed no more prompting than that. She ran full tilt ahead, smashing the wooden barn doors into pieces. Two steps out in the open, her mighty wings extended. With a lurch, she rose into the air. Kale held on tightly to the horn handles in front of her. She tried to open her eyes, but they remained scrunched tightly shut. Wet, cool air rushed into her face, preventing her from forcing her eyes open. She ducked, cowering over the front of the saddle, pressing her forehead against the hard scales of Celisse's neck.

She stayed that way as long as the position of the dragon's body beneath her indicated they were climbing into the sky at a sharp angle. Finally, they leveled off. Kale forced her eyes open. Below them the fog swirled, thinning, breaking up. Trails of misty white hung over pastureland, wooded areas, and furrowed ground. She saw patches of green, a river, a road, and a few buildings.

Celisse banked, her body tilting to one side as she glided in a circle and headed back the way they had come.

"No, Celisse," cried Kale. "Dar said to fly to safety and come back to pick him up later."

Through the dragon's mind she saw little children, a plump woman with a kind face, an old lady in a rocker on a farmhouse porch, and two men, one old and one young, but so alike in looks they had to be father and son. These people were Celisse's family, and Kale felt her own heart clench with grief as she responded to the creature's sorrow. But another emotion was mounting within the dragon's breast. Anger. Wild, intense anger.

The anger became so hot it burned Kale's mind. It grew and lost control and surged out of the dragon's heart as rage. Celisse meant to return to the farm and avenge the deaths of her people.

No, no, Kale begged as the dragon's speed increased.

They flew over the farm now, and Kale saw the tiny figures below. Dar in his bright clothes, a tiny smudge that jumped out of the way of the larger, darker bisonbecks as they tried to capture him. It looked like a game from so high in the sky.

Celisse folded her wings and started a plummeting descent.

NO! You can't. Dar is there in the middle. You'll hurt him by mistake. This is wrong, Celisse. Wrong! You can't kill them. You'll be a murderer too.

Celisse gave no response to Kale's pleas. No coherent thoughts flowed from the dragon's mind, only unrelenting hatred. Kale watched the ground rushing toward them and closed her eyes against the terrifying sight.

A bisonbeck shrieked just before Kale heard a sickening thud. She felt Celisse jerk and knew from the shift in the huge body beneath her that they were climbing again.

She opened her eyes and saw red blood splattered thickly along the dragon's dark neck.

No, Celisse. Kale sobbed. The dragon soared upward, changed directions, and dove for another attack. This time she killed the last three bisonbeck soldiers, one with her teeth and two with a swipe of her tail.

Kale clung to the saddle horn, weeping as the dragon circled rapidly upward. The air became cold and the wings of the dragon slowed to a less frantic beat. Just as Kale began gasping for air, the dragon stopped the skyward climb and began to glide back to earth in large, unhurried loops. Kale's body ached from the sobs that had torn at her while she begged Celisse to stop. A keening wail reached Kale's ears. She felt spasms radiate through the enormous dragon. That's when Kale realized Celisse was crying as she flew back to the farm.

Kale discarded each thought of condemnation as it came to her mind. She would not judge the dragon. Kale had been long enough in the world outside River Away to understand there were things she did not know. She was building a new system of discernment based on truths she had never known existed. Paladin had sent her on a quest to find a meech egg. But maybe on this journey she would discover some important things valuable to her alone.

She wondered how Paladin would feel about the dragon's attack. When Kale asked if Paladin approved of killing, Leetu had said, "Paladin believes in protecting his people." Did Paladin also approve of avenging his people? And wasn't it up to Paladin and Wulder to judge where only they could possibly know all the facts?

She placed a hand on the thick, black scales in front of the saddle's horn. Celisse had fought the monsters who killed her family. She'd won, but she'd need a friend to fight the battle of loneliness ahead.

It's my place to be your friend, Celisse.

Kale shook her head as she realized something. Her "place" used to be village slave. She was to stay in her "place" and do the chores assigned her. Then she'd been given a position in a party going on a quest. In that instance, too, it was an outside force determining her "place." She'd just offered her friendship to someone in need. And it truly was "her place" to do so.

This is what it means to be free. I can choose to do what's right. I choose to follow Paladin. I choose to search for the meech egg. I, Kale Allerion, choose to find Leetu Bends and help her escape if I can.

The words "if I can" echoed in her mind.

Granny Noon said that if a mind was blocked I could get in by saying, "In Wulder's service, I search for truth." What if the means to rescue Leetu is blocked? Will Wulder help me get past trouble? I could say, "In Wulder's service, I search for Leetu." Would that work?

A strong image interrupted Kale's thoughts. A kaleidoscope of books and faces with mouths moving rapidly in speech flashed through her mind. A tornado-like wind swept aside these images. The pictures of a multitude of words were replaced with a heart.

"*Not the right words, but a heart in the right place.*" Kale's eyes widened as she recognized the voice delivering the message. Granny Noon!

21

A Hard Decision

Kale clung to the saddle, limp with exhaustion. The cold wind in her face kept her awake. The hot sun on her back kept her from freezing. The combination of sun and breeze dissolved the remaining mist on the ground. Even so, as Celisse circled, coming lower and lower in the sky, Kale couldn't see Dar anywhere near the farmyard. A new panic rose in her throat. Had he been killed along with the bisonbeck soldiers when Celisse made her reckless attack?

Dar?

"*What?*" The grumpy tone warned Kale something was wrong.

Are you all right?

"*My goldenterm silk court coat has a rip in it.*"

Can you fix it?

"*Yes.*"

Dar's sharp response surprised Kale. Was he angry with her or Celisse or both? She wondered whether his irritation sprang from his coat being torn or from his orders being ignored. Kale tried to read Dar's feelings and tap into his thoughts, but her mind wouldn't cooperate. Her whole body felt as though she'd been harvesting turnips for a week. Her brain must have been as worn out as her muscles.

She needed to get to Dar's side quickly. She wanted to see his face and perhaps be able to read his expression. Mostly, after the harrowing ride on the dragon's back, she wanted to be safe on the ground and with someone she could trust, even if that someone was presently grouchy.

Where are you?

"*I returned to my belongings. I can't wear torn clothing, now, can I? I have certain scruples about my appearance. Our business is important, or have you forgotten? We aren't a troupe of ragamuffin peddlers. We have a quest. We must be on our way. Too much time has been spent battling bisonbecks. Rescuing an emerlindian warrior is next on our agenda."*

His tirade ended abruptly. After a brief pause Kale again heard his thoughts.

"Focus on me so Celisse can get my direction. She should land here and avoid the farm. It's not good for her to dwell on what is past."

Kale silently agreed and did as Dar instructed. Soon the dragon's feet touched the ground in a clearing among tall trang-a-nog trees. Sunlight glinted off the shiny smooth bark, and the huge green leaves fanned the air as the draft from Celisse's large wings disturbed the woods.

The doneel already wore a sporting tunic of crisp green over a white linen shirt. He'd tucked purple breeches, striped with green to complement his tunic, into glossy black high-topped boots.

In imitation of Leetu dismounting Merlander, Kale swung her right leg out of the brace and over Celisse's back, then disengaged her left leg and slid down the dragon's side. However, the o'rant girl lacked the grace of the emerlindian, and her legs were cramped from clinging to the saddle in flight. She landed squarely on her feet and collapsed into a disheveled heap as her knees buckled.

Dar offered her no assistance, so she wiggled around until she sat cross-legged. The great dragon slumped into a prone position and stretched out behind her. Gymn crawled out of his pocket-den and cautiously peeked around the opening of the cape. Kale felt his discomfort. His stomach twinged, and she didn't know if it was hunger or fear. He darted down her front, vaulted from her legs, and took off after a grasshopper.

Dar folded his torn clothes and packed them into his bag. He spoke over his shoulder. "Ask Celisse if she's fully recovered."

Again, Kale did not have to ask the question. The dragon seemed to understand Dar's words as soon as he spoke.

"She said yes, Dar, but I think you can speak to her yourself. She always answers before I ask. So she must understand you."

Dar stopped what he was doing and looked at Celisse. He tilted his head in contemplation. "It *is* possible. Presumably, she's lived among people, away from other dragons, for years. Most dragons can only communicate easily with one person. Merlander and I converse readily. But Merlander shuns connections with any other two-legged beasts, as she calls us. She's quite gabby with her dragon friends, of course."

Dar walked over to Celisse and laid his hand upon her scaly cheek. "You've had a rough time of it, old girl. And you're a very special dragon. I would have been honored to be counted as one of your comrades."

Kale felt the hum of pleasure emanate from deep in the riding dragon.

Dar sighed as if burdened by a weighty grief. "I'm sorry you won't be able to serve Paladin with us."

The hum ceased. Dar trudged back to his belongings with his shoulders drooped and his head hanging.

"Kale, your things are here too," he said. "There, under the fortaleen bush. We have to be going. It's a long way by foot."

Kale didn't understand any of Dar's actions, but for the moment, she was too weary to protest. She shook her head in bewilderment as she moved over to the shrub and looked under the prickly lower branches. One of Leetu's packs was hidden there as well. Kale wasn't about to poke her hand into those sharp briars. She scoured the ground for a long stick. Finding a dead branch, she used it to snag the bags and pull them out.

Once she had them both on the grass before her, she looked for Gymn. The little dragon scurried about on the opposite side of the clearing from Celisse. He seemed totally unconcerned over the emotions of the others. He grabbed insects from the air and scavenged in the foliage for more.

Kale wished she could be so detached. She didn't want to figure out why Dar had turned against Celisse. She didn't want to think about the horrible things that had happened to the dragon and her family. She certainly didn't want to think about the gruesome way Celisse had torn into the guards. She took off her cape, rolled it with Gymn's pocket-den on the outside, and attached it to Leetu's pack.

Dar stood ready to go, not looking at anyone but staring off into the trang-a-nog woods. Celisse lay with her neck stretched out, her chin in the dirt, and her eyes closed.

Kale approached Dar. Her stomach tightened. Her jaw muscles ached from clenching her teeth.

"I don't understand." She pushed her troubled thoughts to the surface and made herself speak. "I thought we needed Celisse. Are we just going to leave her? She has no one, Dar. She's all alone."

"We can't trust her."

Kale glanced at the dejected dragon. "Her heart is broken."

"We can't trust her."

"What do you mean? She's not a bad dragon. She loved her family of people. She cared for them and helped them."

"And because they were killed, she threw all caution to the winds and came back with vengeance in her heart. She had you on her back." His words came out like sharp blows of a hammer. "You who know nothing about riding a dragon. A novice. She knew that. She knew I was on the ground in the midst of the bisonbeck guards. And with hatred in her heart, she dove from the sky to kill. At that moment, it didn't much matter to her who she might kill as long as she got those four bisonbecks."

Kale spoke softly. "I can understand her rage, Dar. She was killing murderers. Those four bisonbecks will never torture, maim, or kill innocent people again."

Dar looked from Kale to Celisse. The dragon still lay motionless next to tall trang-a-nog trees. The large, thick, richly green leaves contrasted sharply against the dragon's dull gray and black scales. Some of the fierceness left Dar's face as he gazed at the despondent creature.

"That's *your* reasoning, Kale, and it had absolutely nothing to do with *her* reasoning." He sighed heavily. "The truth is, she was beyond reasoning. She didn't kill to protect innocent people in the future. No, that's not why she tore through that yard and slaughtered those soldiers."

"Why, then?"

Dar's jaw clenched and the frown grew tighter across his brow. "She allowed anger to rule. That is never the way of Wulder or Paladin. Justice, yes. But not bloodshed to express rage."

Dar pointed to Gymn. The little dragon had eaten his fill and had stretched out on a boulder to sun himself. "Get your friend. We have to go."

Kale scooped the drowsy dragon into her hand and carefully tucked him into his chosen pocket-den. She couldn't help but look with sadness at Celisse. The riding dragon's eyes were squeezed shut, and she'd turned her face slightly away from the people in the clearing.

"Does she understand what we're saying, Dar?"

"Oh, yes, and even if she didn't, she would know the truth in her heart. A follower of Paladin does not demonstrate how upset he is by uncontrolled carnage. A follower of Paladin thinks. He thinks of the consequences of his actions. People in this region instruct their children in these simple truths as soon as they can listen to the stories of old. Celisse has lived among the high races. She has embraced the ways of Wulder."

"What will happen to her?"

"I don't know." Dar shrugged his shoulders and turned abruptly toward the path that led into the woods. "To endanger you and me in order to satisfy her need for revenge shows that Celisse can't be trusted." Without another look at the riding dragon, he started down the shaded pathway. But he continued to lecture Kale. "We may get into another perilous situation, and we need to know that those by our side will follow orders, follow the way of Wulder, follow the teachings of Paladin even under duress. She took off on her own and followed her own inclination. We can't trust her."

Kale shifted her shoulders, trying to settle the packs she carried in more comfortable positions. Reluctantly, she followed Dar. She didn't look forward to this journey. The way would be hard. There was no guarantee they could rescue Leetu. No certainty that Leetu, Kale, and Dar would live to find Wizard Fenworth and the meech egg. Her heart tightened like a fist in her chest. Would she feel better if they could stop for a rest?

No, it's not just being tired that hurts. It's having to accept something I don't like. I wouldn't leave Celisse. I'd give her another chance.

"Dar, I offered her my friendship." She made one last plea.

"You aren't her friend if you accept unacceptable behavior. Leave her in Wulder's capable hands, Kale. He cares more than you do."

The wide path through the woods curved here and there, meandering around bigger trees and sometimes an outcrop of boulders. Two deep ruts showed wagons often used this trail, but Kale and Dar passed no one nor saw any signs of life beyond the usual occupants of a forest. Woodland animals scurried out of their path. Birds called warnings from the high branches, announcing Dar and Kale's progression. Occasionally, a brightly colored halfnack bird zoomed across the lane as if to get a better look at the travelers. Kale looked over her shoulder. Some distance behind her, a huge beast moved like a gray shadow. With head hanging and tail dragging, Celisse followed.

22

CROSSING THE VALLEY

Dar hurried down the path. Kale plodded along, with frequent peeks behind her to see if Celisse still followed. Traveling through the woods was easier than Kale had expected. The huge trunks were spaced far apart with only small, scattered plants for underbrush. Towering trees shaded them. Sudden whiffs of air breezed down the path, shaking the leaves, stirring the dirt at their feet, and cooling the travelers. They walked for more than an hour along the wagon path through the trang-a-nog woods.

Ahead of them, Kale saw a sudden end to the forest. Dar halted by the last tree and leaned a shoulder against its smooth, olive-green trunk while he waited for Kale to catch up. Puzzled, she quickened her pace. From where she was, it looked like the path ended abruptly with nothing but blue sky beyond. She came to a standstill beside Dar and stared with wonder.

The trang-a-nog woods grew right up to the edge of a large valley. The land dropped away within feet of the last tree. The wagon trail veered off to the right and followed the edge in a long circuitous route to the bottom of the cliff.

A river ran through the green basin. Outcroppings of great orange and red rocks dotted the gently rolling hills. Flocks of sheep could be seen as clusters of tiny gray splotches. Rock walls made lines from hillside to hillside. Small buildings looked like toys set among the scenery. Here and there a square of cultivated land displayed the darker green of produce not yet harvested or the yellowish tinge that indicated an early crop.

On the other side of the valley, a sheer cliff rose abruptly. At the top, a dark fortress stood sentinel. Beneath the castle walls, halfway down the vertical rock face, a waterfall emerged and plummeted to the base. A mist rose there, obscuring the bottom of the cascade. A generous stream coursed away from the gray rock to join the river many miles distant.

Dar nodded toward the fort. "Is that where Leetu is being held?"

Kale concentrated, but nothing came to her mind. "I don't know."

The doneel turned and gave her a searching look. "You're tired."

She nodded. She let the pack straps slip from her shoulders and lowered them none too carefully to the ground.

"Kale, I think this sounds like something I've already told you today." A teasing grin spread across Dar's face. "You have a healing dragon in your pocket."

She stared at him blankly for a moment. Then she realized what he hinted at and felt stupid for not thinking of it herself.

He rested a hand on her arm. "Don't be so hard on yourself. You aren't used to having things such as a healing dragon at your disposal."

Dar took hold of her elbow and guided her to a soft clump of tumpgrass in the shade of a tree.

"Here, sit," he told her. "I'll get Gymn out. We'll lay out the moonbeam cape, and you two can take a nap. I feel like playing a bit on my flute. By the time you awake, you'll be refreshed and ready for the next part of our journey. And my soul, which I have to admit is a bit distressed, will have regained some peace."

Dar proceeded to make Kale comfortable, giving her a cup of water from their bottled supply and a biscuit smeared with some of Granny Noon's purpleberry jam.

Kale finished her snack, curled up on the cape with Gymn nestled against her cheek, and listened to Dar's mellow tune from the silver flute. Sleep had almost claimed her when she remembered something she wanted to ask the doneel.

"Dar, I heard Granny Noon's voice."

The music stopped. "Just now?"

"No. When I was on Celisse's back. After the attack."

"What did she say?"

"I was trying to remember just exactly what to say to make sure I got what I wanted. You know, about blocking minds and not getting hurt by wicked thoughts when I tried to find out something. I heard Granny Noon's voice say, 'Not the right words, but a heart in the right place.' I figure she meant that as long as my intentions were to follow Paladin and go the way of Wulder, then if I bungled up the words a bit, it wouldn't matter."

"That sounds right." Dar put his flute back to his lips.

"But I wanted to ask you"—she watched Dar lower his instrument again—"how did I hear her from so far away? Leetu told me there's a limit to how far you can be from someone and still mindspeak."

"Granny Noon is a powerful emerlindian. It could be that she spoke to you. But it could also be that the words you heard were very like something she told you, and you remembered them when you needed them. Or…"

"Or?"

"Or Wulder may have answered your questions, and you heard Him in the voice of one you trust."

Kale sat up. "Wulder mindspeaks!"

Dar laughed. "What's so amazing about Wulder speaking to one of His creations?"

Kale lay down again, not at all happy that she'd revealed again how much she didn't know.

"I just didn't think of Him being around like that. I mean, to talk to, or listen to, or…something."

"You mean you thought He would be busy, too busy to take note of you."

"Well, yes."

Dar played a refrain from the soothing melody he'd started before. When the notes stopped, she held her breath, wondering what he would say.

"I guess you've got to get used to not being a slave. When you were a slave, those in authority over you commanded you to get things done without caring much about how you felt and what you wanted. Now that you've chosen to be a servant to Paladin, you'll have many people who look out for your best interest."

His tune began again. Kale let out the breath she was holding, but she couldn't relax. Gymn nuzzled her cheek, and she stroked his back.

The problem with what Dar says is this: I didn't choose to be a servant. While I was a slave, I was commanded to go be a servant. Do the things Dar talks about count for me? I'm serving Paladin because the village council said I have to.

Dar's serene music and Gymn's healing touch eased her into a tranquil state. Still, her doubt about being Paladin's servant buzzed around in her head like a worrisome bee until the monotonous hum lulled her to sleep.

⊢━━━⊣

When she opened her eyes, the sun had eased down to the western horizon. Across the valley, it blazed red behind the dark fortress. Dar sat propped against a tree trunk, his eyes closed, a soft snore accenting his breathing.

Hurry! The word popped into Kale's mind, and she sat up.

"Dar!"

The doneel woke with a start.

Kale stood. She gazed across the darkening valley to the ominous structure on the cliff side. The sun glared around it, making a silhouette of the tall, straight walls. She squinted, unable to turn her focus from the source of an urgent call. "It's Leetu. She *is* in that fortress. It's the stronghold of Wizard Risto. We must get her out."

"It will take us three days to cross the valley and another two days to climb to the fort."

"We don't have that much time." Kale turned toward the woods. *Celisse, come help us.*

The riding dragon lumbered out of the trees onto the path and trotted the remaining few yards.

Kale transferred her gaze to Dar. His lips formed an uncompromising straight line. His scowl angered her. Gymn trembled on her shoulder, and she reached up to put a protective hand over the little dragon.

"Celisse is willing to help. I know you don't trust her, but if we don't allow her to take us, Leetu will die."

Dar said nothing.

"Fine," shouted Kale. She plucked Gymn off her shoulder and bent to place him in his pocket-den. She gathered up her cape and flung it over her shoulders.

"You walk." She hurled the words at Dar. "I'm riding." She picked up both of Leetu's packs and marched to the dragon.

"Stop."

Kale ignored Dar's command. She tromped over to the dragon and asked her to lie down, standard procedure for mounting such a large animal. Celisse complied readily, and Kale attached Leetu's packs to the proper straps at the back of the saddle.

Dar came up to Kale before she could put her foot on Celisse's leg and give herself a boost up.

"Stop, Kale." Dar placed a firm hand on her arm. "I agree with you, but stop and think. Calm down. You mustn't act on emotion alone. You have to plan."

Kale turned to the doneel, placed her clenched fists on her hips, and stood with her feet far apart.

Dar cocked an eyebrow and blessed her with his most charming smile. "You look like you're about to challenge me to a round of fisticuffs. We're on the same side, remember?"

The sparkle in his eye and the appealing wink he gave her undermined her determination to rush off to Leetu's rescue. She frowned at him.

"Just what is it you agree with?" She growled the question, trying to sound unmoved by his winsome ways.

"We have to get to Leetu quickly, and the only way to do that is on Celisse's back."

"We have to trust her," Kale insisted.

Dar nodded. He went to the dragon's head and placed a hand on her cheek. Next to her profile, he looked very small indeed. But the huge dragon nodded gently, responding to his touch. The doneel looked deep into the dragon's slanted eye.

"You know I don't like this, Celisse. And you understand why." He patted her and stroked the gray scales of her face. "I'm hoping you will do everything within your power to control your anger should we run into a skirmish with the enemy. I'm not only trusting you with my life, but with the life of this young o'rant girl and the life of a very fine emerlindian warrior."

In touch with Celisse's emotions, Kale's heart swelled with the riding dragon's desperate need to have another chance. If Celisse could succeed on desire alone, she would do well. She truly desired to serve Paladin and make up for her rash behavior back at the farm.

Kale pressed her lips together, waiting for Dar's pronouncement. She feared any effort she made to sway the doneel in the dragon's favor might fail and cause more anguish than good.

He stepped back and again faced Kale. "If Celisse will fly us to the other side of the valley and land not too far from Risto's fortress, then we will plan how to enter. You said that Risto was expected at the farm tonight. If he is there, then he is *not* in the castle. We have a better chance of freeing Leetu tonight than at any other foreseeable time."

He looked to the west. The sun had slipped behind the horizon. Only the soft orange glow of sunset edged the cliff top.

"We'll wait ten minutes more to take advantage of the darkness. We want to get as close as possible."

The few minutes ticked by torturously, but finally Dar gave the signal. He surprised Kale by allowing her to take the front seat. He situated his small frame behind her.

Once they were in the air, the frustration of having to wait faded away. Dread, however, crept into Kale's heart. They would probably only have one chance to free Leetu. She didn't worry about the riding dragon messing up their plan. Rather, she worried that she might do something awkward and give them away. Or she might freeze in terror when Dar needed her to be calm and quick.

She tried to think of the words Granny Noon had given her.

My thoughts belong to me and Wulder.

And Dar says You listen to me, and You talk to me too.

Well, Wulder, I thank You for being interested in what I'm doing. Kale took a deep breath. *Please tell me what to do and when, so I don't mess up.*

In Wulder's service, I search for truth. I'm searching for Leetu, Wulder. And a way to get into that castle. And a way to get out. Don't forget a way to get out.

I stand under Wulder's authority. I'm entering into the domain of an evil wizard. Please keep me and Dar and Celisse and Gymn from harm. And Leetu as well.

Celisse soared heavenward. A large yellow moon hung low in the sky. A halo gleamed around it. To the east, stars blinked and glimmered in a stunning array. The beauty of her surroundings almost wiped out the tingle of fear in her heart.

"A little bit of fear is all right," said Dar. "It keeps you alert and helps you react promptly."

Kale did not answer. *Does he read my mind? He says he doesn't, but he's always picking up on what I'm feeling.* She waited, expecting the doneel to make a comment. *If he denies he can read my mind, I'll know he was reading my mind.* Dar said nothing.

They swooped in a large circle and came to rest in a field beyond a wood at the west side of Risto's castle.

"Celisse," said Dar as soon as he and Kale stood on the ground, "you must hide in the trees. You can't come into the fortress with us, but you must be where we can reach you moments after we get out."

Kale sensed the riding dragon's agreement. The rescuers moved stealthily into the cover of the trees.

Dar paused. "Kale, I want you to use your talent to search the area around us. Are there soldiers or guards of any kind nearby?"

Kale relaxed, closed her eyes, and let her mind reach beyond the area where they stood.

"Kimens, there are dozens of kimens all around us." Kale's brow furrowed as she sorted through the impressions coming into her mind. "Dar, I know right where Leetu is, a dark, cold room with stone walls. If we get inside that fortress, I can lead us directly to her. Everything is so clear. Earlier today I couldn't use my talent at all. Now it's like a fog has lifted. I sense Leetu just as clearly as I can see the moon."

"Your eyes are closed, and the moon has a haze around it."

Kale grinned and opened her eyes. She looked at Dar, expecting an explanation from her wise companion in spite of his caustic remark.

Dar rubbed his furry chin with a hand. "The more you exercise your talent, the stronger it gets. This morning you overused it when you healed Celisse with Gymn. On top of all the other mindspeaking, you threw images into the guards' minds. Add the emotional strain of the circumstances, and you taxed your ability to the point of exhaustion.

"You'll have to learn to pace yourself. I can't think of anything more disastrous than to have your talent come to an abrupt stop while we're engaged in something like escorting Leetu out of Risto's stronghold."

"The kimens are coming," Kale announced.

"I'm not surprised. Ever since the Battle of Ordray, they've kept watch on the forces of evil."

"Can such little people help us?" The kimens appeared too fragile for any type of battle.

Dar laughed. "Oh, yes. For one thing, a kimen can light the way through any dark passages we encounter."

Kale tilted her head in puzzlement.

"Kale, kimens wear light. They have no clothing other than beams of light they draw to themselves. They control the color of that radiance and can dim it at will."

"I've seen kimens, Dar. They wear soft, fluttering clothing that floats around them and stirs in a breeze. It looks like the gauzy material Granny Noon wrapped our food in."

"Have you ever touched one?" asked Dar. "Have you ever brushed up against a kimen and felt the texture of his garment?"

"No."

"It's neither hot nor cold. It's not rough or smooth or thick or thin. It's light, and you can't feel it with your fingers."

Kale looked down at her moonbeam cape and remembered Dar tricking her into believing it was made from real moonbeams.

"No, Kale." His voice interrupted her suspicions. "I'm not teasing. Kimens gather light. A kimen is just what we need to guide us in Risto's castle."

23

Into Darkness

The travelers didn't have to find the kimens; the kimens found them.

Kale sat on a log, watching Gymn catch bugs, so she was the first to notice the kimens. The little people appeared as tiny fireflies moving quietly through the woods close to the ground. As they came nearer, Kale realized they were too big to be insects, and then she could make out the familiar forms she'd seen in her own village.

In the dark of the forest, the kimens wore clothing in shades of deep blue, purple, and green. Kale looked closely at the fabric, trying to see woven threads. She saw none, but still she couldn't believe that the wispy material was light and not cloth.

Out of the quiet gathering of tiny kimens, one stepped forward. His green eyes sparkled in a solemn face. His flyaway brown hair sprang from his head in the usual disarray of kimens. Kale looked closely at his blue garments. The flowing fabric looked airy and fragile, but not like any light she had ever seen. He appeared to be a warrior, strong and determined, but he carried no weapons.

A weapon wouldn't be a bad idea, considering where we're going. He could carry a sword or a bow. But…come to think of it, I've never seen a kimen carry anything. Not a sack, not a basket, not a weapon. Oh yes, I've seen them carrying their young.

The kimen gazed at Celisse, Kale, and Dar in turn. But when he spoke, he addressed just Dar and Kale. "I am Shimeran. I have been chosen to guide you."

"You know where we're going?" asked Kale.

A smile lit Shimeran's eyes but only teased at his lips.

"Of course."

Dar bowed with the same respect he had shown Granny Noon. "We would be honored to have your help, Shimeran. I am Dar." He gestured toward the riding dragon. "Our friend, Celisse." His hand moved to indicate Kale, but she spoke before he had a chance.

"I am Kale Allerion."

Shimeran's eyes widened for just a second, and the crowd of kimens around them shifted. A murmur among them quickly stilled as did their unease.

Kale glanced from face to face, trying to decide why they had reacted this way.

Did I say something I shouldn't have? Was it rude to introduce myself?

She examined the faces of the kimens more closely. Their expressions were friendly and calm, no different from the usual expressions of the kimens who visited River Away. She looked directly at Shimeran and was about to ask if something was wrong, but Dar forestalled her by speaking.

"We thought this night would be a good time to rescue our emerlindian comrade."

Shimeran nodded. "Risto is away. The guards have been drinking brillum all day. My kinsmen will cause a diversion, and we may sneak in through the main gate without detection."

Kale wrinkled her nose at the mention of brillum. The ale smelled like skunkwater and stained like black bornut juice. The mariones used it to spray around their fields to keep insects from infesting their crops. Grawligs drank it. Evidently bisonbecks did too.

"All is ready." Shimeran's voice broke into Kale's thoughts. "We should go now."

Dar turned to Celisse. "Will you wait here?"

Kale felt the riding dragon sigh and reluctantly agree. Kale nodded to Dar. She knew Celisse understood Dar, but wasn't sure if Dar could hear the dragon's mindspeak.

They moved quickly through the dark forest, following the kimens.

Three strode several yards in front of the group. These seemed dark in comparison to those close by.

Dar touched Kale's arm and nodded to those ahead. "Scouts." He spoke softly. "There are probably three more ahead of them beyond where we can see, and then three more ahead of them. You notice they've dimmed their radiance. These around us are lighting our way. Those ahead are watching for the enemy so we don't run smack into a band of bison-becks patrolling their boundaries."

One of the nearest kimens turned a frowning face toward Dar and put a finger to his lips.

Kale didn't want to end the conversation. She wanted to know more. She reached to Dar with her mind. *How did the kimens know we came for Leetu?*

"*Logic. They knew an emerlindian in service to Paladin had been taken prisoner. Someone was bound to try to save her. We showed up, so we must be the rescuers.*"

Why didn't they rescue her themselves?

"*Kimens have taken on the role of observers. They will help in time of need, but they never initiate an action.*"

I don't understand why not.

"*They believe that Wulder gave them their talents and diminished size for this purpose. They will not step beyond what they see as their assigned duties unless given a distinct call to do so.*"

I still don't understand.

Dar sighed aloud, and the same kimen hushed him with a sharp, "Shh!"

"*Kale, if you can't understand through my explanation, then you're going to have to use your own eyes and come to your own conclusions. Sometimes a thing makes more sense when you see it. Sometimes words aren't enough.*"

Kale wanted to answer with a loud "huh?" but figured Dar would just go on explaining why he couldn't explain. She decided to study the kimens instead. Maybe she could figure out what material made up their clothing.

She watched the little person directly in front of her. This kimen was a female with the typical wild hair growing out in an aimless way but hanging past her waist. Bits of ribbon and odd, skinny braids, plaited with no particular pattern, adorned the otherwise disorderly brown locks. Blue and purple wisps of material hung from her body almost like the large fan-like fins of a feathered fish. Of course the fish didn't really have feathers any more than this kimen wore light instead of material.

Kale tried to spot seams in the garment but couldn't. The fabric also reminded Kale of butterfly wings, for the dark colors were rimmed with black like the patterns on many of the colorful insects that flew with wings bedecked in jewel colors.

There were also rumors that kimens could fly.

Kale observed the small, lithe figure almost float over the roots and rubble of the forest floor. She studied the kimen's tiny feet and truly could not tell if the soles of her delicate shoes actually touched the ground or just passed above it before moving forward.

A sudden halt in their journey brought an end to Kale's musings. They had reached the edge of the woods and could see the front portal of the towering castle. Dar and Kale crouched behind bushes a dozen yards from the massive open doors while the kimens dispersed to do the tasks they had planned.

The land immediately surrounding the walls had been cleared of all vegetation except for close-cropped grass.

Dar whispered an explanation. "Fortresses, castles, walled cities, all have these clearings around them. The sentinels need an unobstructed view of anyone approaching."

Kale nodded. Her stomach muscles tightened, and she had to swallow hard against the fear rising in her throat. She could not see how she, Dar, and Shimeran could get to the gate and through it without being seen.

A yellow pool of light from a lantern revealed two guards, fully armed, standing at the entry. They slouched and spoke in a casual fashion to each other, but they were neither drunk nor drowsy. A man's voice boomed from the forest where the road emerged onto the castle grounds.

"Yo, the castle, I bring new stock to replenish your stores. Ale, cheese, sweetmeats, and red wine. As the wind blows over the sea, I've had a bad day of it. Come help. My donkey is lame. I don't know that I can make the last quarter mile to your door."

The guards looked warily at each other. Kale saw the shadow of a kimen right at their feet but couldn't see where the kimen himself stood.

"I'll go, Bleak," said the taller guard. "You mind the door." He started down the road with his spear held at the ready. By his casual strut, Kale decided the man had no clue this was a trap.

The dark kimen form Kale had spied at their feet sped before him. The dark splotch flitted across the ground like a shadow cast by the moon on the back of a flying owl.

The guard entered the wood and a moment later called out, "Bleak, come lend a hand. There's plenty here for feasting, and our watch is almost done." He laughed, and the other voice said something Kale could not catch. "Come, Bleak, the merchant will give us each a flask of rich wine before he takes the cart to the castle kitchen."

Bleak hesitated only a moment before abandoning his post and starting down the road.

"There is no one there," Shimeran explained in a whisper. "A kimen has imitated the voice of the merchant. Our people stunned the first guard. Then his voice was imitated to lure the second away. Be ready. As soon as this Bleak passes into the woods, we will go."

In a moment the big form of the bisonbeck guard stepped into the dark shadows of the trees. Shimeran, Dar, and Kale broke from their cover and sprinted across the open field to go through the gaping entryway. Once past the massive stone arch, Shimeran darted to the side and into the shadows. An elevated walkway ran the entire circumference of the courtyard. On this wooden structure, soldiers would stand at slits in the fortress wall to fire arrows at an encroaching enemy or fend off invaders who had breached the gate and entered the castle.

Footsteps clapped along the boards above the rescuers' heads. Someone was on duty. Kale hoped he was as negligent as the two who'd been on guard outside.

Even at this late hour, the castle bustled with activity. As Kale silently listened, she realized carousing bisonbecks made most of the ruckus. Noise of drinking, coarse singing, and raucous laughter came from a room close to the stables.

Shimeran spoke in the darkness. "They have moved this comrade of yours often. There is a prison room in each of the three towers. There is the dungeon, and below the dungeon are natural tunnels and caves. We could find the kimen who watches this emerlindian, but if your mind-speaker can tell us the way, we will save time."

"Kale?" Kale heard Dar's soft voice even though she could not see where he stood in the deep shadows. "Up or down?"

"Down," she answered without hesitation.

As her mind settled on Leetu, she felt the pain and desperation of her friend. She could feel the room, sense the smell of mildew, hear the skitter of unseen small animals, and for that moment, Kale ached as if her bones lay on the rough stone floor. She clenched her teeth against the fear that quivered in her jaw.

"Down," she said again. Her head jerked in a nod of determination. "Down, where it is cold and dark and deadly."

24

Silence?

"Can you mindspeak with me?" Shimeran asked Kale.

Yes.

"Good. I ask this of you. I will lead us to the dungeons. Then I will need your assistance. At that time, please tell me as we come to turns in the passages 'right' or 'left.' Or 'up' or 'down' as we come to steps. As we go through the outer quadrants of the fortress, I will be using all my senses to try to keep us safe. So please do not distract me. Do not mindspeak to me unless necessary."

Kale nodded.

Shimeran's clothing dimmed until the substance looked black instead of deep blue. Only a soft glow hovered at his feet, revealing the stone floor where they must tread without stumbling. He moved swiftly, and Kale followed with Dar behind. Her anxiety increased as she hurried to keep pace with the kimen. He darted around corners, and she feared she would lose him. He abruptly stopped to survey the next segment of their course, and she almost fell over him.

From time to time, Shimeran pushed them into deep shadows, and his clothing gave out not one glimmer of light. Then Kale tried to control her breathing so she wouldn't be heard. Her hand would cover Gymn as he lay curled tightly in his pocket-den. She hoped the cape truly concealed her. Once she thought how nice it would be to shovel out the muck in the tavern stables rather than be crouched behind barrels, with bisonbeck men arguing loudly as they passed a few feet from where the rescuers hid.

Shimeran led them deeper into the fortress. As they traversed the different yards, Kale began to sense the layout of the grounds. Whether she picked up this information from the kimen's thinking or from some intuition of her own, she could not tell. But she knew the general layout of the different parts of the fortress.

A tall stone wall designed for defense circled the entire domain. A second wall of finer stone was actually a ring of rooms. Horse stalls took up a bulk of this section, but there were quarters for the guards, a kitchen, a tavern, and storerooms. The rescuers moved through a feed room among sacks of oats and bales of hay to get from the outer circle to the inner.

Between the second wall and a third lay an expanse of groomed grass. Soft underfoot, it offered no place to conceal themselves should someone come by. Shimeran crossed immediately to the inner quadrant. The next wall was shorter, artistically constructed out of brick and carved black stone. They slipped over it and into a garden.

Here torches lit the pathways. Kale saw plants almost as big as trees and benches clustered as if for visiting as well as resting. Occasionally, as they moved around the center building, they saw porches with marble statues, balconies with engraved balustrades, and arched doorways into the castle itself.

Kale's mouth hung open as she gaped at the castle. She'd been in huts and hovels, fine cottages and rough cabins, barns and sheds and chicken coops. The tallest house in River Away was the three-storied tavern. She'd seen the city Vendela and knew the capital city was far more splendid than this dark and dreary castle-fort. But she'd only seen Vendela from afar, and this fortress, where they might be caught and killed at any moment, was impressive. If it weren't for the fear in her heart, Kale would have enjoyed gaping at the marvels around her.

Once they left the soldiers' domain at the outer rim of the fortress, they encountered only a few servants. They had to hide while two maids sat and complained by a fountain. After only a minute, Kale realized these women were mariones. Her mouth dropped open, and she turned to Dar for an explanation.

Look! Do you see? They're mariones. How can anyone of the high races serve Risto?

He scrunched up his face in a frown and shrugged. *"Sometimes, they serve here because the life is easier, or so they think when they first come. Maybe the high wages attract them, maybe the nice clothes. They pretend to themselves that working here is just like working in a big house in one of our cities. Others are damaged by bitterness and anger. They serve here because they are most comfortable with others who harbor ugly feelings within their hearts."*

The rescuers detoured around two men, a tumanhofer and a doneel, playing cards on a stone bench beneath a torch. As she followed the others quietly around the edge of a terrace, Kale stared at the servants. She tried to see something about their appearance which would serve as a clue to why they chose a life within these dark walls. Nothing showed, save a certain hard look to their expressions. She wondered if the coldness in their faces came before or after they made their choice.

For the most part, Dar, Kale, and Shimeran easily avoided the house workers. The rescuers hid in the shadows and slipped from one place of security to the next. Frequently, Kale touched the slight bulge in her cape that was the healing dragon. Little Gymn helped her to relax, shaking off tension and fear.

Shimeran knew the way to the dungeons. He led them to the back side of the fortress, the part closest to the cliff. In stark contrast to the gardens and castle terraces, a grim enclosure surrounded a great yawning hole that served as entry to the area below. The barren courtyard held little beyond a few wooden benches. The full moon glowed in the night sky, and here, where there were no high walls, trees, or overhanging structures, it cast an eerie half-light. Kale felt more exposed than in any other part of the castle.

A crude ladder made from chopped branches and bound with coarse rope lay against a wall nearby. Shimeran gestured to it, and Dar moved to pick it up. Kale saw the doneel strain against its weight and went to help. Together they maneuvered the end to the edge of the hole and tipped the ladder upright. Hand over hand, they lowered it into the black pit.

Kale wanted to object. Going down that ladder felt like going into a trap, but her bearings on Leetu Bends told her that the kimen was taking them in the right direction.

Shimeran leapt onto the top rungs of the ladder without a sound and quickly disappeared. Dar gestured for Kale to go next, but she shook her head. He stopped beside her, patted her arm, and then stepped down on the second branch rung tied to two long poles. In the gloomy light, Kale watched his ears, perked and twitching, as Dar descended below the rim of the hole.

She cast a glance around the dismal enclosure. Unadorned walls of poorly cut stone looked typical of a poor farmer's barn, not a wizard's castle. No beauty of form rested here. The shades of gray and black shadows obscured any attractiveness. Even in the quiet of the place, there was no peace.

She peered into the hole. Down there, turmoil, evil, and danger danced along roughly hewn stone corridors. She heard echoes of horror and couldn't shake the feeling that this was present distress, not something lingering from the past. Shimeran had gone down the ladder. Dar had followed. Kale reached to touch Leetu's mind.

We're coming! she called, and swung her foot over the top of the ladder, before she could think any more about the terror below.

The wood creaked under her weight. The rungs had not protested a bit as Dar and Shimeran climbed down. But the doneel was half her size, and the kimen so small he could probably float on a stiff breeze. A light flashed into view below her, and she slipped, almost losing her footing. She gasped, clung to the frail ladder, and searched for her companions in the sudden brilliance.

Dar stood beside Shimeran, whose clothing now radiated a golden glow.

"Hope," he said as he smiled up at her.

"Hope?" she echoed.

"The golden light is a symbol of hope. The most perilous part of our journey through the wizard's stronghold is already past. There will not be any guards down here to bother us. Nothing but rats and cats and druddums."

Kale shivered and stepped quickly down the remaining rungs. With her feet on the dirt floor, she put her hands on her hips and eyed the kimen.

"And how about the journey out of the wizard's stronghold?"

"It will require another color." He clapped his hands together and scanned the various routes away from the entry. "Which way, Kale?"

Kale patted Gymn through the cape material. The gesture soothed her brittle nerves. She nodded at a dark tunnel veering to the right. Shimeran started off without comment. His bright light bounced off the rock walls. Chisel marks showed where hands holding metal tools had widened the natural tunnel. Moisture clung to the gray stone, and in places, ran in trickles down to the floor, leaving brackish puddles.

The underground tunnels twisted, following a natural pattern. Here and there man's tools had made tight stretches higher and broader. Some tunnels opened into caverns. Cages made of heavy bars stood empty in these large underground spaces.

Kale stared at hall after hall of unused cells. One looked much like the one before it. None of the caverns were occupied, but all of them were disturbing. Something about the repellent odor also set her on edge. The caverns smelled like an unclean barn. Yet with years of disuse, the granite rooms should smell more like an empty storage shed. She had expected to see suffering and had steeled herself against the horror of this evil prison. Where were the victims of Risto's harsh hand?

They entered yet another ominously quiet cavern. Shimeran's light increased and touched the walls. Chains hung from metal pegs driven into the stone. Doors sat at odd angles, none of them enclosing a cage. Kale shivered at the sight of a pile of rags in a corner. At first she had thought it was a person.

Kale could not shake the unsettling feeling of intense misery. She strained to see into the shadows, expecting faces, expecting some sign of life. "This is a dungeon with no prisoners?"

Shimeran's glow dimmed and changed to a somber blue. "It has been a long time since Risto bothered to keep prisoners alive."

Kale followed in silence after that. Often a cavern had more than two ways leading out. She pointed whenever Shimeran cast her a questioning look, but he led the way in each case. Dar moved quietly, sometimes in front of Kale and sometimes behind.

Kale concentrated on finding Leetu. The thoughts conjured up by the grim sights around them intruded on her ability. She almost heard whispers, soft cries of despair, and rustling like wind in dry leaves. But there was no wind, there were no leaves. Still the eerie atmosphere bothered her.

"Something is wrong," she said as they entered yet another empty cavern. "Are we going around in circles?"

"You are directing us," Shimeran reminded her, walking to the center of the room.

"I know." Kale sighed. Explaining would be difficult. "I feel Leetu is always ahead of us. But sometimes it feels as if we are just a yard or two away. Then it's like we passed her and have a long way again."

Shimeran stopped but didn't speak. Dar's ears twitched, showing his nerves were on edge as well.

Kale continued, "At first I thought they might be moving her, and sometimes we were right on their heels, about to catch up, and sometimes they leapt ahead much farther than could be possible if they are truly going around and around in these same tunnels. Something is very wrong."

"I sense it too," Dar said. "But my worries stem from the lack of life. There have been no prisoners, no guards, and none of the rats, cats, and druddums you warned us of, Shimeran."

The kimen's light dimmed, leaving the walls in shadows. "Let us be quiet."

Kale wanted to object. She wanted to beg the kimen to brighten the room, but she said nothing. She hated the darkness, the quiet. She thought about Dar pulling out one of his instruments and dispelling the gloom with a lively song. It would be nice to break this somber place with a melody.

As the silence gathered around them, Kale strained her ears to hear something beyond her own breathing. Again, she thought she almost heard sounds of sorrow, a sniff, a sob, a pleading voice.

Tears sprang to her eyes. "Dar," she whispered.

"What?"

"The room is not empty. The cages are not empty."

Dar's eyes widened as he looked around. "More light, Shimeran," he called. "As much as you can muster."

Once more the image of Dar playing a tune sprang into Kale's mind. "Music, Dar," she said. "Music. Play something. It's an enchantment."

Dar reached inside his coat to a pocket and pulled out his harmonica.

"We've been blinded by magic." Kale heard the urgency in her voice and couldn't explain it, even to herself. "We have walked past the suffering without seeing. Play, Dar."

The doneel raised his mouth organ to his lips and blew. A melody flowed out with a trill and a lively beat. The air around them wavered, and the image of the empty cavern seemed to melt and flow to the floor. In the room around them, nine cages held thin, worn prisoners.

"They see us," called one in a weak voice. The sobs Kale had heard changed from mournful to joyous. "They see us."

25

ESCAPE!

Many different races sat in squalor or hung from the walls with chains about their wrists and ankles. Some watched Leetu's rescuers with dull eyes. Others croaked out mournful pleas, begging for release, for water, for a crust of bread. A few babbled words that made no sense.

"We have to free them," said Kale.

Both Shimeran and Dar nodded. Dar moved toward a cage and then paused. He turned to Shimeran.

"We can't do this alone. Will your people help?"

"Not many have ever come into the fortress." He looked around. "There are nearly thirty prisoners here. Few of them are in any shape to walk, let alone fight if the need arises. If all the dungeon rooms hold as many, there will be hundreds to guide safely out of this hole."

"We must find Leetu," Kale said.

"Yes," Dar agreed. "We'll find Leetu, and while you and Gymn tend to her, Shimeran and I will come up with a plan."

Kale closed her eyes against the sight of so many hurting souls, but her ears still heard their murmurings, their pleas for mercy.

Leetu, I must find Leetu Bends.

She opened her eyes and trudged back the way they had come, past those she could not help. Following that unseen pull that told her where she would find her comrade, Kale tried to ignore the sights and sounds of misery. She offered the captives words of encouragement, saying they would soon be free. For now, Kale had nothing to give them but hope.

She passed through several tunnels and caverns. None were vacant as they had appeared earlier. Cats, rats, and druddums slunk and scuttled along the passages. Each room held a despairing group of captives. Kale saw mariones, doneels, kimens, urohms, emerlindians, and tumanhofers. With a start, she realized some of the prisoners were o'rants. She had never met another of her race.

Dar urged her forward when she stopped beside an old o'rant man. "I know, Kale, but now is not the time. Tend to Leetu first."

In the corner of the next dungeon, they found Leetu's form rolled against a cold stone wall. Moisture oozed from the rocks and flowed down on the emerlindian. Leetu slept in damp clothing and a shallow puddle that smelled heavily of rusty iron.

Shimeran put his fists to his hips and glowered at the tenants of the dungeon. "Where is the kimen who stands by her friend at this hour?"

The wretched prisoners shook their heads, cowering away from the angry, two-foot-tall kimen.

Dar moved to stand by Shimeran and spoke quietly. "Do you think they even saw Leetu's kimen companion?"

Shimeran shrugged off the question. "I will know why the emerlindian was left alone." He knelt beside Leetu. He felt her forehead and shook his head. "Her skin is hot, yet she shivers. Let us see what we can do for her."

Dar, Kale, and Shimeran moved Leetu's body, limp and feverish, to a drier spot.

"This one is near death," announced Shimeran in a solemn voice.

A fierce denial rose to Kale's lips, but she bit it back. It had taken them a long time to reach their comrade.

I don't really know if Gymn can cure someone so weak.

With help from Dar and Shimeran, Kale laid her cape on the dirty floor and moved Leetu onto the woven moonbeam material. Kale sat down next to her and tenderly pulled Gymn from his pocket-den at the edge of the cape. She held him close to her chest, nestled in her folded arms.

"Wake up, little one," she cooed to the dragon. "We have work to do."

Gymn wrinkled his nose against the putrid smells of the dungeon and tucked his head against Kale's sleeve. With a forefinger, she lifted his scaly chin. The young beast blinked his eyes in the kimen's light. She remembered Shimeran had called the golden glow "hope."

"We must try," she told Gymn. She peeled him off her arm and laid him against Leetu's pallid cheek. The emerlindian did not stir. Kale left one hand on the healing dragon and placed the other on Leetu's soiled arm.

A sparkling voice called to them. "You've come to rescue the emerlindian. What's happened here? Only an hour ago this place was like a tomb. Nothing living but me and the Paladin warrior."

"Seezle!" Shimeran's voice rang with displeasure. "I should have known. Where have you been?"

"Easy, big brother. I went to get fresh water, a blanket, and some food."

Kale looked quickly at the small female kimen. From under the folds of her garment, Seezle produced a loaf of bread, a flask, and a heavy, folded cloth.

Shimeran grunted. "The emerlindian cannot eat. We will dribble some water into her mouth. These comrades will eat the food. I know not when they last ate, but their journey has been long and 'tis not over yet."

Kale gladly accepted the drink and bread. Although they still had some provisions in their stores from Granny Noon, it had been some time since they'd eaten. While Kale's cape with its full hollows was within easy reach, Dar's belongings were back in the forest with Celisse. Truthfully, she hadn't thought about food and how hungry she was until she saw Seezle's offering. Kale shared with Gymn. Dar eloquently thanked the kimen and set right to work on the scant meal.

With the edge taken off her hunger, Kale turned back to her role with the ailing emerlindian and Gymn. She wondered if the healing process would be as exhilarating as it had been when they worked on Celisse's wounds. Leetu's wounds were deep in her being—old, not fresh—and inflicted by an evil touch. Celisse's wounds had been to the surface flesh, relatively newly dealt, and delivered by an arrow rather than the physical touch of wickedness. This would not be a simple healing.

Feeling unequal to her task, Kale positioned herself next to Leetu with Gymn again on the emerlindian's cheek. Hoping Wulder would strengthen her poor efforts, the o'rant girl placed her hands in the correct position to complete the circle.

Kale felt Dar and Shimeran move away. They would plot the freedom of the other prisoners. Kale would concentrate on Leetu.

—•—

When Dar nudged Kale's shoulder, she realized she must have fallen asleep. She lay beside Leetu, her hands still touching the emerlindian and Gymn, making the healing circle.

"Kale." Dar's voice penetrated the fog of her mind. She raised her head without letting go of the circle. She tried to focus on Dar's face but found that his long sideburns on fuzzy cheeks blurred with the rock wall behind him.

He spoke quietly. "Shimeran has gathered all the kimens who live within the fortress."

"They live inside?" Her voice felt hoarse.

"Yes, as uninvited tenants. In fact, Risto doesn't know they are here."

Dar's eyes traveled around the dingy cell. He looked ill at ease. She noticed Shimeran's light had been replaced with a torch on the wall.

Dar fingered a small metal pick and held it up for her to see. "I am undoing the locks while the kimens are gone."

"We're alone?"

"We are never alone." Dar's word echoed strongly on the solid walls. He straightened his shoulders.

She struggled to understand the doneel's words. The intense process of healing Leetu shielded her thoughts from the things going on around her. He had said someone was gone, and they weren't alone. It didn't make sense. "Gone? Who's gone?"

"The kimens. They've gone out to gather more of their people. Those kimens who are used to being inside the walls will guide kimens from outside into the fortress. Our hope is there will be one kimen to help each of these prisoners escape."

Kale nodded. Her head sank back to the ground.

Some time later she felt a touch on her wrist. She opened her eyes. Dar bent over her, fastening a slender green rope on her arm.

"What is that?" she whispered.

"A glean band. It will protect you when the hornets attack."

Kale sat up, letting go of both Leetu and Gymn. "Hornets?" Groggy from her sleep and the healing, she looked around the room for a battalion of stinging insects. Instead, she saw a dungeon devoid of prisoners.

"Not here yet," said Dar as he placed the same kind of bracelet around Leetu's limp arm. "I am learning the most amazing things, Kale. Kimens have warriors and arm themselves with natural weapons. They plan to bomb the bisonbeck soldiers with hornet nests. Clever, don't you think?"

Kale shook the muzzy feeling from her brain. "Dar, what's going on? Did the magic return and cover the people, or are we really alone? How long have I been asleep?"

"Whoa!" Dar sat back on his heels and grinned at her. His ears perked above his head and waggled with excitement. "It's nearly dawn. Awhile ago the captives were taken inside the castle, being fed and given water, and helping themselves to clothing from the servants' quarters.

"But now they are hidden in the third quadrant, awaiting the kimens' diversion. While the outer quadrants are in confusion, they will escape. In the forest, villagers summoned by the kimens will hustle them off to hiding places in the valley. After the prisoners regain their strength, a plan will be made to get them to their homes."

Dar's torrent of words had finally awakened Kale from her befuddled state. "What?" She sat up straighter.

"The kimens arrived about an hour ago. They sneaked in past the bisonbeck guards, which was risky but easier than a normal invasion would have been."

"Invasion?"

"Pay attention, Kale." Dar situated himself in a cross-legged position and leaned forward. "The kimens came into the inner circle without arousing the outer guard. They then went through the castle and incapacitated the servants."

"Incapacitated?"

"They stunned them."

"How can tiny kimens overpower servants?"

"They stun them," Dar repeated. "It's absolutely fascinating. I guess the kimen race didn't like being defenseless. They've come a long way since the days Pretender tried to subjugate them and the urohms came to the rescue."

"Dar!" Kale rose to her feet and glared at the doneel. "Explain what is happening without all this chitterchatter."

Dar frowned up at her, but his enthusiasm soon erased the glower. "A kimen springs out at a servant, leaping in front of his face. Then the kimen produces an explosion of light right in the servant's eyes. I watched them do it dozens of times. The servant drops to the floor like he's been clobbered on the noggin."

"So all the servants were captured while I was asleep?"

"Yes, and then I tied them up, bound them hand and foot. They won't interfere with our escape." Dar looked at Leetu's unmoving form. Gymn still sprawled across her cheek. "You weren't exactly asleep, Kale. You were busy, too."

Kale gazed at the emerlindian. Leetu's complexion still looked pasty. Her breathing came in a long, shallow rhythm. She made no movements other than the rise and fall of her chest, indicating she lived.

Kale fought despair. "I can't see that I did any good."

"We'll take her to Wizard Fenworth," said Dar, rising to his feet. "She needs the healing power of someone skilled against the evil of Risto. Leetu won't die now, Kale. You and Gymn have given her enough strength and us enough time to get her to Fenworth."

Kale didn't bother to say they had already failed at finding the bog wizard. She picked up the blanket to fold as she watched the still form of her friend.

How are we going to carry you? Will the journey make you worse? Dar says you will not die, but I'm afraid.

A flickering ball of light came rapidly down a tunnel and burst into the room.

"Dar, Kale, we must flee." Seezle stopped. Her toes barely touched the rock floor. She seemed poised to run. With a glance over her shoulder, she leapt across the room to their sides. "Risto has returned. He appeared at the gateway of the fortress, cursing his guards, raging with words of destruction. Shimeran has gone to get Celisse and will meet us at the waterfall."

Kale dropped the blanket and moved quickly to Leetu.

"Wrap the cape around her," ordered Dar.

He grabbed the emerlindian's legs. Seezle stood ready to bear Leetu's weight in the middle. Kale hesitated.

"What's wrong?" asked Dar.

"Where is Gymn?"

They all looked around.

"There!" Dar nodded toward a pale green lump on the floor.

Kale stooped to pick the dragon up.

"What happened?" asked Seezle as the o'rant girl slid Gymn into a pocket of the cape and then refolded the material over Leetu's chest.

"Nothing," said Dar. "Hurry, Kale."

"Nothing?" quizzed Seezle.

"The dragon faints," answered Dar, "when something frightens him."

Kale lifted Leetu by the shoulders. Seezle slipped under her waist and supported her there.

"Where are we going?" asked Kale.

Seezle's tiny hands appeared at Leetu's waist. "Beneath the dungeons to the underground river and then to the falls."

A picture sprang to Kale's mind—her first sight of the fortress from across the valley. Midway up the sheer cliff below the black and gray castle walls, water shot out of the rocks and plummeted hundreds of feet to be hidden by a mist at the base.

"Can't we go out of the fortress the same way we came in?" she asked hopefully.

"And face Risto?" Seezle laughed without any humor. "That would be an unpleasant death."

Kale couldn't see that the planned escape route offered anything pleasant at all.

26

OBSTACLES

"Aren't we going toward the entrance of the dungeon?" Kale asked. She struggled to hold Leetu's shoulders without letting her head flop from side to side.

Dar led the way with the emerlindian's feet upon his shoulders. Kale saw him nod. "We have to go up, out of the dungeon, cross to the other side of the east courtyard, and down a well."

Kale thought the doneel sounded very confident. "You've been this way before?"

"No."

Seezle giggled from her position under Leetu's middle. Her little hands grasped the material on either side of the emerlindian's waist, and her disheveled head propped up the small of Leetu's back.

"I have, Kale. I know the way." Her voice almost sang the reassurance. "At the bottom of the well is a river with wide stone banks. It's easy to get from there to the falls."

To Kale, the plan sounded as if it would take them to a dead end. "And once we get to the falls?"

Seezle remained cheerful. "Shimeran and Celisse will meet us."

"I didn't see any place for a dragon to land."

"There isn't any. We'll jump."

Dar halted dead in his tracks, and since neither Seezle nor Kale could stop immediately, poor Leetu's body folded up, bending at the knees and waist like a rag doll. Unconscious, Leetu made no complaint while the three straightened her out. Kale back-stepped, and Seezle, who had been pushed to the ground, stood erect.

Dar twisted to look under his arm at the kimen behind him.

"We're going to jump?" he asked.

"There'll be a net."

Dar's bushy eyebrows drew together in a fierce frown. His ears lay flat against his head, almost disappearing in his shaggy hair. "How can there be a net?" He scowled at Seezle. "You're going to hang a net in a waterfall?"

"No, the net will be wrapped around Celisse. You just step off the cliff as she flies by, fall on top of her, and grab the net."

Dar faced forward and started walking without any warning to those behind. Leetu received a stretching jolt. Kale was glad the emerlindian was oblivious.

"Let me tell you something about doneels," said Dar as he marched, his face firmly directed to the path in front of him. "Doneels are a very social race. We excel in areas of culture. Doneels are comfortable among the aristocracy in palaces and with peasants at village festivals. We are generally blessed with musical, artistic, and literary talents.

"Doneels have been known to dwell among the tumanhofers in their underground cities. Doneels have sailed upon the ocean. Most doneels readily adapt to the rigors of dragon flying. However..." A hard edge sharpened his voice. He delivered his next words with cold precision. "We are not known for reckless feats of acrobatic stupidity."

"It'll be all right," Seezle insisted. Kale could see nothing of the little kimen except her hands on Leetu's waist, a few wisps of flyaway hair, and the glow of her clothing. "Shimeran is in charge of the details. Paladin is overseeing the rescue."

"Paladin?" Kale's attention centered on the muffled voice of the kimen under the midsection of their burden.

"Yes. He's in the forest, encouraging the villagers. I tell you it was hard to come back into the fortress. I would have preferred to follow him around, listening to all he has to say."

"How long will he be there? Do you think we'll meet him?"

"Could be," Seezle said. "But he rarely stays in one place long."

Kale wanted to hurry the others. A chance to meet Paladin filled her with excitement, but the reality of their situation squelched her hopes.

First, we have to get out of here. Then out of the fortress. Then out of the underground river tunnel. Then jump onto Celisse's back and land safely. Then fly to the forest which is probably overrun with Risto's henchmen. Unless Paladin comes to us, I don't think we'll get to him in time.

As they passed through the stone corridors, Kale searched the shadows. All the poor inmates had been rescued. The turmoil that had first alerted her to the hidden presence of prisoners was gone. Yet eerie silence draped every corner with mystery. She and her companions were the only living creatures who remained besides the rats, cats, and druddums.

The cats sat and watched them in various uninterested poses. Kale shivered at their cold stares. The house cats back in River Away had been friendly. These felines looked evil and brooding as if they observed intruders so they could report back to their master. Fingers of dread clutched her heart. She cleared her throat to ask Dar if it was possible for cats to be spies for Wizard Risto.

A druddum hurtled around the corner and slammed into a resting cat. A screech rent the air, followed by an instantaneous battle. Hissing and caterwauling echoed off the stone walls and down the corridors, ringing in Kale's ears. She gladly quickened her steps to keep up as Dar stepped up the pace.

They reached the crude wooden ladder to the entrance of the dungeon. Kale's arms ached from carrying Leetu's body. Although the emerlindian's slight figure shouldn't have been heavy, her dead weight strained the o'rant girl's shoulders. Kale wondered if the kimen and doneel were equally taxed.

Dar motioned to put their burden down. Once they placed Leetu on the ground, he arched his back and rotated his shoulders. Kale watched with a smug smile. He was sore too. The kimen danced over to the ladder and with no visible effort skimmed up the steps. Her clothing hid her legs.

She looks more like she's floating up those steps instead of climbing them.

"The way is clear," Seezle announced from her perch at the top. "Bring your friend up."

Kale and Dar looked at each other, then down at Leetu's motionless body. Dar's strength surpassed Kale's, but his compact body wasn't suited to carrying the long, fragile emerlindian. Kale was taller than any of her companions.

"I'll carry her," said Kale. "Help me get her onto my back with her head and arms hanging over my shoulder."

Dar wrinkled his brow, tilting his head as he looked at Kale with a speculative eye. "Are you sure?"

Kale nodded. "I'll pretend she's a bag of potatoes I'm bringing up from the storeroom in the tavern."

Dar chortled. "She's a lot lighter than those big bags of potatoes." He grabbed hold of Leetu's arms, efficiently pulling her to a sitting position. Kale bent over, and between her lifting and Dar's shoving, they got Leetu's limp body draped over Kale's shoulder.

Kale couldn't straighten up. Dar guided her over to the rickety ladder. "Do you want me to push from behind?"

Kale heard a suspicious bubble in his words. "Are you laughing?" She huffed and shifted her burden a little to the center of her back.

"No, of course not." Dar adjusted the moonbeam cape covering Leetu. "Do you require my assistance?"

"No!"

I can do this, and I can do it quick. I want out of this fortress. I've had enough of smelly, dark holes. I've had enough of adventures. Oh how I wish this were really a sack of potatoes. And I wish this were the tavern basement.

She put a foot on the lowest rung and shifted her weight upward. The branch forming the crossbar under her foot creaked. She swiftly stepped up to the next rung. The thought of grawligs and bisonbecks and mordakleeps and Wizard Risto lurking outside the dungeon entrance, waiting for them to come out, crossed her mind. She closed her eyes and hung on to the rough wooden ladder as her mind reached to the area above. No one but Seezle stood anywhere near them.

Kale forced herself to move a foot up to the next rung.

Adventures like this should be done by people who like adventures like this. I don't like them at all.

And once I get out of here, I'm going to see Paladin. I'm going to talk to him and tell him how I feel. I'm not good at this questing. I'm going to leave Leetu and Dar with Paladin, and I'm going to The Hall.

Maybe after I go learn about o'rants in a part of the country that is peaceful and filled with o'rants and nobody ever, ever goes questing, and after I've been taught properlike in a school that's made just for getting people ready to do things like questing and adventures, maybe then I'll go look for meech eggs and find bog wizards and battle grawligs.

She reached the hole and poked her head out. Seezle's soft glow illuminated the small yard. Nothing had changed since Kale had last seen it. She breathed a sigh of relief and scooted over the edge. Dar popped out almost immediately.

"I'll scout ahead," said Seezle.

Her light went out, and only a whisper sounding like a breeze indicated she'd gone.

"Rest a minute," said Dar.

Kale had barely eased Leetu down to the ground and collapsed beside her when Seezle came back. She whooshed through the arched doorway and settled between Dar and Kale. Her clothing began to glow a soft amethyst as she spoke.

"There's fierce fighting at the main gate. The castle itself is deserted. We can save time by going over the terrace and passing through the banqueting hall and then the kitchen area. The well is just outside."

"How did you find out so quickly?" Kale asked. "You haven't been gone a minute."

Seezle's eyes widened. "Kimens are the fastest creatures anywhere in the world."

Kale frowned. Again she wondered if the tales of kimens flying might be true. But she was too tired and scared to puzzle over the question.

"Let's go," Dar moved to pick up Leetu's feet.

Kale hustled into position, holding Leetu's shoulders, and watched Seezle slip underneath. As the kimen took her place in the middle, Kale noticed how graceful and fluid her movements were, almost like light spilling across the meadow as the sun came up. If her hands had been free, Kale would have reached out to touch Seezle's clothing. Perhaps these creatures did wear light as Dar had said.

In the distance, the clash of swords, the bellows of bisonbecks, and the shrieks of men and animals testified to battle. Kale swallowed the fear rising in her throat and urged Dar to hurry.

"You don't want me to go careening around a corner like a druddum and run smack into a guard, do you?"

"Seezle said the castle is deserted."

"That was a minute ago. Things change quickly in the middle of a fight." His whisper came with a sharp warning. "Keep your ears open and use that talent of yours."

They passed under a stone archway into a courtyard. Gingerly, Kale extended her mind. The encounters with darkness intimidated her. Reaching with her mind had been fun until the mordakleeps took Leetu, and Kale first touched the horrible black void. Concentrating on mindsearching and trying at the same time not to mentally bump into the darkness, she stumbled on the uneven stone bank.

"Watch where you're going," hissed Dar.

Kale bit back a retort. Something moved ahead of them, not within their range of vision but just beyond. Her mind sensed two beings.

"Stop!" she squeaked.

"I'm sorry, Kale. You're right. I shouldn't be barking at you." Dar continued walking. "We'll get out of this. Don't worry."

"Dar, stop moving! There's someone ahead. Beyond that wall."

They came to an abrupt halt and listened. Kale gave all her attention to identifying the enemy.

"Two bisonbecks," she said as soon as she had clearly caught their image.

"Right in the way!" Seezle fumed. "We want to go across that terrace and into the banquet hall."

"Here," said Dar, "put Leetu down under these bushes." He headed to the side of the bricked terrace where a cluster of ornate benches nestled in an alcove of lush green shrubs. They put Leetu between a marble seat and a statue of two dancing maidens.

Once they had the emerlindian on the ground, Seezle darkened her clothing. "I'll go see if these are strays, or if the whole guard force is falling back, deeper into the castle grounds."

She sped away before Dar could respond. He looked annoyed.

"I've been told before," he said, "that working with kimens is a trial."

He stood and walked up the bricked pathway a short distance. Kale followed. Now they could hear the bisonbecks muttering to each other on the other side of the wall. Dar touched Kale's arm. She leaned down to hear his quiet voice.

"Kale, read these bisonbecks' minds. Find out why they're here, and how long they intend to stay."

It took Kale only a minute. "They're looking for a place to set up a hospital for their wounded."

"Tell them this isn't the place. Suggest they look for someplace closer to the stables."

"Why?"

"Because we want them to move."

"No, why would they want to be closer to the stables? I need a logical reason."

Dar rubbed his hand over his chin and closed his eyes. In a moment they popped open with a twinkle. "Because Risto will have their heads if they put smelly, bloody soldiers this close to his living quarters."

She closed her eyes and concentrated. Opening her eyes again, she grinned at Dar. "It worked." Her pleasure evaporated. "Oh!"

"What's wrong?"

"They're coming this way."

Dar put strong hands against Kale's waist and pushed. They dove behind a fountain surrounded by bushes just before two hulking bisonbecks in tattered uniforms came through the gate.

One stopped inside the entryway, grunted, and looked around suspiciously. "Did you hear something?"

27

LOCKED DOORS

The two bisonbeck soldiers snorted and grumbled at each other. Kale couldn't make out what they said. She watched with relief as they ambled in the other direction, carelessly poking under and around the bushes.

Afraid of drawing their attention, she mindspoke to Dar. *What are we going to do?*

"Stay hidden."

That's all right for us, but we didn't exactly hide Leetu. Kale glanced back at the alcove and gasped. *Dar, she's gone.*

Dar's head snapped around and then back at Kale. *"She's not gone. She's wrapped in the moonbeam cape. Kale, try to keep calm."*

Kale bit her lip and turned back to study the patch of ground beside the carved bench and stone maidens. After a moment, she detected the tip of Leetu's boot near the foot of a marble dancer and a tendril of blond hair close to the elaborate seat.

The soldiers worked their way around the far end of the courtyard and started back. She held her breath. As long as Leetu stayed still, she would be practically invisible. That *could* happen. After all, the emerlindian hadn't moved on her own since they found her. Kale's head swiveled as she first watched the bisonbecks and then Leetu's concealed body.

The soldiers rattled the bushes directly opposite their hiding place. Dar touched her arm and motioned her to follow. Darting from a clump of tall flowers to a fountain, from bushes to statues, from one spot of cover to the next, he took them to the area already searched by the enemy. They passed the gate they hoped to use for an exit. From the new location, Kale eyed Leetu's position and then watched the warriors. The

bisonbecks, growling and poking swords into the shrubbery, edged closer
to the statue.

"Tell him to be still," hissed Dar.

"Who?"

"Gymn."

Kale followed Dar's gaze. He stared at a place between the tip of
Leetu's boot and the lock of hair. The moonbeam cape presented a bump
in midair that gyrated, clearly visible.

*Gymn, oh Gymn, don't move. The enemy is close. Be still. Please, be still.
Don't wiggle. Don't move. Freeze!*

Gymn responded. Once again the moonbeam cape served as camou-
flage.

One of the big brutes thrust his sword into the shrubbery behind the
statue. The other leapt onto another bench and peered in and around the
alcove.

Kale thought her heart would pound right out of her chest.

Be still, be still, be still, she chanted in her mind. The words were for
herself as well as the baby dragon. Kale wanted to bolt out the gate.

The soldier on the bench jumped down behind the statue and started
around it. He stumbled over Leetu and fell flat on his face.

"Aargh!" The battle cry came not from the fallen man but from Dar.
He rose up beside Kale with his short sword drawn and charged the man
on the ground. Kale's eyes widened as she watched Dar's blade sweep
across the back of the man's neck. The soldier howled and rolled. Dar held
his sword in two hands now with the point down. The bisonbeck's arm
came out to catch the doneel's leg in a great meaty hand. Dar plunged his
weapon downward. The silver blade stuck in the enemy's chest.

Kale was on her feet, running to help. The second soldier sprang
toward Dar.

"Look out!" she screamed.

Dar tucked himself in a ball. Instantly, his shimmering bubble covered
him like a turtle shell. The blow of the bisonbeck's blade rang off the magical shield.

Screaming his frustration, the soldier jumped at Dar with both feet. He landed on top of the shell, forcing it down with a crackling snap on the bricks.

Kale stopped her forward course and plunged into the bushes, running behind them to a place of better advantage. The soldier either heard her or saw her. He left Dar and bellowed as he approached the manicured thicket. She dropped to her knees and crawled into the underbrush.

What can I do? What can I do?

Make him trip?

Blind him with a flash?

The soldier's huge boots stomped inches from her hands. The branches above her clattered.

Blind him!

She squeezed her eyes shut and thought with all her might.

It worked. Even within the protection of the shrubbery, her eyelids glowed red when the light burst with full intensity around her.

The bisonbeck groaned. His body hit the bricked pathway. Kale stayed where she was, huddled in the dark, panting and trembling.

She listened. Bedlam clamored at the fort entrance, but many walls and buildings muffled the clash of arms. The courtyard around her pulsed with the aftermath of conflict. Tension hung on the air. Silence echoed in sudden stillness.

"Kale, come out," Dar called. "Where are you?"

She tried to speak. "Here." Her voice croaked a broken whisper. "Here," she said again, a bit louder. She inched out of her hiding place.

Dar sat where she'd last seen him, his shell gone. He rubbed his eyes.

"Tell me next time, all right? Warn me." He shook his head as if to clear it. "By all the light on the crystal sea, that was brilliant."

Kale tried to smile in response to his praise, but her lips quivered. A sob rose in her throat. She choked it down and finished easing out from under the stiff, scratching branches. Dar still rubbed at his face, knuckling his eyes.

"Are you all right?" she asked.

"I hope so," he answered. "Check Leetu and Gymn while I try to focus."

She didn't bother to stand, crawling the few feet to the base of the statue. The cape had fallen away and exposed part of the emerlindian's clothing. Kale saw Leetu's chest rise and fall in a gentle, shallow rhythm. Gymn lay inside his pocket-den in a quivering ball. Kale pulled him out and held him securely against her neck, rubbing one finger on the ridges between his ears.

"You're as big a coward as I am," she whispered. "Because you feel what I feel, and I feel what you feel, does that mean we make each other's fear worse? We'll both have to be more brave." She sighed and looked over at Dar examining the bisonbeck bodies. "Like Dar. He's already up and seeing to our safety."

Dar leaned close to the soldier stunned by Kale's blast of light. He prodded the prone man with his sword. She watched him pat the side of the bisonbeck's uniform, locate another long knife, and remove the weapon.

"These soldiers won't fight again," he said. He rubbed at his face as he stood erect.

Have I damaged Dar's eyes? I sent a vision of blinding light into the soldier's mind. How did Dar...?

"Dar?"

"Hmm?"

"I don't understand."

"Hmm?"

"If I sent the suggestion of brilliance into the bisonbeck's mind, why was the light real? I saw the flash even with my eyes closed. The flash nearly blinded you. *No* one should have seen it but him." She nodded toward the man at Dar's feet.

A puzzled frown tightened Dar's furry features. He looked down at the soldier and then up at Kale. He rubbed his eyes again with the back of his hand and squinted at her once more. He opened his mouth and closed it again without speaking.

"Hurry!" The shrill command came without warning. Both Dar and Kale jumped. Seezle's blurred approach created a whistle as she zoomed through the archway and came to a halt. "That light drew too much attention. Let's move. We have to get out of here."

They ran to pick up Leetu.

"Where have you been?" Dar demanded as he hoisted the emerlindian's feet to his shoulders.

Kale let go of Gymn to snatch up her end of Leetu. She didn't want her injured friend to hang upside down off the back of the agitated doneel. Gymn's little claws poked through the material of Kale's blouse as he clung to her shoulder.

Seezle slipped into her place under Leetu. The procession moved down the brick pathway, through the gate, and onto the terrace.

"To the forest." Seezle's voice returned to its natural light cadence. "To see Paladin. I asked if we should join the forces at the fortress entry and help secure the prisoners' freedom."

Dar's ears perked up. "And?"

"He said no. Our priority is to get Leetu to safety. We go through the river cavern."

The doneel's shoulders drooped. He trudged wordlessly across the polished stone surface of the elegant terrace toward the wall of glass doors that gave entry to the castle.

Shouts sounded nearer now. The rumble of determined troops grew louder as boots tramped in the corridors between buildings.

Dar reached the first door.

"It's locked," he said over his shoulder. "Back up a couple of feet."

Once in position, Dar kicked a leg out, his heel aimed at the pane of glass next to the handle. His foot hit the glass and bounced, sending the shock of impact back through the four waiting to reach safety.

Dar growled.

"Enchantment," said Seezle. "It's reinforced by magic."

"How are we going to get in?" Kale looked with apprehension toward

the garden wall that blocked their view of what was happening in the narrow castle passageways. Flickering torches could be seen as they passed on
the other side. Citizens of Risto's castle compound rushed about in the
night. How many of them were soldiers?

Dar caught Kale off balance when he swiftly sidestepped to the next
door. She scurried to follow, struggling to keep Leetu from slipping from
her grip. Dar tried the knob and then quickly went on to the next.

"Look," cried Seezle. "Down at the end. Open windows. See?"

Kale saw what she meant just as Dar took off at a trot down the side
of the building, passing all the doors. Three feet from the ground, a row
of windows stood open. The panes of glass in wooden frames tilted outward on metal hinges attached at the top. Dar put down Leetu's feet. The
others lowered her carefully to the ground.

"Seezle," said Dar, "you go in first. Kale next, and then we'll pass Leetu
through."

Seezle ducked under the pane of glass and disappeared inside. Kale
crouched to get in position.

Dar exclaimed under his breath, "Wonderful!" His tone did *not* indicate pleasure.

Kale lifted her eyes to his face. She followed his gaze at the same time
she heard a commotion. A half-dozen bisonbeck soldiers marched up the
steps at the far end of the terrace. The warriors spotted Kale and Dar. Two
gave a triumphant shout. Twisted grins sprang up on their ugly faces. Kale
took in a sharp breath.

"Go," Dar ordered Kale, pulling his sword from its sheath.

Kale turned away from the window and stood. She, too, pulled her
small blade from its scabbard. She moved to stand next to Dar in front of
the crumpled heap that was Leetu.

The bisonbecks advanced, taking their time. They obviously thought
their prey was cornered. Kale felt a flutter at her leg and knew Seezle had
joined them.

A heavy droning noise from beyond the wall grew louder. Seezle chuckled. The bisonbecks looked nervously toward the outside of the castle gardens. They took a few more uncertain steps toward Kale and her friends. The drone changed pitch, higher and piercing. People screamed, punctuating the inhuman buzz. The soldiers stopped and stared in the direction of the uproar.

A black mist appeared at the top of the wall, a thin trickle followed by a thick mass. At first Kale thought it was a mordakleep, but the darkness was not dense enough to be one of the swamp monsters. And mordakleeps were totally silent. The reverberating buzz came from the cloud.

With a yell of terror, the warriors turned and ran.

Seezle chuckled again.

"Hornets," said Dar.

The swarm turned with a purpose and zoomed after the retreating soldiers.

"They won't hurt us?" asked Kale.

"They pass over those wearing the protection of Paladin."

Kale, totally confused, frowned at the doneel.

"The glean band, Kale." Dar sounded patient. Kale had no idea what he was talking about. "On your wrist."

She looked down at the thin, green rope bracelet he'd fastened on her arm when she first woke in the dungeon.

"Oh." Kale watched as the last of the swarm disappeared in pursuit of the bisonbecks. "How did the hornets get here?"

"My people," said Seezle with a impish grin on her tiny face. "We plucked hornet nests from forest trees and hurled them into the fray." She hopped up and down and giggled.

The menacing hornet drone faded, along with the shrieks from the soldiers being stung.

Kale reached up to her shoulder. "Where's Gymn?" She patted under the collar of her blouse where the baby dragon might have hidden himself. She began looking around on the ground.

"Here he is." Dar handed her the limp creature. "He was under the window."

"Fainted again?" Seezle shook her head in disbelief as she came closer. She put out a finger and touched the little beast cradled in Kale's palm. "Is he all right? He *did* just faint, didn't he?"

Kale squatted beside the kimen so Seezle could see better. The pale blue glow from Seezle's clothing cast a light on Gymn. He breathed in and out. He twitched and curled more tightly into a ball. No marks scarred his body. He hadn't been injured in any visible way.

Kale stroked his back. "I think he's coming around."

They watched as Gymn opened his eyes, blinked rapidly, and then lifted his head.

"He'll be all right," said Kale.

Standing before Kale, Seezle gave full attention to the dragon. Kale reached out with her other hand and tried to touch Seezle's soft, flowing tunic. Her fingers passed through the "cloth." She tried again. This time she paused as her hand entered the material. Light spilled across her palm as if she held it under the glow of a lantern. She wiggled her fingers and felt nothing but air.

Seezle jumped back. Kale looked at the kimen's expression to see whether she was angry. The little face shone with laughter.

"Light!" Seezle exclaimed and twirled away. Kale looked over at Dar and refused to acknowledge the I-told-you-so look on his face.

"I'm hungry," said Seezle.

Both Dar and Kale turned to stare at her.

"We *will* be passing through the kitchen to get to the well," said the tiny creature. "We aren't in any danger now. Don't you think it would be nice to stop for tea?"

Kale turned to Dar. That was something she would expect him to suggest.

"Not this time." He shook his head as he sheathed his weapon. "We still have to go down that well, follow an underground river, and jump onto a dragon flying by. Somehow that doesn't do a thing to whet my appetite."

28

LEAP OF FAITH

Getting down the well wasn't as difficult as Kale anticipated. They sat Leetu in the bucket with her legs straddling the rope, then tied her on. Seezle rode down with Leetu, untied her, and then pushed her off onto the stone bank of the river. Kale climbed in the bucket next, and Dar lowered it. When she stood on the stone bank beside Leetu and Seezle, Dar came down hand over hand on the rope.

Kale checked Leetu for any additional bruises. Even though Kale hadn't been able to come up with a better plan, she hated the idea of Seezle shoving the emerlindian off and letting her fall on the rock. Holding Gymn, Kale let healing flow into Leetu. When she had done what she could under the circumstances, she turned, frowning at the kimen. The bucket on the well rope hung over the edge of the river, not over the stone ledge that served as the fast-moving river's bank.

"How did you drop her onto the bank instead of into the river?" Kale asked. She spoke loudly over the rushing tumult of the water.

"We swung back and forth like a pendulum. Haven't you ever ridden on a swing tied to a tree and jumped off?"

Kale closed her eyes and shuddered. What if the tiny kimen had lost her grip after she untied Leetu? What if Leetu had fallen into the swift-flowing river instead of onto the bank? She would have been pummeled against the stone ledges as the water mercilessly bore her to the end of the cavern. Then her body would have catapulted into midair to be hurled hundreds of feet down with tons of water roaring over the edge.

"Kale." Dar's sharp tone forced her to open her eyes. He stood before her, shaking his head. "We've got plenty to worry about. Don't waste your time worrying about things that didn't happen."

Kale sat up straight and glared at him. "Dar, if I find out you read my mind after you told me you couldn't, I'll be mad as two wolves after the same chicken."

She saw Dar's face lighten with his chuckle, but she couldn't hear his laugh over the water.

He threw her cape into her lap. "I don't need to read your mind. Your face tells it all."

I wonder if that is truly so, Mr. Dar. It seems to me that doneels are full of surprises and mysterious ways. You cook and sew and sing and play all sorts of instruments and fight and travel and seek adventure. You aren't like anyone I ever met.

He grinned at her, and the open friendship in that smile melted her anger. She stood and swung the cape around her shoulders. It felt good to have it on again.

I like having Dar as a friend. And Leetu, and Seezle. I wonder if they think of me as a friend. When you're a slave, you're nobody's friend. Not really.

I think I might like questing just a little, because I have comrades, and comrades are like friends.

They entered the huge cavern with the river running wildly beside them. Seezle's bright light cast a shadow in front of the doneel and behind the o'rant girl. Above them, Leetu's shadow danced on the rock ceiling. A constant mist rose from the tumbling waters. Every surface glistened with a slick sheen of moisture. Their boots slipped on the uneven stone underfoot. The spray mixed with perspiration on Kale's face as she held tightly to Leetu.

"I see lights ahead," said Dar.

They paused, and Seezle dimmed her light.

"I see them," said Kale. "They're like fireflies."

"Kimens!" squealed Seezle. She hopped out from beneath Leetu's middle so quickly that the pull of the emerlindian's slight weight caused Dar and Kale to stumble a step closer together.

"Put her down gently," Kale urged Dar as Seezle skipped ahead of them. Kale collapsed on the stone floor and leaned against the wet wall.

Dar stood with his hands on his hips, watching as Seezle greeted her kin-folk and brought them back. The sound of their merry voices rose over the raging water like melodious wind chimes. It reverberated against the cavern walls with ringing notes accented by laughter.

Every muscle in Kale's body ached. She pulled Gymn into her hands and stroked him, knowing his healing powers would give her enough sta-mina to finish this trip.

She stood to greet Seezle's friends. She held Gymn in her left hand with his head tucked under her chin. Seezle led four bright spots of orange light. The kimens glided over the rough passage.

Seezle hopped over the last small boulder. "Kale, meet Zayvion, Veazey, D'Shay, and Glim." She pointed to each of her companions in turn. "They are the Trio family."

"We got bored," said one of the tiny men. Kale thought he was the kimen named Zayvion.

The second man, Glim, spoke up. "We've been waiting for you at the cliff. Nothing to do there, so we came to meet you."

D'Shay bounced as she talked. "We can help you carry your warrior."

Veazey grinned and blinked her eyes against a sudden spray off the river. "Paladin sent the Trio family, because we're the best airborne escorts."

"Trio?" asked Dar. "There are four of you."

"Airborne?" asked Kale.

"The Trio family is made up of orphans," said Zayvion. Kale liked his deep, strong voice, although it sounded funny coming out of his small body.

"Originally, there were only three," explained Glim, pushing closer to Dar. "The three decided they didn't like being orphans, and they joined together to make their own family."

D'Shay, bouncing on her toes with her clothes flickering between shades of yellow and orange, added her part. "Any kimen orphan can come and apply for a position in the family."

"No one has ever been turned down," said Veazey.

"Gale was, and so was Sweptor," objected Zayvion.

Veazey turned an annoyed face toward the outspoken male and planted her fists upon her hips. "That was two hundred years ago."

"It still counts." Zayvion frowned and looked stubborn. "As long as it happened, it happened. You can't say no one was ever turned down if someone *was* turned down. Gale and Sweptor were both turned down on the same day in the same month in the same year. They were turned down together, and so you can't say no one was ever turned down, because someone was turned down, Gale and Sweptor."

D'Shay stepped between the two. "You're right, Zay. Gale and Sweptor were wild and unruly, and of course they were turned down." She patted his chest with her small hand, and sparks of blue and gold sprayed out at her touch. She turned to Veazey. "You're right too, of course." Her friendly smile drained the tension out of Veazey's face. D'Shay sang her words in the strange melodic cadence of her race. "Gale and Sweptor calmed down and asked Paladin to forgive them for being such a problem. Then they applied to the family again and were not turned down."

She touched her sister's arm, and when she lifted her hand, a rainbow streamed from the palm of her hand to the place where it had rested. Kale blinked as the colored band faded away.

Kale said, "Do that again," but the river noise drowned her request.

Zayvion crossed his arms over his chest. "Took Gale and Sweptor one hundred and sixty-two years to say they were sorry."

D'Shay nodded, and her hair floated wildly around her head. "But Paladin forgave them." She narrowed her eyes at Zayvion but didn't finish her thoughts.

Kale knew what Mistress Meiger would have said. The old marione woman would have said variations of the same sentence for half a day beyond making her point. "If Paladin forgives someone, should another stand in unforgiveness? Does this other person who withholds forgiveness think he is greater than, smarter than, more important than Paladin? What folly!" Oh yes, Mistress Meiger could have scolded interminably on the subject. Kale gave thanks that the kimen was not as long-winded as her marione owner in River Away.

Veazey pointed at Kale. "She doesn't know what we mean by airborne escort."

"My name is Kale." Kale frowned. *I don't like being called "she" anymore. When I was a slave, I wasn't important enough for some people to remember my name. But since I've been away from my home, people have called me Kale, and I like it. Kale Allerion.*

Veazey skipped closer and looked earnestly up into Kale's face. "I'm sorry. Truly I am. I know you are Kale, the Dragon Keeper. Everyone knows about you. You're famous. Paladin has said you are a fine servant. He said you are brave and true. We begged to be chosen as your escort." She turned away and started spinning. Swirls of light came off her clothing as she danced. "We will be famous. The Trio family comes to the rescue, chosen to escort the great Kale, Dragon Keeper. Four of the intrepid Trio kimens joined the warrior Leetu's rescuers and gave their airborne support as the doneel and o'rant jumped from the Risto cliff onto a passing dragon." As she became more excited, her words turned into a song.

"They climbed, they rode, they intervened,
Zayvion, Veazey, D'Shay, and Glim.
When Paladin said, 'Bring them to me.
Leetu, Dar, and Kale must be free,'
Paladin sent the Trio kin,
Zayvion, Veazey, D'Shay, and Glim."

Zayvion and Glim stepped forward, laughing, and caught her as she whirled by. They pulled her toward the unconscious emerlindian.

"We have to be a part of the rescue," said Glim, "before we can be famous and have ballads composed in our honor."

Veazey held up one small arm and cheered. "To the end of the river cavern!"

D'Shay twirled toward the others with both arms raised. "Celisse awaits us." Sprays of light flew off her dress, splattering the walls with tiny colored dots that hit, exploded, and died away.

Kale quickly put Gymn back in his pocket-den. Dar bent to pick up Leetu's feet. Kale hoisted up Leetu's shoulders. The five kimens crowded underneath.

"Do you hear me, Kale?"

Yes, Seezle.

"The Trio family members are always flamboyant, but they do their jobs well. Don't worry. Paladin trusts them."

Do you think it's true?

"What?"

That Paladin said those nice things about me.

"Why, of course. I also heard him praise you."

But he doesn't know me.

"Wulder knows you, and Paladin knows what Wulder knows. They think like one person, because they know each other so well."

A glow of well-being spread through Kale. Gymn had taken the soreness from her muscles. The Trio kimens had lifted her spirits with their silly disagreement and their enthusiasm. Leetu felt extremely light. Kale felt she was doing little more than holding her friend's head while the others carried most of the weight.

As the kimens marched, the colored lights of their garments shifted continuously. Did this reflect their moods? Did they play with the lights on purpose, perhaps to keep boredom at bay? Kale watched with fascination, and the end of the river cavern came quickly.

The sight took Kale's breath away. Beside them, the water plummeted off the cliff edge in a roaring cascade. In front of them, the valley shadows stretched for miles in velvety dark shades of green, blue, purple, and black. Above them, the stars pierced the darkness with tiny pricks of white sparkle. The moon lit the few wisps of clouds with luminous light.

Kale let go of Leetu and pressed her back against the solid rock wall of the cliff. Seezle smoothly moved enough to support the emerlindian's head. Kale breathed heavily. Nothing had prepared her for the immensity of the open space confronting her after the closed-in feeling of the cavern.

The river cascading over the edge made it impossible to converse.

They laid Leetu on the ledge, and, to Kale's horror, the four Trio kimens promptly sat down on her as if she were a log.

Kale heard Seezle's light laughter in her mind. *"They are keeping her warm. It is cool out here."*

We should wrap her in the moonbeam cape. Kale started unbuttoning her cloak.

"No, the kimens need to be able to hold her securely when they jump with her to Celisse's back. Keep your cape."

I hear Celisse. She's coming.

"Tell the others."

Kale mindspoke to Dar and the four kimens at once. A flurry of activity followed. Everyone seemed to know how to help except her. She watched them lift Leetu and carry her away from the waterfall along a shelf to a place where it narrowed into nothing more than a thin lip jutting from the rock face. The five kimens lined up on the narrow ledge of granite and held their burden like a long sack of potatoes across their shoulders.

Seezle gave last-minute instructions to Kale.

"Celisse will carry Leetu and the kimens to Paladin, and then we'll return for you."

Kale felt a moment of panic.

"Wait here with Dar. Shimeran and I will return for you as soon as we can."

In the distance, a black shape approached from high over the valley. Kale could see Celisse's huge wings beating slowly. Kale felt the tension in the dragon's desire to make the pass close to the wall, pick up her passengers, and veer away before hitting the wall of water. From the kimens, Kale picked up an air of excitement that trembled through her as if she would be jumping as well. But Kale couldn't block the horror that clenched her heart with the thought of stepping off the cliff and hoping to land on Celisse's back.

One moment the kimens stood on the shelf, and the next they were gone. Kale fell face forward and looked over the edge. In place of the usual saddle, a netting of white ropes covered Celisse's entire torso. Kale breathed a sigh of relief as she recognized small, lighted shapes clinging to the apparatus. The kimens dotted the dragon's back with a large dark shape pinned in their midst. Celisse made the turn and glided past the waterfall.

They're safe.

"*Now we wait,*" answered Dar.

Kale turned her head and saw he was lying beside her, also watching the dragon fly away.

Too bad you can't play your flute.

"*Oh, I could play it. We just couldn't hear it.*"

Kale started to laugh at the image of Dar trying to play louder than the river, but a horrible dread cut off the humor.

Dar!

"*What?*"

He knows where we are.

"*Risto?*"

Yes, I think so. He's evil. He's strong.

"*Call on Wulder to protect you, Kale. Say the words Granny Noon gave you.*"

I did. I did! Kale grabbed his arm, and her fingers dug into his damp coat sleeve. *Oh, Dar, no!*

"*What? What?*"

He's planning some force, some evil spell. He's so angry. It's boiling within him. He's cursing us and Paladin and Wulder. But he's aiming the evil at us.

"*What's he going to do?*"

Kale tried to sort out the impressions she was receiving. The tangle of dark images confused her. Something was coming apart. Something huge. She gasped.

Dar, he's going to shear away the side of the cliff. He's going to melt the rock under our feet. He's destroying the ledge we're standing on.

Dar looked off after Celisse. "How soon?" he yelled over the thundering waterfall.

"Now!" Kale screamed.

29

Paladin

Kale and Dar rolled away fro—m the edge as the cliff began to quiver. They knelt as close to the stone wall as possible.

Should we escape through the cavern, back to the fortress?

"The whole mountain might collapse on us."

He wouldn't destroy his own castle, would he?

As if in answer to her question, a deafening roar shook the rocks around them. Kale screeched. Dar grabbed her arm and pulled. They scrambled on all fours back toward the waterfall and the wider ledge.

Shards of broken rock pelted them, stinging their skin. Coarse gravel-like pebbles bounced and skittered like hailstones on the flinty shelf around Kale and Dar. The mountain continued to rumble under their hands and knees. A strong shudder knocked them flat on their stomachs. As soon as it passed, they resumed crawling. Kale heard a loud crack and looked over her shoulder. A few feet behind her, a section of the ledge split, hung for a second, and then slid down and away. The exposed rock, several shades lighter than the weathered surface around it, looked like a huge scar on the face of the cliff.

Dar entered the cavern and collapsed with his back against the wall. Kale followed and huddled beside him. The doneel stretched an arm around her shoulders. She raised her head and looked at the dismal scene.

The vapor off the waterfall clouded her vision. From the cavern ceiling a fine spray of gravel fell like a gray curtain. The mountain groaned. Rock ground against rock as the earth travailed under Risto's destructive spell. Kale placed her hands over her ears to block out the grinding noise.

The vibration in the rock made her want to scream and run. But where could they go?

We can't just sit here!

"I know. I'm thinking."

I'm scared!

"So am I."

Back through the tunnel?

"Too dangerous."

Sitting here is dangerous!

"Merlander!"

What?

"She's coming."

How…?

Dar jumped to his feet. "Come on, Kale. She's almost here."

He ran outside the cavern. Kale followed as he darted away from the waterfall along the crumbling ledge. She kept her head down, watching her feet and trying to keep dust from the disintegrating cliff out of her eyes. A shadow passed and then another. Kale looked up in time to see the tail of a white dragon disappear in the mist. As she watched, two small globes of light appeared above them, and then two more. The light became clearer as it descended, drifting closer to where she and Dar stood on the precarious stone shelf.

The mountain shook. Debris rained down on them as the ground trembled. Dar and Kale collapsed in a heap to keep from being tossed over the edge by the violent surges of the rock beneath them. A crash in the distance meant another cliff section had broken away and fallen. When Kale opened her eyes again, four kimens stood around them—Shimeran, Seezle, Zayvion, and Glim.

The little people helped Kale and Dar to their feet.

"The dragons will return immediately." It was Shimeran's strong voice in her head. "We will jump to safety."

Kale's throat closed, and she struggled to breathe. Her muscles felt like boards that would not move, would not jump, but *would* burn with fear as the others leapt onto the passing dragons. A small hand brushed her cold palm, grabbed a few of her stiff fingers, and squeezed. Kale looked down to see Seezle's upturned face. The kimen smiled, her eyes bright with excitement.

"Now!" commanded Shimeran.

"No!" screeched Kale, but a thump on her back, squarely between her shoulder blades, knocked her forward. She tumbled off the cliff.

As she fell, cold air rushed around her, flapping at her clothing and sweeping through her hair. Seezle still held her fingers. The little kimen wrapped her body around Kale's arm. Seezle forced that arm out straight and seemed to pull Kale away from the sheer wall of rock. Another kimen clung to her back. He, too, seemed to be directing her fall.

They hit the dragon with a great thwack. With her free hand, Kale grabbed the soft ropes crisscrossing around the creature's torso. In a moment of scrambling, her feet found toeholds in the netting. Her cheek stung where the impact against the dragon had scraped off tender skin. Tension radiated pain through her body.

Seezle and Shimeran patted her. She heard their melodic voices telling her she was safe. Her fingers clutched the strong, silken cords. She could not open her eyes. She could not speak.

The air cleared, no longer wet, no longer laden with particles of dust and grit. The waterfall's roar faded gradually. The rhythmic beat of dragon wings soothed her fright away. She could feel the rippling of huge muscles beneath her as the great beast breathed the night air and moved almost silently through the sky.

Dar?

"I'm all right. I'm on Merlander. You?"

I'm not hurt.

Silence. Kale searched her mind for a glimpse of the baby dragon's presence. She dared not move a hand down to explore the pocket of her cape.

Gymn was there, groggy and curled up in a ball. She felt his mind stir, shudder in fear, and retreat into unconsciousness. Kale giggled.

Dar?

"*Yes?*"

Gymn's all right. She giggled again and knew the sound had traveled to Dar's mind. *He fainted. Then he came to and remembered what happened and fainted again.*

Kale heard the responsive chortle from Dar. The small sound blossomed into an explosion of mirth. She smiled and giggled again. Then she laughed and clung to the ropes. The laughter shook her with a rolling determination to empty her body of all tension. It wiped away the last vestiges of terror. With her eyes still clamped shut and her fingers wrapped around the ropes, she let her body react. Tears rolled down her cheeks. The kimens stroked her back and arms.

When her emotions settled and she lay exhausted against the ropes, a shiver coursed through her. The kimens moved quickly, tucking the moonbeam cape more securely around her wet body. She felt them scamper lightly over and around her. Being hundreds of feet in the air didn't seem to bother Shimeran and Seezle at all.

Kale opened her eyes and watched as they climbed back and forth across the netting as if it were a tree rooted firmly in the ground. She examined the rigging clenched in her hand. She couldn't identify the fibers twisted in an incredibly fine pattern.

Made by kimens. She'd seen examples of their delicate weaving in baskets sold at River Away's market.

With one finger she touched the white dragon skin beneath the network of ropes. Pearlescent scales covered the hide. Her finger caressed one of the cool, smooth disks. Moonlight twinkled off each of the scales.

Kale noticed the grime on her fingers. Mist from the waterfall and dust from the crumbling cliff had combined to make a muddy coating on her skin. She needed a bath.

Not until I get off this dragon. Kale twisted her head cautiously to view the rider working with the dragon.

A giant! No, a urohm!

Shimeran took two steps along the dragon's ridged back to the huge saddle. With a leap, he landed on the urohm's shoulder and said something into his ear.

The man turned at the waist, reached back, and gathered Kale into his gentle hand. As if she were a large rag doll, he tucked her under one side of his riding jacket.

"Shimeran says you're cold." His deep rumbling voice vibrated through his chest. "We'll be landing in just a few minutes. We'll set you before a fire and dry you out."

Kale nestled within the warmth provided and wondered if this was how Gymn felt in his pocket-den. The urohm smelled of soap and the earthy scent of a man who has worked all day.

Kale listened to the beat of his great heart and felt safe. Pulling Gymn from her pocket, she cuddled him under her chin and enjoyed the flow of health and contentment between them. With each pulse, she gained physical comfort and a feeling of serenity.

Gymn jerked to attention, squirmed out of her hands, and plunged back under the edge of her cape. His fear coursed through her veins before she identified the source.

Fire dragons! Kale gulped. *Fire dragons? Like the evil fire dragon in* The Tale of Durmoil? *Like the monster fire dragons who emerged from the volcanoes in ancient days? Fire dragons are real?*

Kale shook her head. *Why not? Paladin is real. Gateways are real. I'm riding inside the jacket of a urohm on the back of a giant white dragon.*

She wasn't the village slave anymore, and she probably knew as much as the schoolmistress when it came to what parts of legends were real and what was made up. Master Meiger had said Kale didn't know much, but she was learning every day. She would not sit in darkness and let others fight for her.

She struggled to sit upright and moved closer to the opening of the jacket. Her hand clutched a large button that covered her palm as she inched the fleece of the coat out of her way. Ahead she saw four dark shapes in the sky. Dragons flew toward them from the east, but they didn't look any different from the few dragons she'd seen before.

"Nine—no, a dozen," she heard Shimeran's voice from above her. He still sat on the urohm's shoulder.

Kale craned her neck to see him. He sat looking back toward the fortress they'd escaped.

"We have help coming," said the master rider of the white dragon.

"Just so long as it isn't too little, too late," said Shimeran.

Kale looked ahead and understood. She saw four dragons coming to help them. Shimeran saw a dozen coming to defeat them. The ones before them were ordinary dragons. The ones behind them were fire dragons. Kale felt Gymn's panic as he shivered, hidden in his pocket-den. She placed a hand over the bulge in her cape where he lay.

I'm not panicked, Little Gymn, but I'm so weary of all this trouble. One thing after another. Will we ever rest like normal folks in a bed, in a house, by a fireplace?

"They're gaining on us," reported Shimeran.

"Our help is here," answered the urohm.

The four dragons swooped past them, but a moment later they circled to join the white dragon, heading in the same direction. One flew in front, one flew on either side, and Shimeran reported that the last had taken up position behind Merlander.

"An escort," said the urohm. "Now I wonder what Paladin is up to?"

"Look!" Shimeran pointed off to the south. "I think we're going to find out."

Kale pushed herself up and leaned out of the jacket. In front of them, the horizon flushed pink with the approach of a new day. To the south, a gleaming dragon crested a steep hill and cast a shimmering light on the forest below. He soared heavenward and in moments flew over the small band of six dragons trying to reach safety. The regal dragon circled. The riders of the dragons below cheered, waving their swords in a salute to the one above. Then that radiant dragon turned to the west.

Shimeran now stood on the master rider's shoulder and jumped up and down. Kale climbed out of the urohm's coat and stood on the man's thigh. She leaned against his chest and peered over the other shoulder, hanging on to his collar.

Merlander flew behind them, and Kale could see Dar, Glim, Zayvion, and another man who looked like a marione. The marione sat backward in the dragon saddle with one hand waving his hat in the air and the other waving his sword. Kale glanced at the other dragons in turn. Each held riders caught up in the excitement. She squinted at the majestic dragon as it sped toward the fire dragons. The rider wore a golden cape, a shining crown, and held a long sword that sparked with blue lightning.

Beyond, twelve dragons, red in the dawn light with a dark and smoldering sky behind them, advanced with incredible speed. With each breath, flames of fire erupted from their nostrils.

The fire dragons approached.

One man went to meet them.

Paladin.

30

THE BATTLE

Kale forgot the chilly morning air. She ignored the blazing sunrise behind her. The wild cheering of her comrades subsided to a vigilant hush. The formation of six dragons circled to the south in a wide arc so everyone could watch the encounter as Paladin rode fearlessly to meet the opposing forces.

Kale expected a clash of weapons, lightning from that gleaming sword, thunder from the heavens, spectacular displays of force. In the tales told by traveling minstrels in the River Away Tavern, historic wars included an abundance of clamor and bloodshed. She didn't know much about war. She did know it scared her enough to make her palms sweat as she watched the two sides face off for the fight.

Kale didn't like what she'd seen of fighting. Her first battle with the grawligs had frightened her. The horrible screeching, cursing, and howling rang in her ears. Even the hiss of Leetu's arrows as they sailed toward their targets sounded sinister. When fighting the silent mordakleeps, the thud of fists against flesh sickened her. The slash and sizzle when sword drew mordakleep blood turned her stomach. The battle at the fortress included the clanging sounds of sword, spear, shield, armor, and bludgeons. How much more terrible would the clamor be when Paladin released his awesome power upon the swarm of evil dragons?

The fire dragons roared, flames shooting twenty feet out of their mouths and nostrils. Paladin took his position, facing the onslaught. He slowed, checking his racing dragon to a somber pace.

Kale remembered the warhorses she'd seen through Leetu's memory. Urohms rode these majestic creatures in *The Tale of the Battle of Ordray*.

The Valley of Collumna had been lined with men on horseback. Their faces reflected determination. Their bodies stiffened as they carried their lances, point down. Men and horses faced the inevitable with unwavering courage. Now she saw Paladin and his mount take on a similar attitude.

They proceeded with no hurry, apparently not disconcerted by the odds against them. Confidence cloaked the rider like shining armor. Paladin's straight back and steady gaze made Kale blink back tears of pride. What a blessing that she'd been led to enter the service of this great warrior. Against the backdrop of brightening orange sky, his dragon fairly pranced in eagerness to charge.

Kale braced herself as the distance between the line of fire dragons and Paladin narrowed. Flames shot from the evil dragons' mouths and nostrils. They snorted and tossed their heads. Tendrils of fire licked out of their noses. With each blow, the beasts shot forth longer, blazing plumes of red and orange. Periodically, one would roar and let out a stream of fire, casting a glow as bright as the sun peeking over the eastern horizon. Each blast grew more intense. The smell of sulfur permeated the air.

Paladin stood in his stirrups and raised his sword.

In anger the twelve beasts arched their necks, bellowing to the sky above. As one, their heads dropped down. Hideous mouths gaped open. A wall of fire issued forth, aimed at the rider and dragon before them. The inferno rolled across the open space, enveloped Paladin, and moved on.

Kale gasped and held her breath until the ball of fire had barreled clear across the valley and slammed into the ridge of mountains on the other side. She stared in amazement. Paladin and his dragon hung in midair, not singed, not harmed in any manner. Suspended in flight, he held the same posture as before the attack.

Out of his mouth came a command flowing like molten steel from the blacksmith's chalice. *"Enough. Be gone."*

Kale heard an echo and immediately knew the words had come through her mind as well as through her ears.

The fire dragons recoiled. Paladin urged his own forward. He rode into the midst of the twelve dragons. They parted. Six turned to the south and circled back to the west. Six turned to the north and circled away.

In the landscape near Risto's fortress, dark creatures lurked in the shadows of boulder and tree. They slithered and crawled and crept away, melting into the earth and disappearing from the light of day.

A groan erupted from the mountain. A magnified wail of frustration echoed as it hammered the cliffs and rumbled along the valley floor.

Silence followed.

Quiet replaced chaos.

No sound reached Kale's ears save the whoosh of dragon wings steadily beating the new dawn air. A fresh breeze fluttered the leaves in trees below. The first notes of a morning oriole lifted from the meadow. A horse whinnied in a pasture. More birds broke forth in song to be joined by the plaintive bleats from lambs as they sought breakfast at their mothers' sides.

Paladin turned his beast toward the forest and gestured for the other riders to join him. Kale heard the hum of kimen song. Praises to Wulder. Thanksgiving for victory. The music flowed through her and brought back memories of dancing in the cygnot forest, celebrating the presence of Wulder. The tunes rose into full voice. She wept.

She sank down on the urohm's lap and cried. His huge hand covered her, but she did not care if anyone saw her. She had never been so tired before. She didn't take Gymn into her hand to ease away the weariness. Instead she slipped into slumber, preferring the quiet solitude of dreams to struggling with her confused emotions.

31

The Aftermath

Kale awoke to the pleasant smell of wood smoke and the crackling fire in the hearth. A dim yellow light from a lantern suffused the interior of a pine cabin. A wool blanket cocooned her in warmth. She blinked, for the cabin was like many in the village of River Away. The square, squat furniture was built for the bodies of mariones. The dark colors in the curtains and rug reflected marione tradition.

Had she dreamed? How much had been a dream? Was she still a slave in a tiny village in eastern Amara?

She forced her aching head off the hard pillow and struggled to sit. This was not a home she had been in before. She did not recognize the layout of the room nor any particular piece of furnishing, yet she lay on a slave's pallet alongside a kitchen wall.

The front door opened, revealing a brief glimpse of a fenced paddock, a barn, trees, stars, and moon. A man came in, but not a marione.

An o'rant!

The dim light in the room did not fall on his face, but allowed her glimpses of his clothing. Dressed in the elegant apparel of the aristocracy, he rustled as he moved. Light from the fire danced on the shiny material of his jacket and glinted on his finely polished boots. He went directly to the hearth, removed the lid from a pot, and stirred the contents.

Kale's mouth watered as she smelled pnard potatoes laced with savory herbs and butter. The stranger ladled some stew into a bowl, replaced the cover on the pot, and grabbed a spoon. He walked across the room and handed the meal to Kale.

"Thank you," she said, taking the warm bowl.

"Don't burn yourself."

Kale gasped and looked up into Paladin's kind eyes. A young man in the prime of his life, he smiled and lowered himself to sit cross-legged beside her on the floor. His dark hair flowed around his face in soft waves. Blue eyes crinkled at the corners as if he laughed often. His straight nose pointed over a firm, strong mouth. His jaw and chin looked stubborn, but his high forehead made him appear considerate and wise. Kale thought him very handsome and a bit overwhelming.

"Go ahead, eat," he urged her. "You've slept a day and a night. You should be starved."

The fragrance rising with the steam tickled her nose, but a lump pressed in her chest.

"Leetu?" she asked.

"Living, but still unconscious."

"Dar?"

"A rascal still."

"The kimens?"

"All accounted for."

"Celisse?"

"Completely recovered and also forgiven by Dar. She and Merlander are settled in a copse down the road."

Kale lifted her hand to her chest where her little dragon friend often slept.

Paladin smiled. "Gymn is fine as well and has been riding in my pocket." He rested a hand on the full skirt of his court coat. "Sleeping."

Kale took a bite and savored the rich, creamy taste. She took another spoonful and surreptitiously studied the man seated before her.

He smiled. "You can ask any questions you want."

"There are a lot of things I don't understand."

"There's nothing wrong with that."

"Do you really want me in your service?"

"Most definitely."

She liked the enthusiasm in his voice, but she didn't understand why he'd consider her worthy.

"What can I do?"

"Whatever falls before you. No more. No less."

She sighed. The answers to her questions only made more questions in her mind.

"Why do I have these special talents?"

"Which special talents, Kale Allerion?"

"Finding dragon eggs."

"Wulder knew you would be the right one for the quest, so He equipped you for the task."

"The light thing."

Paladin looked down at his hand and seemed to examine his fingernails. "The light thing?"

Kale hesitated, stirring the stewed potatoes, taking a bite, swallowing slowly, and stirring some more.

Paladin said nothing but waited. His attention came back to the o'rant girl. His steady gaze warmed her. Finally peace blanketed her heart, and she felt comfort in confiding in him.

"In the castle garden, when the bisonbeck soldiers came, I concentrated on making the image of light, and real light appeared."

"Ah yes, I remember. I was pleased to see you nab that power so easily, but I do think Fenworth will have a time training your instincts and channeling your energy."

"We'll find Wizard Fenworth?"

"Oh, yes. I've spoken to him."

Kale found this interesting. She paused to think about how easily Paladin solved the problem. Fenworth had not wanted to be found, so he wasn't. Paladin spoke to the reclusive old wizard, and now Fenworth would allow them to find him. Paladin's word was powerful. That raised more questions in her mind.

"You spoke to the fire dragons, and they went away. You didn't threaten them or slay them, you just spoke. Why?"

"Why?"

"Why did they obey?"

"Because my power is stronger than theirs. To their chagrin, they know they cannot defeat me in battle."

She pictured the murderous dragons flying fearlessly across the sky.

"Then why did they challenge you?"

Paladin smiled ruefully and shook his head. "They were angry and not at all rational in their anger."

"Why didn't you destroy them? Why did you let them go? You *know* they'll return."

"They serve a purpose in Wulder's plan. I would not go against what Wulder has ordained."

"But if you destroyed them, then it wouldn't matter. Things like finding Wizard Fenworth, finding the meech egg, taking it away from Risto. Things like that wouldn't be important anymore. And if you'd destroyed all the evil sooner, Leetu wouldn't have been hurt. Those people at the castle wouldn't have been killed. The others wouldn't have suffered. You could do that, couldn't you? You have the power to destroy evil. You could!"

Kale realized as she took a breath that she had spoken in a way she shouldn't have. Paladin ought to be angry at her impertinence.

He nodded slowly, watching her with patient eyes, listening to her rant, not showing any anger toward her presuming to tell him what to do.

She swallowed hard as she saw mist fill the room and their surroundings seem to fade away. She sat opposite the great Paladin with a half-eaten bowl of pnard potatoes in her lap, a dirty spoon in her hand, and nothing around them but swirling gray mists.

"Where are we?" she asked.

"Together," he answered. His hand swept through the air as if waving off an unimportant question. "Kale, Wulder has ordered our world."

"I know that." She answered quietly, ashamed of her string of heated words. Yet part of her still rebelled against the injustice. She strained to understand, chafing because Paladin did not use his power to right the wrongs that evil men like Risto committed.

A light giggle floated through the cloudy air. Kale turned her head to see a small doneel toddle toward them. The baby laughed out loud and clapped her tiny furry hands when she saw Paladin. Without hesitation she clambered into his lap and cuddled in his arms, playing with a shiny gold button on his jacket.

Paladin hugged her and kissed the top of her head between two small button ears.

"By Wulder's design, this little girl will become a renowned seamstress whose fashions are sought after in Vendela as well as other prominent cities."

Kale watched the child stick two fingers in her mouth and rest her head against the soft fabric of Paladin's coat.

"Should I give her a needle and thread now?" asked the strong young ruler.

"No!" answered Kale.

"Why not?"

"She'd stick herself."

"Yes, you're right. To give her the sharp needle now would be of the correct order of things."

Kale's brow knitted in puzzlement. And then her eyes popped wide as the sleeping doneel child vanished from Paladin's lap.

Between the edge of Kale's pallet and the man's crossed ankles, a plant sprouted out of the wooden floor.

"An apple tree, Kale," said Paladin. "Pick an apple for me."

She looked at the seedling and up at the man teaching her. She shook her head. "It won't bear fruit for years."

He nodded. "After it has struggled to put down roots, borne the stretching of growth, enjoyed sun and rain."

She glanced up to see the shadowy presence of an apple orchard surrounding them in the fog. Red apples burdened each branch of each tree.

Paladin surveyed the fruit with a pleased smile.

"These trees are mature and bearing a healthy crop." He pointed to the infant plant between them. "Because the others are ready, should we place an apple on this one?"

A large apple appeared, attached to the tip of the seedling's only limb, crushing the small plant.

Paladin shook his head slowly, a sad expression altering his kind face. The orchard faded into nothing. The mist covered the broken sapling, and when it swirled away, the plant was gone.

Paladin reached out and took Kale's small, callused hand in his.

"Kale, Wulder knows when to do what must be done. I didn't destroy Risto's army of evil because it was not the right time. In this world, people are growing, learning about Wulder, learning about themselves, making choices. Confronting Risto and those like him is part of Wulder's plan to help these ordinary people develop into something wonderful. I would not cheat these good people of the opportunity to be great in the eyes of Wulder."

"It would be easier without the struggles," said Kale, not daring to look directly into Paladin's eyes. She stared instead at his gentle hand holding hers. His perfect skin, smooth and unblemished, looked odd next to her dirty, work-worn hand.

He chortled, a warm chuckle, soft and friendly, coming from deep within.

"Kale, I love you. You are a child of my heart. You have been called to my service. Others have told you to answer the call, and you did. But Kale, now I want you to make a choice." He withdrew his hand. "Do you want to follow me? You can say yes and continue the quest with Dar and the others. You can say no and be free to go anywhere you want."

"Back to River Away?"

"If that is what you want. But you don't have to go there. You could go to Vendela if you want and look for Farmer Brigg's friend Maye at The Goose and The Gander. She would give you a job with wages. She is a nice woman."

Kale weighed the possibilities for a second. Only one choice truly appealed to her. She'd seen Paladin turn back evil. She'd seen him hold a baby tenderly in his lap. She'd felt his touch. She'd seen his smile.

"I want to follow you."

They'd been sitting, but now they stood. Kale couldn't recall standing up. Paladin swept her into his arms and whirled her around. They'd been in a marione house, and now they were on top of a cloud, or at least Kale thought the billowy puffs of white beneath them looked like clouds.

Paladin twirled so fast Kale's legs flew out behind her. Cold, crisp air tingled her skin. She giggled in response to Paladin's deep laughter.

When the spinning slowed, the wooden floor appeared again beneath their feet, and Kale found herself sitting on the pallet across from Paladin. Her fingers were cold, her breath came fast, and she could see in Paladin's expressive face the same exhilaration she felt. Suddenly shy, she ducked her head.

It's like being in a family, an important family. He said he loves me. If only I had something to give him.

He took her hand again.

His question surprised her. "Would you like to give me something?"

Cautiously, she looked up, wondering if he was mocking her. What did she have to give someone like him? His face reassured her. She nodded.

He released her hand and sat back.

A fiddle appeared in Kale's lap.

"Ah, a beautiful instrument," said Paladin. "Will you give it to me?"

Kale felt tears behind her eyes. Would she ever understand what he tried to tell her? She jerked her head up and down and handed over the fiddle.

A ring appeared on her finger. Paladin asked for it, and she gave it. A hat on her head. A bag of coins. A flower. A bottle of perfume. Each appeared, and she willingly gave each to the mysterious man who sat before her. The last item, a picture in a frame, she held limply in one hand.

"What is it, Kale? Why are you distressed?" he asked. "Don't you enjoy giving me gifts?"

She shrugged, fighting the sadness in her heart.

"They don't mean anything to me," she answered. "They aren't mine."

"What would make this painting yours?"

"If I painted it, or if I earned the money to buy it."

"But isn't it easier for me to just give it to you without the struggles?"

Kale watched the painting in its frame dissolve into nothing, leaving her hand empty. As the gift disappeared, a feeling of hope filled her soul.

She lifted expectant eyes to Paladin. He was going to answer her question.

"What is it that I can give you?"

"You've already given me all that I want, Kale. You've pledged to be in my service. You've given yourself. As you continue this quest, give me every thought, every action, every deed. It's so simple, Kale. It's what you are and who you are, what you do and what you think and feel. That is your gift to me."

Kale's heart cringed within her breast. The disappointment tore her with a pain intense and cruel.

"It's too hard to understand. I can't do it."

Paladin took the bowl and spoon from Kale's lap and set them on the floor. He stood before her, reached down to grasp her hands, and pulled her to her feet.

"Dearest Kale, neither Wulder nor I ask you to understand, only to do. Don't waste effort on trying to understand the impossible. Know that the impossible is not impossible for Wulder. The unfathomable is understood by Him. Allow Him to take care of that which is beyond your capability. And you…" He stroked a stray lock of hair off her cheek and tucked it behind her ear. "You concentrate on doing that which is before you."

He grinned. Kale looked upon Paladin's face and caught his enthusiasm, his anticipation of life. She breathed in deep as if to absorb his aura of confidence through the air around him. Her face broke into a smile to answer his. His next words sounded like a cheer in her ears.

"Enjoy your accomplishments, and leave the incredible, the insurmountable, the daunting tasks to Wulder."

"I will," she answered.

The mysterious mist stirred with a sudden, quick breeze and swiftly escaped the confines of the pinewood cabin. Sunshine flowed in the window. Morning birds chorused outside.

Paladin patted her shoulder. "First, may I make a suggestion?"

"Of course." She couldn't help but beam at him. Her heart felt full of love and hope.

He leaned closer and whispered confidentially. "First, let's see if we can arrange a bath. You, my dear, are one unholy mess."

32

Marching Orders

Kale sat on a bench at the plank table under a great oak. A dozen marione children scurried back and forth from the house, putting out plates, cups, and platters of food. Even after a week, it felt odd to sit and be served. But every time she offered to help, she was told she was a guest.

A guest. A guest in the home of mariones. And not just any marione, but General Lee Ark.

Kale looked over to where the famous marione played ribbets with a bunch of wild children. His team of half pints scored again against the older, less organized children. The spectators, sitting on the perimeter of the field, cheered.

Lee Ark had come to her rescue along with the urohm when she was trapped by the grawligs. He'd also ridden Merlander the night she and Dar jumped from the waterfall ledge.

His wife treated Kale as a respected visitor. Mistress Ark had given Kale the most treasured spot in their home, the kitchen, to sleep in, the only room that wasn't filled to the brim with sleeping mariones. In Lee Ark's "cabin," a dozen bedrooms overflowed with eleven children, various aunts and uncles and cousins, and four grandparents. Kale had not been able to sort through all the people.

Leetu lay on a narrow cot in a bedroom full of old women. There, one of the marione elders kept vigil in a rocker next to the dangerously ill emerlindian. At no time was she left alone. Kale wanted Paladin to heal her friend. Could he? She didn't like the waiting and uncertainty that everyone else seemed to take in stride.

The meadow teemed with activity. All the neighbors had gathered at

Lee Ark's home to spend time celebrating the upset of Risto's forces, the presence of Paladin, and each other's company. Members of each of the high races enjoyed the festival atmosphere. Music filled the camp, children scampered about, women sat beneath the trees and did needlework as they visited, and the men played games with each other and with the small ones. Everyone here seemed friendly and joyful, even though they lived in the shadow of Risto's fortress. This was one more thing to ask Paladin about if she ever got the chance.

Since the morning he had given his special attention to her, she had not been able to catch him alone. He was available, but only in a crowd. Every afternoon he sat with the children and told stories. In the eventide he told more tales, but to a gathering of adults who sat on the grass around a campfire and whose children nodded in their laps. As the dark grew thick beyond the light of the fire, sometimes he would explain a deeper meaning to the tale he had just told. Kale loved it all. She thirsted for more of his words, more of his wisdom. How could she ever go on to face this quest if she didn't know everything he had to teach her first?

Paladin came out of the woods on a path edged with late autumn flowers of deep orange, purple, and golden yellow. Dar came with him, tripping along, merrily engaged in conversation. Brunstetter, the urohm master rider of the dragon who had flown to their rescue, marched behind Paladin. During their adventures, Kale had forgotten how short the doneel people were. Next to the six-foot Paladin and the fourteen-foot Brunstetter, Dar's three-foot frame looked miniature indeed. He was tall only next to a kimen.

Paladin smiled at those who greeted him, waved off those who would have joined his small group, and headed straight for Kale. She rose to her feet, her heart speeding up with the joy of seeing him.

"Kale Allerion," he greeted her. "Tomorrow I return to the southern border. Lee Ark stays for a season with his family, and you and your comrades resume your quest."

Paladin nodded to Dar and Brunstetter, who immediately left his side.

He sat on the bench by the table, facing the activities in the surrounding fields. "Be seated," he commanded.

His friendly voice held a note of authority. Kale promptly sat and wondered what orders she would receive.

"Brunstetter is the leader of your expedition. Shimeran is next in command. The kimens will carry Leetu—"

"I can help," offered Kale.

Paladin gave her the slow, thoughtful smile that warmed her heart and made her feel accepted. "No need, Kale. The kimens are very much like ants in that they can carry burdens far heavier than one would expect. And they will be performing special acts toward healing our emerlindian friend."

"Why is she so ill, Paladin? There were few wounds on her body, and those have healed."

Paladin's face grew somber. "The mordakleeps engulfed her. Mordakleeps are the embodiment of nothing. Within their grasp, she was surrounded by nothing. No sounds, no sights, no smells, no taste, not the touch of something against her skin, not even the feel of her skin. Why, even her sense of up or down was hidden from her. Inside a mordakleep, there is no sign of life. In that oblivion, her mind writhed in anguish and shut down against the pain of loneliness and isolation."

Kale pulled her arms and legs in tightly, so that she perched on the bench like a large egg.

Paladin took her hand. "You touched that emptiness when you sought Leetu with your mind. You know how devastating even a glimpse of that void is."

She nodded, unable to respond as she remembered the awful sick feeling that had overwhelmed her.

Paladin's warm hand on hers comforted her. His rich voice soothed even as his words disturbed her.

"Wulder has a place like that. It's used for punishment of those who defy Him with every breath until the very last time they exhale on our world. But that punishment is not meant for Leetu. She will recover. Pretender's imitation of Wulder's void does not have permanent effects when the proper antidote is administered. And you will play a part in that."

At the promise of something to do for Leetu, Kale sat up, leaned forward, and listened even more intently to Paladin.

"The kimens will sing to Leetu as they carry her. They will touch her, stroke her arms and legs, rub her head, run their delicate little fingers over her face. Dar will bring things for Leetu to smell, the best of Wulder's scented flowers and, he assures me, some very fragrant foods he plans to fix at mealtimes. Then Wizard Fenworth will complete the cure."

"What should I do?"

"As you travel, you will project the images you see into Leetu's troubled mind. Beautiful flowers, peaceful meadows, striking sunsets, the funny antics of the kimens, the grace of a butterfly."

I can do that!

"In the evening, you and Gymn will sit with her and make the healing circle. You will allow your love of adventure and your thrill at being part of the quest flow into our emerlindian friend."

Oh, no! "Paladin, I can't. I don't love adventure. I'm scared to death of the quest, not thrilled."

Paladin threw back his head and laughed. Kale pinched her lips together and scowled at him.

When the great man could speak again, after wiping tears of mirth from his cheeks, he winked at her.

"Kale, you're learning more about Wulder every day. You're learning about your talents and how to use them. And on this quest, you will learn some deep truths about yourself."

"You're saying I love adventure and find the quest thrilling."

Paladin grinned, and Kale had the awful urge to stick her tongue out at him just as if she were no more than three years old. He laughed again and got up, reaching into his pocket.

"Here's Gymn. He's missed you just as much as you've missed him.

But I have been teaching him all sorts of little tricks. You will have fun together."

Kale eagerly took the tiny dragon. Paladin walked off to join the game of ribbets. He dropped his coat on the ground, ran into the crowd, and grabbed the ball as it flew through the air. The children on both teams cheered and swarmed around him.

"I *don't* love adventure," she told Gymn. She cuddled him under her chin, and he began to thrum. "I'd rather stay here with Lee Ark's family."

She looked to the outside grill where Mistress Ark turned slabs of meat over the fire. The general's wife put lots of work into caring for her large family. Kale was positive the marione woman derived a great deal of pleasure from her labors. If Kale stayed here, she could help. After all, she knew a lot about household chores. But the thought of staying didn't please her. She squirmed on the bench and turned her eyes in a different direction, seeking her friends. Although Kale didn't have a family, she did have comrades: Dar, Leetu, the kimens, and Gymn. Now Brunstetter would be joining them, and the quiet giant intrigued her.

Kale watched the game of ribbets. The teams ran helter-skelter back and forth across the same ground over and over, chasing a ball the size of a chicken.

"I do *not* get a thrill when I think about the quest," she muttered. Gymn hummed. It was one of Dar's marching songs.

She held him away from her and gave him a suspicious look, her eyes narrowed, and one eyebrow crooked.

"What has Paladin been teaching you?"

The little dragon sighed, licked his lips, and blinked.

A quiet thought flickered from the creature's mind to hers.

She yelped. "Hatch another egg? Not now. When we get to The Hall there will be plenty of time to hatch another egg."

Gymn's thought grew more urgent. One word drummed in Kale's mind. *"Now, now, now."*

"Not now," said Kale.

33

On the Way Again

Kale sat back to back with the urohm Brunstetter on his major white dragon. She faced the direction from which they had come. His huge body blocked the wind for her.

The second seat afforded her a good view of the smaller flying dragons behind the lead. The leather apparatus had two seats, one large enough for the urohm to be comfortable. The second seemed a little big for Kale's backside but had riding hooks for her knees at the right place. Celisse flew beside Merlander. No longer the dull colors she had been when they first rescued her, Celisse's scales flashed like silver and polished onyx in the sun.

Packs of supplies surrounded Kale. Gymn perched on Kale's shoulder, enjoying the clear morning view. A second dragon egg rode in the soft scarlet pouch hanging around her neck and tucked into her blouse.

Paladin had agreed with Gymn.

Paladin had looked over the dragon eggs as Kale displayed them at the ruler's request. Her treasure looked like a row of chicken eggs on Mistress Ellie Ark's kitchen table.

"I've never seen so many," that good woman commented to all those who'd gathered to witness the event. It seemed all the Ark clan and most of the neighbors were in her spacious kitchen.

"Nor have I," added Lee Ark. "It's a sign, I'm thinking, of troubled times ahead."

"Nay, don't say so," said Ellie and looked to Paladin's serious face for reassurance.

Paladin put a hand on each egg in turn and tapped his chin with a finger of the other as he contemplated the row. Finally, he picked one out and handed it to Kale. Then he smiled, and everyone in the crowded room heaved a sigh of relief and nodded to one another.

Kale tucked the precious egg away with a different kind of sigh. She didn't want to deal with another baby dragon. Not that Gymn was any trouble...

Paladin patted her shoulder and gave her a wink. Kale didn't much appreciate his nonchalance.

There're times when I wish this great man were a bit more serious minded. He could use a good dose of Master Meiger's pessimism. Paladin keeps handing me more and more duties. Find the wizard. Find the meech egg. Go questing. And oh, by the way, hatch out and mother a bunch of dragon babies while you're trekking from one end of Amara to the other.

Paladin's shout of laughter surprised her. He gave her shoulders a squeeze, whispered, "You can do it," and left the cozy home amid friendly farewells from everyone but Kale.

He heard what I was thinking.

"I did."

Kale jumped. Paladin stood outside the door. With one hand clasping the elbow of a doddering grandma, he rested the other on the stooped shoulder of the grandpa. Paladin didn't appear to be paying Kale one bit of attention. He spoke to the older couple, nodding at what they said in return.

You listen to my thoughts?

"Whenever you speak to me, I will."

How is that possible? You're busy. Even now you're busy with someone else. And you'll be so far away.

"I seem to remember a conversation we had about allowing Wulder to take care of the impossible. Wulder and I will be keeping an eye on you, Kale."

He was moving away, talking to various people as he left. Kale went to the door and stood, leaning against the side. She watched him walk down the hillside, then in front of the barn and fenced pasture. He passed most of the crowd, and his stride lengthened as he headed for his shining white mount, saddled and waiting. It was not the same dragon he had ridden into battle. Even in the morning sunlight, this dragon looked as if he had been carved out of the glowing moon.

"I'm not leaving you, Kale. Talk to me when you need to."

Will you answer?

"Always. But not always with words."

But it would be so much easier if you just spoke to me.

His words were kind and patient as he mounted the regal dragon and waved once more to the people nearby. *"We've had this conversation before, as well. Take care of what is put before you, Kale. I will see you again."*

Her own questing party departed soon after.

Dar rode Merlander. The kimens with Leetu rode Celisse. Brunstetter, riding point, directed his dragon, Foremoore, toward Bedderman's Bog. The other, smaller dragons followed side by side. Kale's stomach was full, her body was warm, and she had a comfortable seat with nothing to do but play with Gymn. She wondered if the tiny trickle of excitement along her skin was a thrill of adventure.

They left the valley behind them, soared over a heavily wooded area, and soon viewed a vast, fertile plain. It had taken Dar and Kale a lot of walking to cover the same distance. Kale enjoyed making the trip back on the huge white dragon Foremoore. She gazed at the scenes below and projected them to Leetu's silent mind.

A recent rain had swollen the brooks. The waters danced along the banks, hurrying to the rivers. Sunlight glistened off the trees, and a breeze ruffled their limbs, making the green leaves flicker from dark to emerald. Fall had brushed some of the landscape. Kale happily relayed all this to the unconscious emerlindian until she noticed a few farmhouses burnt to the ground, then a few more, then a village completely destroyed.

Risto.

Paladin had stopped him for now. What plan did Wulder have for the wicked wizard? How would their quest to rescue the meech egg turn out?

Well, it's impossible to know that, and I'm supposed to leave the impossible to Wulder.

Still, the sight of the bisonbeck army's destruction distressed Kale. She deliberately turned her attention to the leaves turning brilliant colors. She projected the lovely image to Leetu's mind. Rich green blanketed most of the landscape, but vivid orange and yellow splashed trees at the crest of a few hills. Radiant red mingled with the almost purple-blue leaves of the common armagot trees.

If Kale had been back in River Away, she would be taking the younger children out in the woods to collect armagotnuts. Mmm! One of Mistress Meiger's armagotnut pies would be wonderful.

They flew over another forest. She passed along to Leetu the image of dazzling birds flitting among the foliage. Carefully, she noted the beauty and wonder below them. She didn't want to miss one single picture that might aid in the emerlindian's recovery.

Immediately after noon, when the sun shone directly overhead and their shadows kept pace right below them, Brunstetter signaled for them to descend. They landed in The Midways. Bedderman's Bog with cygnot trees and marshy pathways lay within sight.

The kimens put up a tent for Leetu. Dar unpacked his cookstove. Brunstetter efficiently removed the burdens and saddles from all three dragons, fed them, watered them, and sang rumbly songs in a deep bass that they evidently liked. All three were humming along with their eyes half closed, swaying their heads in the peculiar way dragons do when they are content.

Kale sat beside Leetu, sending the image of the tent. The fabric was not made of light but of threads so fine that Kale wondered if they'd come from kimens' heads. The reddish brown certainly matched the shade of most of the little people's hair.

A voice roared through the air. "What is this, a camp?"

Kale jumped to her feet, knocking down one side of the tent. She had to battle her way through the cloth to get outside. Brunstetter stood with his hands on his hips, eyeing a scraggly tree and a stump that had appeared between where Dar prepared a meal and the resting dragons.

"Do you not hear me?" The voice was louder, so loud Kale covered her ears. Still the words sounded like thunder and were hard to distinguish. "I asked a question. Question. Quest. Not a camp. A quest. Tut-tut-tut."

Kale heard muttering and then the booming voice again.

"A tree? I am *not* a tree. I'm a wizard."

More muttering.

"I *am* speaking softly. Have to, you know. Scare the creatures not accustomed to wizards if you don't treat them gently. Oh dear."

Kale strained to hear the reply but could hear only a murmur.

"I am not a tree. Quit saying so. You, however, do seem to be a stump. Tut-tut."

The wizard's form had become more o'rant and less treelike as the argument progressed. The wizard tilted his head toward the shorter man. "Do you hear thunder?"

Now his face pulled together in a furious scowl. "Me. *Me!* I'm *not* roaring like thunder, and I am *not* shouting!"

The volume of the last words knocked all but Brunstetter off their feet. The wizard stopped roaring. A muttering of two voices replaced the bellow.

Kale lifted her face from the grass and watched the tree turn into a tall, willowy old man with a long beard. Leaves and twigs clung to his wrinkled robes. Beside him, the stump transformed into a short, round man who came up to the older man's waist. His brown clothes bagged around his small stature, and Kale recognized the style of clothing as that of an academician.

From where she'd fallen on the ground, Kale drew herself up on her elbows for a better look. *The short man might be a teacher from The Hall. And the wizard is definitely the man I saw in The Bogs.*

The little man was a tumanhofer, one of the mountain people. A little taller than Dar, with a florid complexion and short black hair, the man growled between clenched teeth. His bushy eyebrows closed over his nose as he scowled up at his companion. Glasses perched on his bulbous nose.

Small, dark eyes squinted behind the frames. A tiny pointed beard accented his pointed chin. A thin line of mustache crossed over pouty lips.

Dar hopped to his feet and ran to meet the two.

He swept a deep, courtly bow. "Wizard Fenworth, we are delighted that you have joined us. And is this the famous Librettowit? You are spoken of highly in all the universities of Amara."

The two men turned as one to glare at the doneel.

"Humph!" they said in unison.

"Tea?" offered Dar.

34

Mislaid Castle

Dar served sandwiches, fresh fruit, sweet pastries, and, of course, tea. Before they sat down to eat, the tumanhofer went around to each person and introduced himself as Trevithick Librettowit, a librarian. Fascinated by the wizard, Kale watched Fenworth eat with gusto everything the doneel placed in front of him. During the entire meal, the old man said little besides an occasional thank-you and many requests to pass one dish or another. Midway through his second helping, the wizard reached into his tangled beard, pulled out a mouse by its tail, and set it on the ground. The tiny creature scampered away.

Kale barely kept from laughing out loud. She coughed to hide the gurgle that rose in her throat. She wouldn't want to offend the man. He *was* someone who fell into shouting easily. She looked to see the reaction of the others in her party. Everyone looked busy, almost too busy, as if they were purposely not watching Wizard Fenworth.

Perhaps it's rude to notice when a wizard does something strange.

The tumanhofer ate more slowly, occasionally scribbling a line or two in a book he balanced on his knee.

"Well then," said the wizard, standing and brushing crumbs from the front of his robe. He also dislodged brown, dried leaves, a nest of beetles, several moths, and a lizard. "Let's go questing."

Librettowit put his book away and stood. "Yes." He looked up at the wizard with a cautious expression. "But first, home to prepare."

The stout tumanhofer sighed his relief when Fenworth accepted his suggestion. Shimeran made a gesture to his fellow kimens. They scrambled to take down the tent and prepare a litter. Dar doused his fire and packed his culinary tools.

Fenworth paced for a few minutes, deep in thought. Abruptly, he turned to Kale. "You can't go, of course. You're too big."

Kale's disappointment at the announcement overcame her reluctance to talk to someone as important as the bog wizard. "Too big?"

"Yikes!" Fenworth rapidly crossed the distance between them and stopped to tower over the o'rant girl. "Who are you?"

"Kale Allerion, sir. We met in Bedderman's Bog." Kale remembered clinging to the cygnot planking, trying not to slide through while the wizard stood by saying, "tut-tut" and "oh dear." Then she remembered the bird. "You didn't help me. And you pretended you weren't even there!"

And now he said she couldn't go on the quest because she was too big. Paladin had said she could go on the quest, and she was going to go.

"I'm *not* too big!" she shouted.

"Of course, you're not too big. What are you talking about?"

"You just said I'm too big."

"What nonsense! As if I couldn't tell you're just the right size. Best size for an Allerion. Best size for an o'rant. Best size for a girl. Why are you complaining? Questing is no place for whiners."

"You said I couldn't go. I'm too big."

"You're not too big! Quit saying so!"

Kale had to cover her ears now. The wizard's voice was taking on thunderous volume.

The tumanhofer came up beside his distraught companion and spoke clearly, pointing behind Kale as he did. "You said the urohm can't go and is too big."

Kale glanced behind her to see Brunstetter standing by the dragons and grinning. Annoyed that she'd misunderstood Fenworth and been trapped in a ridiculous argument, Kale glared at the gleeful urohm.

"Of course he's big," roared Fenworth. "He's a urohm, Librettowit. Happened centuries ago at the Battle of Ordray. Not to him, of course, because he is younger than that, but to his people. A good thing, too. Urohms come in handy at times, but not in The Bogs. Dragons aren't welcome, either. No dragons, no urohms, but little girl o'rants can enter at any time. That is, if they are questing. And this one is questing." There was a pause as the wizard tugged on his beard and glared down at the tumanhofer. "Where did I leave the castle?"

"In a pumpkin patch."

"Ha! That was a diversion. The times are perilous. I changed my mind and moved it." Fenworth put his hand over his chin, closed his eyes, and frowned.

"A beehive?" suggested Librettowit.

The wizard shook his head. A score of bees flew out from his hair and zoomed away.

"A lily pad?"

Fenworth groaned and frogs dropped from the sleeves of his robe. "Do be sensible, Wit. I left it someplace safe."

"You've left it on a lily pad four times in the last month," grumbled the tumanhofer.

"Aha!" Fenworth snapped his fingers and opened his eyes. "Feather on a bird."

"And you remember which bird?" Librettowit did not look hopeful.

"No, but he is to come to me when I give the secret signal."

"And you remember the signal?" The tumanhofer sat down and pulled out his pen and book once more.

"Well…no."

"You wrote it down somewhere? You left yourself a clue?"

"See here, Wit, you are not to be difficult about this."

The tumanhofer shook his head and began writing in his book, evidently giving up on an immediate departure of the questing party.

The kimens and Dar slowed their preparations to leave. Fenworth strode back and forth, occasionally stopping to converse with a butterfly or a plant. Kale sat down beside Leetu and projected the images of the odd man's afternoon antics into her sleeping friend's mind.

Fenworth sat in the grass and a dozen rabbits gathered around him as if having a conference. He spoke to each one of them. Wondering what language they used, Kale was tempted to use her mindspeaking abilities to listen in on the conversation. Remembering Leetu's instructions on the polite use of her talents, though, she did not eavesdrop.

Later the wizard sat on a large rock and didn't move for an hour. He began to look like a bush entangling the boulder. Kale repeatedly blinked her eyes to keep the man in focus, or else he blurred into part of the landscape. Several birds swooped out of the sky and perched in his branches…on his arms. They flitted away after moments of intense chattering.

The rest of the afternoon, Fenworth went about visiting just as if he were a host making sure his guests were acknowledged and made to feel welcome. At some time during this aimless chitchat, he asked the members of their group to tell him their ages. With each revelation, he would exclaim. "Ha! See? I am older than you."

Seezle tilted up her chin, and with mischief in her eye, said, "Now how am I to know that for sure? You haven't told us how old you are."

The old man fumed. He harrumphed, blew in his beard, clapped his hands against his robes, and glowered at the tiny creature before him.

Seezle's smile only grew broader. "You don't remember, do you?"

"Sixty," Fenworth barked. "Seventy. Maybe eighty-something." He stood straighter, and his expression brightened. "Seventy-two. Something very close to seventy-two, I believe." He turned and walked away, humming the little ditty every child sang at birthday celebrations.

Seezle giggled and plopped down next to Kale and Leetu.

"Seventy-two years old?" Kale's face pulled into a puzzled frown. "He looks a lot older than that."

"He's talking about centuries, not years," explained Seezle.

Kale gasped and watched the sprightly old fellow with new admiration.

At dusk a black bird flew into their camp and landed on Fenworth's shoulder.

"Oh, yes," said the old man, "I remember now. The sun falling over the side of the world, that was the signal for Thorpendipity to bring me my castle. Makes sense, you see. Nighttime. Suppertime. Bedtime. Want to be at home. My own table. My own bed. Comforts. Don't you see? Questing can be such an uncomfortable business."

For one second Kale observed the befuddled expressions of her comrades. A burst of light filled the meadow, making it impossible to see anything. She squinted, put her arm across her eyes, and felt as if her body were being sucked through a hole.

She heard horses neighing, a duck quacking, and bacon sizzling. She smelled the bacon, but also flowers, and then strong lye soap.

"Now where's the key to the front door?" She heard the wizard mutter practically in her ear. She turned toward the sound and reached out, but felt nothing but moving air. The swirling wind astonished her as it made almost no noise. Odd sounds, a drum beating, a door opening and shutting, a cat's meow, could be heard distinctly.

Fenworth's voice floated on the air. "Yes, you see, I am the leader, because I am the oldest. I asked, and I am definitely the oldest. The senior wizard on the expedition. Well, actually the *only* wizard on the expedition. That is, the only one on the good side of things. There are other wizards involved who are not. But of course, these wizards are not in our party of questers but are, more specifically, the reason for the questing."

Odors rode on the currents as if picked up from faraway places and passed under her nose. She smelled leather, baking bread, apples, and she wrinkled her nose against dirty barn fumes.

Kale smiled as she heard Dar declare he didn't want to lose his pack with his flute in it. She heard kimens' laughter, and Fenworth said, "Here's the key. Now where's that door?"

Kale placed her hand on the pouch holding the egg to be hatched. No problem there. She moved her hand to the bulge made by Gymn in the moonbeam cape.

Fainted.

Kale patted the little dragon absent-mindedly.

Oh, Gymn, this is exciting, not scary.

She first realized she no longer sat on the grassy ground when the wooden floor beneath her shuddered and thumped as if dropped. She put her hand down and felt the wood grain and edges of old boards worn smooth by years of use.

"Ah," said Wizard Fenworth. "Of course I remember. How could one forget an Allerion? A new apprentice. Will she be as talented as her mother?"

Kale jerked her head around and tried to see him, forgetting how the dazzling light hurt her eyes. Her eyelids flinched against the brilliance but not before she saw an outline of the wizard closing a massive wooden door.

The wind ceased. The light faded. Kale opened her eyes to view her surroundings. Wizard Fenworth, Librettowit, Dar, Leetu, and the kimens all crowded in a small room. All but the wizard and the emerlindian sat on the floor. Leetu lay among the cluster of kimens. Fenworth stood with his hands on his hips and a satisfied smile on his face.

The room resembled Granny Noon's cozy home. Even General Lee Ark's pinewood cabin was more elegant than this humble abode. Most of the homes in River Away had newer furniture. Fenworth needed a maid with a dust rag. In no way did this hovel look as Kale thought all castles would.

Fenworth extended his arms in a gesture of welcome.

"My home is your home. Welcome to my castle."

35

Wizard at Home

Kale soon learned why Librettowit, the librarian, spent his time with Wizard Fenworth.

In the "castle," a common room served as the main gathering place. It was the only square room in the castle. The kitchen took one corner of this space. A table and benches nestled close to the oven. On a small rug, a cluster of stuffed chairs made an excellent place to sit in front of the hearth.

To the right side of this huge fireplace, a door led to Fenworth's bedroom. To the left was Librettowit's room. The wall across from the fireplace held a double wooden door that led to the outdoors. The door with its beveled glass windows *did* look as though it belonged in a mansion.

Round windows of various sizes spotted the walls in no clear order. In the middle of each of the remaining walls stood one circular door that lead to a tubular hallway. Along these labyrinths of corridors were round rooms with floor-to-ceiling bookcases, each overflowing with books.

Hundreds of books. Old books, new books. Big books, tiny books. Thick books, skinny books with no covers. Books with leatherlike pages, books with colored pages, books with no pages but pictures inside that moved and changed constantly. In one room a table sat in the center upon which four books lay open. As Kale watched, words appeared on the page of one of these books. When the lines of script reached the bottom, the page turned and new words surfaced on a clean sheet as if they floated to the top of a pond.

In the days while Kale waited for Wizard Fenworth to be ready, she wandered around in these rooms. Each room had one large, comfortable chair and lightrock lanterns to use. Occasionally, she picked out a book from the shelves to read.

She also got lost in these rooms and hallways. The best thing to do when lost in the castle was to find a door to the outside. From the exterior, the castle appeared to be a giant cygnot with a gathering of slightly smaller trees around it. The round hallways Kale walked through in the castle were limbs connecting those trees.

Librettowit had shown her around the maze of halls and rooms.

"Fenworth's castle is the center of The Bogs," the tumanhofer explained. "This tree is the oldest living tree in Amara. The trees around are not much younger." He beamed at his surroundings when he showed her his study room. "Fenworth's collection of books outshines all others. It is a privilege to be his personal librarian, although he does forget exactly what my duties are from time to time."

"What are we doing to prepare for the quest?" asked Kale. It seemed to her that they did little beyond reading, eating Dar's good meals, and sleeping in the hammocks the kimens strung from bookcase to bookcase in various rooms.

"I am gathering information on Risto, his history." Librettowit peered over his thick glasses. His small eyes examined Kale. He sighed. "There is so very much that can be learned from books. It is most often not necessary to figure things out for oneself. One only needs to read the proper book on the subject. For instance, I am also researching known facts on meech dragons. They are rare, you know, but still there are valuable accounts of them. And I am copying maps to send with Fenworth to aid in the journey. Actually, I will give them to Brunstetter. Fenworth would misplace them."

"You aren't going with us?"

"Oh, no. I'm a librarian."

⊱━━━⊰

Kale tried to corner Fenworth for a talk. He had said a number of puzzling things. He mentioned her mother. No one had ever mentioned her mother. She tried to tell herself that the way crazy things came out of his mouth in no particular order was a sign that she shouldn't believe anything he said. But she wanted to ask just in case.

The man had a talent for disappearing. She would follow him into a corridor, but he'd turn off into a room or down another corridor. No matter how quickly she ran to catch up, the room or the hallway would be empty.

He could be within sight and totally inaccessible. Sometimes she would see him sitting in the top tree limbs among a gaggle of birds. When she tried to climb that high, the thin branches swayed and bent, depositing her gently on a lower level of the cygnot network. They felt like fingers grasping her clothes and then releasing her when she found secure footing.

Each night Fenworth retired early to his chamber. In the morning he rose before the sun to converse with animals of nocturnal disposition. In fact, he spent a great deal of time visiting with animals who came to call.

All this time, Leetu showed no signs of getting any better.

Kale asked Dar when they would be on their way.

He smiled over the pot he was stirring. "It would be a grievous mistake to leave before the wizard is ready. And since Paladin ordained the wizard to accompany us…" He shrugged and went back to fixing a noontime feast out of the wizard's surprisingly well-stocked cupboards.

She asked Shimeran.

"No sense in hurrying a wizard," he told her.

She asked Librettowit.

"No idea. Not going. So not much interested. It will be nice to have the libraries to myself once you and your party are gone. We haven't had this much to-do in a hundred years or more. Usually, it's rather pleasant, living with Fenworth. Quiet. Time for study."

The kimens were no help at all. They contentedly read or joined Dar in making music. They took care of Leetu and played with Gymn. Worry did not seem to be a part of their makeup.

Kale found a whole room full of books by famous o'rants. She took one down from the shelf and started through it, looking mostly at the pictures.

"I think we will wait for Metta to hatch."

Kale dropped the book, slapped a hand to her heart, and whirled around at the wizard's unexpected voice right at her shoulder.

"Metta?"

"The minor dragon riding in a pouch suspended from a seventeen-and-a-half-inch thong around your neck."

Kale moved her hand on her blouse and felt the familiar pouch beneath the material. "Oh."

Fenworth turned away.

"Wait," cried Kale.

When he turned back, she took a deep breath and plunged in. "I've wanted to ask you questions. What did you mean by apprentice? When will Leetu be well? Do you know my mother?"

"Oh, we mustn't speak of her. That's dangerous. When we above mention those below, it puts them in deadly peril. So, of course our lips are sealed."

Kale tried to protest, but found her lips were indeed stuck together.

Frowning fiercely, she used her talent. *You may have stopped my mouth, but I can still mindspeak. Is she alive? Where is she? How do you know her? And my father? Do you know my father, too?*

Fenworth for once looked directly into her eyes, and she saw compassion before he covered it with a stern expression.

"Yes, of course, you can be rude and naughty and impatient and cause all sorts of trouble even though you've been warned. But you won't. You don't want further harm to come to the dear woman we are not speaking of."

Kale opened her mouth. "You're right."

"Now for your other questions. Although we will pretend you only asked two for security reasons, of course. And therefore, we shall now address the first of your two questions. What do I mean by apprentice? I think you shall have to ask Wit. He's a librarian, you know. He should have a good dictionary somewhere. And the third question: 'When will Leetu be well?' First, you must answer my question."

"I'll try."

"Who is Leetu?"

"The emerlindian."

"I know many emerlindians, my dear."

"The emerlindian we brought with us. The one who is sick."

"Four thousand, six hundred, thirty-two emerlindians." Fenworth tapped one bony finger against the palm of his other hand. "That's how many I know. Living, of course."

Kale feared the wizard would get off track, and she'd never bring him back to the subject of her friend's health.

"Leetu Bends. Paladin assigned her to the quest. She was injured by mordakleeps. We've been helping her, but you must cure her."

"Why would I do that, my dear?"

"Because Paladin said…"

"Oh yes, of course, I do remember something…Where is this Leetu?"

"In your kitchen, in a hammock the kimens put up."

"Ahhhh." The wizard tapped a finger to his temple. "I know which one of my guests you speak of. Quiet young woman, speaks nary a word. Rather uninteresting on the whole, but we shan't hold that against her. Mordakleeps, you say? Nasty."

He started walking down the hall in what Kale hoped was the direction of the kitchen. She would have had to go out the door and around the castle to the main entrance to find her way back.

After many twists and turns they came into the warmth of the cozy common room. The kimens and Gymn sat on one of the stuffed chairs while Dar read to them.

Fenworth marched across the room and stood beside Leetu.

"Time to get up," he barked. "Enough already of dwelling on your misfortune. Revolting creatures, those mordakleeps, but that's behind you now. If you're going to live, get up and live."

Leetu opened her eyes, blinked twice, sat up, and swung her legs out of the hammock.

"Hungry, I bet." Wizard Fenworth patted her rather awkwardly on the shoulder. "Dar will take care of that."

He turned to Kale. "You come with me."

He bolted out the front door with Kale scrambling to make it outside before the door slammed behind him. That was another one of Fenworth's tricks for disappearing. Grateful that the planking around the castle was tightly woven, Kale scurried to keep up without having to mind her steps too carefully.

"I'm going to answer another question for you." Fenworth stopped and leaned against a tree, suddenly relaxed, as completely relaxed as he had been energized one second before. "Only fair. No, not the one you didn't ask, because we've forgotten all about that one. This is a bonus question, one for free."

Kale stood panting. She nodded.

"I have been given information that leads me to conclude the probable purpose Risto intends for the meech egg. I know what he's up to! No good, of course.

"Part of this information comes from Librettowit's excellent summation of Risto's past deeds, which reveal his interests. Part of it comes from my informants, various intelligent animals who can get close to almost anyone without that person, Risto in this instance, being aware.

"Risto thinks he can best Pretender." Fenworth gave a mirthless laugh and shook his head sadly. "That's the problem all too many times, ambition, pride. In some cases it's dangerous to want to be better and prove it. Think of me trying to be better than Wulder. Preposterous! Think of me trying to create something. Foolish beyond measure. I am a lowly wizard privileged to use the gifts of Wulder, and then only in the way He designed them. Yet these imbeciles go about doing evil, and if that isn't bad enough, they try to top each other in just how evil they can be."

"What is Risto planning to do?" asked Kale quietly. She dreaded the answer, but she wanted to hear it. She wanted to know what they were facing. She didn't want Fenworth to talk and talk and never get around to telling her.

"He is going to create another race to do his bidding. Pretender has tried seven times and failed seven times. But Risto thinks with the meech egg he has found the secret."

"Has he?" asked Kale.

Fenworth tenderly put his old hand against her young face, cupping her smooth cheek.

"There is so much you do not know yet. But you are learning. No, Kale. The secret is you must *be* Wulder in order to create. Risto will fail, but he will hurt many. His failure may very well walk the world like bison-becks and mordakleeps. Unless we stop him."

He moved his hand to gently tap her on the shoulder. "But we've got some circumstances on our side. Stumbled on the meech egg, Risto did! Stumbled. Doesn't have your talent for finding dragon eggs. Very few people do. But he stumbled on it."

"That's in our favor?" Kale didn't think Risto's finding the egg by accident was a good thing.

"Wasn't prepared, you see. Didn't have his geese in order. No, I think that's ducks in a row. Ducks and geese also lay eggs, as do alligators and a peculiar mammal called a platypus. But dragon eggs. So rare. One must be particular about all the details in hatching. Risto had to keep the egg separate and isolated, so it wouldn't be quickened by a warm-blooded creature. He has many plans to work out in order to succeed in using the energy of the egg after it quickens and before it hatches. Time's against him and in our favor. Of course, Wulder is for us and against Risto. Of course, we don't know where the egg is and Risto does. But of course we have friends to help us find it, and Risto doesn't have friends. Has henchmen, though. Nasty creatures doing his bidding. Slaves he forces. Other things like him who do evil just because they like to. Don't understand that. Don't particularly want to."

Kale tugged on his sleeve. "Will we be in time?"

"Well, now, that is our hope, is it not?"

36

A New Start

Kale watched Leetu across the room. The emerlindian sat in a hammock, reading a book. She looked just as she had before the mordakleep attack, except her hair had been moonbeam white. Now it resembled golden honey when the honeycomb is held up to the sun. Creamy skin replaced the alabaster tone of before. And maybe her eyes were a deeper blue. Emerlindians grew darker as they aged and gained wisdom. Leetu was but a few weeks older. How much wiser was she than before? What had she learned while going through this ordeal?

"I'm fine, Kale, just fine." Leetu looked up from her book. "Quit staring at me."

Is she really fine?

Gymn jumped from Kale's shoulder and flew the short distance across Fenworth's common room. The small healing dragon landed on Leetu's head, making her giggle and bat playfully at him. He scampered around her head twice and then moved down to her heart. He crisscrossed her body, darting down to where her feet dangled out of the hammock. He perched on her toes for a moment, looking at Kale. He blinked.

Kale's face broke into a grin, and she laughed. "Gymn says you're fine. He's examined your internal organs and found nothing lacking."

Leetu threw back her head and joined the o'rant girl's laughter. Kale had never heard the emerlindian respond to humor with more than a gentle chuckle.

Prickles ran down Kale's arm. Her hand flew up to grasp the bulging red pouch that hung from around her neck.

Leetu sat up abruptly, disturbing Gymn's balance. He flew off, indicating his displeasure with throaty grunts. He winged over to land on Kale's shoulder.

"What is it?" asked Leetu, her eyes trained on Kale's face.

"Metta is hatching."

"Metta?"

"Fenworth told me her name."

Kale took the thong from around her neck and carefully removed the dragon egg from her red pouch. Gymn crawled down her arm and perched on her wrist. He tilted his head and contemplated the egg nestled in Kale's palm. He began a thrum. The vibration tickled Kale, but she didn't ask him to stop, nor did she move him away from the hatching egg. Leetu eased out of her hammock and crept closer. She maintained a respectful distance, but Kale noticed the emerlindian's face light up with wonder.

"Why is it that the birth of a dragon is so much more spectacular than that of a chick?" Kale asked her friend.

"The beginning of any new life is wonderful," answered Leetu in a soft voice. "Dragons are said to carry the heart of Wulder."

Kale wrinkled her brow. "That doesn't sound right."

"It isn't," agreed Leetu. "There are a lot of things said that are not true. It sounds nice so people repeat it. Actually, that bit of untruth originated in a fairy tale."

"How are people supposed to know the difference between fact and fable?"

"Those in Paladin's service make it a point to study the true tales of Amara. Once you have learned the truth, you begin to hear the false note in a legend of ersatz."

"Ersatz? I've never heard that word."

"But I'll bet you have heard many ersatz stories, particularly in the tavern on a Saturday night."

"The tales told by the traveling minstrels? I thought those were based on true history."

"Some of them are. That is where the danger lies. Enough truth is mixed with deceit to make the deceit sound truthful."

Kale shook her head at Leetu's words, but her eyes remained on the crack widening along one side of the egg.

Leetu lowered herself gracefully to sit cross-legged on Fenworth's tattered rug. "When you go to The Hall, you will mingle with people who have followed Paladin for many years. You will read works written by those caught up in quests like ours. You will hear tales from master storytellers, and these tales will be the uncorrupted versions. As you begin to know who Wulder is by the evidence given you, your heart will become sensitive to His truth, the *only* truth. You will then know when someone is trying to deceive you for an evil purpose."

Kale frowned and looked down at her hand. The egg rocked gently as the dragon within struggled to hatch. Leetu's ideas all sounded too complicated. Kale could hardly believe she had been entrusted with the care of minor dragons; now it seemed she was expected to discern between good and evil.

"I am just an o'rant slave girl, Leetu."

"Nay, Kale." Leetu's whisper was strong with conviction. "You are chosen by Paladin. You have a destiny."

Kale cupped her hand a little tighter around the soft, leathery egg. It had been a long time since she'd thought of her destiny. Once she thought it was to live in The Hall, wearing pretty clothes, learning from wise and wonderful scholars. Mostly she had thought of what it wouldn't be: cleaning out chicken coops, walking squalling babies, peeling vegetables, gathering rushes from the banks of the river. She figured if she was to wash dishes, at least in The Hall they would be beautiful china plates, silver cups, and golden bowls instead of the earthen pottery of River Away homes.

Gymn scooted up her arm, circled her neck, took a moment to rub his cheek against her chin, and then raced back down her arm to take up his vigil over the hatching egg. She chuckled in response to his hurried affection.

Part of the shell fell away, and Gymn's thrum became higher and louder. He stomped his hind feet against her skin.

"Purple," Kale announced as she saw a bit of the dragon's skin.

"A singer," said Leetu.

Kale nodded. The book had said purple dragons sing. "But I don't see why Paladin would choose a singer. How will a singer help us on our quest?"

Out of the corner of her eye, she saw Leetu shrug. "Perhaps Paladin didn't choose this dragon with our quest in mind. Perhaps one of us needs the ministrations of a singing dragon."

"Ministrations?"

"A singing dragon can heal emotions much the way the healing dragon cures a cold."

The baby dragon kicked a chunk of shell out of her way and stretched her tail and hind legs across Kale's fingers. Gymn's thrum changed to encouraging chirps. Kale held her breath as Metta used her tiny front legs to push the rest of the shell off her head. Gymn leapt into the air and gave a triumphant cheer that sounded like the *caw* of a blackbird. Even without appropriate fanfare, little Metta shoved the covering off her face. Her newborn eyes focused on Kale and then on Gymn. Gymn settled down, lying along Kale's forearm and watching with rapt attention as the baby stretched and rubbed against the palm she lay in. Kale gingerly stroked her delicate skin with one fingertip.

Kale jumped as the door to Fenworth's room swung open and banged against the wall. Her hand closed instinctively to protect Metta.

"Time to go," said the old wizard. He strode across the small room and charged out the front door.

A burst of light filled the room. Kale doubled over, shielding both little dragons with her body. She heard the wind rip through the wizard's castle. An eerie silence followed. She felt her body being drawn away from her surroundings.

"No warning!" Kale heard Dar's complaint.

"What? Not me," Librettowit hollered.

Chickens clucked. A cuckoo clock sounded three times. Kale smelled apple pie rich with cinnamon. She felt a thousand feathers brush against her neck and back. Cold air made her shiver. Warm air washed over her like a major dragon's breath.

"Come, come now. Don't dawdle." Fenworth's voice sounded far away. "Oh dear. Tut-tut. Do hurry."

The wind ceased. The light faded. Kale opened her eyes to view her surroundings. They were in the meadow where they had left Brunstetter and the riding dragons. Lee Ark and the urohm stood staring at the new arrivals.

Kale's stomach felt queasy from the sudden motion and then the abrupt stop. The kimens, Leetu, Dar, Librettowit, and Wizard Fenworth swayed a little as their bodies adjusted to being still again. All around them, bits and pieces of clutter lay strewn across the grass.

Dar shook himself and muttered something about rudeness. He began to pick up his clothing from among the things on the ground. Kale looked more closely and realized all their belongings had been swept up and brought with them. Leetu's books lay scattered about. Her bow and arrows and quiver poked out of the foot-high grass. Dar's cooking equipment was spread out over an acre.

Librettowit stamped his booted feet and shook the quill pen he still held in his hand. "See here, Fenworth. I'm not going on this quest. I'm a librarian. I provide information. I don't go adventuring."

With a long, steady stride, the wizard marched over and clapped the smaller man on the back. "Ah yes, friend, but I keep forgetting what you tell me. We are going into the Mount Tourbanaut, and I thought you'd like to visit your mother."

"Leave my mother out of this." He stamped his feet again and shook both fists in the air.

"You don't want to visit your mother? Well, of course, I shall explain to her you were busy. I'm sure she'll understand."

Librettowit's face grew redder. "She will *not* understand. See what you know about mothers? Nothing!"

"Well, of course. Tut-tut." The old man shook his head sadly. "So many things I don't understand." His face brightened, and he again laid a hand on the tumanhofer's shoulder. "But then, you're a scholarly sort. You'll take up the slack, no doubt."

He rubbed his hands together and started across the meadow toward the waiting marione and urohm.

"Lee Ark! Glad you're to join us. Brunstetter! Always good to see you. Let's get organized, shall we? Got a quest to quest. Got to get moving. Can't quest while sitting in one spot, now can we? Tut-tut, such a lot of to-do to do, you know. I like questing, generally speaking, except for the uncomfortableness of it all."

Lee Ark and Brunstetter grinned at the old man. The kimens skipped in the grass, picking up their own things and delivering various items to their proper owners. Dar muttered about the uselessness of ironing when your clothes were transported in such a helter-skelter fashion. Leetu found her quiver first and began to fill it.

Metta crawled up on Kale's shoulder and lifted her chin to the sun. Out of her tiny mouth came a song. No words formed with the melody, just syllables of smooth tones to match the mellow tune. Kale felt hope rush through her, and joy.

Everyone stopped to listen. It only lasted a few minutes. Joy bubbled in Kale's heart as the notes trilled through the air. Her spirits lifted and soared, and she thought she would just have to laugh out loud. The feeling embarrassed her some, but not enough to destroy the elation. As the last delightful note faded away, Fenworth raised his hand in a salute to the baby dragon.

"Exactly what I was thinking, little Metta. Good job! Well done! Thank you, my dear." He turned to survey the rest of the questing party. "Well now, a new start to the quest. Part two, you might say. Onward. Except that we are going into a mountain. Downward, then. No, that doesn't sound quite right." He stopped and pointed to the ground. "Aha! My walking stick."

He picked up a long, gnarled branch. Kale thought it might have been part of the natural debris of the countryside.

"Glad I didn't forget this."

Leetu started to laugh. Dar at first cast her a disgruntled look, but then a grin broke across his face, and he began to chuckle. The kimens tumbled about, doing acrobatics that matched their lighthearted laughter. Even Librettowit succumbed and chortled, his body shaking in merriment. Lee Ark and Brunstetter laughed so hard, they leaned against each other and wiped tears from their eyes.

"Tut-tut. Oh dear. It seems Paladin has assigned me a bunch of flibbertigibbets for a very serious task. I shall make the most of it. Adds to the challenge, no doubt."

37

Blimmets

They rode in comfort high above the countryside. Kale sat in the riding master seat on Celisse with Librettowit, Shimeran, and Seezle as her passengers. The two minor dragons rode for long periods of time on Kale's shoulders, but they would get cold and dart inside the moonbeam cape to warm themselves in their pocket-dens. Dar carried Leetu with him on Merlander. Brunstetter took the Trio family kimens with him. Lee Ark, the appointed leader of this portion of the quest, escorted Wizard Fenworth.

The old man muttered about his age and his position as leader due to wisdom gained "through the ages, bleak ages, blessed ages, boring ages, and blasphemous ages." Last Kale had heard of his mutterings, he was trying out other *b* words that might describe ages he had experienced. "Bothersome. Yes, indeed there were plenty of those. Tut-tut. Bilious. No, not quite the right word. Boisterous? Hmm? Battered. Yes, I like battered. Very descriptive. Must have been some battered ages along the way."

Librettowit graciously accepted his part in the quest after a period of scowling and stamping about the meadow, picking up his belongings, mostly books and pens and paper, three pairs of reading glasses, and a pot of razterberry jam. After he had said his piece about being dragged along, he turned out to be a delightful companion.

On the back of Celisse, as her strong wings carried them farther and farther from The Bogs, the librarian told stories one after another. The kimens and Kale listened intently as he pointed out landmarks below and related historical facts, tidbits of local tradition, and fables reflecting the citizens' heritage. His entertaining lecture lasted all day, even when Seezle handed around packets of food prepared by Lee Ark's wife for their noon-time meal. Occasionally, Metta would sing a folk tune.

"Librettowit, how does she do that?" asked Kale. "She's only a few hours old. How can she know these songs?"

"She plucks them out of your mind. Well, my mind in this case. She's a mindspeaker, of course. If you have the memory of a song, even one you have only heard once, she will appropriate it. She will also give back to you words you've forgotten so you might sing along."

"And she can give me the words to a song that you remember, and I've never heard?"

"That's right."

The idea intrigued Kale and her kimen passengers. They spent several hours in the afternoon singing songs from myriad heritages: kimen songs of praise; marione songs of planting and harvesting; tumanhofer songs of earth, sky, and sea; and dragon songs of clan and ancestry. Kale discovered that Celisse and the young minor dragons had a fierce pride in their genealogy. Librettowit provided Gymn and Metta with heroic tales of minor dragons.

An hour before the early autumn dusk, Lee Ark signaled for their descent. The four dragons landed in a vale with a stream for water and a stand of trees offering wood for the campfires.

Brunstetter took off on foot to bargain for a herd of sheep from a local shepherd they had passed over. He carried a heavy purse of coins and came back with enough mutton to satisfy the hungry dragons. Kale gratefully watched the urohm lord escort the dragons to the other side of the trees to meet their dinner. She didn't mind Gymn's, and now Metta's, antics as they looked for food, catching bugs in the air and gobbling them down. Even the snaring of an occasional mouse did not upset her. But there was nothing entertaining in watching a large dragon devour an animal whole.

Pleasantly tired after the uneventful day of traveling, the troupe soon finished an evening meal and bundled up to sleep warmly in tents and blankets. The moon hid behind a bank of snow-filled clouds. The fires smoldered as glowing embers. No more flames leapt. No sparks shot heavenward from brightly burning logs.

In the darkest hour of the night, the blimmets attacked.

Kale heard a terrified screech and sat up. In that moment, shrill cries of panic multiplied to fill the air.

She crawled hastily out of her small tent and sprang to her feet, trying to decipher meaning from the clamor. She heard Lee Ark's strong voice call out, "Blimmets!" and then she knew. Weasel-like creatures with luxurious dark fur and razor-sharp teeth, blimmets devoured warm-blooded animals.

The cacophony of shrieks came only partially from the victims of the attack. Blimmets gave full voice to harrowing screams. The noise frightened and confused those they descended upon.

To Kale's ears, the chaos sounded like hundreds of women and children screaming as they were torn apart. But the questing band numbered only eighteen including the dragons. It was the slaughtering blimmets who numbered in the hundreds.

"Light!" Lee Ark's voice trumpeted above the havoc around Kale's tent.

She rushed to the nearest fire and grabbed a stick. She stirred the coals, throwing on kindling that had been gathered for morning. A blaze leapt up.

Not enough! They need a blaze above us to light the whole camp in order to fight off blimmets.

Holding the stick ready to swing at an attacker, Kale listened to the contest for life. Her comrades defended the camp. The large dragons roared. They would stomp on the small enemy and crunch those they caught in their mighty jaws. But blimmets won by sheer numbers in most cases. They swarmed out of the ground, attacking anything in their way. They did not engage in a battle but in a feeding frenzy.

Kale ran to the next campfire. She brushed past a tall figure, and only knew it was Wizard Fenworth when she heard him speak.

"What are those two things that make water?" he asked.

"Hydrogen and oxygen, Fen," Librettowit's words came between grunts. His breathing sounded labored.

Kale wondered what he was doing as she stirred the next bed of coals. She coaxed a flame to dance above the wood as she quickly fed twigs into the hesitant fire. Her eyes darted back and forth, searching out the shadows. Why the blimmets had not overtaken this small, central part of the camp, she did not know. The light from the fire extended only a few feet and did not illuminate the tents on the fringe.

Am I helping? Is this firelight enough?

She saw silhouettes of two people swinging swords in a downward motion. Lee Ark and Dar. The blimmets were mere shadows undulating around their legs.

"One part hydrogen to two parts oxygen?" Fenworth puzzled aloud.

Kale wanted to scream at the old man to do something useful. How could he talk such mumbo jumbo when their friends were in mortal danger?

"No!" Librettowit screamed. "The other way around."

"Light!" Lee Ark commanded again.

Where do I get light? Illusion? Can I make a light like I did in Risto's garden? No, that was an accident.

A swirl of white blinded Kale. Cold wet flakes stung her cheeks.

"Wrong temperature," yelled Librettowit.

"Oh dear, tut-tut."

In an instant the snow disappeared. A swooshing sound drowned the screeches of the blimmets and the cries of the questing comrades. A blast of water fell from the sky with enough force to knock Kale flat.

"Now that's better," said Fenworth from the ground near her. "Should I do another?"

"Perhaps once more," Librettowit answered.

This time when Kale heard the swoosh above her, she covered her head with her arms and squeezed her eyes shut. The second deluge did not catch her off guard.

The fires were out. Pitch dark engulfed her. The smell of wet, charred wood filled Kale's nostrils. She moved back.

The horrible screeches had ceased. Around her, moans oozed through the black night. She shivered and sat up.

She wanted her cape. She wanted to check on Gymn and Metta. She wanted to *see* something. The darkness felt heavy against her skin. Her heart raced. She fought the urge to cry out for Dar or Leetu to come rescue her. What had happened to the wizard and his librarian? Why didn't they *do* something? She had to have light. She *had* to!

A pop and sizzle above her turned into a long glowing cord of light. It hung over her, some twenty feet above the campsite. It grew as she watched, the ends extending outward like tendrils of a vine. She rose to her feet, her neck still bent backward as she stared at the slender rope gently pulsing with a soft glow.

Wizard Fenworth and Librettowit both came to stand beside her. They, too, stared upward as the light wormed its way through the black night, dispelling the dark. The tube twisted and then branched out. Thin fingers of willowy light popped out of the side, sizzled a moment, and then began to stretch. As each new appendage grew, it, too, sprouted new limbs of glowing tubes.

"Remarkable," said Librettowit.

"Unique," said Fenworth. "Well done." He turned and placed a hand on Kale's shoulder. "You and Gymn are needed this night. Librettowit and I will practice the art of healing in our way. You minister in yours."

Kale tore her gaze away from the intricate lacework created by the intertwining vine of light. The shadows of night disappeared under the moon-white glow from above. A circle of clear ground encompassed the wizard, the tumanhofer, and Kale. At its edge began a gruesome spectacle, piles of blimmets, sodden corpses, their sleek black fur glistening on lifeless forms.

"We have no time to waste, my dear." Fenworth stroked Kale's shoulder. "Go to our friends. Stop the bleeding. Stop the pain. Put each into a deep sleep and move on to the next. When we have relieved their suffering and the immediate threat of death, then we will return and repair the damage done to their bodies."

Kale looked up into the face of the old man. His strength shone through the sadness in his eyes. She nodded and moved back to the tent, crawled in and found Metta crooning over Gymn's still body.

"Wake up, Gymn," she said. The sound of her own voice surprised Kale. Her tone held authority as if she were suddenly in the position of Lee Ark, responsible for their safety and unwilling to brook any nonsense.

Gymn stirred. Kale picked him up. Metta flew to land next to her neck and leaned under her chin. The touch of the singing dragon comforted the o'rant girl.

When Kale stepped over the line of blimmets piled in a circle around the inner camp, she realized they had been held back by some force, though she did not have time to figure out what. Fenworth and Librettowit moved among the felled dragons. Kale approached Lee Ark. His shredded trousers barely covered his bloody legs. His wounds freely bled. Kale dropped to her knees beside him.

Lee Ark turned his head to her, and a twitch at the corner of his mouth told her he tried to smile. His expression told more of great pain and courage. "Next time," he whispered, "I go to bed with my boots on."

Kale nodded, not trusting herself to speak. She put Gymn on his barrel chest and concentrated. Vaguely she heard Metta singing as she and Gymn worked to heal their leader.

No pain. Sleep. Stop the lifeblood from flowing out.

She felt Gymn shudder. When she looked at Lee Ark, she saw his handsome features relaxed in sleep. She moved on.

Dar was already unconscious. She repeated the procedure, following Fenworth's instructions even though she wanted to stay and completely heal her friend.

Leetu had fallen among the ravenous blimmets. They had shredded most of her body, digging with sharp claws as if burrowing into their victim, and at the same time, biting and tearing away small mouthfuls of flesh. Curled in a ball, Leetu had protected her face and chest.

Kale cried as she and Gymn saved the emerlindian's life and then rose to search for the kimens.

They found them huddled together. Their wounds were less severe since they had leapt into the trees as soon as the attack began, except for Glim. He had been the first one assaulted. Zayvion cradled Glim's lifeless body in his arms.

38

Moving On

Wizard Fenworth, Librettowit, Kale, Gymn, and Metta worked until dawn. Dar and Lee Ark regained their strength first, enough to set the campfires blazing again. They had to go into the woods to gather dry wood. Fenworth's deluge had saturated the immediate vicinity. The frigid air turned the water on the ground to ice. Everyone wore wet clothing, and the warmth of the fires felt good.

Leetu and Brunstetter had suffered many wounds, but responded to repeated healings administered by Kale and her minor dragons. Wizard Fenworth and the tumanhofer gave aid to the large dragons. Then they helped heal the two-legged members of their questing party.

As the sun came up, the fine lace network of lighted vines overhead abruptly stopped growing and faded away. The people of the countryside walked over the nearby rolling hills to congregate around the camp. They offered to help in any way they could.

If Kale hadn't been so tired in body and in spirit, she would have been amused at the sidelong glances they aimed toward Fenworth. Each woman bobbed a curtsy. The men nodded. Kale didn't doubt they had turned out to help those who were victims of the blimmet attack. It was something the people of River Away would have done as well. But a wizard walking among them certainly stirred up curiosity.

The farmers and townspeople thanked Wizard Fenworth for slaying the blimmets, then set about digging a huge hole in the ground. When they finished, the local people layered the blimmet bodies and wood doused with deckit powder in the crater. No one touched the beasts but used shovels and picks to move them.

This done, the kimens invited Metta to go with them into the stand of woods to bury Glim. Kale watched with sadness as the little people marched in a dignified procession away from the crowd. They carried Glim's remains in a shroud of golden light. As tradition demanded, those who waited sat in a mourning circle.

The local women went back to their homes, leaving the children to ask questions.

"Why did Pretender make the awful blimmets?" asked a young boy sitting in his father's lap.

As the oldest member in the circle, Wizard Fenworth nodded to Librettowit, indicating that the tumanhofer should answer the question. The broad little man stood and went to the center. He would answer the children's questions until he came upon one he could not or did not wish to answer. Stroking his beard, he looked the crowd of men and children over, cleared his throat, and began.

"For each of the high races of Wulder's creation, Pretender tried to make his own race. The blimmets are Pretender's failure to make a race like our friends, the doneels."

"Did Pretender send the blimmets to kill us?"

"No." Librettowit paced around the center of the circle and then faced the young man who had asked. "Pretender has no control over this evil creation of his. That is one of his failures, and I'm sure it goads his ego. However, blimmets charge blindly from one act of destruction to another, and that surely delights Pretender's wicked heart."

"Where did these blimmets come from?"

"From the ground. They burrow rapidly through the earth. Sometimes their movement can be seen from above as the ground bulges and sinks in a line above their tunnel. After they have eaten, they sleep for months, then wake up ravenous."

"Will they come back?" The little girl's chin trembled, and she held tightly to her father's arm.

"This pack is dead."

"Why did the water kill them?" The tall boy sat upright beside the other male members of his family.

"Blimmets do everything quickly, in small fierce movements. They breathe in gulps. They pulled water into their lungs before they knew what was happening. Also, they are not intelligent. Those who survived the first drencher would not have realized they only needed to hold their breaths in order to survive."

"They're pretty," a little girl said around the thumb stuck securely in her mouth.

Librettowit looked at her kindly. "Yes, my dear little one, they are. Their fur is gloriously shiny for all their digging in the dirt. It is incredibly smooth and silky. It even has a pleasant odor, somewhat like baking nut pie, sweet and rich. However, if you take a blimmet pelt and make some garment to wear, it attracts other blimmets, and you meet a nasty end."

Librettowit put his hands behind his back and glanced over to Fenworth. The old wizard nodded.

Librettowit sighed. "It is also said that the meat is tasty. Roasted blimmet is a savory culinary dish. I tell you this not to tempt you, but to warn you. Once you have eaten the blimmet meat, you will want more. I cannot imagine a more unhealthy occupation than hunting blimmet. Yet there are men who do so. Young men...they do not grow old."

"Is that why we burn them?" asked another child.

"Yes, and we put in the deckit powder to make the fire burn hot." His voice rose and for the first time sounded stern and impatient. "Deckit powder also leaves a bitter taste that would discourage any fool from the idiotic notion of sampling the meat just to see if the stories are true."

"I have a question," said Kale.

Librettowit nodded to her.

"Why did the blimmets only attack outside the circle we stood in?"

Librettowit's shoulders eased back, his chest puffed out, and a pleased smile lifted the corners of his mouth.

"I did that."

"Wit." Fenworth said the name low and slow.

"Well, it's true I couldn't have done it without Fenworth right there feeding power into my spell, but you can't live with a wizard and organize his library for centuries without learning at least a thing or two."

Kale remembered hearing the tumanhofer grunting and panting during the attack. If Librettowit could cast a magic spell, could anyone? Provided that anyone was given the right training, of course. She didn't think she should ask that question here, but one of the younger children must have been wondering the same thing.

"Was it hard?" a little voice piped up.

"Quite," answered the librarian.

"Sir?"

Librettowit turned to a girl sitting snuggled up against a slightly older sister.

"Yes?"

"What was the pretty light we saw in the sky? It was after the screaming stopped. It wasn't high enough to be the moon or the stars."

Several voices spoke up, defying tradition of allowing the spokesman to answer any question. The phenomenal light caused more interest than the peculiarities of blimmets.

"Wizardry."

"The wizard did it."

"Wizard Fenworth made the light."

Librettowit turned to face Fenworth.

"Aye," said the old man. "Wizardry made the light, but it was not me."

Kale stared at Librettowit. Had the tumanhofer performed such an astonishing spell?

No, he was just as bewildered as I was. And if Fenworth didn't do it, who did? Librettowit and I were the only ones who were not hurt. No, that's not true. Gymn and Metta. But Gymn had fainted. Metta?

The song of the returning mourners drifted from the woods. The people rose to their feet out of respect. From one direction came the five kimens and Metta. From the other arrived the women with the rejoicing feast. A few in the crowd hummed the song the kimens sang in strong, sure voices. Metta flew ahead of the walking procession and landed on Kale's shoulder.

Dar pulled out his flute and joined the music. Kale heard several fiddles pick up the melody as the people responded to the unspoken call to worship. The o'rant girl recognized the praise song she had heard kimens singing in the cygnot forest after the mordakleep attack. Now she knew the words. Metta sang in her sweet, high voice, and Kale began to sing as well, knowing the little purple dragon gave her the words from a kimen's memory.

In the past, Kale had participated in the custom of celebration when a citizen of River Away died. She understood that death meant a passage to another time and place. In River Away, the villagers thought the more boisterous the revelers, the more likely a dead person would enter a place of happiness.

It's like Leetu said. Some things I knew were right are wrong. I'm changing so much on the inside. I keep learning things that seem to me I should have known all along.

It isn't how much we dance and sing and enjoy the rejoicing feast that gets a dead person to a happy place. It has something to do with the person, not us. It has something to do with Glim's life, not his death.

She walked around among the dancers until she had examined each of the kimens' faces. Shimeran, Seezle, Zayvion, D'Shay, and Veazey all looked content. They sang with joy but not with absurd fervor. Kale relaxed. They truly celebrated Glim's departure, assured he would reside in a happy place.

I don't know how I know it, but I do. Not all these people understand. But the kimens do. And Dar and Leetu.

She looked among the dancers again, this time climbing onto a farmer's wagon to get a better view.

She spotted the urohm and their marione leader quietly consuming a quail apiece.

Brunstetter and Lee Ark know what is right and what is wrong. Do the questers know more because they follow Paladin?

Fenworth's voice interrupted her thoughts. *"The questers are in the position to learn more, Kale. Because they follow Paladin. None of us knows it all. Only Wulder. Only Wulder."*

Kale whipped her head around until she caught sight of the wizard. He had a little girl on his knee and held a cup to her lips for her to drink. He winked at Kale.

"Another thing, o'rant girl, you must learn to control your use of light."

Me?

"Yes, you!"

39

Mount Tourbanaut

Kale stomped up the path, grumbling under her breath at everyone who came to mind. Her night had been filled with bad dreams. She startled awake at every slight sound, thinking another pack of blimmets was outside her tent. Metta had come awake each time, and her soothing voice crooned Kale back into slumber.

The first morning they had bade Zayvion good-bye. He would travel back to Glim's homeland and inform the Trio family of their loss, Glim's gain.

After days of flying north, the dragons delivered the questing party to the base of Mount Tourbanaut. Their wingspan prevented them from flying into the narrow canyons, and so the large dragons were left behind with D'Shay and Veazey.

Librettowit beamed as he came across each additional landmark familiar to his youth. He bubbled with enthusiasm to be back in the land of his birth, but even he could not keep up a running commentary on their surroundings. Just like the others in the questing party, the tumanhofer had to concentrate on breathing as they tramped up the canyons. The entrance to Dael, the tumanhofer's principal city, nestled between two peaks of the same mountain.

Cold winds, a spattering of sleet, sore feet, and too many questions all plagued Kale's peace of mind. The moonbeam cape warmed her body, but her cheeks and nose felt like ice. Her fine boots rubbed against her toes and heels and made her limp.

The worst part of going on a quest is the walking. And not knowing where you're going. And having cheerful people surrounding you who don't seem to realize the danger behind us...

She thought of poor Glim and the hideously beautiful blimmets, attractive even in death. She glanced over the edge of the path and realized a drop-off had formed while she trudged along. She had better watch her step and quit stomping lest she cause the narrowing ledge to crumble.

…danger beside us…

Lee Ark said they would reach Librettowit's city before nightfall, but unless the guard recognized the wizard's librarian straight off, they would probably have to camp until morning when the tumanhofer would go through the gates alone and secure a pass for the rest.

…and danger before us…

Once they gained admittance to Dael, they would briefly visit Librettowit's family. Then the tumanhofers would provide a guide to take them deep into the mountain beyond where their people built towns. The questers would pass into territory where Risto's henchmen had taken up residence. Fenworth said there was a barrier of some sort that they would have to break through.

But when Kale asked who had built the barrier, the tumanhofers or the enemy, Fenworth hemmed and hawed and changed the subject.

He's not very good at answering questions.

Leetu Bends' voice startled Kale. "What's the matter, o'rant girl?"

"Nothing."

"You look angry."

"I'm not."

Leetu said nothing but walked directly behind Kale until they reached a wider spot in the path. The emerlindian lengthened her stride to come up beside Kale.

"You're limping," Leetu said. "Why don't you let Gymn heal you?"

"Gymn is little more than a baby. He worked hard after the blimmet attack. He deserves a rest."

Leetu shrugged. "Stubborn," she muttered, but Kale heard her.

"What?"

"A comment upon immaturity."

Kale narrowed her eyes and turned her face to the wind.

"You're mad," said Leetu, "because Fenworth won't answer your questions."

"You won't answer my questions either. And Paladin didn't answer my questions."

"He didn't?"

"Well, yes, he showed me things, but that was a long time ago."

Leetu hummed the chorus of one of Dar's favorite marching songs before she spoke again. "To demonstrate her anger, the young o'rant girl resorts to sullen behavior toward her comrades, grumbling against her leaders, and stubbornly refusing help."

Kale said nothing.

"Immaturity," said the emerlindian.

Kale stopped and faced Leetu. "Yes. All right. I'm immature. I'm tired, confused, frightened, immature. There! Does that help any, now that I've agreed with you?"

Leetu nodded, and Kale resisted the urge to give her a hearty shove.

"You are still putting one foot in front of the other, Kale." Leetu stepped around a boulder in the path. She looked back at Kale and gestured for her to come on. "Give yourself credit for not giving up. You haven't slowed down our expedition, and you've been a valuable member."

"Most of the time I don't know what I'm doing."

Leetu chuckled. "Most of the time *I* don't know what I'm doing. My advantage is more experience. Many times I know what is expected of me, and I do that, whether I am confident of success or not."

Kale allowed Leetu to go first as the trail narrowed and rose steeply but came up next to her again as soon as there was room for the two to walk side by side.

Leetu offered Kale a long, thin breadstick and took one from her pocket for herself.

"As for being confused, you know what you're to do now. You are to follow Dar, who is just ahead of you. You trust him to be following Shimeran."

"I want to know if I made that light-thing in the sky, and if I did, how? Fenworth won't tell me anything."

"He's a very old man, Kale, and probably tired. This quest is asking a lot of him. Have some patience and more compassion. Work to make things easier for him, not harder."

"But he's a wizard," Kale protested.

"And you think wizards have endless strength, endless knowledge, the answers to everything, and the means to fix all troubles?"

Kale thought about Leetu's words. After a minute, she answered reluctantly. "Yes."

Leetu did not speak up.

Kale sighed. "I suppose this is another instance where what I don't know is greater than what I do know."

"It's hard to unlearn falsehoods, but Paladin knows you can, or he wouldn't have entrusted you with this quest."

The ledge topped a bluff, and to their left stood a small wood of majestic evergreens. Beyond that, another cliff rose sharply toward the sky.

"Frightened," Leetu continued. "Well, it is a lie to face scary things and pretend you are not frightened. Just as it is deceitful to look at the beauty of that scene"—she nodded toward the mountain range—"and pretend the grandeur does not stir your soul. Perhaps not false, but folly, to take in with the eyes and deny with the heart."

The emerlindian paused and gazed with wonder at their surroundings. Then she turned her attention back to Kale.

"Immature. You've heard Dar say I am young. I am certainly no Granny Noon. But when you beat back that pride that wants to say, 'I'm big,' then you are in the position to learn."

Kale had an image of a little marione, Dubby Brummer, with his dimpled fists planted on his broad hips, a pout on his face, and one foot about to stamp the ground. How often she had taken care of the troublesome toddler who always wanted to do what the big children did. The image of his grubby, stubborn face made Kale laugh. The path narrowed again.

"Put your hood up," said Leetu as she fell behind, "and the veil over your face, o'rant girl."

They crossed the small mountain meadow and started up another incline. The wind calmed, and a few flakes of snow drifted lazily around the travelers.

Kale looked ahead. Lee Ark led them. Shimeran and Dar followed. She held the fourth position. Behind her Leetu helped Librettowit climb over a fallen tree. Brunstetter and a clump of brushwood hid Wizard Fenworth and Seezle. Kale caught her breath and looked again to the front of the line and to the back. Her eyes swiveled to look at the mountain pass— boulders, trees, a cliff in the distance, gray light as the clouds holding snow obscured the sun.

The mural in the tavern! Even the details of clothing matched exactly the figures in the picture. This scene she walked in was the scene depicted of the members of the seven high races crossing a mountain passage. Kale had seen it every day of her life. She'd dusted it. She'd even wiped ale from the surface when a careless customer had swung his full mug too heartily.

Kale looked back just as the old wizard and the tiny kimen came around the bend. Now the picture differed from the painting on the wall. But even the brushwood that had hidden the last two members of their quest was in the picture in River Away. She'd always thought the brotherhood of travelers looked eager to face their adventure. She felt tired and weary, eager to find a warm bed.

Who had painted the picture? Master Meiger said it was a traveling man who paid for his meal and board by drawing the art upon the wall.

She scurried to catch up with Dar. Maybe he would have an idea. Around yet another twist in the trail, she found those ahead of her had stopped.

An old o'rant woman dressed in shabby attire stood bent and shivering before Lee Ark.

"I've waited so long." Her scratchy voice carried a note of pleading.

Kale felt uncomfortable. Why did Lee Ark look so formidable? Did he have to look angry, as if he would, at any moment, raise his heavy hand and beat the poor ragged soul? One old woman could not endanger them. Surely their leader should be more hospitable. Kale clenched her fists under the moonbeam cape, fighting an odd tremor flowing through her body.

The old woman bobbed her head. "We knew you were coming—a wizard, Paladin's choice warriors, and the o'rant girl known as the mighty Dragon Keeper."

The old crone held out two mittened hands cradling a large egg. Her withered fingers poked through the holes in the knitted black yarn. The yellowed egg she held was larger than her head and perched precariously in her shivering hands.

Leetu, Librettowit, and Brunstetter came up behind Kale and then stopped.

"Who told you we were coming, old woman?" asked Lee Ark.

"A trader. He said it was important to get the egg to the o'rant girl." Again the whine in her voice scraped over Kale's brittle nerves.

"Then why didn't he bring it?" Lee Ark snapped. "Why send an old woman?"

"He didn't want to come on Mount Tourbanaut. He said the tuman-hofers had no love for him. That Risto would know he had carried the egg and come after him."

Kale eyed the egg. She didn't feel the draw that she had felt before, the enchantment that urged her to reach out and pick up a dragon egg. Something dark wavered in and out of her mind as she concentrated on the old woman's offering.

Lee Ark's low voice sent a shiver down Kale's spine. "Why send *you* to the top of an unfriendly mountain when the autumn weather is so uncertain? Why not send a strong shepherd, a young man?"

"I've lived on this mountain all my life. My father was a shepherd." The old woman snorted. "No one else was willing. The trader said he'd taken the egg from someone who'd stolen it from Risto."

Wizard Fenworth came up to them and promptly sat down on a rock. He was winded and seemed more interested in opening his flask of water than in the stranger accosting the troupe.

Librettowit, is it the meech egg?

"*Wrong size. Wrong color. I don't trust this woman, Kale.*"

Leetu spoke up. "She got the egg from a bisonbeck, Lee Ark."

The woman's head jerked up, and she glared at Leetu. "Not all people are afraid of those unfortunate ones who have not pleased Risto and have been cast aside. Gorrad is a trader and an honest one. He took the egg, because he heard rumors that Risto had stolen it and Paladin wanted it back. But he's had bad dealings with Risto. Who hasn't? He was afraid. Who wouldn't be?"

Lee Ark broke in. "Yet you, an old woman, are not afraid to bring the egg to us?"

"My life is almost over. I came slowly. No one would suspect 'an old woman' to be carrying something of great value."

Fear gripped Kale's stomach. She wanted to rush forward and knock the egg out of the unkempt woman's hands. Yet another force told her to run the other way, to order everyone to run.

"I don't want that egg," said Kale. "It has no value. It is evil."

The woman stood upright, now more than two feet taller than Lee Ark. She raised the egg above her head and a screech tore from her throat.

"Run!" screamed Kale.

The woman hurled the egg down to the rock path at her feet. Kale and her comrades jumped away, bolting for shelter.

A roar, billowing smoke, and choking fumes erupted as the old woman cackled and shrieked.

Kale and Leetu ran to Fenworth, still sitting on the rock and drinking from his flask. They each grabbed one of his arms, and between them, hauled the wizard back down the trail.

He muttered complaints at them. "Up, not down. The gate is up. Who is making that hideous noise? Hold on, let me get my feet under me. Where's my walking stick? Best walking stick I've had in ages. Did we lose it?"

40

✝HREE HEADS ARE ∏O✝ BE✝✝ER ✝HA∏ O∏E

"I don't suppose the water spell would work again?" Fenworth pulled at his beard. He'd taken his hat off and crumpled it into a wad.

"No, probably not," agreed Librettowit.

Kale crouched between the tumanhofer and a wall of stone. Two bulky boulders protected her and the wizard and his librarian from the three-headed monster raging along the mountain path. Kale's eyes darted back and forth between the menacing beast and the two old men. She searched the outside area for the mysterious woman and could not find her. The giant lizardlike creature paced around in a ponderous circle, preventing any of the travelers from getting past.

Fenworth sat at the rear of their little refuge. He continued to stroke his long gray beard with one hand and clutch his hat with the other. His beard took on the look of swamp moss, and leaves sprouted from his robes. "Fire spell?"

"Too unpredictable."

"Shriveling?"

"Takes too long."

Impatient with their conversation, Kale pulled out her small sword and repositioned herself on her knees so she could peer out beside Librettowit and watch the beast. Her fingers tightened around the hilt until her knuckles shone white. She forced her hand to relax and took several deep breaths. She set about locating each of her comrades.

Leetu had scrambled to a perch above them beyond the monster's reach. She straddled an odd bush growing out from the cliff and shot arrows down upon the angry creature. They penetrated its skin and stuck out like quills. Brackish blood drizzled from each wound, but the arrows did not hinder its movements.

The beast roared and charged Kale. She and Librettowit fell back as one of the monster's heads abruptly stopped outside their hiding place. The thing prodded at the boulders with its snout, but the small opening prevented it from thrusting any closer.

Kale sucked air into her mouth with a hiss as she tried to pull herself into a shadow as far from the opening as she could get. A long, skinny black tongue flicked out of the head's mouth and explored the crevice. The wizard, the tumanhofer, and the o'rant girl cowered, pressing their backs against the rock wall. In desperation, Kale jabbed with her sword and nicked it. The tongue jerked back with a slurping sound, and the head moved away from their shelter.

"One should never," said Fenworth, sternly, "transport *any* monster in the confines of an egg shell. Being cramped like that makes it cranky."

Another head hovered over the opening in the rocks near Kale and Librettowit. Kale braced her feet apart in a fighting stance, took a firm grip on her sword, and sliced deliberately as the tongue snaked in. The end of the monster's tongue fell at her feet and writhed there. With a squeal that did not sound a bit like a soldier, Kale backed away from it as if it were a serpent. Librettowit grabbed the ugly thing and threw it out of their hiding hole.

"This is not a librarian's job," he complained. "This has nothing to do with books and research."

While Fenworth muttered about spells—wet, dry, cold, hot—Kale peered over the boulders, trying to locate the other members of their quest. One monster head moved close to a ledge littered with small boulders. A sudden flash of light sent it snapping back.

At least one kimen is in there.

Kale saw the third head plunge downward. She screeched as Lee Ark darted from one rock to another. Hideous teeth snatched at his back. Dar's trumpet blasted the air. At that precise moment, Brunstetter jumped out and drove his long sword into the monster's neck beneath the jawbone. All three beast heads howled. The wounded one continued to bellow. Then that head and neck fell limply to the ground. Now as the monster moved, it had to drag the lifeless portion along.

Fenworth had risen and crouched beside Kale.

"No more heroics." She heard him mindspeak to them all. *"Just be patient a minute. I've almost got a handle on this calcification spell."*

It's about time! The thought sprang up in her mind, and she jerked around to see if it had been heard by the old wizard. His frown seemed to be for his concentration on the deed at hand. He didn't seem to notice her at all. Kale breathed a sigh of relief, but none of the tension left her body.

The beast still trudged back and forth, and it knew where each of the members of the quest hid. Frustrated, it growled and made passes at the rocks with the two remaining heads. One head came at Kale again, and she backed up, raising her sword. Instead of flicking its tongue in the space above the boulders, it rammed its massive head against the rocks. The blow shook their little stronghold. Dirt and grit showered down on them, covering their clothing and hair with dust.

Kale looked over to see Librettowit and Fenworth whispering to each other and casually brushing dust off their heads. She gritted her teeth.

Will he have that spell ready in time?

The creature moved off toward Lee Ark's sheltering rocks. Kale watched. The third head dragged the ground. The beast stumbled and struggled. His movements seemed more encumbered than just from the fallen head.

"His tail is turning gray," she reported to the men behind her.

Librettowit rose to spy over the boulders.

"It's turning to rock. Good job, Fen, but how about starting at the other end. It would be nice to have those disgusting heads turn to stone first."

Fenworth ran his hand over the top of his head. Kale noticed for the first time a bald spot right on the crown, surrounded by the long fringe of gray hair. The wizard's fingertips made a circular motion on the exposed scalp.

"Let's see, that would require a number of adjustments... Yes, it could be done."

"Never mind," said Librettowit. "The process ceased while you were contemplating the change. Just go on. The beast will quit moving as soon as you get to the legs."

Librettowit gave a yelp of approval. "That's the way. That last bit charged up the remainder of his tail. He's hauling around a city building's worth of stone on his backside. Oops! That seems to have irritated the fellow."

Two roars competed in ferocity. One of the heads reached over and nipped the other. Kale held her breath as she watched the hind legs pause, stiffen, and then change color from green to gray.

"Be a little quicker, will you, Fen?" said Librettowit. "The thing is going to suffer now." He turned his head away.

"Right," said Wizard Fenworth and closed his eyes to concentrate.

Kale turned away too. Then she covered her ears as the beast moaned. She welcomed the silence a moment later and looked back to the mountain path. A stone statue stood with one head hanging over the cliff edge. The two upright necks twined around each other and bent back along the creature's spine.

Dar, Lee Ark, and Brunstetter cautiously came out of their hiding places. Leetu began her descent, and the kimens skittered across the open space to stand with Kale as she emerged.

"Well, then." Fenworth climbed awkwardly over the rocks. Lee Ark and Kale moved to help him.

He crammed his hat back on his head and dusted off his robes. Then he slapped his palms together, knocking off the dirt.

"That was an uncomfortable situation. Warned you, didn't I? Quests are quite interesting except for the uncomfortable parts. I don't suppose that unpleasant woman is still here." He looked around, even stretching to stand on his toes and peer beyond the monster. "A female wizard. Didn't recognize her, but I suspect she was that Burner Stox woman. Married Crim Copper. Beastly wizard. Can't say they get along at all well."

The others began to move. Kale felt as if she had awakened from a bad dream. A giggle bubbled up in her throat, and she repressed it, knowing the others would count it for just what it was, nerves. She watched as Leetu picked up the few arrows that had bounced off the monster when it was still alive to threaten their lives.

The arrows stuck in its hide were stone now.

Dar rejoiced that his pack had not been trodden upon. Brunstetter and the kimens quickly gathered more of the scattered belongings and brought them to the wizard.

"My walking stick." With one finger, Fenworth patted Seezle on the shoulder. "Thank you, my dear."

He glanced up at the monstrous statue. "You know, I really think we must be going. I can't remember if this spell holds or not."

Kale had no problem with clearing out of the vicinity of the solidified creature. Lee Ark again took the lead, and the rest followed. Minutes later they heard a grinding crunch, and then a massive shudder vibrated under their feet.

"Crumbles," said Fenworth. "I remember now. Crumbles. Good thing we weren't standing under it. Wit, you're going to have to explain to your kinsmen why one of their mountain passes is now filled with rubble. Should sit better with them, coming from one of their own."

"Right," said the tumanhofer, nodding his head and glowering.

"Perhaps you could write a history of the occurrence," suggested the wizard.

"I'm a librarian. I *read* books. I don't write—"

"Hmm? Well, then. Tut-tut. I could—"

"I'll see to it, Fenworth."

41

City of Dael

The path widened as it joined another mountain trail. The snow fell in earnest. The sun had been behind clouds for hours, and now the gray light grew darker. The veil of loosely woven moonbeam cloth over Kale's face protected her from the chill and aided her ability to see. But as the afternoon faded into night, she began to worry about losing their way in the mountain passes.

"Not much farther," Librettowit called to his companions.

"Stay close together," ordered Lee Ark as he moved down the line, checking on each of the trekkers.

On his way back to the head of the line moments later, he repositioned the kimens. He sent Shimeran to the front. Seezle walked directly before Kale.

"Shine," barked Lee Ark as he strode against the quickening wind to the front of their procession.

The kimens produced a bright yellow light. Even so, Kale barely made out Shimeran's form, and Seezle's glow cast just enough light to make the path between the o'rant girl and the doneel visible.

The others must be having it harder than I am. I have the moonbeam cape.

They'd packed heavy winter clothing. After the encounter with the woman wizard and the three-headed monster, they had reached an altitude where the wind pressed like icy fingers into their skin. Lee Ark had paused long enough for everyone to put on the extra clothing. The kimens, of course, had no need for anything other than their usual light attire. Kale had gratefully tucked her feet into extra socks and her hands into mittens knitted by Granny Noon.

"Not much farther," Librettowit called again.

Kale's feet sank in the snow as it piled higher on the path. Lee Ark tramped back again. "Put a hand on the shoulder of the person in front of you."

This time he brought Brunstetter to walk directly behind Shimeran and Wizard Fenworth behind the urohm. The giant walked, shuffling his feet, deliberately clearing a trail for those following.

Kale's fingers on Dar's shoulder grew numb. She switched hands, pulling the cold one into the warmth under her cape. Seezle held onto the back of Dar's pant leg. Kale wondered if the little creature was warm, and if her light warmed the back of Dar's leg.

"Not much farther," Librettowit repeated.

Kale had no warning when they came to the massive wooden doors that made up the gate of Dael. Even standing huddled next to the others with Brunstetter applying his massive fist to announce their arrival, she could see only a dark bulk stretching out of sight to either side. The wind howled, and the snow swirled in a blinding curtain. Only one lantern beside a boarded window in the gate flickered a grudging welcome.

The wooden shutter swung back from the gate window. A square of light appeared and then was blocked by a head bundled in a dark scarf.

"What? What?" the gatekeeper growled. "No admittance after dark. Go to the caves for shelter and come again in the morning."

The shutter started to swing shut, but Brunstetter caught it.

His low voice rumbled pleasantly as if he were explaining to a child some simple matter of courtesy. "We've Wizard Fenworth with us, and we're on Paladin's business."

"That won't work here," grumbled the gatekeeper. His hands covered in thick gloves jerked at the edge of the shutter, trying to dislodge it from Brunstetter's massive grip. "Here now, let go of that. Go to the caves like any decent citizen and wait for morning. Wizards, indeed. Using Paladin's name as if it were a password. Shame on you, and *let go!*"

Librettowit pushed to the front. "Trevithick Librettowit here. I'm not interested in sheltering in the caves tonight. Let us in."

"Wit? Wit? You don't say? Bumby Bumbocore here. How've you been, you old bookhound?"

"Busy," Librettowit snapped. "And cold."

"Oh yes, just a minute." He started to move away from the gate window. "Tell your friend to let go."

Brunstetter released his hold on the shutter. The square patch of light disappeared. A moment later the rumbles and groans of gears meshing and grating together signaled that they would be admitted. The noise went on for a long time before a large door set in the bigger gate swung open.

Why would such a simple wooden door require all that ruckus to get it open?

Brunstetter stepped aside, allowing Fenworth to enter first, followed by Librettowit and the rest of the party. The urohm had to stoop to get through the entry. Gatekeeper Bumbocore shut the door, abruptly cutting off the sound of the howling wind.

Kale threw back the hood of her cape and shook snow from her clothing. She stamped her feet and hoped they all would soon be someplace where she could put her frigid toes next to a fireplace.

Librettowit introduced the gatekeeper. "A cousin," he explained. He and Bumbocore did a lot of backslapping and questioning. They asked more questions of each other than they bothered to answer.

"Ahem!" Wizard Fenworth cleared his throat. "Mustn't keep your mother waiting, Wit."

Bumbocore looked startled. "Is Gloritemdomer expecting you? I just saw your father today at noonmeal, and he didn't say a thing."

"Now isn't that the way of a quest?" Fenworth tapped his walking stick vigorously against the stone flooring. "Risto knows we're coming. That Burner Stox woman knows we're coming. Probably that no-good husband of hers, Crim Copper, knows we're coming. Even sent out a three-headed monster to greet us, but do our people know we're coming?" He started muttering and shaking his head, pulling his beard with one hand, knocking newly sprouting leaves to the floor as he did so.

Bumbocore paled. "R-risto? Burner St-stox? Monster?"

Fenworth patted the short man on his back. "Been bothering you, too?

Tut-tut. We'll have to do something about that. Good calcification spell works if you remember to move briskly afterward."

He cleared his throat and gestured to his librarian. "Nice talking to old friends, but we must be going. Gloritemdomer makes a good supper, and we don't want to be late. Rude, you know."

Librettowit led the way through the wide streets of the stone city. Lightrocks shone in a variety of colors along the way. Kale wondered why they were spaced so far apart. The cheery colors brightened dark passages but were not grouped together to illuminate the entire area. After a while, she grew used to the effect of the subdued lighting and thought it was a pretty way to brighten the constant gray of the granite.

"Now you see," said Librettowit, doffing his hat to those he passed as he went on instructing his traveling companions, "tumanhofers don't take granite from the mountain, chip it into blocks, haul it across the country, and stack it into buildings. Such an inefficient way to build a city. Our homes are carved out of the rock. Our streets are not paved, because they are rock to begin with. Therefore we can spend our time on more worthwhile things."

Leetu?

"Yes?"

What do tumanhofers think are worthwhile things to do?

"Digging."

Digging? As in dirt?

"Sometimes, if you count their extensive agricultural research programs. But more into the way things work. Librettowit digs into books and finds interesting facts. Some tumanhofers dig into different ways of doing things. There are more inventors, scientists, and scholars among the tumanhofers than any other race. In Dael alone, there are six universities."

Does anybody need that much learning?

"The tumanhofers do. It keeps them happy."

Kale unbuttoned her cape, and the two dragons scrambled out to sit on her shoulders. They chittered excitedly. Kale caught the gist of what they said by listening with her mind.

She grinned as she realized they were saying things she wanted to exclaim herself. Metta and Gymn were uttering, *"Look at that. Did you ever see...? What is that used for? Ooo, that's pretty,"* over and over in different variations of the same, awed thoughts.

The questing party walked a long, long way before the house fronts began to look like homes instead of stores and inns. Their tumanhofer guide quit talking as he rounded a corner and quickened his pace. Down the street a door flew open, and a stout woman rushed out. She trotted to meet them and embraced Librettowit.

"Mama!" he exclaimed and enveloped her in a big hug. A man appeared and joined the hug, adding slaps on Librettowit's back and exclaiming, "Well, well, welcome, son."

Neighbors poured out of the nearby homes and gathered in the street. Kale stood back and watched. This was unlike anything she had ever seen. Mariones did not display their affections. These tumanhofers spent twenty minutes greeting each other and making introductions. They laughed and hugged. Librettowit's father, Grundtrieg, took over the introductions once his son had led him around and made known the names of each of his companions. Grundtrieg introduced Kale to a young tumanhofer girl named Estellabrist. She pulled the o'rant girl around to meet at least fifty neighbors, relatives, and friends who had come over from the surrounding streets.

Finally the visiting travelers were escorted into the house. Kale sank onto a soft cushion next to the wall. Dar lowered himself beside her.

"Would it be rude to take off my boots?" she asked the doneel. "My feet ache."

"Not a bit. You've been accepted as an honored guest."

"Honored guests can take their boots off?"

"Most definitely."

Kale pushed the cape off her shoulders and let it fall behind her, then went to work on her boots. With double socks beneath, they seemed determined to remain on her feet.

Dar braced himself and helped her tug. Then Kale returned the favor and marveled at how comfortable she felt with the doneel after all this time together. In River Away, no one would have helped her remove her boots, not that she'd ever had any. She would have been ordered to assist Dar. As they settled down again, she grinned at him just because it was good to have a friend.

Wizard Fenworth had been given the biggest, most comfortable chair next to a cozy fireplace. Brunstetter sat on the steps of a stairwell. Lee Ark and Leetu Bends sat at the table with Librettowit and his father. The kimens had found a corner where they wouldn't be stepped on as Mistress Librettowit and her daughters bustled around making supper.

"Librettowit is happy here," said Kale.

"Tumanhofers enjoy family."

"Do you have family, Dar?"

He nodded, then closed his eyes and leaned his head against the wall. "Lots."

Kale thought about Fenworth's comment about her mother. Could it be true her mother was alive? Could the old wizard know where she was? She almost asked Dar's opinion when she remembered Fenworth also said that talking about her mother would put her life in danger.

I want my mother to be alive. I would like to find her. She let her eyes roam over the room watching the tumanhofers exchange smiles and affectionate pats as they passed. Librettowit's mother kissed his cheek as she set a basket of bread on the table. His father gave his wife a hug around the waist. *I wonder what it feels like to be part of a family. I think it would be nice.*

"You belong, Kale." Dar's soft voice interrupted her thoughts. "You are part of Paladin's legion. We are your family."

Kale gave him a hard look. He still leaned with his head against the wall, his eyes closed. He looked tired and innocent of any mischief.

"Are you sure you don't read my mind?"

"Positive. You are altogether too predictable to even have to bother."

"Could you read my mind if you wanted to?"

"Nope. Haven't got the talent. I can only converse with you if you initiate the mindspeaking."

Librettowit's sisters brought around bowls of warm, soapy water and towels. They washed for dinner there in the parlor of Librettowit's home. Kale thought that was a quaint custom. Another sister soon provided each guest with bread on a platter, a steaming bowl, and a spoon. Dar sat up and smiled his most charming as he thanked her.

"Don't eat yet," he whispered to Kale as the tumanhofer woman walked away. "Grundtrieg will say a blessing on the meal first."

When everyone was served, the father bowed his head and repeated a simple grace. Then he thanked Wulder for the company and the pleasure of seeing their son. He added that he and his family were honored to assist in Paladin's plan in any way put before them.

Kale looked down at her bowl. In the dim light, she could not tell what was in it, although it did smell delicious.

"What is this?" she asked Dar.

"Tumanhofers live underground, so it could be roots or mole stew or grubs."

He lifted the spoon to his lips and took a slurping sip. Across the room, Leetu's head jerked up, and she frowned at the doneel.

Dar ignored her. "It's good, Kale. Now it would be rude not to eat what they have put before you. Just enjoy it."

"What is it?"

Dar heaved an exaggerated sigh. "Flatworm soup."

Kale bit her lip and looked around the room. No one noticed she wasn't eating. Metta and Gymn scurried around the base of the walls, looking for insects. The little dragons liked worms and grubs and things. Would they eat cooked flatworms?

"Take a bite," said Dar. He dipped a chunk of bread in the broth and popped it in his mouth.

Kale swallowed hard. She would *not* insult her hostess. She dipped her spoon in the soup and only half filled it. Closing her eyes, she lifted it to her mouth. It *did* smell good. She tasted it. Her eyes popped open.

"Onions!"

Dar laughed.

Leetu's voice entered Kale's thoughts. *"I told you he's just like a big brother. He teases even when he's worn out and too tired to sit at the table."*

Kale grinned across the room, answering Leetu's friendly smile with a wink.

Just like a brother. I'll have to learn to tease him back.

"I might be willing to help you with that project."

Kale sighed and dipped her spoon in the onion soup. She would like to stay here. But tomorrow they would go on.

Deep into the mountain.

Looking for the meech egg.

Walking straight into Risto's lair.

42

†HE BARRIER

Blue sky, white clouds, green grass.

After half a day of trudging down gray granite tunnels toward the center of Mount Tourbanaut, Kale wanted sky above her head and grass beneath her feet. She tried to remember that outside the mountain was a frenzied blizzard and walking was certainly easier within.

I don't really want to go questing on the icy slopes of a mountain with a furious wind trying to push me off and hard pellets of snow pounding against me.

She looked at the grim walls revealed by the lanterns they carried. *I'm certainly not cut out to be a tumanhofer.*

Librettowit walked up front with their guide, Tilkertineebo Rapjackaport. Kale found it hard to remember even part of the tumanhofers' names. The names for places in the tumanhofer mountain were short. They had passed through small towns, Glep, Tras, and Burr. Soon they would reach Fiph, and then a stretch of tunnels where no tumanhofers cared to roam.

Fenworth trundled along in a wooden cart pulled by a burro. No danger threatened them for this part of their journey, and the old wizard slept most of the time. Dar sang his hiking songs. The kimens and Metta joined in. Kale sang too, but her heart couldn't keep up with the happy beat.

I'm not really afraid, just realistically cautious. After all, we're going into Risto's territory. Someone should be worried about the things we may have to face.

They ate noonmeal at a tavern in Fiph.

The long tunnels of Penn stretched for miles in a mazelike structure. Rapjackaport explained that hundreds of years ago the tumanhofers had mined this region. Now only druddums careened through the passageways.

Mile after mile, Rapjackaport led them deeper into the mountain. Shades of gray mottled the walls of the large tunnels. The floors had been leveled of all bumps and ridges. The walls were hewn smooth by tumanhofer tools. So far, this final approach into Risto's stronghold was exceedingly dull. The only breaks from monotony were old miner signs at each corner, telling directions. They indicated the four points of a compass with an arrow showing which direction the tunnel followed.

Kale resisted the urge to ask how much farther they had to go.

I'll be glad when we get to where we are going, retrieve the egg, and hurry out of here.

"The Cavern of Rainbows," said Rapjackaport. "This is where I leave you."

Kale's head jerked up at the sound of the tumanhofer's voice. His hearty words bounced off the walls. They'd entered a gigantic cavern.

Huge, glistening crystals hung from the ceiling in the brilliant hues of a rainbow. The floor was a rippled rock substance that looked as if it was once a thick porridge of pastel shades. Kale imagined someone pouring it out and watching it harden. Round craters dotted the area. They reminded Kale of the dents made by bubbles in the top of porridge cooking in a kettle, only these were quite large. Kale could have put both feet in the one nearest her. Another was wide enough Dar could have lain in it. Three walls were solid lightrock but not the blue she'd seen most often underground. These walls glowed with a clear, silvery light.

"I'll take the cart and burro back with me," said Rapjackaport. "If you get through the barrier, you'll find miles of natural tunnels. Some of these passages are not big enough for a wagon of any sort."

Brunstetter looked uncomfortable at this. He eyed the small wagon and his own bulk as if comparing sizes.

Leetu and Librettowit helped Fenworth climb out of the cart. He sat down on a boulder that glowed a soft pink. Having just awakened from another nap, the old wizard gazed at the vast underground cavern with sleepy eyes, yawned, and stroked his beard.

"Thank you, dear Rapjackaport, for guiding us." Fenworth's quiet voice echoed faintly around them. "We understand your eagerness to return. We won't detain you."

The tumanhofer bowed with more precision than elegance and turned to his cousin. "Take care, Librettowit. This is an odd job for a librarian."

"I'm aware of that, Port. But we do what we must do."

They embraced. Lee Ark and Dar unloaded a few supplies from the cart and helped turn the burro. Kale remembered to say her thanks as the tumanhofer left them, but her eyes were on the magnificent cave. The glitter and vivid colors had almost blinded her to a mar of ugliness seeping out of a crevice on the opposite side. In contrast to the beauty of the great stone hall, a mound of black coarse sand, rocks, and boulders spilled out of this one wide crack.

Fenworth, leaning heavily on his walking stick, crossed the uneven floor with his eyes trained on the deplorable deformity. A few yards from its base he sat down again, this time on a lavender boulder. The others started setting up camp, but Kale went to stand by the old man.

After a moment he sighed. He propped his walking stick against his shoulder and placed both hands upon his knees. He leaned forward and squinted at the black, ragged pebbles as if reading written lines amid the pile. Eventually he reached to take Kale's hand in his without looking away from the crumbly-looking mass in front of them.

"Crim Copper. That's who made this atrocity, Kale. Crim Copper." He patted her hand. A mouse fell out of his sleeve and scampered away, ignored by both of them. "Risto, Burner Stox, and Crim Copper working together. Can't be good. Oh dear, oh dear. Can't be good."

Dar fixed an especially good supper and played soothing "digestion music" afterward. Metta sat on his shoulder and sang her syllable-song. Kale listened patiently as Librettowit explained again that the little purple dragon's snout wasn't formed for making words like the seven high races used, but the minor dragons had a language of their own. Therefore the gifted creatures could communicate mentally in the common language, but voiced their thoughts with what sounded to us like a string of nonsense syllables. Kale thought the music Metta made without words was lovelier than any ballads she had heard sung by minstrels at the tavern.

The kimens joined the singing and danced. Their beautiful clothing changed with each movement. With the pastel lava rock beneath their feet and the vibrant jewel tones dripping as crystals from the ceiling, the spectacular performance kept Kale's attention—except for the few times her eyes wandered over to the old wizard.

Fenworth had scarcely touched his meal, and anything Dar cooked usually had his admiration, or at least his attention. The wizard often complained about Librettowit's lack of culinary skill, to which the tumanhofer replied, "I'm a librarian." Fenworth also enjoyed music. It was peculiar for him to ignore Metta, Dar, and the kimens.

This night Fenworth ate a few spoonfuls and put the bowl of green stew aside. He sat contemplating the barrier.

Kale worried every time she noticed how totally occupied the wizard was with Crim Copper's black blight on the beautiful cavern. Fenworth grew leaves and didn't bother to shake them off. He drifted into the appearance of a massive trunk that dissipated any time he moved. Occasionally he stood and paced. Kale tried once to reach into his mind, but as she'd found from earlier experiences, his thoughts were guarded.

A disturbed wizard is not a comforting sight. Why do the others ignore him?

The music drew her back to the activities in the camp, and she began to ask herself questions. *All the songs are about friendship… Is it coincidence? No, they're celebrating our brotherhood in the quest… On purpose?… Probably… Why?*

She quit trying to figure it out. The next song had many verses, and she had heard it often. She called Metta to fly to her shoulder. Kale wanted help in remembering the words. Turning her back on Fenworth's brooding figure, she gave herself over to enjoying this evening with her comrades.

In the morning Fenworth still sat on his lavender boulder, keeping vigil over the black barrier.

Kale sat next to the tumanhofer with a platter of fried mullins to share for breakfast. She nodded over at the wizard, who was mostly tree this morning. "What is he doing, Librettowit?"

The librarian picked up a hot stick from the platter, took a bite, and looked over at his longtime friend. "Thinking."

"Could you help him? I mean, with some fact from your research."

"Humph! A librarian needs books in order to do research." He chewed for a moment and then swallowed. "I have remembered several incidents in history when a wizard was called upon to break down walls. I even remembered one where a wizard moved a mountain. But he was on the outside of the mountain, not within it. There's a difference."

"What will he do?"

"Think some more."

The others sat around and let Fenworth think. Sometimes he paced while he thought. He carried his hat in his hand and wadded it into an unrecognizable clump. He often muttered. But Kale couldn't see that he made any great discovery with all the thinking and pacing and wadding and muttering.

Night came, and the music was about Wulder and the many wonders He had performed.

Kale watched the pondering wizard. *We need Wulder here now.*

The next morning brought no better results. Fenworth trailed a long, bushy vine off his robes whenever he paced. The little dragons kept close to the old wizard. An abundance of insects scattered out of his leaves every time he moved.

Around the campfire that night they sang of Paladin's mighty deeds. Kale sang along, but her heart yearned for some kind of action. *We need Paladin here now.*

The next morning she could no longer stand the patience of everyone but her. She wanted nothing more than to go pummel the wizard with a thousand questions and maybe stir his old bones into doing something.

She climbed up the wall that sloped toward the black barrier and found her own lavender boulder to sit on. Her moonbeam cape flowed from her shoulders but gave her no sense of being part of a great quest. Gymn and Metta nestled in their pocket-dens and offered no companionship. She sat with her elbows on her knees, her chin on her fists, and her face turned toward Wizard Fenworth as he sat on his rock, starting to look like a bush.

She glared at him, then glared at the black barrier.

He should do something. This is a waste of time. Why can't he just say, 'Move!'?

Fenworth sprang to his feet and looked straight at Kale. His alarmed expression told her before the rumbling in the ground that she had done something terrible.

Kale reached down to balance herself on the shuddering boulder. The black mass beside her began to shift. Down in the campsite, her friends scrambled for cover. Leetu and Lee Ark sprinted to the wizard and dragged him, protesting, away from the cascading black gravel. The barrier was coming apart.

Thick dust filled the air. Kale fell backward and tumbled down the rocky incline. She heard shouts but couldn't look. Her main concern was to keep from whacking her head as she turned over and over, faster and faster down the slanted wall. She coughed and sputtered and tried to keep her arms wrapped over her head.

When she hit bottom and the tiny black rocks kept sliding down around her, she curled up in a ball and tried to breathe through the cape.

Finally the mountain quit trembling. Kale sat up, starting another tiny landslide as the mound of gravel covering her fell away. The air was full of thick black dust, so she kept the edge of her cape over her nose and mouth. She blinked dirt from her eyes.

The natural light of the magnificent cavern glowed dimly through fine black powder as it settled. The gravel and dust lay over everything, blanketing the former brilliance. Only a half-light showed Kale the small cave surrounding her.

When she stopped coughing against the gritty air, she reached into the cape and pulled out Metta and Gymn, one in each hand. Metta raced to perch on Kale's shoulder as close to her neck and under her chin as she could get. Gymn lay limply in the palm of her hand. She stroked his backbone and let out a sigh of relief when his tail twitched.

"Fainted again," she said to Metta. "He'll be all right."

Kale said it more to reassure herself. She felt battered. Her arms and legs ached. Gymn would heal her bruises. She examined herself and found only scratches under a black coating of dust.

I'll be all right. Nothing is broken. I just have to find the others.

I hope no one is hurt.

Looking around, she examined the small, separate cave created by the landslide. The rocks formed a new barrier almost completely surrounding her. She spied a small tunnel yawning open to the rear. Disoriented from her tumble down the slope, she could not think where it might lead.

To the others, I hope.

Kale tucked Gymn away in the cape. She crawled on hands and knees through the opening. Metta hummed an encouraging tune in her ear. Long and straight, the tunnel took them to another, larger cave.

Kale stood and stretched, feeling her aching muscles.

This stone room looked much like the one they had camped in for several days. Great clouds of black dust had blown through the tight tunnel.

Kale took stock of her situation. She had the moonbeam cape and her two dragons. She had food, among other things, tucked in the cape's hollows. She wasn't badly hurt, nothing Gymn couldn't fix.

Not too bad. She swallowed the lump in her throat. *I wonder where the others are.*

43

THE MAZE

Leetu? Kale reached for the emerlindian with her mind.

Gymn peeked out of the cape, then darted to her shoulder to sit next to Metta.

Leetu?

"*Are you safe? Metta and Gymn?*"

Yes, we're fine, and you? The others?

"*Wizard Fenworth is unconscious. Librettowit has a nasty cut on his fore-head. Lee Ark has a broken arm. A boulder hit Brunstetter on the head, and he's dizzy. Otherwise he's all right except for cuts and bruises. Shimeran and Seezle are dirty but whole. Dar is too dirty to speak intelligibly. He's limping around. And he favors one side as if he has some broken ribs. He's muttering about his soiled clothing, not his injuries.*"

Kale almost smiled, imagining the doneel's disgust at the sooty dust on everything. But she pictured the old wizard, pale and still. *Fenworth?*

"*Librettowit thinks he tried to stem the landslide, and it was too much for him. I can't find any broken bones. He seems all right from what I can see. Gymn could tell us more.*"

Kale remembered the horror on Fenworth's face as he looked up at her. She shivered at the memory.

The black barrier had collapsed, and somehow Kale had made it happen. Now her comrades were hurt.

But if Fenworth had not been able to move the mass in three days, how could she have been responsible? She shook aside the unsettling feeling that her thoughts had sent the black rocks and gravel cascading down upon them all.

Where are you?

"*Still in The Cavern of Rainbows. But when the black barrier collapsed, the walls shifted. Several tunnels out of here appeared.*"

Should I try to come to you?

"*Yes, if you can. We need Gymn to help with the injuries.*"

Kale knew exactly which direction to go to find the others now. She could feel Leetu's presence. However, choosing the right tunnel proved difficult. There were so many.

Blue lightrocks studded the walls of some of the tunnels. Other tunnels were pitch black. Some were twice as high as Kale was tall. Some were barely big enough for her to squeeze into. A sickly sweet smell poured out of one. Others stank of damp and decay. Two smelled like cabbage boiling. Kale dreaded going into any of them.

Crawling through yet another tunnel that seemed to lead nowhere, she muttered, "At least you two are with me." She stroked each of the dragons, took a deep breath, and let it out slowly.

Reaching into one of the cape's hollows, she pulled out the lightrock and handed it to the little dragons. Then they went through the opening closest to where Kale could feel Leetu's presence. Metta and Gymn sat on her shoulder, holding the soft glowing lightrock between them.

Sometimes Kale walked.

Sometimes she crawled.

Hours later Kale had discovered how futile was her search. None of the tunnels they explored took them to her injured comrades. Some tunnels veered off in the wrong direction after she had crawled for what seemed miles. Others came to dead ends, and Kale had to inch backward to a spot where another tunnel converged with the one that went noplace.

All of the tunnels were filled with bugs and druddums. The insects crunched under her feet or crawled over her hands. They fell from the ceiling and slipped under the collar of her blouse.

The druddums tore through the stone corridors as if being chased, their normal speed accelerated by a frenzy, probably set off by the landslide. Kale never saw one slow down for anything. They slammed into her at irregular intervals. Sometimes she'd be hit and knocked over, then trodden upon by others following the first.

She grew weary and disheartened and more convinced than ever that all of this was the result of some rash act on her part. "I thought, *Move!* and the barrier fell apart. But it's ridiculous to think I could cause such devastation. I am just a slave girl."

Metta and Gymn did not respond to her words.

"I *was* a slave girl. Now I'm a servant of Paladin. That doesn't make any difference. I'm still an ignorant o'rant girl."

She backed into the most central cave she'd found and sat down in despair.

"Don't give up!" Leetu Bends' voice admonished her.

We've explored every tunnel going out of this cave. I'm so confused I don't remember which branches of which tunnels we've already been through. Kale knew her frustration rang in her words even though they were not spoken. She struggled to control her emotions. The last thing she wanted was to give the emerlindian another chance to say *"immature"* in a disdainful tone.

"Then mark them."

You mean start over? Go back through all the territory we've already explored?

"Sometimes you have to."

Leetu's patient tone irritated Kale. The o'rant girl spoke to her companion dragons instead of the emerlindian.

"How are we going to mark the tunnels as we go through them?"

Gymn jumped off her shoulder and glided to the entrance of the tunnel they had just left. He put his front foot in front of his face and spat. A fine green spray coated his paw. He stamped that foot on the wall. Metta leapt in the air, did a somersault, and let out a gleeful squeal. She zipped over to Gymn and proceeded to imitate him. She left a tiny purple paw print beside the green.

The system worked, but still it required hours of walking and crawling. Each time they rested for a few minutes, Gymn healed Kale's new hurts. Under the influence of his healing, she could have forgotten to eat.

But Metta liked mealtime and snacktime and naptime. She sang mealtime tunes every so often. The words would flit through Kale's consciousness and remind her to eat.

Kale watched Metta catching bugs, sometimes bringing extra ones to Gymn, who sat on his friend's lap and thrummed. The healing vibrations did much to ease Kale's discomfort physically, but her nagging thoughts remained hurtful.

"I don't understand why you think stopping to eat is better than eating bugs along the way," Kale snapped at the purple dragon.

Metta dropped on her haunches and stared at Kale.

Kale looked away from the dragon's sad eyes. "I'm sorry."

Metta flew across to land on her favorite spot, tucking herself under Kale's chin. She began to sing.

Kale chuckled and stroked the purple scales on the dragon's side with one finger. "Do you know a tune for every occasion?"

After a rest, Kale again began her hunt through the maze of tunnels. "We are so close this time." She sat beside another dead end.

Leetu?

"I know. You can't be more then a few feet away. Let me ask Brunstetter if he can move these boulders from this side. Perhaps we can break through."

In a few moments, Kale heard stone scraping against stone. The wall of rocks making up the blockage trembled. With a surge of hope, she picked up smaller stones and moved them away. In a matter of minutes a slanted hole appeared, and Kale looked into Brunstetter's smiling eyes.

"Welcome back, little stray," he said and winked. Kale laughed.

The urohm's huge face disappeared, and Leetu's popped into view. She, too, smiled and laughed. "Haven't you had a minute to wash your face, o'rant girl? You look like a thousand-year-old emerlindian."

Librettowit showed his face next, and when Kale saw the bloody bandage on his head, she gasped.

"Here, take Gymn. He can start the healing while we make the hole bigger for me to get through."

The librarian shook his head gingerly. "No, Kale, his power only works with you nearby, best if you can actually make the circle of healing by touching."

"Move aside, tumanhofer." Brunstetter ordered good-naturedly, his deep voice rumbling in a way that comforted Kale's raw emotions.

She leaned toward the opening to see if she could spot Fenworth, Dar, and the kimens. Dar and the kimens sat around Fenworth's still form. As Kale watched, their heads snapped up, their attention riveted by something out of Kale's line of vision.

Dar jumped up and pulled his sword from its scabbard. Kale heard the battle cry of a bisonbeck. Brunstetter dropped the rock in his hands and ran toward the camp. Leetu raced after him.

A swarm of soldiers descended on her friends before they had a chance to defend themselves. Shimeran and Seezle jumped in the air, but a net shot over them and captured the kimens as it fell. Dar didn't have a chance to duck into his shell. He moved slowly, and Kale knew Leetu was right, his injuries must be worse than just bruises.

What can I do? An explosion of light? Move mounds of dirt?... I don't know how!

She watched in helpless horror as Lee Ark and Brunstetter fell under the assault of dozens of bisonbeck warriors. When the fighting stopped, each of her comrades had been captured. Chains bound Leetu, Lee Ark, Brunstetter, Dar, and Librettowit to each other at the ankle and around the neck. A net entangled the kimens so tightly that they lay in a huddled heap. Four guards stood around Wizard Fenworth as if the old man would arise and smite them all. Kale cringed at the pointed spears inches away from the ancient and vulnerable wizard.

Not one of her comrades glanced toward the small opening where Kale's eyes peered through, watching as the bisonbecks destroyed the tents and scattered their belongings.

Leetu, what should I do?

"Stay out of sight."

Yes, but I can do something, can't I? To help you get free?

"Find the meech egg, o'rant girl. And get out of this mountain."

But—

"Follow orders, Kale. And don't play with your talents. Treat them with respect, or more disaster will fall upon your head."

The bisonbeck commander roared. His troops fell into military formation. A soldier roughly lifted the old wizard and slung him over his shoulder. Her friends began the march out of The Cavern of Rainbows.

Kale ground her teeth. "My talents. I don't help anyone with my talents. I cause disaster. Why? Why give a stupid o'rant slave talents?"

44

In the Stronghold

As soon as the last soldier marched through the exiting tunnel, Kale began to claw away loose stones around the small opening. Minutes later she crammed her body into the narrow hole and pushed and wiggled and squirmed until she fell out the other side. She tumbled and slid before coming to rest against a boulder covered with black dirt. Metta and Gymn flew through the shallow slit she'd made and landed beside her.

She stood and walked around in a daze. She picked up Fenworth's pointed wizard hat and bunched it into a wad, much the way the wizard did when he was thinking. She walked aimlessly around the destroyed campsite. Metta and Gymn followed, making sad chirruping noises to each other.

Kale stooped to pick up Dar's flute. A dent in the side showed rough treatment by the vicious bisonbecks.

"Dar will want this," she said to the dragons. "Maybe he can fix it." She wiped it off with the wizard's hat and stuck it into one of the hollows of her cape. She picked up Dar's smashed harmonica and several other small musical instruments, all variously damaged, and quickly stowed them away.

The tumanhofer's stack of books had been kicked over and thrown in all directions. Kale gathered them, dusted off the sooty grime, and fitted them into a hollow. Picking up a pair of Librettowit's reading spectacles, she noted a cracked lens and put it with the other things she had collected.

Collapsing on a boulder, gray with Crim Copper's smudge, Kale dropped her head into her hands, fighting the urge to cry.

With a shudder, she sat up. "It's no use pretending things aren't bad."

The dragons flew to her shoulders. "We've got to consider what's best to do and then do it."

She stared at the debris around her, absent-mindedly putting Fenworth's hat on her head. She shook herself as if trying to wake up.

"Keeping broken things won't help."

She pulled out the spectacles and intended to throw them as far as she could. Gymn hopped on her shoulder and trilled. The high-pitched warble pierced the silent room.

"What?" Kale lifted a hand to rub against her ear. Gymn's excited squeal had been all too close to her eardrum. At his urging, she looked at the broken lens. "It's fixed!"

Kale jumped to her feet. The dragons lost their balance, fluttered beside her for a moment, and then landed on the rocks. Kale pulled out the books and found the pages unwrinkled, untorn, the book covers pristine clean. The flute was dentless. She lifted the harmonica to her mouth and blew. A reedy chord resounded merrily in the forlorn cavern. She marveled at the undamaged instruments as she laid them in a row on the ground.

"You'd think somebody would have told me."

She repacked the items in her cape and continued to rummage through the mess left by the bisonbecks. She picked up items belonging to each of her comrades except the kimens. Again she puzzled over the fact that she had rarely seen them carry anything.

"Do you suppose they have hollows in their light clothes?"

The dragons didn't offer an opinion.

Kale picked up Leetu's bow, broken into two pieces. She looked from the pieces in her hands to the dragons watching her with expectant faces. Kale could feel them urging her to try it.

She fitted the two ends of the bow together. The shaft stretched taller than she did. Kale slipped it into the hollow opening. The bow slid in easily, moving down and down until the whole bow disappeared. Kale held her breath and pulled it back out. The jagged edges where she'd put the two pieces together had mended; no sign of breakage existed, not even a seam.

"Look at that! Wait till I show Leetu."

The emerlindian's words echoed in her memory. "Follow orders, Kale. And don't play with your talents. Treat them with respect, or more disaster will fall upon your head."

Kale looked quickly at the dragons. Both had turned their heads aside and refused to look her in the eye.

"This isn't my talent. It's something the cape does."

The dragons made grunty noises in their throats.

Kale growled back. "All right. Guilty," she said, and her shoulders slumped. "When will I ever learn?"

She shoved the bow back into the hollow and gathered Leetu's arrows into the leather quiver. When she finished, she gazed around The Cavern of Rainbows and sighed over its dulled appearance. Her eyes rested on one of the many tunnels leading out.

"Well, Gymn, Metta, we have things to do."

Kale marched across the disheveled room exiting the cavern by the same tunnel the bisonbeck warriors had used earlier.

I'm supposed to be looking for the meech egg. It is probably kept in the center of Risto's stronghold. The bisonbecks were probably returning to their underground fortress. It is reasonable to follow them. Now, if I just happen to come across my friends on the way as I'm looking for the meech egg, and I happen to see a way to help them escape, then that wouldn't be disobeying orders.

She could feel the direction she needed to turn each time she came to tunnels branching off, just as she could judge the distance between herself and the last of the marching soldiers. She put the hood and veil over her head so she could see in the dimmer passageways. Following her captured friends was not difficult. However, staying out of the way of citizens of this underground community became a problem.

For a while the stone corridors were eerily empty. No druddums, no insects. Kale concentrated on the movement of the troop of soldiers surrounding her comrades. Gymn and Metta darted about, unsuccessfully looking for snacks. As they approached one bend, the two dragons bolted for Kale and dove into their pocket-dens. She got the distinct impression someone was approaching around the blind corner and flattened herself against the wall, remaining still so that her cape hid her. She heard heavy footsteps slamming against the stone floor.

Five seconds later, two soldiers, large and surly, tramped past her without one look in her direction. She soon discovered that Gymn and Metta could hear someone's approach better than she could. As they neared the center of Risto's stronghold, the dragons warned her repeatedly when someone was coming.

The humid air became harder to breathe. A stale, rancid odor burned her throat. The dragons coughed, objecting to the unpleasant atmosphere. The tunnels widened, and they met carts pulled by donkeys and people on horseback.

Just when Kale thought she would not make any more progress with all the stopping they did for traffic, the army marched down a wide staircase and entered a less populated region. Kale and the dragons followed, and followed again, when the prisoners were taken down another, narrower set of stone steps.

The dungeon!

Gymn, Metta, soon they'll put our friends in cells and leave them. Maybe then we can do some good.

Once more the tunnels branched, this time in three different directions. The major part of the bisonbeck guard marched off to the left. A few took the weary prisoners down the central corridor. When Kale got to the intersection, she turned right.

She stopped and turned around, coming back to the point where the tunnels merged. To her left was the way back from where she had come. Straight ahead she could sense more bisonbecks than she had ever encountered before. To the right lay the dungeons, she was sure. Her body turned and headed back down the wrong hallway. She stopped again and tried to turn.

I don't know! she answered the dragons' inquiries. One foot moved forward, and Kale strained to keep the other from following. She lost the battle and took several steps before she could stop again.

She peered down the dark, rocky hall and saw nothing beyond dreary walls and a few dim lightrocks. She took a few steps forward before she even realized she was moving.

"I want to follow Dar and Leetu." She tried to turn. "But I can't." She stomped her foot. "What's down there? Is this a trap? Maybe it's the meech dragon egg pulling at me." She shivered as she looked at the cold stone walls of the wizard's domain, realizing she was far away from home, friends, and anything good. "Maybe Risto has some kind of enchantment that lures trespassers into his clutches. And I'm the next victim."

Metta and Gymn exchanged a nervous chitter. Kale understood they wanted to stop her in some way. Metta began to sing, and for an instant Kale felt a release from the pull. When it came back, it tugged so hard she ran a ways before she could slow herself down. She couldn't stop. Ahead she could see two bisonbeck guards standing at attention beside a large archway.

Probably Risto's hall where he receives visitors. He's probably waiting in there to see what his enchantment has brought him this time.

Don't go in with me, Metta, Gymn. Fly away, hide. There's no reason for you to be caught as well.

The soldiers ahead spotted her. They lowered their spears to ready position.

"Halt!" one ordered, but she was helpless to do as he commanded.

Metta began to sing, a slow melodious tune, soothing and peaceful.

Thank you very much, Metta. But my nerves are beyond succumbing to your ministrations. I'm about to be killed, I think.

The second guard took a step forward. "Halt!"

I'm trying. Believe me, I'm trying.

Metta crooned.

Why did Paladin choose a singing dragon? A fighting dragon, a fire dragon, an invisible dragon would have been useful.

Metta flew forward and circled the heads of the guards. They did not seem to notice her but stared at Kale's approach.

Maybe Metta is invisible.

Gymn gave an excited flip in the air and landed back on Kale's shoulder.

Neither guard challenged her again. Kale walked up to them and studied their faces as she passed. They breathed, but they did not blink. The pupils of their eyes were mere dots. Their gazes were locked on some point down the hallway where she had been moments before.

They don't see me. They don't hear me either? Metta continued to fly slowly around them, singing her soothing syllable-song. *She entranced them.*

Gymn somersaulted in the air. Kale turned her head to observe the room she entered.

Who will be here to greet me? More guards? More mesmerized guards, I hope... No one?

She searched the corners of the room with her eyes while she continued to step toward a wooden cabinet. Her palms itched to open the elaborate carved doors set in the opposite wall. Her hand went up to the knob, twisted, and pulled as soon as she reached it. The door swung open noiselessly.

Inside, a huge egg sat in a velvet-lined basket. It was twice as big around as Kale and as tall as she was from her waist to the top of her head.

Gymn chirruped a note of victory.

Kale put her hand tentatively on the hard shell. The surface shimmered with a pearlescent luster. *Don't be so happy, little friend. How am I supposed to lift something this big?*

45

THE VOICE OF EVIL

"Gymn, now I *have* to go get the others. Brunstetter could carry this, but I can't." Kale rubbed the cold surface of the giant meech egg with her fingertips. Colors surfaced on the glossy white shell and rippled like oil in a rain puddle.

Gymn flew into the huge cupboard and circled around the egg. His eyes glowed with admiration, and he voiced his excitement with a constant stream of trills and chirrups.

"It is beautiful," Kale agreed. She tried to step back from the meech egg to get a better look. Her feet did not respond and her hand stuck to the shell.

"No!" She pulled again. She grasped the stuck hand with her other and yanked. The palm resting on the egg burned as if she were ripping off her skin.

Tears welled up in her eyes. "Is this a trap? Do I have to stay here until Risto comes?"

"Ah! The o'rant girl." A deep voice filled her mind. A gloating laugh followed the words. *"I suspected ten years ago that your existence was a myth. I'm actually gratified that you have come to me."*

Who are you?

"Wizard Andor Tarum Risto, and you are Kale, the last of the Allerions."

For one second, Kale wanted to ask him about the Allerions. But she realized that evil had access to her mind, and Granny Noon had warned her about the dangers of communicating with the wicked in any form.

I stand under Wulder's authority. As she repeated the words the old emerlindian had given her, she felt Risto receding from her thoughts. *I stand under Wulder's authority.* She heard his sinister chortle before his presence completely left her mind.

"I stand under Wulder's authority." She looked quickly around the room, expecting the evil wizard to appear.

"We have to get out of here. Surely, he's coming."

She pulled away from the egg and fell over, sitting down hard on the stone floor when her hand was released. She tried to jump to her feet, ready to run from the large chamber, but her legs would not obey.

Gymn chirped at her.

"I *can't* take the egg with me!" She turned on Gymn and blistered him with a frustrated glare. "Think of something useful."

Kale clenched her fists and drew her arms inside the moonbeam cape, folding them over her chest.

I can't carry it. What can I do?

"Nothing, o'rant girl." Risto's voice mocked her. The taunting words sounded as if they came from somewhere in the room. Kale whirled around but saw nothing in the shadows.

"I stand under Wulder's authority," she shouted. She clapped her hands over her ears and tried to block any word Risto might hurl at her. The cloth of the cape came up as well in her haste to cover her ears.

"The cape," Kale whispered. "If I can get the egg onto the cape, I might be able to push it into a hollow. Then I could carry it!"

She whipped the cape off her shoulders and spread it on the floor, lining side up, in front of the cabinet. Gymn flew around her as if inspecting her actions from every angle.

"I don't think I will hurt it if it drops," she said. "But I'll try to ease it down just in case."

Kale put her arms around the egg and braced her legs, ready to lift with all her strength. She gave a mighty heave and discovered the egg weighed less than Leetu. She lost her balance and staggered backward. Gymn flipped several times in the air and landed on the floor just as she steadied herself. She carefully lowered the egg onto her cape, then stood shaking her head in amazement.

"Weight's not a problem," she said after a moment. "But the opening to the hollow is way too small for the meech egg." With Gymn sitting close, intently watching her struggle, Kale tried to get the hollow opening to stretch.

It's hopeless.

"Ah yes, o'rant girl. It is hopeless. But your task is unnecessary at any rate."

Kale wrinkled her brow and tried to think. Her head hurt now as Risto mindspoke. She needed to concentrate on how to solve the problem of moving the egg. The talent that attracted her to dragon eggs would not let her leave without the meech egg.

"I would like to discuss my plans with you. Would a new race be such a bad thing? Did Wulder really say new races should not be created? I merely want to supply the world with a work force."

Kale regretted not ever having read the great tomes which told the history of Wulder's involvement with the world. She knew the general story from tavern songs and bedtime stories. Wulder molded the land and sea and air out of His thoughts. He'd taken a bit of land and sea and air and formed each of the seven high races. But there were many things she did not know. She didn't know if Wulder had said not to make any more races.

The ache in her temples eased a bit. Now she remembered that in all the tavern songs the making of the seven low races resulted in tragedy. A sharp pain streaked behind her eyes. Kale bent over and held her head in her hands.

"Did you like cleaning chicken coops? Scrubbing floors? The race of beings I propose will actually get pleasure out of doing things the high races disdain. This is not a bad thing. You are not wise enough to make judgments against me, Kale Allerion."

The way Risto said her last name made Kale shiver. He hated her. She knew it.

I stand under Wulder's authority. I stand under Wulder's authority.

The pain in her head subsided. She sank to the floor, feeling drained.

Mistress Meiger's blue scarf! I can make a sling like the ones I used for carrying an infant while I worked.

Gymn dove into a pocket and returned in only a moment with the long strip of soft cloth. Kale tied the bottom two corners of the cape to one end of the scarf and the top two to the other. The large meech egg hung as if in a snug hammock. With the scarf over one shoulder and across her chest, the cape cradled the egg against Kale's back. She felt no weight to speak of, but the shifting bundle was bulky and cumbersome.

"It's the best we can do, Gymn. Let's get Metta and get out of here."

Metta continued to fly around the two guards and sing until Kale and Gymn had raced down the corridor away from the room.

"It is hopeless, little Allerion. Hopeless."

I stand under Wulder's authority.

Metta caught up with them. Kale wondered how long the effect of the purple dragon's song would keep the guard immobile.

Better to hurry and not waste time wondering.

Kale could feel in which direction the masses of Risto's minions were gathered. She figured she could avoid pockets of concentration. She needed to go higher as quickly as possible to reach a tunnel leading outside. Her plan was to avoid meeting anyone and move upward at all times.

At the first corner she met a parade of people moving down the hall as if they all had a common gathering place in mind. Few of these citizens of the underground stronghold were soldiers. The smattering of high races among the bisonbeck women and tradesmen puzzled Kale. She watched for a moment or two before turning back into the tunnel she'd already traveled. She'd have to find another, less crowded passageway.

"You see, o'rant girl, not all your people are so stubborn. Some embrace the benefits of joining me in my efforts to make the world a more pleasant place to live, an easier place, a place where individuals struggle less."

I stand under Wulder's authority.

I won't listen to Risto. If those people are so thrilled to follow him, why aren't they smiling? Those poor people looked as mesmerized as the guards did when Metta sang to them.

Granny Noon said never to mindspeak with one of the evil ones. They get a foothold in your mind that way. I won't listen to him.

I stand under Wulder's authority. I stand under Wulder's authority.

After several false starts, dodging people, backtracking, and hiding, Kale found herself trudging down a stone hallway with branches sprouting off every few yards. Small niches in the wall where boulders had crumbled and fallen into the corridor offered places to hide. Kale was ready to jump into one at any moment. The feeling of a great populace of bisonbecks nearby made her edgy.

Gymn and Metta flew for the most part instead of riding on her shoulders. Grateful for their vigilance in spotting trouble, Kale also longed for them to be constantly near.

"I walk beside you, dear o'rant girl." Risto's voice came rich and warm into her thoughts. *"I am not in the habit of sending my friends into dangerous situations alone. I find it reprehensible that you must face these hardships without proper training, without comrades. Who prevented you from going to The Hall? Who allowed your friends to be hurt and captured?"*

Before Kale could repeat the words that closed off Risto's intrusion, Metta and Gymn darted back around the corner. Kale scrambled into one of the stone pockets in the wall behind fallen boulders and flattened herself on the floor. She knew as long as she was still, the cape would cloak the egg from sight.

Kale held her breath as the bisonbeck soldiers stopped a few feet from where she hid. She could see something of their movements between two rocks. Two argued vehemently over whether or not the men had time to go to the alehouse before evening duty. Three men, waiting for the arguing two to come to a decision, leaned their massive shoulders against the walls and rested. One man came and sat on the boulder shielding Kale and her friends.

Kale felt Gymn trembling within his pocket-den. Her own heart pounded. She clenched her fists, willing herself to stay still.

"You see the peril you are subjected to. If you were under my command, these men would be no threat to you."

Leave me alone!

"But I don't want to leave you alone. I care about what happens to you.

Ask yourself, Kale Allerion, who is beside you in this time of trouble? Paladin? Wulder? No. I am. I offer help."

Again Risto's tone of voice, smooth and coaxing, slipped on the name *Allerion.* A bitter edge poisoned the sweet, persuasive speech.

Kale gasped. She had been listening to him. *I stand under Wulder's authority.*

Just as she felt the heavy presence of Risto leave her mind, a strong hand grasped her shoulder and jerked her out of hiding.

"The o'rant girl!" A coarse voice bellowed in triumph.

"Surely it is not the one Risto seeks."

"You fool, who else would it be?"

"One of the peasants."

"A drudge. Look at the burden it carries."

"They are all at evening discourse. None would be brave enough to forgo the instruction."

"Let's see what it carries."

Kale twisted in the bisonbeck's hard hold and kicked out. He grunted but did not loosen his grip.

"Aargh!" cried another. "My eyes!"

Kale spotted an irate soldier wiping purple dye from his face. He pawed at his eyes. "I can't see!"

"Minor dragons! It *is* the mighty Dragon Keeper. Hold fast, Deemer. It will be your head if it escapes."

Kale squirmed against the iron grasp. Both Metta and Gymn flew around the bisonbecks' heads, spitting into their faces. When a spew of green or purple liquid landed directly in a soldier's eyes, he doubled over in pain, clawing at his face, trying to wipe away the thick spittle.

The last one to get sprayed was the one holding Kale. His hands jerked away from her shoulders. She ran. The little dragons zoomed beside her. Their wingtips brushed her hair and cheeks. The outraged cries of the blinded men echoed in the stone corridor.

The meech egg bounced against her back, reminding her that she could only duck into tunnels large enough for its unwieldy bulk.

She passed several small crawlways and turned into a dark burrow she hoped would be a tight squeeze for the soldiers should they recover enough to follow. The passageway narrowed. She ducked her head out from under the blue scarf strap and dragged the egg behind her. She came to a fork.

Which way?

"You are inside my stronghold, o'rant girl. Each way leads to me."

I stand under Wulder's authority.

The two dragons sat before her, peering down the small dingy tunnels. "Do you know which way to go?"

Metta and Gymn looked at each other and exchanged a few words Kale couldn't understand. But she understood their thoughts. Each would take a tunnel and explore. Kale was to rest.

Kale almost laughed when Metta's motherly suggestion to eat something and take a little nap settled in her mind. But the idea of their leaving her, if only for a few minutes, struck her heart with terror.

What if Gymn runs into something scary and faints?

The little green dragon gave her a disgusted look.

Yes, I did notice you fought that last bunch of bisonbecks. She answered his prodding question, even though, until that moment, she hadn't realized what an accomplishment the skirmish had been for her dragon friend. *I'm proud of you.*

Gymn nodded his satisfaction with her praise and zoomed into one of the tunnels. Metta disappeared into the other.

Eat? I guess I have to.

She took out a package from inside her cape and nibbled on tasty cheese sticks made by Lee Ark's wife.

In a moment, Metta came back. The tunnel had ended in a pile of rubble. She sat in Kale's lap and shared the cheese, turning her nose up at the bread. When they finished, the purple dragon curled up on Kale's knee and hummed one of Dar's "digestion" songs.

Kale squeezed her eyes shut against sudden tears.

"Most of my people are settled in their homes for the night. A hearth

glowing with a warm fire. The smell of stew and fresh baked bread left over from dinner with their families. You don't have to be alone."

Kale sighed, weary from a long day filled with troubles. *I stand under Wulder's authority.* She heard Risto's mocking laugh and then welcomed the silence. Her chin dropped against her chest, and she dozed.

The dungeon! The dungeon! A hole. Leetu, Dar, Fenworth!

Kale awoke to Gymn's frantic explanation of what he had found. Kale reached for the blue scarf and followed the excited dragon. After a long crawl, Kale stopped behind Metta and Gymn as they hovered next to a natural slit in the stone wall. She heard Wizard Fenworth's scratchy voice.

"Uncomfortable things, quests. Not always predictable. A bit boring when nothing is going on. But then dungeons are always boring. Quests! What a bother. Lose things, find things. Meet the most unpleasant people. Present company excepted, of course."

46

Some Things Can Be Moved, Some Can't

Kale peered through the little hole and almost whooped with joy.

Leetu sat with Librettowit, deep in a discussion. Lee Ark, Dar, and Brunstetter leaned against one wall, eyes shut, looking pale and unhealthy. Shimeran and Seezle were not in sight. Fenworth sat cross-legged in the center of their cell. One arm looked very treeish. But the other hand rubbed across his bald spot, keeping that side free of leaves and twigs. Without his hat, the old man looked very forlorn.

A wizard should not be without his hat. He looks so old.

As soon as the thought flitted across her mind, Gymn dove into the cape and came out, pulling the large pointed hat behind him. Kale grinned and nodded. She took the hat from him and stuffed it through the small hole. There she wiggled it back and forth, waiting for it to catch someone's attention.

"See," said Fenworth. "You lose things, you find things. Now there's my hat, and it's about time."

Leetu jumped up and ran to snatch the hat out of Kale's hand. The welcoming smile on her face transformed into a glare almost immediately.

"You're supposed to be searching for the meech egg."

"I've got it right here."

"Then you're supposed to be taking it out of the mountain."

"I've been trying." Kale glared right back at Leetu. "That's not such an easy job. There are miles of tunnels down here, and most of them go in circles."

"Here now, mustn't quarrel." Fenworth came up behind Leetu and reclaimed his hat. He smoothed the brim, straightened the pointy crown, and placed it on his head. "Ah, now that feels better." He smiled broadly at Kale. "I assume you have your dragons with you."

"Yes sir."

"Let's have Gymn, then, and if he doesn't mind assisting me, we'll patch up our comrades' aches and woes. Metta could sing us some encouragement."

Gymn wiggled through the opening and flew to the old wizard's shoulder.

"I thought Gymn could only heal with me." Kale frowned as both her dragons attached themselves to Fenworth.

Leetu put her fists on her hips and frowned. "Only you and any wizard in the service of Paladin." Her frown deepened. "Actually, I think an evil wizard could also force Gymn to heal, but I also think it would hurt him."

Kale started to tell Leetu that Risto had spoken to her, but she hesitated. Shame washed over her as though she had done something bad. Instead of confiding in her mentor, she turned back to the egg in its moonbeam cape sling and undid the knots so she could more easily get to the hollows.

She called Leetu back to the hole. "Here is your bow. Where are Shimeran and Seezle?"

Leetu took her weapon, running an experienced hand over the wood, checking for damage. "They are being kept someplace else. It would have been too easy for them to escape this cell."

Kale looked across the small room and noted the wall of bars. The kimens could have walked right between them. She passed Dar's flute and harmonica into Leetu's waiting hand. Some of the instruments were too big to fit through.

"I have your books and Librettowit's, but they won't fit either."

"Why did you bother?"

"I don't know. I thought you'd want them."

"I seem to remember telling you—"

"I know, Leetu, I just picked them up. I don't know why."

Kale pushed Dar's small sword and scabbard through the hole. She had difficulty fitting the hilt of Brunstetter's sword through, and the sheath would not fit through even with Leetu pulling and Kale pushing. When she had passed as much of her friends' belongings as she could to Leetu, she peered into the small room to see what progress Fenworth and Gymn had made.

Dar sat up and gave her a wave and a wink. Lee Ark and Brunstetter carefully inspected their returned weapons. Librettowit had his reading glasses on and was reading a small volume of poetry.

Fenworth walked over to the opening where Leetu stood on one side and Kale on the other.

"Food would be helpful, dear girl. And water."

"Food?"

Leetu sighed. "You picked up books but not food."

"I have some left from my provisions." Kale handed over all that she had.

"You see, they don't even appreciate what you've brought them."

"I stand under Wulder's authority."

Both Fenworth and Leetu's heads turned sharply as she uttered the phrase with anger.

"Risto?" asked Fenworth with an eyebrow raised.

Kale nodded and then realized he probably couldn't see more than her nose and mouth from where he stood. "Yes," she admitted.

"He's been badgering you?"

"Yes," she whispered.

"How like him." Fenworth shuffled off to the others, carrying parcels of food in his arms.

Leetu moved closer to the hole and leaned forward. "Kale, you haven't been talking *with* Risto, have you?"

"No!" Kale shifted uncomfortably. "Not much."

The frown disappeared from Leetu's face and compassion registered in her eyes. "Are you all right?"

Kale took a big breath. "I think so."

"He lies."

"Yes."

"It sounds like truth."

"Yes."

Leetu grinned and winked at Kale. "If you were an emerlindian, you'd be a shade darker."

Kale's eyes widened and her mouth dropped open. She snapped it shut before Leetu could say something about her not knowing anything or having a lot to learn.

Dar sprinted across the prison cell, waving his harmonica.

"Kale!" He reached a hand through the opening to touch the one she had resting there. "You are a sight for sore eyes, what little I can see of you. You have the meech egg?"

She nodded.

"She needs to take it out of here." Leetu sounded practical and gruff again. "We have our weapons. We can escape. You go on before us. Don't wait."

Kale shook her head. "I'm getting nowhere. I need help."

Lee Ark joined them. He no longer held one injured arm cradled against his chest. "I agree with the o'rant girl. Leetu, you assume too much. Her talents are strong, but she is untrained. Paladin chose her, which certifies her ability, but he also chose us to accompany her. We are stronger together."

Dar looked into Kale's eyes and gave her another wink. He turned to Lee Ark and nodded pointedly at the hole through which Kale stared. "It seems to me that we have a problem in this togetherness thing."

Their marione commander gave a decisive nod and walked back to confer with Brunstetter. The little dragons flew back to the hole and squeezed through. Both were exhilarated over their success. They chattered to each other until Kale interrupted.

"I don't think Brunstetter can move any of this rock."

Metta and Gymn both cocked their heads and inspected the wall of granite as they sat on her shoulder. They muttered to each other, and Kale got the gist of their thoughts. People had the strangest notions of how to spend their time.

"They want to get out of the dungeon," she explained. "Can you look further down this tunnel and see if there is a way out?"

They darted off without responding. Brunstetter looked the hole over. Fenworth examined it as well.

"Tut-tut. Some things can't be moved easily. I could make Kale smaller if you want her in here with us," he offered. "But it would be more to the point for us to go out there with her. Can't say I like these accommodations. Food is inedible as well."

"They haven't brought us any food," said Librettowit at his elbow.

The wizard jumped. "Don't scare me like that, Wit. Why aren't you at your books? Proves my point though. Can't very well eat food that isn't served. Therefore, it is inedible." He turned and whispered to Dar in a voice loud enough for all to hear. "Sneaky, quiet fellows are librarians. One moment he has his nose in a book, the next he's dragging a decent, respectable wizard off on a harrowing quest. No respect for my age and station in life. Librettowit's useful, I have to admit. Still, he can't cook. He's my friend, though, and you have to make allowances for friends. None of them are perfect. Very few of them can cook."

"Harrumph!" grunted Librettowit and tramped away. The wizard, shaking his head in befuddlement, watched the tumanhofer stomp across the cell.

Kale's attention caught on the flutter of leathery wings. Metta and Gymn had returned.

"They've found Shimeran and Seezle," Kale told Lee Ark. "I'm going to go see if I can get them out. Then we'll come back for you."

Lee Ark nodded.

"You might remember," interrupted Leetu in Kale's mind, *"who is in command. It is more proper to ask Lee Ark if you can go, rather than tell him."*

Kale felt her face burn red. She looked quickly from Leetu's disapproving face to Lee Ark's amused one. She heard Dar chuckle and looked at him.

"I think," said the doneel with a cocky grin, "our little o'rant slave girl is doing a good job of thinking for herself."

Are you sure you don't read my mind?

"Never. Go see if you can help our kimen friends."

Kale followed Metta and Gymn, dragging the meech egg on the cape. The passageway came to an abrupt end, opening into a chamber. Kale crouched in the tunnel about halfway up one wall.

In the center of this stone room, a sphere floated. Smaller than the ones Kale had seen from a distance, hanging over the city of Vendela, this orb contained the two kimens. Kale caught her breath. Shimeran and Seezle sat back to back, legs crossed, knees pulled up to their chins, eyes closed, and their arms folded and resting on their knees. Their hair fell limply around their shoulders and flowed to their feet. As still as stone, they looked liked lifeless carvings.

Kale examined the empty room. She could drop to the floor some six feet below her, but how would she reach the floating sphere?

"Can you fly to them?" she asked her companions.

The emphatic *no* surprised Kale.

"Shimeran? Seezle?"

No response.

Shimeran! Seezle!

Still no response. She wouldn't give up. Around the room many tunnels led out of the chamber. If she could find something to aid her in one of those tunnels…

She tied the blue scarf to the corners of the cape once more, slipped the makeshift sling onto her back and sat down on the rock edge, preparing to jump to the ground. Her legs and feet felt cold as if she had submerged them into Baltzentor's Pond near River Away.

It must have something to do with whatever it is that floats the ball.

Both Metta and Gymn objected, chittering warnings about the room, but their thoughts came in an overlapping rush. Kale couldn't sort them out, and she was in no mood to wait. She pushed off the shelf created by the end of the tunnel and plunged into air as thick as water.

She fell but did not land on the floor. The meech egg thumped against her back. Kale bobbed upward like a cork on a fishing line. It felt so much like being in the pond Kale instinctively kicked her legs and "swam" toward the orb. She put both hands on the surface of the sphere and felt the transparent material give under her palms. She pushed harder but did not break through. However, in response to her shove, the orb floated away from her.

I wonder if I could get this ball back to Fenworth. He could probably open it.

She looked back at the tunnel where Metta and Gymn sat anxiously waiting for her.

That direction only takes me back to a tiny slit in the wall.

She looked at the numerous other openings leading out of the small chamber. She made up her mind almost immediately.

That one looks the right size and the right direction.

Kale shivered against the cold air surrounding her.

Best get moving before I freeze.

She put her shoulder to the sphere and pushed, moving her legs in a strong swimmer's kick. The meech egg dragged behind her, making her movements clumsy. Finally, she bumped into the wall above the tunnel she'd picked out. She pulled herself to the top of the kimens' prison and sat on it to push it downward. After several tries she pushed it into the rock opening.

The sphere burst, spilling Shimeran and Seezle onto the hard floor. A sparkling light filled the room for an instant. The kimens curled into balls, rolled over a couple of times, then sprang to their feet. They shook their heads, sending their already wild hair flying in all directions.

Shimeran placed his hands on his hips and surveyed his surroundings. Seezle squealed with delight and sprang across the expanse to hug Kale's neck.

"I thought you were dead." Kale laughed with relief. Seezle's warm body tickled a little.

"Whyever did you think that?" asked Shimeran.

"You were so still."

"We were waiting."

"Your lights weren't shining."

Seezle giggled. "You saw our underwear."

Shimeran gave his sister an impatient look.

Kale wrinkled her brow, trying to remember what the stonelike figures of the two kimens looked like. "Uh, I don't remember seeing anything but a lot of hair."

That sent Seezle into another round of giggles accompanied by acrobatics.

Shimeran sighed. "Kimen skin is very much like a covering, like a finely knitted stocking without seams." He scowled at Seezle. She quit prancing and stood in one place but continued to quiver with glee. Shimeran focused on Kale.

"Where are the others?"

Kale pointed across the room behind her. "Gymn and Metta are waiting over there. Fenworth and the others are in a prison cell."

"Can you find them from here?"

Kale took a moment to get her bearings and locate Leetu. She tilted her head toward the tunnel behind them. "They should be down that way. But half these tunnels end abruptly, and you have to backtrack."

The kimen leader nodded. "Do you need help fetching the minor dragons?"

"No."

"Then do so quickly."

He could have said thanks.

The thought startled her. Had Risto said that? No, it was her own thought. Where was Risto all this time? Why was he so quiet and not pestering her?

Kale dove into the room and swam across as easily as if she were swimming to the opposite shore of Baltzentor's Pond. The dragons would not fly in the room, but rode back across on Kale's head. Their clawed feet dug into her scalp. They jumped off into the opening just as they reached it and stood huddled together looking fearfully at the now-deserted chamber.

"Why do they find that place so dreadful?" Kale asked.

"The heavy air would have clogged their tiny lungs," said Shimeran.

"I didn't feel anything."

"No, you probably could have lasted an hour or more before you real-ized you were drowning."

Kale looked back into the clear air and wondered what other hidden dangers they would encounter on this quest.

She shifted the sling on her back and turned to follow the others down the passageway.

The meech egg thrummed. A loud thrum. It vibrated her shoulder blades. It could be heard distinctly in the stone tunnel. It echoed and grew louder with each beat. Surely every bisonbeck in the region could hear the meech egg's contented thrum.

47

WHICH WAY OUT?

As Shimeran, Seezle, Kale, and the dragons approached the dungeon cell from one end of the long tunnel, four bisonbeck guards approached it from the other.

"We heard you coming," said Dar when they reached the cell.

"So did they," Kale answered, nodding to the burly men out of the prisoners' sight.

Shimeran dropped to one knee beside the locked door and placed his hands in a cup to receive his sister's tiny feet. Seezle stood on this makeshift boost and reached a hand inside the keyhole. In a moment the door swung open. Lee Ark, Brunstetter, Dar, and Leetu jumped into the corridor with their weapons ready. The bisonbecks charged.

Leetu slew the lead soldier with an arrow. Dar let fly two small daggers and downed another. Though Lee Ark and Brunstetter were massive, they moved with quick precision. The marione and urohm dispatched the remaining two warriors in a brief flurry of hand-to-hand combat.

"Is there any way to quiet that egg?" Lee Ark asked as he cleaned his blade before sheathing it.

The egg's monotone thrum, drowned out in the din of battle, now sounded loud in the rock corridor. It hung against Kale's back, gently vibrating.

The marione commander looked straight at Kale, and she suddenly felt guilty. "No, I mean, I don't know." She looked at Leetu and Dar. Both shrugged and looked to Fenworth. He shook his head and turned to his librarian.

"Well?" The wizard cocked an eyebrow.

"I believe," said Librettowit, "Kale is carrying the book containing a reference to meech eggs in her cape."

Kale slipped the sling off her back and quickly located the books. She pulled out a heavy brown volume.

Librettowit frowned and shook his head. "No, smaller."

He rejected each book Kale found until she reached her arm into the hollow up to her shoulder and recovered a small blue leather book with ancient yellowed pages.

The librarian frowned as he opened it. "Someone has been restoring these volumes." He leveled a glare at the o'rant girl. "Risky business. You could do a lot of damage."

Kale shook her head and spread her hands in an innocent gesture. "Not me, it was the cape."

Librettowit carefully turned the fragile pages until he came to a passage of interest. He harrumphed a few times as he read.

"I could send it to my castle," suggested Fenworth.

"No," said the tumanhofer and scratched his brow.

"Use it to bake a cake and then do the backward spell once we're out of this hideous mountain."

"No," said Librettowit and squinted fiercely behind his spectacles.

Lee Ark, Brunstetter, and Leetu stood at attention. Dar shifted from foot to foot. With big yawns, the minor dragons disappeared into their pocket-dens. Fenworth stroked his beard, dislodging a whole family of mice and a sparrow.

"Just as I feared," Librettowit said.

"What can we do?" asked the wizard.

"Nothing."

"Nothing? You went to university so that in a time of crisis you come up with nothing? Preposterous. We should have brought a plumber instead of a librarian."

He turned to address Lee Ark. "I knew it at the time, but he mopes if you leave him at home."

The tumanhofer's face went red beneath his whiskers. With his book tucked under one arm, he stepped in front of the old wizard and with a pointed finger jabbed him in the beard at waist level. "I didn't want to come on this quest. I told you I'm a librarian, not an individual given to questing."

Fenworth bent forward and growled. "You should have told me you were a plumber! I would have left a plumber at home. In fact, I did. I *did* leave the plumber at home and brought a librarian."

Librettowit shook his fist in the wizard's face. "You don't even know a plumber."

Lee Ark stepped forward, separating them. He stood between the angry men and patted each on a shoulder. "If the bisonbecks don't hear the egg, they will hear you. I suggest we leave."

Fenworth straightened and looked at the floor strewn with bisonbeck warriors slain minutes before. "Quite a good idea, actually. It's getting crowded down here." He looked down the dungeon corridor in both directions. "Which way would you suggest we go, Wit? You've always had a good head for directions. Especially underground."

Librettowit signaled for the others to follow and led them back the way Kale had come with Seezle and Shimeran. As they passed the room where the orb had floated, Kale touched Leetu's arm and whispered.

"I haven't heard Risto's voice in my head for a long time. What do you suppose he is up to?"

"He's up to capturing us again. You haven't heard him because the rest of us put a shield around you."

"How?"

"The same way you blocked him with the words Granny Noon gave you. We knew you were in peril so we kept up the block for you."

"You can do that?"

She nodded.

Kale looked at her companions trudging through the tunnel, following the tumanhofer. "All of you?"

"All of us in the cell."

"What did you say?"

"We stand together under Wulder's authority and offer a shield of protection from Risto's poisonous words around Kale's mind."

"And the words worked?"

"The words didn't work, Kale. Wulder worked."

Another four bisonbeck guards barreled down the corridor at them. Lee Ark and Brunstetter sprang in front of Librettowit.

Leetu pushed Kale behind Dar and the wizard. "Keep that egg safe," she ordered and ran forward to enter the fray.

The wizard changed into a tree. Dar stood ready with a dagger and his short sword drawn. The bisonbecks did not break through the comrades' line of defense.

Kale gingerly stepped over the legs of one of the fallen warriors when Lee Ark gave the all clear and Fenworth was persuaded to change back into himself. The sight of blood still made her queasy. The still forms of the dead soldiers looked capable of jumping up and resuming their fierce battle.

Kale and the wizard fell into step together. Dar and the kimens guarded the rear, Lee Ark, Brunstetter, and Leetu followed directly behind Librettowit who seemed confident about his directions.

"Why can't you just whirl us out of here, Wizard Fenworth?"

"Whirl? Whirl! What type of scientific activity is whirl?"

She decided not to let him distract her. "Whirl, as in move people without regard to time or distance from one place to another, as when you whirled our party from The Midways to your castle. Whirl, the useful action of a wizard in times of necessity."

The wizard scowled at her with narrowed eyes but kept walking.

"You didn't happen to pick up my walking stick, now did you?"

"No, I'm sorry. I didn't see it."

"You didn't place it in your cape hollow?"

"No sir."

Fenworth turned his attention to those in front of them. Kale peeked at the wizard's frowning face. He didn't look open to any more questions.

They moved on. The egg thrummed. Kale shifted the light weight to the center of her back. "About the whirling out of the mountain."

"The walking stick would have been useful."

"You could put your hand on my shoulder, sir."

He promptly clapped his wrinkled hand over Kale's blue scarf strap and gave her a gentle squeeze. They walked on, turning occasionally and once climbing two flights of stone steps. Soldiers in groups of four tried to stop them twice.

She could sense the whereabouts of the underground populace. She knew Librettowit was leading them to an uninhabited region.

"Wizard Fenworth, can you do something to get us out of here safely?"

"You know, dear girl, you have a mind like your mother's."

She held her breath, hoping the old man would say more.

He took a deep breath, coughed a little, and squeezed her shoulder. "The cape did not mend the items you put in the hollow."

"It didn't?"

"Not by itself."

She puzzled over the statement. "I didn't do anything, sir. At least, I don't think I did."

"No?"

She tried to remember what she was thinking at the time. Something about doing something useful instead of sitting around in a daze. "I don't think I did anything."

"You didn't happen to be wearing my hat?"

Oh no! I was! I wonder if it's a great crime to put a wizard's hat on your head. I mean, if you aren't a wizard. If you're just a slave girl. I mean, a servant.

There's no use trying to keep it a secret.

"Yes sir. I believe I did. Just to have my hands free to sort through the debris and pick things up. I didn't mean any disrespect, Wizard Fenworth."

"The combination of the hat and the cape and your talents as an Allerion mended the broken items you put in the hollow." He patted her shoulder. "I shall enjoy having you as an apprentice, I think. That is, if we get out of this mountain alive."

"About whirling, sir?"

"No, Kale."

48

Moving Heaven and Earth

With each tunnel they turned into, the questing party moved farther away from the underground populace. No bisonbeck guards challenged them after they entered a natural cavern deep in the mountain. The ceiling here vaulted high above their heads. The scattered tiny lightrocks looked like stars in the night sky. A trickle of water ran in a meandering stream across the footpath. The travelers had to cross and recross as they followed Librettowit.

"Clever, very clever," muttered Fenworth under his breath at regular intervals.

"What's he done?" asked Kale, looking ahead at the tumanhofer librarian as he trod purposefully forward.

"Not, he. Me." Fenworth leaned heavily on Kale's shoulder as they walked. "Bringing a plumber would have been a total waste of time. Librarians are handy. Tumanhofer librarians, when you are under a tumanhofer mountain, are especially useful."

"Where is he taking us?"

"Who?"

"Librettowit."

"Out of the mountain."

"He knows the way? He's been here before?"

"Librettowit is a history buff. Knows about old mines. This one probably hasn't seen a tumanhofer pick in over a thousand years. Thing is, Wit knew it was here, and he knows where the gate is."

Kale's shoulders straightened. "A gate out of the mountain?"

"Tumanhofers like gates. And onions. And cheese. Books, of course. And mechanical things. Handy in an agricultural way, as well."

Kale spoke quickly, trying to stop the wizard's flow of conversation before he got completely off track. "Will there be tumanhofers at the gate?"

"Wouldn't think so."

They moved on, watching their footing on a particularly rough patch.

Fenworth coughed, having some trouble clearing his throat. "Do hope the gate's open. Likely to be shut, though. Tumanhofers like things closed up and tidy. Old gate. Might not open if it's shut. Might not close if it's open." Fenworth had another fit of coughing.

"We'll stop here to rest." Lee Ark gestured to a grouping of flat rocks that looked as if they might have been placed for people to relax and converse. It had the feel of the common room in Fenworth's castle.

Kale sat next to the wizard and removed the sling from her back. The meech egg thrummed steadily. She rested her arm over the bulky package of her cape and contents. The minor dragons climbed out of their pocket-dens and blinked at the surroundings. Once they saw the others in the party resting, they darted off to look for food.

"A cup of tea would be nice," Dar said as he eased himself onto a rock and stretched out on his back, his hands cupped behind his neck. Black grime dimmed the bright yellow of the doneel's clothing. His brocade jacket had a rip in the arm seam. Stains spattered his ragged pants, and scuff marks obliterated the high shine of his boots.

Lee Ark and Brunstetter took out their weapons and began sharpening the blades. Kale shivered at the sight and looked over her shoulder. She could not sense anything lurking in the shadows. It had been quite awhile since she had noticed the presence of any bisonbecks either near or far.

Leetu sat down and pulled out an arrow. She fiddled with its feathers and then changed it for another. Kale wondered what she was doing.

The emerlindian looked up at her. "Kale, look in the things Granny Noon gave you. See if you can find moerston bark. We can chew on that."

Kale remembered the bumpy bark and Granny Noon's advice to use it when hungry. "It has some nutritional qualities," the old emerlindian had told her. "But for the heart, it is much more helpful. The little bit of food you get from it will seem like much more, because it tastes good and refreshes your mouth."

Kale dug in her cape and pulled out the packet. She got to her feet to pass the contents around. She put the last piece in her mouth and bit down. It tasted like a tea Mistress Meiger brewed and then chilled to serve in the tavern on summer days.

The cramp in Kale's stomach eased. She longed for the peaceful days of a slave when she was often tired, often lonely, but never hungry. For a moment Kale wondered if she would see the old emerlindian Granny Noon or Mistress Meiger ever again.

That's not very profitable thinking. She chastised herself and went to sit with the librarian.

"Can you tell me if the gate was left open or shut?" she asked him.

He had taken off his shoes and rubbed his feet with his broad-fingered hands. "It was left closed, but reports through the years indicate that the mechanism that triggers the opening and shutting has become unreliable. Tumanhofer gates are elaborate. The gate at the entrance of Dael is an example. Looks simple, but it requires a trained man like my cousin Bumby Bumbocore to open and close it after it has been set for the night."

"I remember the door in the gate made a lot of noise before it opened."

"Yes, well." Librettowit looked down, embarrassed. "Could have used some adjustments. All that racket wasn't strictly necessary, but I think it makes the gatekeepers feel important, shows what a lot is going on while they're working to open the door. People standing outside are impressed rather than impatient if they think the gatekeeper is struggling with quite a few gears to allow their admittance."

Kale nodded. "How is this gate made? Will we be able to open it if it's shut?"

Librettowit stared off in the distance for a moment before he answered. "Yes, I'm hoping so. Tumanhofers study the great gates in school as youngsters. The lever for this gate to the old mine is in the center of a tunnel-like structure. When the gate closes, the middle of this corridor squeezes shut so that the gate looks like an hourglass on its side. The lever itself is not complicated, but the walls that move and twist in on the tunnel are intricate."

A soft note from Dar's flute echoed through the large chamber, bouncing off rock walls ninety to a hundred feet high.

He played a restful tune first. Metta flew to perch on his knee and joined him. They chose a rousing marching song next. When they were finished, Lee Ark smiled at them and ordered everyone to get ready to move on. Librettowit couldn't get his shoes back on his swollen feet. Gymn came and, with Kale, healed the ache and the swelling.

"Sorry for the delay," the tumanhofer said. "Librarians aren't used to being on the march, you know."

"Don't worry about it, friend," said their marione commander. "I'm not used to traveling with a healing dragon. It seems prudent for us to take a few more minutes here and allow Kale and her small friend to minister to us all."

In a half an hour, while Metta and Dar provided music, Kale and Gymn refreshed all the members of the party, except Shimeran and Seezle, with a brief healing.

The party fell in behind the tumanhofer again, and they headed out. The minor dragons ran back and forth across Kale's shoulders in a game of tag, until she caught each one and put them inside the cape at her waist. She felt them burrow through the cloth folds to their pocket-dens.

"How much farther?" Leetu asked Librettowit.

"Two more vaulted chambers, a twisty tunnel, and the main cavern."

In the twisty tunnel, Kale's nerves began to zing. She caught up to Leetu. "I feel something."

The emerlindian nodded. "Something is following us."

They walked on a few more minutes, Kale looking twice at all the shadows and over her shoulder repeatedly.

"Leetu, I think there are hundreds of them, whatever they are."

"Yes, they follow Risto's command to stop us before we leave the mountain."

"Shouldn't we tell Lee Ark?"

"I already have."

"Oh." Kale looked at Lee Ark. He walked with every nerve on alert. Towering next to him, the urohm moved his head from side to side in constant vigil. "Brunstetter?"

Leetu nodded. "And the kimens, and Dar."

"What is it out there?"

"Schoergs."

Kale closed her eyes for a moment. *I'm not going to be surprised. After all this, I should have known that schoergs weren't made up to scare little children into being good. I wonder if they look anything like how the old fairy tales describe them.* She shuddered and opened her eyes.

Now she watched the shadows for something as tall as she was, wiry, covered with black fur, having a thick body, skinny arms and legs, huge yellow teeth, and small beady eyes. They could crawl up and down walls like huge spiders. They could flatten themselves and slip through small holes.

The questing party came out of the twisty tunnel and into a huge cavern. Across the expansive floor a smaller tunnel led straight out of the mountain. Kale could see the round arch of daylight from where she stood. She could also feel the anticipation of a thousand fierce schoergs waiting to attack.

"Run!" Lee Ark's command came a second before a screech cut through the cavern. In one moment, every surface of the wall behind them and to the left swarmed with rapidly moving dark, shaggy bodies. Brunstetter scooped Wizard Fenworth over his shoulder and took off across the open space. The meech egg bounced against Kale's back as she ran, almost as if it wanted to push her forward with its own panic.

Lee Ark, Dar, and Leetu reached the entry to the gate tunnel a moment after the kimens. They all turned to face the enemy with their weapons ready. Brunstetter set Fenworth down and joined the line. Librettowit and Kale arrived last.

Lee Ark's stern face turned to the o'rant girl. "Go through the tunnel, Kale. We'll hold them here. You will see the o'rant town of Kringlen. Go there if we don't follow."

Librettowit and the wizard had their heads together, arguing about the fireball spell.

"Necessary," shouted Fenworth.

"Unreliable," the librarian countered in a voice twice as loud.

Kale ducked into the tunnel and ran. Five yards ahead, the sun gleamed on new-fallen snow. She looked back over her shoulder and saw Brunstetter's legs with the back of Leetu on one side and Dar on the other. The howls of the frenzied schoergs followed Kale, sounding like a steady roar in the tunnel.

Her toe caught on an almost covered rod in the flooring, and she pitched sideways, slamming against the wall and a vertical metal bar. She fell flat on her face. Scrambling to her knees, she looked behind her at the floor.

The lever! I knocked the lever down. She looked at the walls around her. *Nothing's happening. It doesn't work anymore.*

Then the floor shuddered. The walls shivered. A shrill scraping noise filled the air around her.

She sprang to her feet and bumped her head on the ceiling as it lowered and twisted. Her legs buckled under her as the ground also moved, rising and twisting.

Running, crouching, falling, crawling, Kale made it out and fell into a snowbank. She flipped around and stared down the tunnel to a six-inch opening in the middle. The lever lay across the small hole on this side of the gate.

They're trapped!

Kale started back into the tunnel to lift the lever. The meech egg on her back hit the top of the shrunken tunnel. She backed up, ducked out of the cape sling, and left the egg and dragons in a bundle beside the entrance. She crawled into the tunnel. In a matter of a few feet, she had to lie on her stomach and wiggle closer to the lever. Through the small opening, she heard the clamor of battle.

She came to a place too narrow for her shoulders, and she still couldn't reach the lever. She stretched one arm out ahead of her and wiggled just one inch closer. Her fingertips were two inches away from her goal.

She pushed with her feet, her knees. She squirmed and gained an inch.

"I've got to reach it. They can't get out."

She strained, scraping her shoulders against the rock.

"I have to move it. I have to—"

The lever jumped toward her. She clamped her fingers around it and pulled. It didn't give. She pushed. Nothing. She shook it back and forth, and the bar slid an inch to her right. She tried again and it slid further into the wall. The ground rumbled under her. The floor shifted to the side. Kale rolled. The gate began to open.

As the circle widened, Kale saw the furious fight for survival playing out at the cavern end of the tunnel. Flashes of light attested to the kimens' activity. Or was the wizard using the fireball spell? Kale heard swords cutting through the air with a whoosh and then thudding against tough schoerg bodies.

"Leetu! Dar! The gate is open. Hurry!" Her scream barely rose above a second rumbling of the rocks surrounding her. The stone wall next to her shattered and came down in a thick mass of gravel, sand, and fist-sized rocks. The floor beneath her heaved upward. She slid back toward the outside of the mountain.

"Dar! Fenworth!"

A boulder crashed next to her and pinned her pant leg. Kale tugged frantically, tore the material, and clambered out of the tunnel. She tried to stand, but the rolling ground threw her back down on her hands and knees. With the dirt-encrusted sleeve of her blouse, she attempted to wipe dust from around her eyes. She turned and saw a fissure opening up behind her. The white snow tumbled into the expanding rocky breach.

The cape bundle slipped away from Kale and toward the crevice.

"No!" Kale dove for the moonbeam cape and missed.

Gymn! Metta! Fly to me! The eggs!

Kale struggled through the snow, trying to catch up to the cape as it skidded toward the black gap. The mountain continued to stretch and break its boundaries. The ground underneath Kale gave way. She fell downward with snow cascading on top of her, burying her. As soon as her feet touched something solid, she fought her way upward. When she surfaced, the cape and its contents had slid into a bush. The bare branches quivered with vibrations from the earth beneath it. Kale scrabbled toward it, determined to snatch the prize from its limbs.

The mountain quieted. The ground grew still. Kale hauled herself to her feet and plunged through the shifted snow. She stumbled but fell forward, and her hand caught the smooth moonbeam fabric. Crawling forward, she pulled with all the strength she had left. The tangle of winter branches held on like bony fingers.

A shriek reverberated through the rocks beneath her, like the death wail of some hideous monster. The earth surged beneath her one more time, a rift opening right at her feet. The momentum of the mountain pitched her backward, wresting the cape from her hands. Cape and bush flew through the air in the opposite direction.

Kale lay on her back, staring at the brilliant blue sky. A lone white cloud peacefully floated above the tortured mountain.

Turning away from the mockingly tranquil sky, the o'rant girl sat up and crawled to the edge of the newly formed chasm. She reached with her mind to Gymn and Metta.

Emptiness.

She tried to connect to the meech egg.

A void.

Tears streamed down her face. Voices brought her head around to stare at the misshapen entrance to the old tumanhofer mine. Dar and Leetu sat with a singed Fenworth propped between them. Librettowit lay stretched out with Brunstetter kneeling over him. Curls of smoke rose from his charred clothing. His fancy mustache and beard were stubble. The kimens examined the librarian with their usual speed and efficiency. Lee Ark, bloodied and weary, limped toward Kale.

"You saved our lives, o'rant girl."

"I lost the cape." She looked away from him and down the jagged sides of the gorge.

Lee Ark did not respond. She couldn't say she had lost the minor dragons, the meech egg. The words stuck in her throat behind a lump that cut off her breathing as well as her voice.

A sob broke the stranglehold. She bent forward, weeping.

The marione's calm voice washed over her. "We will build two litters for the wizard and the tumanhofer. Aid will come from the o'rant valley soon. They will have noted the disturbance and sent help."

He left her and went back to take care of practical matters. Kale saw him leave through a blur of tears.

They should go on without me. I don't want to go any farther. I don't want anything. I failed. Oh, Gymn and Metta, I failed you. Paladin, I'm sorry.

49

HOME

O'rant hands lifted Kale out of the snow. Someone wrapped an o'rant robe of fleecy wool around her bruised body. More o'rant hands passed her with tender care onto the back of a blue and gold dragon. O'rant arms carried her in the flight down the mountain into the valley.

A citrus smell clung to the clothing of her rescuers. The sharp, slightly sweet fragrance had always been a part of Kale's bedding at home. Mariones had an earthy odor clinging to their bodies. Kale had noticed when she was quite young that her skin smelled different from the babies she rocked for the village mothers.

Kale nestled against the strong chest of the o'rant male who cradled her wrapped in soft, citrus-smelling blankets. The sorrow in her heart wanted to bury itself in this sensation of being surrounded by something curiously familiar. Kale didn't want to figure it out. She didn't want to think too much. She closed her eyes and shut out the world.

She awoke in a soft, warm bed in a room with painted walls and a rug that covered the floor. Warmth radiated from a crackling fire in a brick fireplace. A landscape painting in a gilt frame hung above an oak mantle. Curtains draped the windows. Sunbeams danced through multiple beveled panes of glass set in a finely carved sash.

The room smelled of citrus.

Kale sat up and looked out the window. Thick snow blanketed the countryside. Two stone walls topped with frothy caps marched down a straight country road. Bare-limbed trees in an orchard held aloft puffs of frosty snow. The sun sparked reflections on a myriad of tiny ice crystals covering every field, tree, bush, and building.

Kale closed her eyes against the brilliant beauty.

There should not be any beauty left in the world.

Merry whistling and light footsteps announced the approach of someone beyond the polished wood door. A slight tap and then the sound of the door shushing across the plush carpet preceded a cheerful "hello."

An o'rant woman entered with a tray. The tray had legs to fit over Kale's lap. The woman wore a rich blue skirt with a matching short jacket, an ivory blouse underneath, and a lace cap on her head. She smiled with straight, white teeth looking pretty and natural in her pleasant face. A few wrinkles sprang out from her eyes and lips as if they had been etched by years of friendly good cheer.

"Tea and toast." The woman walked briskly across the room. "Then more sleep for you. You needn't get up today or tomorrow if you don't wish it."

She set the tray down on the bedside table.

"Here, let me help you pile those pillows so you can sit up proper and eat a bite."

She grabbed three pillows and stacked them against the headboard. "Try that." She reached for the tray. "My name is Mistress Sanci Moorp. I'm the head housekeeper here at Ornopy Halls."

Kale sat back against the pillows, pulling the covers up around her waist. She stared at her hands.

"I'm clean." She held out her arm and inspected the delicate linen nightshirt sleeve. "How—?"

"Oh, you were exhausted all right when you came in late yesterday afternoon." Sanci Moorp fit the tray over her guest's legs and poured a cup of tea. She dipped two spoonfuls of fine white sugar into the brew and stirred vigorously. The silver spoon chimed against the porcelain. "You don't remember soaking in the warm tub?"

Kale shook her head.

"Drink that now. It has herbs to help you sleep and heal."

Mistress Moorp sat on the chair and watched as Kale picked up the cup and took a sip. The lace cap bobbed on the housekeeper's head as she nodded her approval.

"You were chilled clear through. All of you were. Your wizard has caught cold. The tumanhofer has broken legs. Cuts and bruises the like I've never seen, on all your friends. But they're on the mend. We have good doctors here in the valley. Librettowit will have to curtail any adventuring for some time. But he doesn't seem to mind. He's been mumbling about books and was right pleased when I had a footman carry books up from Master Ornopy's library. The tumanhofer gentleman cannot sit up yet, but he seemed comforted to have a stack of thick tomes on his bedside table."

"He's a librarian." Kale spoke around a mouthful of toast.

"So I have been informed. Also that he does not go questing. Your wizard is a very old man. I don't think it was the wisest thing for him to have gone questing, either. But wizards have remarkable stamina. Let's hope rest and good food will be enough to cure him."

"Dar?"

"The doneel?" At Kale's nod, she smiled. "Oh, I love a nice doneel. They are such pleasant houseguests. He's busy replenishing his wardrobe. Called for material and thread. His feet were injured, and he had a gaping wound in his back."

Kale gasped.

"Not too bad," Mistress Moorp assured her. "More than a scratch, less than it could have been. He's content to putter around his room until he has time to put together some suitable clothing."

She hopped up to replenish Kale's empty teacup.

"Your other friends are sleeping. Even the kimens. At least, I assume they're sleeping. They take care of themselves, you know. I did get to serve them some of my sweet cakes and a berry juice I put up last summer. Such dear little creatures."

"Leetu Bends is all right?"

"The emerlindian?"

"Yes."

"She's sleeping, which is what you should be doing. You are getting drowsy, aren't you?"

Kale nodded and raised a hand to cover a tremendous yawn.

Mistress Moorp smiled with satisfaction and took the tray. "You cuddle back down, and when you awake, I'll have a nice bowl of chukkajoop for you."

Kale slid under the covers, knocking two of the pillows aside in the big bed. "Dar once told me chukkajoop is the o'rant national dish. I've never had any."

Mistress Moorp chuckled. "Well, if we had a national dish, I guess chukkajoop would be it." She pursed her lips in a comical moue. "Doneels love to tease. And they make good friends. You are fortunate to have him among your companions. He's been worried about you."

Regret intruded on Kale's comfort. She hadn't been a very good friend to any of her companions. This room, the food, the good housekeeper's kind attention, none of it should be wasted on her. "I don't deserve to be treated so well."

Mistress Moorp frowned fiercely at her young charge. "In this house we don't wait for someone to deserve to be treated decently, my dear." Her voice had a hard edge, and Kale realized she had in some way offended the woman.

"I'm sorry. I didn't mean to…"

Mistress Moorp's expression softened. "No dear, I'm the one to apologize. I forgot you haven't been taught the ways of the o'rants. But that will change now. You can stay with us as long as you like. Master Ornopy has already said he'd take you in as one of his daughters. He's a generous man, and your story touched his heart."

"My story?" Kale struggled against the sleep that pulled her away from Mistress Moorp's words. "Who told him my story?"

"Why, Paladin, dear. He was among those who went out to rescue you."

"Paladin?" Kale tried to sit up again, but she could not even keep her eyes open. Tears slipped down her cheeks. She didn't want to face Paladin. He would be so disappointed in her.

"Rest, dear, and heal." The shush of the door opening and closing over the carpet followed Mistress Moorp's soft words.

┼═┼═┼

A tangy smell of something delectable pulled Kale out of a deep sleep. The fire crackled and sparked, warming the room with its golden glow as well as a pleasant heat. In the chair where Mistress Moorp had sat earlier, a man rested, his head against the high, cushioned back. His long legs extended straight out with polished black boots crossed at the ankle. Kale blinked and looked closely as the fire played a flickering light over his features.

"Paladin!" She sat up abruptly.

His eyes opened slowly, and a gentle smile spread across his lips.

"Little Kale, it's good to hear your voice." He reached for a bowl on the table at his elbow. "Mistress Moorp sent up chukkajoop. I'm partial to this stew myself, and Mistress Moorp makes some of the best I've ever tasted."

Kale crossed her legs under the blanket as she took the thick ceramic bowl into her hands. It fit in one, and warmth spread through those fingers as she picked up the spoon with the other hand. Hunger rose up at the smell of the rich dark stew. She took a mouthful and savored the flavor.

"I *do* like it."

"You sound surprised."

"Dar said it was made of things from underground. Only roots and things."

"Doneels." Paladin shook his head gently. The grin on his face widened.

Kale took another bite and peered into the bowl. There was not enough light for her to see it very well. "He also said it was blood red."

A dark candle on the table sizzled. The unlit wick suddenly burst into flame. Paladin picked it up and held it over Kale's bowl.

"It is!" Kale grinned up at Paladin. "The broth is red."

"Eat it, Kale. It's good for you."

Paladin sat comfortably stretched out in his chair while she ate the entire bowlful and scraped the last drops out of the bottom with her spoon. She handed the empty bowl to him, and he put it down on the table. Only then did it strike her as appalling that Paladin himself had served her and sat quietly beside her while she ate. She hadn't even offered him polite conversation as the mariones did around their fancy tables with important guests.

"Now, Kale." His voice held a note of reprimand. "We've been very comfortable together. Why have you gone tense, and why do you look ill? Did the chukkajoop not sit well in your stomach?"

She knew the last question was a jest. It sounded very much like something Dar would say. Of course the delicious stew had not made her sick. Kale looked down at her hands folded in her lap. *What does he want me to say? What should I say?*

Only two words came to mind. "I'm sorry."

"Sorry?" He quirked an eyebrow at her.

"Gymn and Metta are dead."

"I know what happened to Gymn and Metta."

"I lost the meech egg."

"I know what you did."

"I hit the lever and made the gate close. When I opened it again, it fell apart. Everything fell apart."

"I know."

"I didn't do one thing right. And Gymn and Metta are dead."

"Wulder is in charge of life in our world, Kale. He gives it, and He takes it away. And when He takes life from one of His creatures here where we stand, He moves it with His infinite care to another place we know very little about. You are not mighty enough to be in charge of the giving and taking of life. Not your life. Not Gymn's life. Not Metta's life."

Kale scrubbed the tears off her cheeks with the back of her hand. Paladin offered her a handkerchief.

"Blow your nose," he ordered kindly.

The noise embarrassed Kale, but everything about being with Paladin now embarrassed her. He should be visiting with Wizard Fenworth or Leetu or Dar. Not her.

Paladin reached out and took her hands in his. He leaned forward and smiled a small, tender smile that somehow warmed her with love and peace. "I want to visit with you, Kale. You are more than my servant. You are my friend, my child, my vision of the future."

She shook her head slowly from side to side. Paladin could not be wrong. But what he said didn't make sense. She was a slave girl who didn't even follow orders very well. Who didn't do the right thing. Who caused all sorts of problems. Who caused terrible things to happen.

"Kale, what happened when you first found the meech egg and you tried to walk away?"

"I was stuck."

Paladin nodded. "Sometimes we cannot walk away from our responsibilities. What happened when you left the cape and reentered the tunnel to open the gate?"

"Nothing. I mean, the meech egg didn't hold me."

"Sometimes the order of importance of our responsibilities shifts. What was crucial at one moment moves down to second place, or third, under different circumstances."

Kale wrinkled her brow, trying to understand.

Paladin squeezed her hand. "What do you think Wulder wanted you to do? Sit and cradle the meech egg, or try to help your friends?"

"Help?"

Paladin nodded. "You did the right thing, Kale. You didn't sit and reason it out. You jumped up and did the right thing. You are a better person than you think. Wulder is pleased with who you are."

"But it was my fault."

"You have the power to crack a mountain in two? Amazing! I thought you were just a slave girl." The twinkle in his eye took away the sting of his words.

A smile played at the corner of Kale's mouth. "I guess not."

"You have choices to make now, Kale." Paladin let go of her hands and leaned back in his chair. "You can return with Dar to The Hall. Or you can stay here in the o'rant valley. Either choice is all right with me. If you go to The Hall, you will be trained, and much will be required of you.

"If you stay here, you will learn more about your people. Things will come across your path that will require you to help friends and even strangers."

Paladin sighed and leaned back in the chair. He looked perfectly content and at ease, not troubled by wicked wizards and all the evil they created. "It is quieter here. The likelihood of adventure is less. But still you will be my servant. I will be pleased with you. You are mine, Kale, and I do not scorn those who have given their service to me. You won't be bored here, either. There will be plenty of opportunities to do good.

"You don't have to decide tonight. In fact, you can wait until spring." He stood up and stretched.

Kale watched him. His strong body silhouetted by the fire looked much like that of any young man, yet Paladin had been around since before the Battle of Ordray. Her eyes widened at the thought. Wizard Fenworth was that old too. Paladin was special in ways Kale could not understand, and he had claimed her as his friend, his child.

She looked down at her callused and scratched hands. She didn't seem a good candidate for service at The Hall.

"I didn't much like questing," she said, barely above a whisper.

Paladin nodded. He didn't look surprised or upset over her admission. Kale remembered Fenworth's words. "Questing is often uncomfortable."

Paladin smiled, and Kale knew he recognized the wizard's thinking.

"Unpredictable," he added.

Kale nodded, looking into his eyes and knowing he would not condemn her for her choice, no matter what it was.

He left, carrying the empty bowl. Kale got out of bed and sat in the window seat, gazing out at the peaceful countryside. Its blanket of fresh snow glowed under a full moon in a clear sky.

There must be a million stars in that sky. Librettowit said that Wulder knows each of their names. Paladin knows my name…so does Wulder. She tucked her chilly toes beneath the long nightgown. *I don't have to decide tonight. I don't have to decide until spring.*

⊢══╡

The days that followed gave Kale a most wondrous taste of belonging. She sat with Ornopy's girls and learned to sew at Dar's instruction. Librettowit regaled them with hours of stories and taught them history. They danced with the kimens and did chores with Mistress Moorp. And the chores were not drudgery, but fun because of the companionship.

Librettowit and Fenworth told legends and tales of old. Leetu and Dar demonstrated juggling feats. Everyone gave it a try but only ended up laughing more than catching the objects thrown in the air. Brunstetter and Lee Ark knew an astounding number of games. Members of the household and guests played every afternoon in the light of the sunroom. Contented, Kale took pleasure in each moment she spent as a part of this happy entourage.

The days lengthened. Crocus and springbuds poked their colorful heads through the last of the snow. Birds flew back into the o'rant valley from the south and began nest building. Lambs, calves, and colts frolicked in the pastures.

Kale made her decision.

One day, when the breezes chased away puffy clouds that had sprinkled the newly sown fields, she looked at the broken slopes of the shorter peak of Tourbanaut and sighed.

"There is one thing I must do first," she said to the empty road. "I must go find the meech egg, or what's left of it." She did not look over her shoulder at the massive bright walls of Ornopy Halls. She didn't go back to gather provisions from the ample supply of kitchen cupboards. She wrapped the shawl she'd knitted at Mistress Moorp's hearth around her shoulders. She set her eyes upon her goal and started the long walk back to the wrecked entrance of the abandoned tumanhofer mine.

50

Standing Together

Muddy waters swirled in the streams coming off the mountain. With the spring thaw, melted snow washed down the slopes, creating rivulets that ran together, making tumbling brooks and swift, quiet rills. White mountain dewdrops, tiny flowers on mosslike plants, covered the ground.

The smell of new grass, damp earth, and sweet dewdrops filled Kale with exuberance. She climbed rapidly, using paths well worn by shepherds and their flocks. As the sun began to sink to the west, she stopped and surveyed the countryside now spread below her. Sighing, she sat on a boulder and gazed with contentment at the valley of the o'rants. She easily picked out Ornopy Halls, three beautiful buildings with an elegant wrought iron fence around them and a straight road running out its front gate.

It's been home to me as if I'd never had a home before. But Paladin put a claim on my heart as well as my life. I want to go to The Hall.

She stood and began the more arduous climb up broken granite and shifted crags. The cool mountain air penetrated her clothing. Shivering, she wished she'd brought something a little more practical than the shawl.

Granny Noon's moonbeam cape always kept my body warm. I must find the cape and the eggs.

Her foot slipped on some loose rocks. Some of the pebbles fell into her boot. She sat down to remove it and shake out the debris, but as soon as her backside touched the ground, she sprang up again.

Kale frowned and bent to sit down. Her legs straightened and she took two more steps up the mountain. Every muscle in her body strained to go forward.

"The eggs! I'm being pulled to the eggs." She gave a whoop and grinned. "I'll find them. I can't help but find them."

Kale climbed more vigorously while the sun went down and the moon rose. She reached a flattened area that looked vaguely familiar. When she spied the twisted entrance to the tumanhofer mine, she knew why. She turned her back on the gaping black mouth and headed to the cliff where the moonbeam cape and its precious contents had slipped over the edge.

Bright moonlight cast the region in a stark contrast of light and shadow. To the right was a slope of boulders which might be easier to descend than the spot at Kale's feet. She took a few steps in that direction. A light at the bottom of the crevasse caught her attention.

A glowing cloud hovered at the base of a rockslide. It constantly shifted. The edges grew thin and drifted into nothing. The center remained unchanging, a roundish mass of eerie green light.

"I don't much like the looks of that." Kale spoke her doubt even as her feet moved toward the easier descent and the mysterious luminescence.

The day's walking and climbing, the lack of food, and the cold night air began to wear on her. She tried singing some of Dar's marching songs to keep alert. She struggled to slow down against the ever-increasing strength of the meech egg's pull.

She mumbled to herself, "Making your way down a crevasse side is no place to fall asleep on your feet."

An almost forgotten nudge in her mind caught her off kilter. She sat down with a thud on a hard jagged rock.

"Ouch!"

Even the pain couldn't disguise the persistent niggling in her mind.

"Gymn?" She stood up. *Gymn!*

Kale moved cautiously down the rocks. Gymn's thoughts, and then Metta's, bombarded her. She wouldn't go to sleep now, but she also found it hard to concentrate on where to safely put her feet.

Slow down. I'm not understanding it all.

You're all right, and so is Metta.

The meech egg is fine.

The worm is a nuisance.

Worm?

Kale shuddered as she got Gymn's impression of the worm—big, slimy, slowly stalking them. Kale caught the image of the two minor dragons picking up rocks and flying over a massive roundworm. They dropped the rocks on the squirming beast. Pelting it discouraged its advance, and the worm slithered back into the rock walls. According to Metta's account, this happened often. They also spat on the creature, leaving green and purple splotches that hurt the worm and caused it to turn back.

So it's very dumb and very persistent. Kale chuckled at Gymn's tirade. *And you are glad I am coming, because you and Metta are tired of it.*

It was so good to have those choppy, chaotic thoughts of the minor dragons flitting through her own thought pattern, Kale laughed out loud.

She learned Metta and Gymn had spent a comfortable winter in a cave that boasted three hot springs and plenty of insects and small rodents. The minor dragons knew she would come get them. They had felt it their duty to protect the meech egg from the worm. The mention of the worm sent Gymn off on another lengthy description of the clumsy beast's constant stalking. Apparently when it captured a victim, the worm surrounded it and went to sleep, absorbing the captive directly through its oozing skin.

Kale grimaced with distaste. Clearly, the worm was an undesirable creature to winter with in a cave.

She reached the bottom of the ravine. Broken rocks littered the floor. She picked her way toward the glowing mist. The air smelled musty and unpleasant. It stung her eyes as she passed through. On the other side, a gap in the rocks gave entrance to the cave where Gymn and Metta guarded the meech egg. Kale heard its thrum, deep, constant, and strong. As she entered the chamber behind the mist, steamy air clung to her skin. Streaks of lightrock material mottled the cavern walls, giving off an even blue light.

Gymn and Metta flew to greet her. Tears of joy slipped down Kale's cheeks. She uttered a praise of thanksgiving to Wulder as she cuddled each little dragon's slim body against her face. She walked with them on her shoulders and collapsed beside the bush holding her cape and the meech egg. There she gently rubbed the two dragons' scaly backs until she felt calm and rested.

As Metta sang a song of rejoicing, Kale's spirit revived. The small piece of her heart that had been discontent even while she enjoyed the company of her own people now felt at peace. Gymn's healing touch took away her aching fatigue.

Before settling down for the night, she carefully broke away the dead branches of the bush that ensnared the cape and egg. She explored the pockets and found all six unhatched dragon eggs safe. She delved into the hollows and discovered treasures from her travels and from Granny Noon. She wrapped herself in the moonbeam cape, and the sticky heat of the cavern no longer bothered her. Metta assured her she could drink the spring water, so she drank her fill. At long last, she lay down, curled herself around the thrumming meech egg, and let its soft vibrations lull her to sleep. The minor dragons would take turns watching through the night against a visit from the worm.

Kale awoke to Metta bouncing on her shoulder and chirruping a warning. Sunlight filtered into the cave. Kale saw clearly the huge worm slowly advancing across the open space. Worms on a fishhook had never been a lovely sight. A worm the size of six cows walking one behind the other made Kale sit up and stare. Pinkish gray flesh undulated as the creature inched forward. It moved sluggishly, rippling and sliding toward a tree near one of the hot springs.

Kale blinked at the sight of the stubby tree. She didn't remember it from the night before. A tangle of long moss hanging off one side caused her to sit up even straighter and squint at the thick limbs.

"Wizard Fenworth!"

Metta and Gymn left her and flew to the tree. They circled Fenworth, chattering in high-pitched squeals. Kale stood and grabbed a long branch she had broken off the dead bush the night before. She charged the worm, hitting its head. It recoiled and turned away. Its retreat was slow and cumbersome.

"Well, if I have to face an enemy alone, that worm will do."

Gymn landed on her shoulder and scolded.

"Excuse me," said Kale. "Of course I wasn't alone."

Fenworth stretched and began to look more like a wizard. He yawned and shook his head. His hair and beard flew about him.

"Tut-tut. Shouldn't sleep sitting up at my age. Puts cricks in my shoulders."

"Good morning, Wizard Fenworth," said Kale. "Did you follow me yesterday?"

"Follow you?" The wizard harrumphed. "I didn't follow you, my dear. I led the others."

Kale looked around the cave. No one lurked in the shadows as far as she could see. "Where are they?"

Fenworth glanced around in puzzlement. "Oh dear, where did I put them? No, no, I remember. I came on ahead. Got tired of walking."

He watched the tail end of the worm disappear through one of the many cracks in the cave walls. "What a dreadful existence. Makes one glad one's a wizard."

"Yes, being a wizard is much preferable to being a worm."

Kale recognized the voice before she turned to see Wizard Risto. Amazed, she realized how closely the evil man resembled Paladin. They were about the same build and had the same coloring and similar facial features.

He stepped into the cave from where he stood by the entrance. "But being a wizard who has taken his destiny into his own hands is infinitely preferable to being a wizard who lives to please another."

"Tut-tut." Fenworth shook his head and slowly stood. Shaking out his robes, he dislodged a lizard and a mouse. As always, leaves fluttered to the ground as he walked over to Kale and put a hand on her shoulder. "He means me, you know. Not the first part, the 'destiny in his own hands' part. The second part, about pleasing." He shook his head again. "I don't think Risto has ever given me a compliment before. And really, I should compliment him back. Polite, you know. But I can't think of anything nice to say. Oh dear."

Risto sneered at Fenworth. Kale saw any resemblance to Paladin melt away. Where compassion and wisdom enhanced Paladin's face to make him attractive, Risto's contempt shadowed his face with hard, ugly lines.

Wizard Fenworth leaned closer to Kale's ear. "He had to wait for you to show up, you know. Couldn't find the meech egg on his own, even when it was at his back door, so to speak. He hasn't the talent for finding dragon eggs as you do, my dear. Galls him. He wants to be all-knowing, all-powerful. Galls him that a mere o'rant girl can find the meech egg, and he can't. Had to follow you. Galls him."

An angry, guttural growl emanated from the evil wizard. "Hand over the meech egg, old man."

"Oh, I couldn't do that." He looked at Kale. "Perhaps Kale would like to…"

Kale found she was too scared to speak. She shook her head.

"No," said Fenworth sadly, "I didn't think so."

"You're no match for me, Fenworth."

"No match. Haven't got a match. I've got a good fire spell, but Librettowit doesn't like me to use it. Librarians can be incredibly picky about details."

Risto took a step forward and roared. "Fenworth!"

"Yes?"

"You bore me with your prattle."

"Oh, regrettable, that. Why don't you go seek the company of someone who doesn't prattle? Seems like a good solution to your problem."

"Enough of this nonsense." Risto marched across the cave.

Kale ran.

She flung herself over the egg and cringed, expecting to feel Risto's large hands grab her and hurl her out of his way. Instead she heard laughter: the soft chortle of Dar and Leetu, the shimmering giggles of kimens, and the bark of hearty laughter from Brunstetter and Lee Ark.

"Foiled again." Librettowit's voice bubbled with merriment.

Kale looked toward the entrance of the cave. Her friends filed in and came to stand with Fenworth.

"You're late!" said the wizard.

"Ran into an angry group of grawligs," said Lee Ark.

Kale rolled off the egg and sat with a thump on the hard cave floor. "Why didn't he grab the egg?"

Librettowit came to her side. He extended a hand and helped her to her feet. "You were between him and what he wanted, and you are Paladin's servant."

"I'm not a very powerful servant."

"Doesn't matter. He wasn't prepared for resistance." The librarian looked over at the frustrated wizard. Risto's face had turned dark with rage. His eyes bulged as he glared at the line of opposition. "*Now* I think he is prepared. Let's go stand with our comrades."

Kale stayed close to the tumanhofer's side. "Will there be a battle?"

"More a contest of wills."

For the first few minutes, Kale thought nothing was happening except a lot of staring. Then she noticed her friends fading. At first the colors of their clothing became pale, and then she could see through them like a mist. She no longer watched Risto, but stared in horror as one by one, her comrades disappeared to be replaced by a gleaming green cloud like the one at the cave entrance.

"My little friend, Kale Allerion."

Kale looked up at Risto and saw his expression had changed. Now he looked again very much like Paladin.

"This has been a trial for you. But you have passed. You are worthy of being my follower."

You're Risto.

"Of course I am, dear o'rant girl. I am sorry for all the confusion. It was necessary to make sure you were the last of the Allerions and not some impostor."

I don't understand.

"The Allerions have always worked with me. You were stolen from us at birth. We welcome you back."

Kale looked to her friends to see their reaction to this news. She saw nothing but the glowing mist shapes.

They might not have heard him mindspeak anyway.

"That's right, Kale. Because they aren't really there. You stand alone. You always have. You have no friends. It was all an illusion I created. I've gone to a lot of trouble to draw you into our family circle. And I am not the only one who awaits your arrival."

In her mind, Kale saw a castle turret with an o'rant woman sitting by the window, gazing longingly across a forest. Kale fought a panic rising in her chest.

"I have cared for you ever since I met this woman who loves you." Risto's voice in Kale's head caressed her loneliness with warm, soothing tones. *"I've kept you safe when I could, and agonized when you had to suffer. You must see that to come with me will make not only me happy, but you as well."*

Kale looked into Risto's face. He looked so like Paladin, except for a hard glitter in his eyes, stern lines of disapproval around his mouth, and the tight angry line of his jaw.

"Believe in me, Kale. I will teach you the wonders of your powers. No one else can give you the answers you need because no one else is like you. I am the perfect guardian for you, Kale. No one wants to help you as I do. No one can but me.

"I would be greatly distressed should anything happen to you, and if you leave me, I'm afraid disaster will befall you. You would be destroyed. There is no doubt about that. Make the wise decision, Kale. Go, pick up the meech egg, and come."

Kale remembered Pretender had told the kimens that he had mastered their weather and had the power to destroy them. He had lied.

She remembered Leetu saying that when Risto lied it sounded like truth.

She remembered Granny Noon's advice.

"I stand under Wulder's authority." Kale spoke the words aloud.

Risto grimaced.

Her friends appeared with not even a wisp of the gleaming clouds clinging to their clothes. Metta sang. Her song soared with praise. Its trills and runs echoed off the stone walls. Shimeran and Seezle twirled in place and then began to dance. Dar pulled out his trumpet and blasted the air with a triumphant call.

Risto glared at them all.

"We won?" Kale asked Librettowit under her breath, keeping her eyes on the volatile wizard.

He nodded. "He tried to weaken each of us with evil words in our minds. We all stood firm in our allegiance to Paladin."

Fenworth put a hand on Kale's shoulder. "Caution, my dear. Do not assume. Tut-tut, my dear librarian. I think you spoke too soon. Look at our enemy's demeanor."

Kale glanced at Fenworth's serious face, and then her eyes went back to the evil wizard. The man shook with anger. As each second passed, the tension in his body escalated. The energy of his hatred radiated from his eyes. Kale wanted to duck behind someone. Fenworth and Librettowit, who were wise. Lee Ark, Leetu, and Brunstetter, who were strong. The kimens and Dar, who somehow always gave comfort by their presence. Kale hoped Paladin would walk through the glowing mist at the cave entrance and banish Risto. Out of the corner of her eye, she saw the giant urohm scoop up the meech egg and cradle it protectively in his arms.

The stone floor quivered under Kale's feet. The air around the wicked wizard crackled. Rage poured out of his body into the small cavern. Vibrations of malice intensified, and the rock walls began to shake. Kale trembled, but she couldn't tell if it was fear within that made her shake or the undulating world around her.

"Come close now," ordered Fenworth. "Time for an exit. I think we'll whirl. Kale likes to whirl. Hold hands. Let's stay together, children. I want no one lost."

Metta and Gymn flew to Kale, darted under the edge of the moonbeam cape, and burrowed into their pocket-dens. At the same time, her comrades gathered around Fenworth. A blinding light burst into the cave.

A roar of anger filled her ears and gradually diminished as if a distance was growing between her and the one who roared. Risto had been left behind.

"Destination?" Fenworth's voice came to her, although she could not tell where he was.

She held someone's hand. She thought it was Dar's, small and slightly furry. A racing wind buffeted her.

"Oh dear, oh dear. We're being followed."

The fierce cries of wild animals surrounded them. Sharp teeth nipped at Kale's heels. She could not open her eyes to look, and yet she could see in her mind the black shapes of huge hounds racing beside them. Their red eyes pierced her soul and made her want to scream in terror. Throaty snarls raked along her nerves, and the air filled with a fetid smell of rancid meat.

"Detour!" Fenworth exclaimed, and the next moment water splashed against Kale's legs, soaking her trousers and boots. The water stung small wounds at her ankles inflicted by the hounds' teeth.

Even through closed eyes, Kale sensed the brilliance around her fade. The air turned bitter cold. Some barrier now muffled the sound of the wind. She peeked but wasn't able to make out any shapes near by. She couldn't even pick out the form of the one holding her hand.

"Oh dear, oh dear. I need help now. All of you, stay together and call on Wulder."

How do I call on Wulder? Just talk to Him?

A streak of blackness hurtled past Kale's right ear, sizzling the air and burning the side of her face.

Oh, Wulder, I don't know if Fenworth is wise enough or any of us strong enough to get out of this mess. Please, help us.

In the distance, she heard dragon wings flapping against the air. She heard cattle lowing and blackbirds screaming, warning of an intrusion. The light intensified again, and she squeezed her eyes shut. The wind whistled.

Fenworth chuckled. "Reinforcements. Ahh! Now, where was it we were going?"

Reinforcements? What? Where? Again her mind captured an image her eyes could not see. White-winged dragons, the dragons themselves of a multitude of colors, men in shining armor, Paladin on a great shining dragon, weapons that blazed. Too many formed in the darkness for her to count. They drove away dark, swift shapes and gave chase.

Kale felt as though she was being dragged through bushes. She lost her grip on the hand she held and felt an odd cylindrical structure form under her so that she sat straddling it in midair. The wind ceased. The light faded. Kale opened her eyes to view her surroundings.

She and her companions sat on the branches of a towering trang-a-nog tree. Close by stood an o'rant farmhouse, a barn, and a wagon. In the distance, Ornopy Halls stood elegantly basking in the bright spring sunshine.

Fenworth looked around anxiously. "Most uncomfortable! Did we lose anyone? Head count! Lee Ark, Leetu, and Brunstetter. Three. Should we count the meech egg? No, I think not. Don't drop it, Brunstetter. I'm to take that home and raise it. Ridiculous, being a parent at my age. Where were we? Oh yes, three. One o'rant, two kimens, two minor dragons. Eight. A librarian and a diplomat. Ten. We're missing one."

"Who's the diplomat?" Kale asked Librettowit who sat on the branch above her.

"Dar. Doneels are often considered quintessential ambassadors." He cleared his throat and raised a hand to catch Fenworth's attention. "You forgot to count yourself."

The wizard bristled. "Nonsense. I'm the oldest, so I counted myself first."

"You're the oldest, and you didn't count yourself at all."

Three mongrel dogs charged from the open barn door, barking furiously. They surrounded the base of the tree. One stood with front paws against the smooth olive-green trunk and issued a challenge to the interlopers in its tree. Another leapt in the air, snapping at Brunstetter's heels dangling just beyond its jaws. The third raced pell-mell around the base of the tree and furiously barked its opinion of anyone who dared enter its territory in such an unconventional manner.

The farmer and his wife appeared in the door of their home and gazed with amazement at the scene in their front yard.

"Bring a ladder, man," commanded Fenworth. "We return, the conquering heroes."

The farmer's wife nudged her dumbfounded husband. He nodded to her and darted for the barn, coming out a minute later with a long ladder under his arm.

Kale turned to Dar sitting in a clump of broad trang-a-nog leaves on another branch. "What happens next?"

"We celebrate…and we go home."

The words sounded as sweet to Kale as music. Home. Not to the Ornopy Halls, but to The Hall, The Hall in Vendela, Paladin's Hall.

ALMOST THERE

Dar traveled with her. Paladin had given him permission to enter The Hall and train for service.

Veazey and D'Shay had flown with the large dragons over the mountain pass as soon as the weather permitted. Merlander and Celisse carried Dar and Kale on the lengthy journey south along the Morchain Range. When they reached an area Kale recognized, she insisted they land beside the trade road.

"This is where I left Farmer Brigg's wagon, Dar."

She stood beside the bustling road and stared across the valley at the beautiful city of Vendela. Metta and Gymn flew around her head in excitement. They touched down on her shoulders, only to take off again, chittering to each other and turning loops in the air.

Spring had come and gone. The approaching Summer Solstice Feast Day had brought many travelers to Vendela, capital of Amara. The sun sparkled on the city's sheer white walls, shining blue roofs, and golden domes. Spires and steeples and turrets towered above the city in a vast variety of shapes and colors. More than a dozen castles clustered outside the capital, and more palaces were scattered over a hilly landscape on the other side of a wide river.

"This time I'm going in," said Kale to her companions. "This time I'm not afraid of the proddings in my mind that say there are too many new things in Vendela for me to even count." She felt again the pulse of the city, the many minds filled with their own thoughts and spilling into her consciousness. She easily blocked the torrent, controlling the flood of humanity and retaining her own identity. Her mindspeaking talent no longer made her uneasy.

"This time I'll be able to ask questions and get answers. I'll learn about Wulder and Paladin, and I'll learn more about me as well. I may even learn about the Allerions."

She put her hands on her hips and sighed with pleasure. "We're almost there."

"Almost there is not there. Come on, let's go," Dar said as he walked back to Merlander. "This time tomorrow you'll have your leecent uniform."

"Leecent? What's leecent?"

"The lowest rank in Paladin's service. Not that you'll be treated badly for being the lowest, not in Paladin's service, but—"

"Wait. Are you saying I'll be Leecent Kale?"

"Sure."

"And Lee Ark? The Lee means...?"

"Highest rank. Actually, he is General Lee Ark, higher than Major Lee or plain Lee."

"Leetu?"

"Two steps down from Lee. Didn't you know that, Kale?"

Kale shook her head slowly. *Master Meiger was right. I don't know anything.*

She grinned at her doneel friend. "But I'm learning!"

Tonight she'd sleep at The Hall. Tomorrow she'd wear a leecent uniform. There was a festival to see, and she had teachers to meet, classes to attend, a life to live.

Kale ran across the little hillside and jumped onto Celisse's saddle. "Let's go!"

GLOSSARY

Amara (ä'-mä-rä)
Continent surrounded by ocean on three sides.

armagot (är'-muh-got)
National tree, purple blue leaves in the fall.

armagotnut (är'-muh-got-nut)
Nut from the armagot tree.

Battle of Ordray (ôrd'-rā)
Historic battle where Bisonbeck army threatened to overcome kimens. Urohms, aided by wizards and dragons, fought to save them. Ordray is a province occupied mostly by urohms in a southeast Amara, a wedge of land between the Morchain mountain range and the Dormanscz volcanic range.

beater frog (be'-ter frôg)
Tailless, semiaquatic amphibian having a smooth, moist skin, webbed feet, and long hind legs. Shades of green; no bigger than a child's fist; capable of making loud, resounding boom.

bentleaf tree
Deciduous tree having long, slender, drooping branches and narrow leaves.

bisonbecks (bī'-sen-bek)
Most intelligent of the seven low races. They comprise most of Risto's army.

blattig fish (blat'-tig)
Freshwater fish often growing to a length of two to three feet, voraciously carnivorous, known to attack and devour living animals.

blimmets (blim'-mets)
One of the seven low races, burrowing creatures that swarm out of the ground for periodic feeding frenzies.

The Bogs
Made up of four swamplands with indistinct borders. Located in southwest Amara.

borling tree (bôr'-ling)
Having dark brown wood and a deeply furrowed nut enclosed in a globose, aromatic husk.

bornut
Nut from borling tree.

brillum (bril'-lum)
A brewed ale that none of the seven high races would consume. Smells like skunkwater, stains like black bornut juice. Mariones use it to spray around their fields to keep insects from infesting their crops.

broer (brôr)
A substance secreted by female dragons through glands in the mouth, used for nest building. It hardens into a rock-like substance resembling gray meringue.

brook dabbler
A freshwater fish having silver scales on the belly, a coal black back, fins are the colors of a sunset.

brushwood
Spiny, dense shrubs having delicate purple flowers in the spring and black, poisonous berries in late summer.

chukkajoop (chuk'-kuh-joop)
A favorite o'rant stew made from beets, onions, and carrots.

cygnot tree (si'-not)
A tropical tree growing in extremely wet ground or shallow water. The branches come out of the trunk like spokes from a wheel hub and often interlace with neighboring trees.

crocodile melon
Shaped like a cantaloupe with hard, dark green, bumpy rind. Tastes bitter but not poisonous.

deckit powder
Yellow crystalline compound used for explosives.

doneel (do'-neel)
One of the seven high races. These people are furry with bulging eyes, thin black lips, and ears at the top and front of their skulls. They are small in stature, rarely over three feet tall. Generally are musical and given to wearing flamboyant clothing.

double-crested mountain finch
A small, colorful bird with a double crest on the crown of its head.

Dormanscz Range (dôr-manz')
Volcanic mountain range in southeast Amara.

druddum (drud'-dum)
Weasel-like animal that lives deep in mountains. These creatures are thieves and will steal anything to horde. They like to get food, but they are also attracted to bright things and things that have an unusual texture.

drummerbug
Small brown beetle that makes a loud snapping sound with its wings when not in flight.

emerlindian (e'-mer-lin'-dee-in)
One of the seven high races, emerlindians are born pale with white hair and pale gray eyes. As the age, they darken. One group of emerlindians is slight in stature, the tallest being five feet. Another distinct group is between six and six and a half feet tall.

ersatz (er-zäts')
Imitation, substitute, artificial, and inferior to the real thing.

Fairren Forest (fair'-ren)
A massive forest of mostly deciduous trees in southwest Amara.

fire dragon
Emerged from the volcanoes in ancient days; these dragons breathe fire and are most likely to serve evil forces.

fortaleen (for'-tuh-leen)
Bush with two-inch long thorns.

glean band (gleen)
A bracelet delicately woven by kimens out of vines from the glean plant. It wards off wasps and other stinging insects, as well as poisonous reptiles.

grand emerlindian
Grands are close to a thousand years old and are black.

granny emerlindian
Grannies are both male and female, said to be five hundred years old or older, and have darkened to a brown complexion with dark brown hair and eyes.

grawligs (graw'-ligs)
One of seven low races, mountain ogres.

greater dragon
Largest of the dragons, able to carry many men or cargo.

gum tree
Tree with sticky leaves and yellow, rayed flower heads, the center of which may be plucked and chewed.

hadwig (ad'-wig)
A sling-type weapon with a spiked ball at the end.

halfnack bird
Brightly colored, medium-sized bird.

jimmin
Any young animal used for meat. We would say veal, lamb, spring chicken.

kimen (kim'-en)
The smallest of the seven high races. Kimen are elusive, tiny, and fast. Under two feet tall.

lightrocks
Any of the quartzlike rocks giving off a glow.

major dragon
Elephant-sized dragon most often used for personal transportation.

marione (mer'-ē-own)
One of the seven high races. Mariones are excellent farmers and warriors. They are short and broad, usually musclebound rather than corpulent.

meech dragon
The most intelligent of the dragons, capable of speech.

minor dragon
Smallest of the dragons, the size of a young kitten. The different types of minor dragons have different abilities.

moerston bark (môr'-stun)
When chewed, it soothes hunger and freshens the mouth. Bumpy, brown, and thin.

moonbeam plant
A three to four foot plant having large shiny leaves and round flowers resembling a full moon. The stems are fibrous and used for making cloth.

Morchain Range
Mountains running north and south through the middle of Amara.

mordakleep
One of the low races, associated with freshwater sources, shape shifters.

mountain dewdrops
Small white flowers growing close to the ground in an almost moss covering.

mullins
Fried doughnut sticks.

nordy rolls
Whole-grain, sweet, nutty bread.

o'rant
One of the high races. Five to six feet tall.

parnot (par'-not)
Green fruit like a pear.

pnard potatoes (puh-nard')
Starchy, edible tuber with pale pink flesh.

Pomandando River (po'-man-dan'-do)
River runnning along the eastern side of Vendela.

quiss (kwuh'-iss)
One of the seven low races. These creatures have an enormous appetite.
Every three years they develop the capacity to breathe air for six weeks and
forage along the sea coast, creating havoc. They are extremely slippery.

razterberry (ras'-ter-bâr-ee)
Small red berries that grow in clusters somewhat like grapes on the sides of
mountains. The vines are useful for climbing.

ribbets (rib'-bits)
Ball game played between two teams, similar to soccer.

River Away
Marione village in eastern Amara.

rock pine
Evergreen tree with prickly cones that are as heavy as stones.

ropma (rōp'-muh)
One of the seven low races. These half-men, half-animals are useful in herding
and caring for beasts.

scarphlit (scar'-flit)
An oily substance used in medicinal potions.

schoergs (skôrgz)
One of seven low races. Hairy, short, and lean.

speckled thrush
Small bird with white speckles on a brown background.

Tale of Durmoil (der-moil')
Folktale relating when the fire dragons emerged from the volcanoes.

trang-a-nog tree
Smooth, olive-green bark.

tumpgrass
A tall grass that grows in a clump, making its own hillock.

urohm (ū-rome')
Largest of the seven high races. Gentle giants, well proportioned and very
intelligent.

Vendela (vin-del'-luh)
Capital city of the province of Wynd.

Wittoom (wit-toom')
Region populated by doneels in northwest Amara.

ABOUT THE AUTHOR

Donita K. Paul comes from a family of storytellers and teachers, so it is only natural that she loves spinning imaginative tales interwoven with lore. A retired schoolteacher, she keeps her hands in the mix by being one of the professional storytellers in the Sunday-school department of her church.

Donita has two grown children, two grandchildren, and two dogs. She currently lives in Colorado Springs, Colorado, in the shadow of Pikes Peak. When she's not writing, she enjoys reading all genres, from picture books to biography.